Because a Fire Was in My Head

Flyover Fiction
Series Editor
Ron Hansen

LYNN STEGNER

Because
a Fire
Was
in My
Head

University of Nebraska Press
Lincoln and London

3/07

literaryventuresfund

investing in literature
one book at a time

providing a foundation
for writers around the globe

www.literaryventuresfund.org

The University of Nebraska Press is grateful
to the Literary Ventures Fund for its support
of this work.

Publication of this volume was assisted by
The Virginia Faulkner Fund, established in
memory of Virginia Faulkner, editor in chief
of the University of Nebraska Press.

*Library of Congress
Cataloging-in-Publication Data*
Stegner, Lynn. Because a fire was in my
head / Lynn Stegner.
p.   cm.   — (Flyover fiction)
ISBN-13: 978-0-8032-1139-1 (cloth: alk. paper)
ISBN-10: 0-8032-1139-2 (cloth: alk. paper)
1. Relationship addiction—Fiction.
2. Self-esteem—Fiction. 3. Women—Fiction.
4. Self-perception—Fiction. I. Title.
PS3569.T33938B43   2007
813'.54—dc22   2006032399

Set in Minion by Bob Reitz.
Designed by A. Shahan.

For Allie

I went out to the hazel wood,
Because a fire was in my head,
And cut and peeled a hazel wand,
And hooked a berry to a thread;
And when white moths were on the wing,
And moth-like stars were flickering out,
I dropped the berry in a stream
And caught a little silver trout.

When I had laid it on the floor
I went to blow the fire aflame,
But something rustled on the floor,
And some one called me by my name:
It had become a glimmering girl
With apple blossom in her hair
Who called me by my name and ran
And faded through the brightening air.

Though I am old with wandering
Through hollow lands and hilly lands,
I will find out where she has gone,
And kiss her lips and take her hands;
And walk among long dappled grass,
And pluck till time and times are done
The silver apples of the moon,
The golden apples of the sun.

WILLIAM BUTLER YEATS
"The Song of Wandering Aengus"

Because a Fire Was in My Head

Kate

They were stopped on a hill at a red light, Kate Riley and a man.

There was always a man. Did it matter which? Perhaps it might have mattered if she had been willing. Or not afraid.

They were stopped on a steep hill, the red light at the top crowning the intersection, with several cars in front, so that theirs — it was new and dark—tilted sharply up toward the summit. Until she glanced to her left there were the usual sounds of afternoon traffic in the town of Monterey. The sun was out, a temperate day, an ordinary moment from the flow of impersonal and familiar time. Until she saw the young woman there was sound, the calico busyness of suburban scene, the smell of new leather, the man beside her, his hand resting lightly atop her—she could not see his face, but she noted with satisfaction the space filled in by his shape. He had just concluded a long sentence with her name as its caboose—*Kate*—gently rocking at the end, a reassuring lilt that, to some extent, she knew she did not need, even while she took pleasure in its small ritualized caress. Then it all vanished, or it dropped its claims, ceased to move; the camera had stopped forward action, and the moment fell from above like a single pebble into her hand.

On the sidewalk to her left was a young woman. She alone went on, lived on. A black Labrador sat beside the woman, alert, watching the traffic, his nose lifted slightly, his head shifting one way then another—he seemed to be hoping that someone would come along to help. The young woman was slender, even . . . cadaverous. Her left hipbone jutted out and up at a distorted angle, and the modern, hip-hugging slacks she wore struck a sad note of complicity—she was blind and could neither see and enjoy her conformity with the fashion of the day, nor realize how slightly, fatally it missed the mark. Someone else—not family, Kate could not imagine a family—a friend or a store clerk perhaps, had chosen the clothing for her. Kate could not imagine a family because of the dignity; dignity of that sort was self-generated and independent. Dignity could not be borrowed, it was wrung from the smallest of acts repeated over time.

The cropped shirt revealed a swath of tummy, flat and pale, not unattractive—men liked looking without being seen, yes, Kate thought, even the man sitting next to me, all of them. The young woman's hair had been cut with ease of care—or utility—in mind. The eye locations were shadowed, like charcoal smudges, and sunken in against the nose in the way that was typical of people blind from birth. It was as if the muscles surrounding the eyes, having never been called to action, retreated permanently. With her left hand she gripped the animal's heavy leather harness as she tugged a plastic bag over her right hand, using her teeth in the end. There was something wrong with the arm . . . it kept springing up, bending inward, like a wing that did not want to be extended. Finally she half-knelt, half-squatted on the curb, all awkward limbs and angles; this girl had more than simple blindness to deal with. But there was something exciting, even aesthetic about her distortions—a figure in a dream by Picasso. In fact, the whole thing became a marvelous, lurid dance, and Kate was completely transfixed by the sightless cadaver with her one wing and her dog so true.

Kate glanced ahead, up the hill; the light had still not changed.

In the town of Monterey dogs had to be leashed; they had to be cleaned up after by their owners. The first was a municipal code, and the second simply a local code of conduct encouraged by discreet signs and the occasional plastic bag dispenser in parks and along popular walkways. The young woman's Seeing Eye dog had defecated in the gutter. It had never crossed Kate's mind, or she had never associated this natural function with Seeing Eye dogs who were immune, like priests and nuns and doctors, to the imaginings and degradations of the public eye.

The stools left by the Labrador were round and hard, and these attributes, combined with the steep slope, had sent them rolling downhill about four or five feet.

Her hand sheathed in the plastic made a sweep of the gutter—nothing. Again, she swept the area where she knew her dog had hunched moments earlier and where she naturally estimated his leavings should be found. Beside her the Labrador waited, perhaps embarrassed by what he had done, confused by her actions, worried. But Kate could see that he trusted his mistress, despite the long delay, or that he was at least willing to put up with things as they were.

The light would never change . . .

Kate thought about mentioning what she was witnessing to the man beside her, but even before the thought had concluded she decided that she did not want him to see it. Who would want to share so remarkable a moment? But she *could not* share it, either. It was like trying to call out in the middle of a dream—the effort was overwhelming. She felt paralyzed by the narrative.

Now the young woman dropped clumsily to both knees, the one normal arm and hand still linked to the dog's rectangular harness, and the other, the wing fluttering out beyond the safety of the gutter into the actual lane where cars, which had turned right from the cross street above, were now passing with the swift, carefree momentum of descent. Down down down they rushed toward her innocent arm . . . and just below, out of reach, the three brown stools sat like three blind mice.

Christ, let it go, Kate Riley thought, *just let it go. Surely, you are not required . . . you may excuse yourself.*

The light changed. Time resumed, gathering its skirts and fleeing before them. The car surged forward, the seat pressing itself with the sudden authority of the present tense into Kate's body. *You are here*, it said, *now*, it asserted. But she thought that she would look back, she felt sure that she would look back, she even wondered if some part of her, some imagined, allegorical remnant of Kate Riley would ask that they stop . . . and she would get out of the car, cross over, be the one the dog waited for, the person who was going to help. And Kate was aware, she *marveled*, that she did not look back. She felt herself to be in a kind of shock. She could not even turn her head. That was the thing that surprised her most—that she could not even *make* herself look back, there was so little will left, there was so little will left . . .

Because it was Kate who was in the grip of her own momentum, it was she who sped down down down into the broken wings of innocents.

Are you afraid? His question as they passed under the green light, which hung like heavy mistletoe over their heads. She kissed him. Brave Kate. Or perhaps it was only that she was aware of behaving bravely. She was pretty that day—on the thinner side of things—and felt not only that it was safe, but that she deserved to bestow a kiss. She was important, too; that day she was more important than he, more important than anyone they passed. Even the blind girl.

And they arrived at the hospital precisely on time.

June 3rd, 1970. Before the days of CT-scans and MRIs. Before they could look inside without making an actual entry, without making themselves an instrument of scientific faith.

His first name was Jim . . . he was important, they were all so important, but she could not even remember his last name.

It was a small Catholic hospital with a reputation for decent, workmanlike medicine. Jim had urged something more cutting-edge, a large medical center with a university attached, but Kate insisted on the unpretentious, and since she knew that he secretly approved of that, and as it wasn't his brain about to be probed—she couldn't help but note—he acquiesced. The sixties had only just concluded; faded bumper stickers continued to announce *small is beautiful*. And though she had never been a child of the sixties, had never been rich enough or idle enough to indulge in it, Jim, her newest one, had the philosopher's fondness for pretty ideas.

Under the hospital porte-cochere, he turned off the engine and strode with a masculine sense of purpose inside, long legs, arms pumping easily back and forth. She liked the way he walked, for that day *she* was his purpose. Five minutes later at her door stood Jim with a nurse pushing a wheelchair. Kate made some jocular remark—*it's not my legs, it's my head that hurts*—and they smiled, relieved and impressed—*brave Kate*—and said their lines, reaffirming that today was her day, today Kate Riley was special and everything about Kate overruled, and from everything Kate would be excused. It was just as she had fantasized it, the whole thing, the whole wonderful farce, and so real that, now more often than not, she found herself believing it.

Most of the rooms they passed were doubles, a vinyl accordion wall separating patients, but an entire room had been reserved for Riley comma Kate. The airy, wash-worn, hospital gown lay waiting on the coverlet, along with a shrink-wrapped plastic tub containing a cup, straws, toothbrush and paste, comb, hospital socks with a white rubber chevron pattern on their soles, the kind they make for toddlers, a turquoise aspirator, some brochures, and the ubiquitous bean-shaped vomit dish. Jim placed her overnight duffel bag near the bed and said, "I'll be right back." She felt a sudden hollowing in her stomach—was he going to make a call? Now? Was he actually going to place a call now to the office? Would the new secretary be there, Sandra in her summer sandals? Did she know, she must know, about the headaches, the blackouts, the exploratory surgery? They all must know. Surely he was excused . . . somewhere she had heard that thought before, somewhere recently . . .

"Can't it wait?" she asked. "My head, it feels as if a horse has kicked me."

Jim was a modern-day ascetic, lean and haphazardly clothed, but clean, very clean, with eyes that were always gazing a little too deeply for comfort, especially at that moment as he tried to be intensely comforting. He was so sincere that, under different circumstances, she would have laughed.

"I thought you were off this deadline . . . didn't they get someone else to do the piece? You promised . . ."

"Kate. I'm just going to the restroom."

She stared back at him. He was the purest of them all. "Oh you."

By the time he returned she had already changed into the gown, arranging herself with poignant neatness beneath the covers, like a little girl waiting to be tucked in.

"My hair," she said, not really thinking of it yet—cueing it up.

"It will grow back, exactly as it is now," he said, lifting the cool heavy mass, rolling his hand back and forth beneath it, then he must have checked himself; it would not do to appreciate her hair today, he seemed to realize. And again Kate remembered why she liked this man.

Behind his chair there was a window and through its upper half she could see yellow California hills studded with live oaks, blue sky, a single cloud stretched and flattened by the wind off the sea, and the sea itself, just a slim wedge of blue-gray. She would remember that scene, the colors, the one long cloud, for the rest of her life. If she lay down partially she did not have to see through the lower half of the window where a cemetery spread in tufted, green undulations down to the river that flowed to the nearby sea, though even then, during that first hour in the hospital, she did not feel its genuine weight, its very real pull, and avoiding it was a matter of pretense—part of the show.

Later on a nurse came in carrying a white enamel tray, and in it, several items: scissors, a razor, tweezers, electric clippers, a tub of antiseptic shaving gel, a rubber band, a clear plastic bag, a tiny paper cup containing a single pill. "Would you like a sedative? It helps to relax."

Kate looked at the neatly folded towel draped over the nurse's forearm like a barmaid's, and smiled. "No."

"Yes," said Jim at the same time. They laughed. "Well, I need one," he added, still smiling in a way that was meant to be boyish and pleasing.

When Kate had moved to the stool and the plastic smock was snapped around her neck, Jim rose. They had agreed beforehand that he would go away during the haircut, and while he fished out the new hat—a light blue cashmere beret—she brushed her hair into a single bundle and bound it with the rubber band. Then he stepped outside the door and waited. Arrangements had already been made with a wig man over the hill who worked quickly and expertly with human hair. Jim was to take the hair to him immediately, then return. By the time she was released from the hospital in a week the wig would be ready—or at least that was the plan.

"I'm sorry," said the nurse.

"Well . . ." Kate offered a light, ecclesiastical shrug, accepting fate with the equanimity of a nun.

"It's beautiful hair."

"My grandmother's," she murmured as if in a dream. Then she closed her eyes as the scissors made their way through the thick bundle. The sound of the scissors laboring, a slick chunking sound, was unique in all the world. Then it was over. The nurse placed the hair carefully in the plastic bag, and handed it out to Jim who departed without a word.

"Do you want to see?" the nurse asked as she took her seat again.

"Yes." In her excitement Kate grabbed the mirror. "Oh." She pulled what was left of her hair out to the side, shook her head, and tugged again at the dark ragged halo. "It's perfect, perfectly awful ... I look like, well now, who do I look like?" Fiddling with the clippers in the tray, the nurse seemed to understand that she was audience, not participant. "That blind girl with her choppy hair, that's who I look like. How strange. I wonder what it would be like to be blind." And then she thought about that as a possibility.

The nurse was staring at her.

"I'm ready," Kate said.

Again with the scissors until it was uniformly short, then out came the clippers, which *clacked* sharply before settling into a steady buzz, mowing front to back, front to back, the cold fingertips of the tines vibrating and the clumps of hair dropping like small furry animals she was giving birth to, one after another, except that there was nothing to them, they were all hair.

Now the nurse—her nametag said Betty—plump, motherly Betty would not allow the mirror. "Let me use the razor first, Mrs. Riley. Your head has a nice shape." Against Kate's naked scalp her palms were warm and intimate, and she seemed proud of her work as she spread the shaving gel and drew the razor about, making short orderly paths. A warm wet towel at the end, some antiseptic lotion, and Nurse Betty was finished.

"I think I'd like to be alone," Kate said in a quivery voice, "seeing for the first time."

Betty offered an understanding nod, "Of course," sweeping up the bodiless fur creatures, letting the door close behind her with a distinctly soft regret.

On the tray table the mirror lay face down; Kate picked it up and looked, instantly casting her gaze to the yellow hills, the one long cloud, then down at the squares of gray linoleum, crawling back up to her hand holding the mirror, to the mirror itself, irresistibly turning it. "You."

She was thirty-nine, and it was the first time she had seen her face, not as someone who owns it or possesses it, but as a witness to a true, if strangely static, event. When you had no hair it wasn't your scalp you noticed, it was your face. And hers was a tired face, a hard face, a face she did not recognize except as someone she had seen once long ago on a street or in a crowd. Or maybe in that distant doctor's office . . . maybe that was the last time Kate could bear to see the woman she was. The eyes looked smaller, the lips thin and drawn down, the wrinkles were determined, there for the duration, and not at all evanescent as she had made them for so long through the eyes of others. *A face of certain experience*—those words came to mind. Even the dimples—small depressions that a veteran actress had practiced into their very existence—strained for an old recognition—the recognition that there had been someone innocent once, just a girl with dimples.

And at the same time, Kate Riley knew this face, she knew it like a dull pain in a place one hopes to be able to forget. She knew it and hated everything about it and there could be no forgiveness, none.

In redemption she was not interested, only in the moment freed of the past, all tethers neatly cut away. What would it be like? Who could imagine such a thing? The rarefaction, the light like the black at the center of the sun, and no memories, and without them, no one to have remembered them. No Kate.

The doctor came in, and several minutes later, two more, one of them female, and Kate hated her too. The anesthesiologist. The men wrote on her head, lines and numbers in purple ink, and used an instrument that reminded her of a sextant as they plotted their course across the seas of her mind; they made their preliminary calculations while the anesthesiologist waited. They murmured Kate's chances as if soothing a child, and even then, even then, forgetting for the moment what she had seen in the mirror, she made light of their task and of the future it put into question. Because they were men. Oh, the men, the men, the wonderful men . . . they would all cure her, wouldn't they, hadn't they? One of the doctors was especially masculine—strong hands and a steadiness in his eyes that bordered on angry determination. He would not easily fall. It would be worth it, Kate thought idly, to feel him fall.

These men were preparing her for exclusion from the future, the silent ongoing party that *was* the future . . . *an invitation has been sent, Mrs. Riley, of course! but mail service being what it is, the invitation may not arrive.*

When they left at last the female asked her question: Was there anything that concerned Kate, with regard to the anesthesia?

"Waking up," Kate told her.

"Many patients prefer a sedative beforehand," she suggested, neatly sliding her small freckled hands into side pockets. Her lab coat was spotless—no stains, no wrinkles, no blood.

"Piss off," Kate said.

Bright blue orbs with pinpoint pupils, flipped hair, enameled smile—all were impervious to Kate Riley, room #321 at St. Whose-its in the town of Monterey. Impervious as a billboard. "Well," quoth the billboard, "if you change your mind . . ."

If she changed her mind . . . my god, she could, but if she did, if she changed her mind, it would ruin everything, it would undo all . . . Kate seemed to know that much. If she got up and walked out she would lose her entire life, she would lose Jim, Kate Riley, her identity, and she would gain that face, that hard, unforgivable, pinch-eyed face in the mirror. She would be alive. There was that. Back in the old violence.

The anesthesiologist left without closing the door—another affront—Kate had become public property in a public place, the now proverbial potted plant—and she leapt from the bed to shut it. Outside the window, the long cloud had broadened to a ceiling, low and ominous; the yellow hills had grizzled beneath it; the trees seemed distant and man-made, props from an old stage set; and the sea . . . despite its slight appearance, she knew that the sea was as huge and ongoing as death. Except for the blue duffel—*her* bag, Kate's—the room was a colorless rectilinear assortment of glass, plastics, and stainless steel, commercially laundered fabrics, antiseptically altered air. Into this . . . appliance, she had freely entered.

She recalled that Mother had shaved her head, once to deal with lice, and a second time to deal with the boys who were worse than the lice, Mother said, the boys with their calf-eyes who came skulking round the house.

Poor head, Kate thought, poor undressed scalp, and she let her hands feel the exposed skin, which resisted slightly, like fine sandpaper, the motion of her fingers; she caressed the exposed contours of underlying bone, her head, her baby-bare mortality, smaller than a honeydew melon. Inside, like gray custard—as she had been told by the lout in X-ray—was her brain, full of memories, Kate's memories, Kate's pattern of impulses, responses, gestures, expressions, the sovereign land of Kate with its defining cartography of experience, a whole world, Planet Kate, spinning freely along, utterly self-contained and intact, a perfectly pure global entity which would be invaded the next morning.

With some surprise she realized she was afraid. Many times in the past fear had come, but then it was different, it was cloaked, disguised, burrowing through secret tunnels beneath the daily streets of her life. This fear now seemed to pool around her, a dark and appalling water that rose so quietly, almost as a circle of friends might, friends who were about to betray her, filling every corner as it crept upward to the small smooth buoy that was Kate altogether, Kate bobbing along on a dark unrepentant sea.

She called Jim's secretary—Sandra of the Sandals—knowing that he would stop by after he had driven her hair to the wig-maker. She couldn't let him see the face her scalp had perversely made public. But there was something else, something she could not make out yet but which she seemed to know was on its way, like a train whose approach one can feel trembling in the iron rails. "Tell him not to come. Tell him I've taken the tranquilizer and want to rest, and to come in the morning before . . . before it begins."

"Mrs. Riley," Sandra began, and Kate could hear the shapely words lining up, she could hear the whole chorus behind her, Sandra the secretary.

"Yeah, thanks," she said, and hung up. She thought of Jim. He had adored her, but that had faded. It was hard to make out the word anymore. He had resumed regular work hours, no more stolen afternoons, no more time with Kate spreading wildly, amorphously, abjectly throughout his day. Time with Kate had assumed its proper, squared-off place in his schedule, and she had diminished proportionately, just as the time had. Until the brain tumor—that had restored her dominion.

Surgery was scheduled for 9:00 a.m. At some point a nurse arrived with a sleeping pill, which Kate hid from her. So there was the night, the long night, not with a man as she was always hoping, as she had spent so much of her life anticipating, but with eternity stretched out before her like a sated lover. That was how she felt the possibility of her death, not as loss but as all of it gained, love sated, love worn out—the deepest and most irreparable sort of emptiness.

There was still the night to cross, though, and her mind began to move upon the silence, slow and aimless, remembering this, remembering that, like the hand of that sated lover over the body he has just possessed.

Then a strange thing happened, a tiny shift in perspective—she could almost hear the muffled *click*: she began to see herself as one might a twin sister, or as the imaginary obverse to whom she had long ago given the name, Ramona Moon; she began to watch and to account for Kate Riley just as the brain tries to account for the mind. In this way, and perhaps only in this way, she might save herself. For if she could not stop the Kate Riley who had entered this hospital, there was a very good chance she would kill both of them.

No, a flake had to be chipped from the block of time, Kate's time on the planet, and that flake had to be polished to a lens, and she had to look through that lens to see herself. And she had to do it for the boys. And for the she-child.

Slipping out of bed, she opened the window, letting the California night seep slowly into the room. Even on a moonless night, a Western sky glowed secretly blue behind the black, and was never bluntly dark the way a New England sky became on summer nights. It was something she had noticed when she visited upstate New York with the musician, one of the reasons, she told him, she was leaving.

After several moments she could see well enough the hospital room, the clock on the wall, the hand mirror lying prone on the tray table. Perhaps she had never felt so alone, perhaps it was irresistible, the way ugly things are, but she picked up the mirror and gazed again at the unfamiliar face, as if to try to make a friend. And what she saw first in that midnight blue glow were the whites of her eyes sharply white, like neon, and what she felt was the cool breeze on her bare head, and the questions—who are you and how did you get here—that had risen like twin sentries on either side of the door to the hospital room could be heard again clambering heavily to their feet. And suddenly, with a homesickness that was beyond repair, it was not 1970, it was 1941, and Kate Riley stood on a wooden platform in Netherfield, Saskatchewan with C. J. Pettigrew, or Scoop as he was known, because he was the station agent and often heard news from nearby villages first. That day Scoop Pettigrew seemed to know more than he wanted to say.

"Come in and have some tea, Kate Riley."

"But I can see the steam. I can even see the light," she added, though she could not. The tall white plume was rising, rising and coming toward her—she seemed almost to feel it rising from the very top of her own head, like a wonderful idea.

"It's still a good ten minutes off. Come and have some tea so you're nice and warm for their arrival." When Mr. Pettigrew smiled his cheeks became two tomatoes.

She squinted back at him, embarrassed by the tomatoes, and peered up the track. Now she could in fact see the CPR engine's cyclopean eye boring mightily through the distance, and through the cold, too, which crept upward in an ashen fog from the slough that lay to the south of the village. The whole day had been ashen-colored and dull, the cold dull too, like a weight upon the skin that only the wind could lift, and then the cold tucked in behind the sharpness that was neither hot nor cold, only a rasping pain. It was ten below. The Eaton's catalogue pages that she had layered beneath her coat crackled when she moved—another reason not to enter the Pettigrews's rooms above the station. They were one of the wealthiest families in town, their eldest daughter, Miriam, Katy's best friend, though she was a year older, but she did not have to use paper for insulation, and the Pettigrews did not have much to do with the Rileys, "because we're Irish," Katy's mother told her. "He has the high airs of the English. And she's French." No further descriptive was required when it came to the French, apparently.

"When are we going to get one of the new locomotives, Mr. Pettigrew?"

"Not for a long while, Katy. This is just a branch line. But your mother and father rode something fancy, I'd wager, once they reached Minneapolis. They've one called the *Hiawatha*, I've seen pictures of it."

The two stood for a minute or so, gazing up the tracks, Mr. Pettigrew with his hands knotted behind his back, and Kate, impatient, rolling up and down onto the balls of her feet, leaning forward now and then in that stiff, overbundled manner winter imposed on movement, to see around Mr. Pettigrew. Behind and above them, the Union Jack snapped back and forth against the pole. The flag was still relatively new, left over from the royal visit of King George VI and Queen Elizabeth just two years before, and the colors were bright and festive against the pale sky.

The frozen February air was so dry that whenever the wind rustled up a drift of snow, the powder was a fine dust that burned like the alkali from a dried-out summer slough. Kate had forgotten her hat and she was unusually cold. Without her father's help, her ringlets hadn't been quite successful, and the vestigial coils hung from long segments of lank red hair like the harness swings in the schoolyard where her friends at that very moment were playing. She had been released in order to meet the train.

But after all, Kate was cold, she had forgotten her hat, and her oldest brother John hadn't made it in the day before as he was supposed to have; there had been line trouble outside Moose Jaw — frost heaves. Colin was to meet the westbound train in Winnipeg; he had gone off to Camp Borden north of Toronto to become a flyer for the big war in Europe, but they had given him a special leave. So Kate had had to ask the neighbor widow, Mrs. Eustace Winget, to help her prepare the house for everyone's arrival, to haul the ashes and lay in the coal, to bring parsnips up from the basement, beets, and a handful of Prince Edward Country apples they kept in a deep barrel, and a jar of Saskatoon preserves and some pickles; to air linens, and to fill the missionary pot and set it to boiling on the stove; to sweep and clean. And she was not to bellyache, her mother had told her before leaving two weeks ago, no, she was not to bellyache . . . but it did seem to Kate that she deserved a cup of tea at least. So she told Mr. Pettigrew that she thought she would, and he ushered her over to the door that led up to their rooms.

Stiffly, she entered the Pettigrews's parlor, preferring to stand, she told Mrs. Pettigrew in a formal, better-than-Irish voice, as she dolloped large amounts of cream into her tea so that she could gulp it down quickly and return to the platform. Sitting would reveal the insulating presence of the catalogue pages, and Kate did not want Celeste Pettigrew to hear them.

There were a lot of fine rugs and big furniture, small delicate items made of pink glass, chairs covered with chintz, and even a bronze bust of someone famous. Highfalutin, Mrs. Riley called it, gaudy, she declared, but Kate could not help being enchanted by the rich colors, the wood shining darkly like furnishings from a castle, and there were even silk tassels hanging from the lampshades that danced whenever a train pulled into the station. Now here came jellied pastries. Mrs. Pettigrew seemed especially nice that day, commenting on Katy's red hair and her lovely "aristocratic" skin, so that when the train whistle blew Katy was not actually waiting on the platform, she was rustling down the stairs with queenly flounces and the satisfaction of knowing that she had had sweets without her mother's knowledge.

The train had already arrived. Behind Fiona and Hugh Riley it loomed, breathing steam and smelling excitingly foul and industrial, everything faraway brought before her, Kate Riley, so that even the grain elevators towering silently above the engine were as easy to dismiss as three old deacons at a bonspiel. Her father was hanging oddly, like a scarecrow, between Scoop Pettigrew and her brother Colin, and all she could see were yellow eyes, yellow, as yellow as new mustard, fixed with a kind of pleading apology on her. Just then an icy wind swirled around the corner of the station house and against the back of her neck, penetrating her thick hair with the stunning sharpness of an angry hand.

Kate heard a sound, a piercing whimper, the kind a rabbit lets out if a wolf or a dog catches it, and it seemed to have come from her . . . But she did not say, "What's wrong with your eyes, Poppy?" She could not seem to say it, to admit that she had seen. It contradicted everything she understood about Poppy. Instead, she gave her head a shake, as though there were something annoying nearby, then snapped herself to a regal attention and announced with a shiver, "I forgot my hat," and Hugh Riley seemed relieved, grateful even, to have the focus turn so swiftly to his darling Kate and her cold, uncovered head. He dropped his eyes, smiled wanly as they helped him into Scoop's old Model T, fumbling all the while, digging into his coat pocket even as they eased him into the backseat and pressed a red blanket over him.

At last a triumphant grimace; he called her, and she pushed

through the two men. Her father's cheeks were hollowed and his teeth looked enormous and too long, the lower ones much more obvious than the uppers in some dark shift of fortune. His starched white shirt collar poked up stiffly around his chin, creating an emptiness just below; the shirt seemed to have been borrowed from someone, it was so big and white. Above the whiteness his yellow eyes were even more shocking. He was aware of their effect—she could see that—and dropped his gaze as he thrust out a clawed hand, reaching blindly for her other hand to help take a small brown package. Kate backed away slowly. Inside the brown paper lay a carved Indian girl wearing a leather shift and a beaded headband; on the bottom of her feet, burned into the wood, were the words *Sioux Indian Squaw*. Kate was still examining the figure as the Model T pulled away. There had been no room in the car, but her mother had thought to pass her woolen hat out the window, and Colin sneaked a little bag of rock candy into her pocket. He looked so much like Poppy, except younger and without the hump, that whenever Colin was in town Kate almost couldn't decide whom to cotton up to. Now here he was in a smart new uniform. And now, too, here were the other eyes.

She waited to watch the train leave, and still she waited, sitting on the bench against the outside wall of the station, glancing up the tracks now and then, as if there had been some mistake. Another train would arrive, another father would emerge.

A delinquent gust menaced around the station, slapping past her, poking up a dirty pile of snow. Huddled inside her coat she could still hear the flag snapping above, and the train whistle thinning into the west, and then just the wind beyond the tracks, planing one way and then another across the snow-rippled flats as if hunting for something it had lost so long ago that it could not remember what it was. *Poor wind*, Kate thought, *poor old wind*. When she heard Celeste Pettigrew put a record on her phonograph, Kate stood. It was fancy music, music without words, and this time Celeste's taste was vexing somehow. Kate picked up a tune her mother was always humming . . . *oh when Irish eyes are smiling* . . . but the words made a terrible echo in her mind, and she clamped down on them and walked in silence along the platform, turning at the end toward the village.

The train tracks marked the southern boundary of Netherfield; beyond them lay the open prairie and the sky rising and fanning overhead with a dizzying omnipresence that held both motion and suspended motion; an overwhelming show of emptiness as strong as a blow to the head that blanked out everything, coupled with a tyranny of sheer freedom, sheer possibility that tended to straighten spines and fill lungs and run the mind along a ragged edge. Oh, it was big. Again and again it began the same way wherever she went, and seemed never to end—the end of ends. Perspective was all out of whack: for that sky, for that land flowing out to a horizon that kept receding, for that sky all over head, *all over*, and the sameness of the land so that sometimes the sameness became the thing, not the land, the sameness of even the tiny outcroppings of makeshift civilization, each crowding up to a grain elevator like believers to a traveling faith healer; no, a human being could not provide contrast—at least not a healthy one.

The sky, the space it took up in Kate's mind, yet did *not* take up but emptied out, created a funny little contradiction inside, a worry she couldn't quite get rid of, that drew her head down as surely as a weight at the end of her nose might. Thus, Kate Riley walked home through the village of Netherfield, its weathered miscellany of houses, sheds, false-fronted businesses, school, and churches—a lot of churches—the assorted rudimentary needs of society laid out in a snug and faithful crosshatch as if it mattered, *as if it mattered*, and was no less poignant or more audacious in that vast rolling prairie sea than the very idea of life blinking into the twilight of the abyss—or so Kate Riley was thinking as she drifted back to her hospital room.

She gazed again into the hospital mirror at the whites of her eyes, a bright, healthy white. Though it was June, the breeze from the open window was cool. She tugged the blue knit beret down over her shaved head. His eyes, yellow . . . her head, cold . . . these together were the small, unmarked keys that opened memories.

What had happened then? Where was the rest of Netherfield, the rest of her life there, and then her life after? How had it led inexorably to this place, to this moment that was a place? This place that might end all her moments to come? The future of the future.

Memories came at her from all directions; there was no orderly lining up of events . . .

It had begun to snow as she walked through the village, big flakes the size of cotton balls which the wind made frantic and silly, darting one way then another.

She was smiling as she reached the house, the Model T just pulling away. "Better get on in and have a cup, Katy," Scoop Pettigrew hollered to her, forgetting that his wife had just given her tea.

How could he forget, she wondered. And then: *it's not good, all this tea and candy and stuff.* She looked at the Sioux Squaw, then shoved it back inside her coat. Poppy never forgot her and he wouldn't now either, she decided, standing before the iron gate. But she seemed to know that he would forget her, that he had already begun, that nothing would ever be the same.

The house was a tall narrow clapboard that sat on the corner, one street over from Main, two blocks from Lonegren's Store, and far enough from the school that Kate had more than enough excuse to dally coming home. Once it had been painted yellow, but the paint had been scoured down to thin yellow lines in the creases between the clapboards, and vague patches on the leeward side of the house. The small wallpapered rooms arranged themselves around the stairwell, which rose directly from the front door landing. The pine plank floors were painted brown; the glass was wobbly and never quite honest, especially with the storm windows secured to the outside. The kitchen counters were covered with oilcloth that had been tacked down; the shelves were open, cluttered but clean.

Kate loved her home; though not the finest, it had a lilac bush, and a Hawthorne hedge along the iron fence, and three little birches where the biffy stood, though they now had indoor plumbing. There were Irish linens in the cupboards, and doilies tatted by her grandmother draped along the arms and back of the chesterfield, lace curtains, a teacup collection and six tiny thin glasses, delicately pink, for sherry drinking on special occasions. Her own small bedroom had cozy angles in its ceiling, and a dormer niche that just held a small table where she did her schoolwork, and made clothes for her cutout dolls. Poppy, as she alone was allowed to call him, had made the table himself. There was an iron bed, a varnished dresser, and several pictures from old calendars tacked to the wall.

In her mother's face an aimless fear wandered; she seemed too tired to bring it to a focus, to think about the details ahead, probably there had been so many at the Mayo Clinic. Now it was just the one big thing she could look at; she kept walking around it and pointing to it in a quiet shocked way. "He's going to die," she told Kate. "That's the story of it." She was standing on the stairs, going up to him, and she had merely turned when Kate entered as if to tell her to put some water on, or to wash her hands—a trifle. Even her tone seemed to have nothing to do with her words. And so Kate replied, "Yes, Mother," and went to find Colin.

That's the story of it, her mind repeated.

The next day John arrived, tall and thin, and always neatly though not too impeccably dressed, which would have drawn attention. No, John was a modest sensible man with the kind of face that was hard to recall, a clerk at the Bank of Commerce—with prospects, his mother liked to remind Eustace Winget. "It seems to me that something will have to be done," he kept saying. Fiona murmured vaguely in response, and then later Kate would hear him enunciate the same words again, "It seems to me that something will have to be done."

Colin played cards with her when he wasn't helping Fiona or fixing something—the copper mesh in the screen door, the sewing machine, something to do with the cistern. It was Colin who regularly emptied the white enamel pan that sat under his father's bed. And unlike her mother or John, Colin never said anything that burned inside her head; his words were light and airy and as hard to hang onto as a spring breeze, and yet the feeling never failed to linger, tingling somewhere behind her ears, like the magic coins he was always finding there.

So they were all together in Netherfield for one week that February of 1941. The wind blew relentlessly and the dry granular snow drifted up against the house and the townspeople talked about the Rileys' bad news, *may God bless them*. After several days Hugh recovered enough from the travel to join them at the dinner table one night, though his head drooped downward like a buzzard's, and the hump on his back rose triumphantly above; his eyes stayed yellow, because the cancer had moved from his pancreas to his liver and was not going to leave. He breathed through his mouth, and his lips were so cracked that scabs had formed. Fatigue had relaxed his jaw, which then accentuated his lower teeth, crooked and bad. In such a face the tired sweet smile he had for everyone would have been unbearable, except that none would hurt him by looking away or wincing. None but Kate. At the once incontrovertible head of the table he was a sagging and pitiable sight to the others, but to Kate he was an act of betrayal, a beast, a lowdown thief who had somehow taken over her father, and who now seldom gave but demanded all of the attention.

He could not help it, but why didn't he? Why didn't he just put things back the way they had been? She felt his smooth hands in hers as they skated around the rink; she saw him behind her as he playfully styled her hair to look like Shirley Temple's; she watched him arrange his delicate watch tools . . . it was all gone. There was nothing to look forward to, there were only the lost things which she was discovering one by one now, like flecks of broken glass, some of them surprisingly far-removed from the occasion of the first shattering impact.

The pot stew steamed, the bread was still warm and yeasty, the conversation ambled along quiet side streets, avoiding the main topic of their days.

Colin carried in the bread pudding, serving his father first, then the others, and at last he came to his sister.

"Kate won't have any," Fiona said calmly, making a small abrupt sign with her hand, flicking something invisible away. It was a gesture she used so often that it had acquired the potency of symbol and was understood instantly regardless of circumstance.

In the silence that followed, Hugh struggled to clear his throat; lying on his back most of the day, his chest filled and went half stagnant with "sputum," as Fiona called it—one of the new words in the house that Kate found repulsive. Finally, without lifting his eyes, without moving anything but his lower lip, which had become red and wet with the effort, he uttered her name, "Fiona." Then he had to clear his lungs again. "Some pudding," he said, still not lifting his yellow eyes. "The boys are here just the week."

"Kate is a mite fleshy."

"At her age it's right to have extra. Why, I recall a snap of you . . ."

"It isn't healthy. Look at Mrs. Duff, it takes her twenty minutes to get up her own front stairs."

John began to gently drum his middle and index fingers on the table beside his plate—*ta-dum, ta-dum, ta-dum*—a sign that, for the time being, he would reserve judgment.

Colin was still standing beside Kate's chair, the bowl of bread pudding hovering near her cheek and taking on the sudden appearance of flesh as it jiggled slightly in his hands.

"Sit down, son," Fiona said quietly, firmly, "Kate won't have any."

"Kate won't have any what, Mother?"

A brief trapped expression fled across Fiona's face; she glanced at her husband, then back at Colin. "Son . . ."

Ta-dum, ta-dum, ta-dum.

"I don't really care for any," Kate mumbled, wanting only to end the talk.

"What is it Kate won't have any of," Colin persisted, his voice rising, "pudding? Your pudding or is it your . . . ?"

"It seems to me," John said sharply, but there was a guttural sound at the head of the table, a twin yellow flash of eyes, and he cut short what he was about to say.

"It's Mother's love that brings on her concern," Hugh stated, his voice clear and strong, his eyes yellow like a wolf's. He stared at his wife. "Of course it is." Tugging the napkin from his neck, he made as if to stand; both sons leapt to his side and eased him toward the stairs. "Cleora Duff does have a terrible time of it," he said softly as they helped him up to bed.

Fiona gazed silently at Kate for what seemed hours, but Kate could not return the gaze; she watched her empty plate as the side of her face seemed to melt. "Look what you've done," rasped her mother.

Later, Colin delivered a dish of bread pudding to Kate's room. "A little more for the boys to hang onto," he whispered, and Kate made a face and gave him a poke.

"Colin," she said, "why does Mummy . . ."

"Oh, never mind about that. She's in a snarky mood. Can't blame her, I suppose."

In the half-dormant, half-mad world of a prairie winter, time lost all precision, the minute ticks and nicks of living blunted to a dull and seamless existence. But that winter there were other markings, traces of life sharpened by suffering. Kate measured the length of her father's illness by the length of townsmen's hair; Hugh Riley had been Netherfield's barber for twenty-five years. In that time the women had lost the knack, but it wasn't until Fiona brought him home from the Mayo Clinic that the town saw it would have to recruit a new barber. At the back of the barbershop stood a billiard table, and a small desk where Hugh repaired watches and eyeglasses on the side. Which meant, one way or another, he was always bending over something—a man, a billiard ball, a pocket watch—and with the years his back had humped accommodatingly, as if to bring his head closer to the task at hand. But in spite of his deformity he was a handsome man with dark hair and lively blue Irish eyes and a soft, wounded way of holding his mouth. It was his mouth, his sensitive suffering mouth and the kindness it implied, Fiona said she had loved first. Kate had heard their story many times—it was part of the household mythology.

They met in a village south of Portage La Prairie when she was seventeen. During the warmer months of the year Fiona's father allowed their home to become a Stopping House, with the women sleeping in the front room and the men out in the stable. "Him I catches smoking I'll thrash," he would say to the men. He was too shy to speak to the women. In the morning there was porridge with chokeberries, salt pork, and tea. Hugh was passing through, headed west, looking for work, but he stayed after the porridge, and he stayed through the threshing season, working for Fiona's father, and then because Mr. McCory could see his calf-eyes and the direction of things, and because he let it be known that he didn't want his only daughter marrying a thirty-year old fellow with no more prospects than a pair of scissors, the two eloped. That was 1911.

There was a first child stillborn in 1913. John came in 1915. Later, twin girls who quickly succumbed to the great influenza pandemic of 1918. Colin arrived in 1922. And then in 1931, with the Depression beginning its slow deep swing across the decade, Kate appeared, red-haired, green-eyed Kate with her sassy temper and her dimples and her little bit of extra everywhere, blowing through their world like a warm Chinook in the dead of winter.

Netherfield's barber waited until spring to die, as a final kindness to his widow, they said.

The wild crocus that spread down the almost imperceptible slopes of the vast prairie land swells, and the prairie rose, palest pink, that grew along the coulee banks; the buttercups in the low areas, the tiger lilies and huge spikes of gladioli in the garden, the delicate sweet peas in the black earth on either side of the front stoop—all were making their annual appearances. The slough was alive with mallards, their new nests snugged into the tules. In the creases and coulees the spring melt ran knee deep, a muddy foaming wash, while overhead willows swayed, and the tentative green leaves of the aspen, newly unfurled, shimmied in the dazzling light. Beyond the village, caught here and there in the short tough prairie grass, were the traveling cottony seeds of the cottonwood trees, forgiven entirely their look of litter. Small patches of melt water dotted the widening expanse of land as evenly as the fair weather clouds across the sky overhead, and the two seemed to vie one for one, puddle for cloud.

Dawn. Kate had come downstairs and out onto the verandah, and looking down at her bare feet, feeling a hint of early warmth in the wood, the almost muggy mildness of the air, she decided to go further.

He had died an hour or so earlier. She had heard, or seemed to remember hearing, a single note that did not sound human torn from her mother, then the rumbling voices of the men, her brothers, and then she had simply retreated back into sleep, hiding in its frayed edge like a wild animal in the grass beside the road where large unknowable things were passing with alarming speed. It was the silence across the hall that had eventually drawn her fully into the day, and that confirmed his death. They were all sitting in there. Praying, she supposed. She herself had never believed in God. How could anyone believe in something that was not physically present, or at least visible on a regular basis? No, almost from the beginning Kate Riley had cast her lot with the present, with the urgency of immediate desires and their proximity to possible requital.

So far as Kate was concerned, her father, Hugh Fergal Riley, died that day at the train station. Circumstances—his illness—had pinched their relationship down to practically nothing. Without that, he did not seem to exist, or he existed in a way that was hateful to her. There he was at the center, hustled along by his illness, and everyone else plodding obediently beside him, the road obvious, the end inevitable. Kate's father had not been a separate individual with separate experiences; in her mind he lived only as connected to her. Once when a schoolmate's mother mentioned seeing him over in Virden, Kate found she could not really believe it; and whenever anyone recalled events before her birth, a holiday the Riley family took to Kenosee, or her father's part in building the house they lived in, his years as a local curling champion, it all seemed to have come from a boring storybook. In fact, it vaguely irked her to have to hear about other times, other places. It could not be called a failure of imagination, for Kate had a vivid, even wild fantasy life. In a sense it was a failure of reality, which simply did not make the proper impression on her, or which allowed itself to be colored to suit her needs or fancy.

She stepped down off the verandah, lifting the hem of her nightgown over a puddle at the base.

Her mother would wait to call Dr. Bartholemew. Like any physician in the Prairies, he was the most respected man in the area; he would have to drive down from Moosomin, followed by Mr. Hawkes, the undertaker, in his Packard hearse, which served as the area's ambulance as well. She would not want to bother the doctor until after he had had his morning meal; and she would want the time in order to tidy the house and to put on her good dress and to have one of the boys pick up something from Lonegren's to serve the doctor after he had finished the examination. Fiona had been through this before with the twins and with Eustace Winget when her Fred had passed. She had always been very good with illness and death, neutralizing the charged atmosphere with an orderly, businesslike manner. It was almost as if Fiona Riley were playing a sort of game—a serious game—at which she aimed to be better than competent.

Kate cut over to Main Street. The early morning light was flat and total, laying down instantly the long shadows of the town buildings in a serrated pattern east to west. Heading north, she traced the pattern in the gravel with her bare feet. When she came to the semi-circular shadow of the Ukrainian Church with its onion domes, she slid her feet gracefully along the curves, as if practicing a dance movement. At the end of town prairie chickens had come out onto the road to gravel up; Kate could hear their busy *chuck-chuck-chucking* as she approached, and then when she crossed the road they scattered, and she padded along the ditchbank path for awhile. The sun was exactly before her now, hard and white and still riding low in the sky so that, briefly, it seemed to be her own height, to have paused even, in order to have a word with her, the big shining head of the sun exactly opposite her human one.

Squinting, she stopped and in a voice that was both girlish and imperious said, "Well?"

For a while she listened to the wind and the silence it was always trying to conceal. She looked down at her toes; they seemed a long ways away, and separate. She had grown a lot that year, had started to develop bud-like breasts and even some curly wisps in her private area. The breasts were fine, but the hairs frightened her—it seemed foreign, like a little invasion.

Beside her in the ditch where the snow had gone, leaving a muddy trickle, she noticed a duckling from last summer perfectly preserved in the mire, its tiny bill shaped in happy anticipation of the life it did not get to live. Just above it, tonguing down from the edge of the path the little orange flowers of the false mallow were just beginning to bloom. She picked several of the buds and dropped them onto the duckling, pretending that it had been her pet, that she had just found it after a long sad winter's search, and that she would not cry, she would be brave, she would *chin up*, as her mother liked to say. Then Kate found a stick, drew a heart-shaped coffin outline around the creature, dug the stick in the mud at its head, and resumed her journey.

The air moved past her gently, as if not wanting to disturb. Out in the short furry new grass meadowlarks burst from underfoot. Without knowing where she was going she kept walking, and when she saw the cemetery past where the road curved toward Virden, it became her destination as if it had been her destination from the outset — the iron fence, the protective cypress trees bent away from the wind that came down from the north and west, the stone markers knocked crooked by frost heaves and which, from a distance, looked like her father's bottom row of teeth. She could see the figure of a man as she approached . . . no, not a man but a boy. Jan Larsen. A classmate two years older. His people were poor; they had moved in from the outback only a couple of years ago, picking up odd jobs where they could: tending the cemetery was one of them. The job had apparently fallen to Jan. He was there with a rake, pulling the moldered debris of winter away from each of the stone markers and along the fence lines. Though he had not lifted his head or faced her, she knew that he had been watching her come since she had abandoned the ditchbank path. Any vertical figure on the prairie steppes was viewed with an uncanny visual hunger, the eyes, as if magnetized, returning again and again to the slender shape that rose from the flats and grew like a quiet contradiction. And knowing that he had been watching her come, she decided that Jan Larsen had been waiting for her. Probably he had already noticed the bare feet, the nightgown, but Jan would make no comment. The Larsens were Swedes — silent, reliable, brutal hard-workers.

Without pausing she walked straight through the gate and came up so close to him that the hem of her nightgown fluttered against his leg. "Where does it all come from," was the first thing she said.

He peered up from his raking. "What?"

"That dead stuff," she said, pointing at the sodden brown vegetation he was raking.

"Why, all over," Jan said. "The wind blows it up against the stones and then the snow buries it."

"I've never seen that kind of leaf."

With the tines of the rake Jan teased the big leaf from the mess and laid it aside for her. "Doesn't belong here. Somebody must've brought it with 'em and planted it in their yard, or maybe raised it from seed."

Kate picked it up and opened her palm beneath it. "It's like a hand," she said, "like a brown hand sleeping in mine."

Past the cemetery, in the field below the irrigation dugout, they could hear the ringing cries of red-winged blackbirds hunting for morning seed.

"I don't guess I belong here either," she said in a kind of whisper, closing her hand around the leaf, and watching the wind as it bore her words away. *Now that he's gone,* she thought.

From under his cap Jan glanced at her nightgown, then poked aimlessly at the debris.

Though she hadn't thought about saying what she'd said, once the words were out, they seemed right to her, if only for their being heard that morning—the morning her father died. *My father is dead,* she thought.

She gazed up at Jan's broad Scandinavian face; there was no trouble in it. He seemed to be waiting for something to come along, or not. "My father died this morning," she said. "When I was asleep."

His brow furrowed briefly. He gave a nod.

"There was no last good-bye," she said, looking right into Jan's scoured blue eyes.

"Too bad," he managed to say.

"I was sleeping, and off he went . . ." she made a dramatic gesture with her arm toward the open and empty prairie, "without a last good-bye."

"Ah, that's the too bad of it." There was a long pause. "Being your father, he'd've known, though."

"Known?"

"How you felt 'n all."

"Oh yes," she said brightly, "Poppy knew so much." She heard the tinny sound of the *knew* and was pleased with her quick adult adaptation, even while there was something unreal about it. "Poppy knew a lot," she added sadly. "Everything."

Jan cleared his throat and for a moment gazed east out into the empty plains rolling away from them in every direction with a fierce persistence. The wind whipped past them suddenly, dropped, picked up again and shoved along the cypress trees. Then Jan Larsen did something that startled her: he hugged her. The rake was still in his hand and she could feel part of the long handle pressing into her back, while through the thin fabric of her nightgown the buttons of his barn jacket ran right up her front, like finger footsteps. When he released her he went back to his raking, his face tense and flushed.

There had been something exciting about Jan's hug and the buttons on his jacket and her nightgown and the wild space all around them, and right in the middle of it, the faintest warm scent at the base of his neck. And her father's death . . . it was exciting too. It was somehow secretly connected to Jan, as if he had been waiting in the cemetery that morning in order to comfort her, to help her to say the words—that she did not belong in Netherfield, and that Poppy knew, he understood, he would always understand no matter what she did.

A week later at the funeral she thought about Jan. Her mother sat beside her, a black shawl over her hair, and the brooch Hugh had given her on their twenty-fifth anniversary pinned to her breast. The brooch was formed in the shape of a single red rose with a genuine ruby, and Hugh Riley had saved two full years to buy it for her. John and Colin stood behind; there was a clot of friends around the grave, and beyond them the empty prairies radiating away and away, like rings of water, Hugh Riley at the center and beginning of it all, going down like a stone. The priest finished, his last words swiped by the wind. Handfuls of dirt rattled against the coffin lid. Kate stood, people hugged her, she thought of Jan.

"It seems to me this cemetery has never looked so well tended," John observed.

Jan did it, Kate thought, *Jan did it for me.*

"Oh, Hugh," Fiona wept.

"I wish it had been me," Colin said sadly.

"Oh, my hubby." But then Fiona peered at Kate and her expression changed, grew confused.

"What is it, Mum?"

"This way, Mother," Colin said, guiding her to the undertaker's car.

Most of the townspeople walked, there was so little money for gas because of the war, but the Smiths had hitched a team to their Ford and were hauling back several of the older villagers, including Mrs. Duff. And Ted Lonegren Jr. had a roadster gleaming in the morning light, which the women mostly disapproved of, even the two who were riding in it.

Miriam asked to walk with Kate, and together they followed the small crowd back to Netherfield.

In spite of the crocuses in bright lavender patches here and there, in spite of the puddles and pools of melt water, in spite of the sweet wisps of something about to bloom or already blooming far off, maybe primrose, the land seemed painfully exposed and wind-blasted. She could not seem to shake the sensation of something rude, a vast affront. She even glanced sharply at her friend. Had she said something? But Miriam Pettigrew walked along in a companionable silence, letting her hand gently bump Kate's, whereupon she clasped it perhaps a little too earnestly, for it annoyed Kate and she found excuse to withdraw her hand.

Maybe it was just the place, the having to be there without him. The having to go on.

At the edge of town in an abandoned farmyard there was a corrugated iron grain elevator still standing, and the wind slapped its broken door back and forth, whistled around the structure as if looking for a way to knock it down for good. Abruptly Kate went over, found a heavy rock and lugged it against the door, just to shut up the wind.

Several members of the crowd stood staring.

"It's bothersome, isn't it?" Miriam offered.

Katy shrugged. "Not to me much."

Miriam looked at her shoes. The two went on.

Not a cloud cast a shadow; the sun was everywhere at once, blinding and omnipotent. Someone in the lengthening crowd remarked that it would be a scorcher of a summer, and from the receiving silence it was clear that the pronouncement had the authority of experience. The last decade had seen depression, drought, dust, hoppers—all of everything, and Canadians did not want to be caught expecting anything else. If they were going to be beaten they wanted at least the pride in watching it come from the edge of the world, like a great yellow cloud of dust.

Down Main Street the crowd made its way, gathering before the barbershop where Mr. Nicholson hung one of the cemetery wreathes, and everyone dropped his head, or crossed himself before continuing on to the wake at the Rileys where there was sure to be some Irish whisky.

Kate felt withered and faintly sick, and no remedy she thought of seemed promising. She swallowed against a hard knot in her throat and kept her eyes on the planks of the sidewalk. Every now and then a strange panic almost overtook her, but she clenched against it each time and it stayed somewhere behind her. It was like a flash from a nightmare she could not remember, and she felt herself groping for the day's littlest and most tangible things, like the clay mud sticking to the edges of her good shoes, and Miriam Pettigrew's dress that had come all the way from Paris, France, and her brother John nodding at her, as if to say *be a good girl today*, and through the window of her father's barbershop the big white chair, pale and waiting in the dusky light.

For the first time since last summer the air was warm enough to arouse Netherfield's accumulated bad smells from the nuisance ground, and for reasons she could not explain, she made a point of inhaling it as deeply as she could, taking it all in.

All right, she thought, *all right, then.* And again she inhaled the foul smell. What the words meant she didn't know, but they seemed to marshal her for what was to come, the way that the townspeople, in saying that it would be a scorcher of a summer, were bracing themselves.

Her father had been dead six weeks, the period of acute mourning had passed, the excitement of the death was over. Her brothers had come and gone, their father's male possessions divided, or given away, or placed in the keepsake chest. The barbershop lease was legally terminated. Domestic matters had been arranged: coal would now be delivered, larger bags of staples as well, anything that a man would have carried. John established a contract with the Larsens to come by the house once a week and do the chores, the repairs, the hauling that Fiona and Kate could not. Then he went back to Moose Jaw and Colin returned to Camp Borden. And the two women—the one that had been and the one that would be—were left to each other.

Many observed that Hugh Riley had waited until spring to die, as a kindness to Fiona. They knew him to be that sort of man. Seven years later, when Kate left, it was well into fall, with all of winter for her mother to face—and this too was noticed by the people of Netherfield.

But even one more day would have been impossible for the young Miss Riley, for every day except the very last had been the same:

"I'll be dead by the time you get home from school."

"I can't go, Mum. I won't go."

"Oh, you'll go."

"Please let me stay. Let me make you some tea."

"Do you want to be ignorant? Do you want to be an ignorant Irish girl, talked about and pitied? What would Dad think? He bent his back over that chair year after year for you, and made so much of you, and now he's gone. Do you want to shame his memory? I'm a widow," she said, spitting out the word as if she had suddenly discovered something poisonous in her mouth. "In this place." Through the lace curtains she gazed with the same dull contempt Kate had seen in her eyes the day before, and the day before that, all the days that had trailed forward like dusty steps from the long-ago oasis of his life. "I'll be gone by the time you get home from school," she murmured in rote fashion, her eyes glazed over.

After the first several weeks, racing home, Kate understood that her mother was not going to kill herself. She was not going to take gopher poison the way Fran Weatherston had five months after her husband was lost in a blizzard; she was not going to hang herself with binder twine like Mr. Wilbur; she was not even going to be driven to the mental hospital over in Weyburn where Rose LeBlanc, it was rumored, would no longer use words, answering every question with an eerie charade of the wind. No, Fiona Riley may have missed Hugh, a man that made her a woman and a husband who defined her place in Netherfield; she may have felt the shame of widowhood in a landscape that was hard on solitary women, but once her daughter left for school each morning she was somehow able to rouse herself, to dress with a tidy feminine resoluteness—a pair of gloves, a small feathered hat, an umbrella tucked under her arm—and go into the village to conduct the matters of the day. Dr. Bartholemew had arranged for her to earn a nursing license at the General Hospital in Winnipeg. He had noticed her natural, practical skill with the sick, her distanced sort of caring that discouraged self-pity. So within a year the matters of the day included visiting the sick of Netherfield, consulting Dr. Bartholemew but only as needed, since a good many of the illnesses were psychosomatic, and arranging for the pills and powders from the chemist.

Yes, once the girl was out of sight her mother was able to set aside what she had lost, to contain it. The girl reminded her of him, not in the way that everything reminded Fiona of Hugh, and not because Kate was their child. No, it was because he had belonged to her, to Kate. In a sense, then, Fiona lost her husband the day the girl was born. He had given Kate what had once belonged to Fiona, which was more than love, not even love, though that was there, too. He gave his daughter his own original innocence, which had long ago retreated to its little room at the forgotten center of things. Nothing he had ever learned about human nature, about life, about the world around him, could hope to penetrate the flawless armor of his relationship with Kate. Together, they had contrived a kind of unspoken ideal, he for her, and she for him, to which no one else had access. Kate so identified with her father that she felt herself merged at all times with him, with his opinions, his tastes, his feelings, even those feelings that applied to her, and even his adoration of her—especially that—so that without him she found herself at a profound loss. He was gone. He wasn't there to love her, so the love was gone too. The love had taken up space and made things happen the way the wind filled the sails of the little boats on White Beat Lake, and pushed them from one shore to the other. Without the wind, the sails, suspended against the masts in dejected layers, practically disappeared. And without the love, in some terrible, inexplicable way, Kate Riley was gone, too, folded in on her own emptiness.

She poked at her dimples, as if to revive the charm they had once produced; she swished about before the hall mirror, searching for the exact flounce that used to catch his eye; she drew her lips down in the irresistible mock pout, she bounced her curls, she quipped operatically to the now absent audience—but it was all ordinary. *She* was ordinary, suddenly, dimmed to the backdrop of life. Inside, she felt a dry well from which only Poppy had been able to draw water.

Then she did something she could never understand: she slapped her own face as hard as she could.

Around the village, at church, during bonspiels, town gatherings, with the doctor and his patients, on visits to neighbors, Fiona Riley trod forward, and was respected for surviving so handily. Survival was more admirable than success, particularly individual success, which called attention. But at home with Kate something dark and wretched, even ominous boiled up inside her. She would not eat meals at a table with her daughter. It seemed to disturb her, the look of the two of them at a table. She ate in the parlor alone, sitting on the edge of the chesterfield like a guest at tea, her supper placed in a saucer, while Kate ate in the kitchen. At first Kate didn't mind the arrangement—it meant she could eat all she wanted. But as the weight began to mount she longed to be told *Kate won't have any*. It would have been something.

There was more than solitary feeding. Fiona developed a habit that involved exercising her lower lip against the rim of her false teeth. The habit never appeared outside the house. She insisted that any object that had been shifted or removed be returned to its exact place, and one day broke down completely when a teacup from her little collection had been turned with its handle to the left, not to the right. After that, Kate was allowed to dust only when her mother was present and keeping track of locations.

Alone, the girl seemed to trouble her, like an apparition or a stranger she did not expect and for whom she was not prepared. Kate often felt her mother staring at her, but with an eerie blindness, her head cocked, her lips quivering over a rush of silent words.

"Did you say something, Mummy?"

"Quiet."

"But is there something you want to say to me?"

Fiona's lower lip would begin its rolling massage of the denture rim.

"Is there something you need?"

Eventually her mother came around, often with the same words: "Haul the ashes," though every morning Kate hauled the ashes and never needed to be told.

Even at age eleven Kate was aware that her mother would have preferred the death of another child to the death of her husband; that there was something both surprising and galling about Kate's presence.

The boys were gone, off living their own lives. John had announced his engagement to Miss Vera Murdock. Colin was based "somewhere in England," the war ministry would not say where. France had crumbled, Britain was threatened; Colin might not ever come home. Prime Minister Mackenzie King was urging Canadian citizens to buy war savings certificates in addition to paying the higher income taxes to fund the national effort—the two together amounted to almost 40 percent of every earned dollar. Wheat farmers had been practically ruined by the glut of unsalable grain, though the government was buying some of it at salvage prices. What luxuries stores carried few citizens could afford. There was rationing—sugar, butter, liquor, coffee, tea, and gasoline. Netherfield, along with every other prairie town, had been gutted of its male youth, all of whom were clamoring to join the fight overseas, so many that there weren't enough left to meet farm labor needs. Even two of the single women in town had moved to the cities to work in defense factories, including Miss Phillips who had been Kate's teacher. She had enrolled in the Ottawa Technical School to become a welder, which offered better wages. Mr. Bowles took over the school. Bowles had a clubfoot and a bad temper because of it, but he was an old bachelor with money of his own, the only one around who could do the job, and nobody dared object.

To Kate the war, the half-empty store shelves, the elevators spilling grain that no one wanted, Mr. Bowles's ugly foot—all were natural components of her father's death, like the aches and pains that went along with influenza. She might have even expected it. He had abandoned her to a world that lacked few of the necessary supplies.

After Hugh Riley's death Kate was often sick. It was hard to stay well at home, the atmosphere was so glum. Earaches were common, stomachaches, tiredness that the doctor suggested was anemia but a simple blood test proved otherwise. Fiona nursed Kate as she would have any of her patients. Outside the ritual exchanges that had become their sole commerce, these were the times they actually spoke to each other, and so they became the times Kate felt that her mother cared. *You were always so dear when you were sick, Kate, so very appealing*, she told her daughter years later.

About two years after Hugh Riley died Kate reported another earache. The day broke with a freezing fall rain; the school had been shut down for chimney repairs, and the prospect of a third empty day at home, no friends, no distractions, was practically unbearable. The wind rattled the storm windows; the sink pump had jammed up, and Kate had had to draw water from the well out in the yard. Carrying the buckets to the house, some of the water had slopped against her wool boot-hose, freezing instantly. She began to feel, or to imagine, a pressure inside her ear, and after an hour it was even painful to swallow.

"So you've another earache, Kate." Since Hugh's death it was never Katy, it was always Kate, or young lady, sometimes simply *daughter* or *girl*.

"My throat hurts, too." She swallowed, and added, "When I swallow."

"Sit here at the table," Fiona said, patting its surface. The gentleness of the gesture vaguely worried Kate.

Her mother opened the stove and with a poker, shoved the coals about until they glowed orange. Then she replaced the lid, set a small pan on it, and poured in the oil.

"You've another earache. Such a raw day with no school to dash off to. It's easier to forget when you're in the middle row with Miriam."

Kate offered a wary smile and admitted, "It is a little easier."

"You're mouthy in school, I hear tell." Rummaging through the medicine cupboard, Fiona emerged from behind its door with an eyedropper, and said with a note of motherly humor in her voice, "I never did guess I'd have a mouthy child." She was already dressed for her visits to the sick, better dressed than usual because Dr. Bartholemew was making his twice a month journey to Netherfield that day. The cream-colored blouse and brown wool suit looked prim and feminine, and the small, clip-on onyx earrings gleamed in the dim kitchen like the eyes of a rodent.

The oil hissed and spat against the side of the iron pan. Kate watched a faintly smoky steam curl up suddenly; it was much hotter than usual. It was burning, in fact. With a slow, exaggerated grace, her mother lifted the pan and set it atop a trivet, then she drew the hot oil into the dropper, folded a tea towel over her arm, and addressed Kate.

"Have you seen my brooch, Kate?"

"What?"

"My brooch."

"No, Mum."

"The brooch Dad gave me for our anniversary." Her voice was dangerously singsong.

"No."

"I've looked high and low and I can't seem to find it." She had the palm of her hand against the side of Kate's head and was easing it over, the dropper of hot oil poised in her other hand.

"Mummy, the oil, it looks awfully hot."

"The brooch with the ruby, Kate. The ruby rose. You liked it so much, but he gave it to me." A strange half-laugh escaped her. Her hand with the dropper of hot oil scribbled about in the air.

Kate's hand shot reflexively to her ear.

"Poor Kate, having another earache."

"I do, Mum."

"Then you'll be wanting the oil."

"It's too hot, it looks too hot this time."

"Are you well, then?"

"But Mum . . ."

"I have to think you're well then, to not be wanting the oil."

It was confusing, it was all so confusing. Hand still clamped over her ear, Kate answered, "I suppose so," because there didn't seem to be any other way out.

Her mother put on a shocked face. "Dr. Bartholemew is coming this morning. There are people to see who are sick." Frowning as though confounded, Fiona straightened and took a step away from the table. "I ought to give you a clout alongside the head for the lying. Young Mrs. Carthy's hemorrhoids was so terrible last week that every time she had to have a movement she fainted away. What kind of stunt do you think you're pulling, when Mrs. Carthy and the others are needing me? Her with a baby coming. And Dr. Bartholemew driving down from Moosomin . . . I've got my own complaints, you never think of that, do you . . . war taxes taking another jump . . ." Fiona's fingers brushed the vacant lapel of her neat brown suit, and like a blind woman discovering a message in Braille, her eyebrows leapt to alarmed arches. "My brooch."

Kate bolted for the door. "I'll help look for it, Mum. I'll go and look for it."

When she returned, empty-handed, she found her mother bent over the table, the dropper of oil on the floor lying in its own innocent puddle, the brooch apparently forgotten. Fiona looked up at her as if at a stranger. "I still pine for him," she said.

"Yes, Mum," Kate said, stroking her mother's coiled dark hair.

"He loved you but it's me that pines for him."

Kate was silent. She did not talk about Poppy, about her and Poppy, with anyone. It would have been a violation, though she could not have said exactly how.

"No brain can stand this, no brain can stand this," Fiona cried, her sobs as dry and barely audible as cat-coughs.

For Kate that night of all the nights marked the end of one thing and the beginning of another. It was like a long journey by train during which, without the traveler realizing it, perhaps while he is asleep and the cars are rocking rhythmically along as they have been, and the stream of air seems to take time away, a halfway point is crossed: now it would take more effort to go back than it would to go on.

Evenings after supper tended to be better. The only times her mother could stand to look at Kate were when she was sick, but after their solitary suppers, Fiona allowed Kate to wait upon her, to rub her feet or set her hair, or simply to agree, with a word or a sound, to her running appraisals of various neighbors and their shortcomings, none of whom, it seemed, could be trusted. And all talk found its way back to the old days with Hugh.

"Mrs. Clay, that woman is a real nosy. She came in Sunday and didn't know when to leave, it being a beautiful day and I had decided to get some sun, by the time she left it was too late . . . wanted to know if John was married yet, and I have never shown her any friendship, but still she hangs on. She is a real nosy. She started in on the old barn dances, John and Colin were small and I had to take them with me, and Dad would come in time for lunch, I was popular even though I was married, what with the bank boys and the station boys I got me share of dancing. The Homemakers put them on. I would bring cake and sandwiches. Netherfield had a good bunch of nice people then. Then there would be a box social and my box would go sky high even though I would not tell anyone, they just seemed to know. I seemed to get the first prize. Once a poor fellow got set back fifteen dollars for mine."

In the morning, after Kate had hauled the ashes and stoked the fire and made the tea and served the porridge, it was always the same: "I'll be dead by the time you get home from school."

One day she went walking with Jan Larsen beneath the poplars in the coulee east of the village, and Jan, in his silent Swede way, put his hands on her breasts. She was fifteen, he was seventeen; it was spring, the poplar leaves shimmying in the soft breeze, the ground still wet with thaw, and neither of them caring. Her father had been dead four years. It was the first time since then that she felt something good, something warm and welcome and valuable rush into the dried out hollow his death had made of her life. To Kate it was as if Jan Larsen had found a piece of her, a piece of her that had been lost since that day at the cemetery; he had found it and he was giving it back to her. There in his broad hands she liked it very much; she liked who she became with him, she felt strong and happy.

After that there were more walks and other boys; there were the Saturday night rowdies; there were the shadows beyond the boilerful of barley coffee at the edge of the rink where she gathered with friends after school; there was the hayloft above the barn floor they had flooded to make an extra curling rink during the big '47 Championship bonspiel; there was Sullivan's farmhouse, abandoned ten years, where she and George Harcourt found a red Hudson's Bay blanket, receiving it as a sign of Life's approval; there was even Mr. Mapes, the town's general repair man, though he seemed to recoil from what he'd done and afterward took to church every day. Best of all were the soldiers who returned from the war, but most of them could not stay with their people. The big new combines with their rubber tires had replaced threshing gangs all over the Prairies, and young men had to keep heading west to find work in the cities and factories, this despite the general prosperity that the war had brought on for Canada.

Everyone seemed to be leaving the Prairies. A pale new light exposed Netherfield for what it was, or for what had been its destiny from the very beginning. It was like a child who carries a defective gene. The Prairies were too harsh, too dry, too cold, the rain unreliable, the native species so ancient, so subtly adapted that they and whatever value they possessed were mostly invisible to the immigrant; the towns were too remote, the living too hard. Netherfield was one of hundreds of small collections of imported culture thrust on an innocent land. Shoulder to shoulder, the churches stood up from the flats in the snow of winter and the dust and heat of summer, in the wind that offered no apology, no remorse; the churches lined up their ramshackle pageantry of human faith—and made not enough of a difference. The place might have taught if any had been willing to listen. Then the War came along, and the big combines, the rubber tires, the faster mechanized methods, the automobile too, and even the prosperity of the forties—it was all part of a vast force driven by Time itself that was undoing the big dream of the West just as it seemed to be awakening.

And Kate was desperate to be a part of it, to let it sweep her away.

"Quite a gang of boys," Fiona Riley said. "Mrs. Winget tells me there was quite a gang at the dance . . . if I find out you've been nasty . . ."

"Mother."

"You'll go to the Gray Sisters, I'll see to it. They've a place in Montreal, a stone convent for girls who go wrong. Incorrigibles."

It was easy to lose the weight with the boys calling, though Kate was still an ample girl. Smooth broad shoulders and large breasts, and as Jan liked to say, the best set of legs around, she developed a slack way of moving, hips leading the way, that nevertheless possessed a certain rhythm that suggested determination. There was no doubt in anyone's mind that Kate Riley was going places. She had a penetratingly sexy gaze softened by the dimples, the cuteness. She was tall, not too tall, not so that it bothered the boys. And her voice was low and professional, a receptionist's at a bank, or it was peppy and girlish, or sometimes when she was feeling sexy Jan told her it was *furry*. Kate Riley could adapt to anyone, anyone male.

These attributes she discovered one by one, like the contents of a keepsake chest—items that had been hers when her father was alive, hers, but different, hers as potential. There were still the dimples, the full mouth, and these combined with the newly found womanly traits created an enchanting effect.

When she was sixteen and a half Jan asked to marry her; so did a soldier from Gimli who was going into the furniture business. And on the train to visit her brother, John and his wife, Vera, she met a man who said he would arrange a job for her, said he knew people, in Vancouver, who ran a big hotel.

"Canada's evergreen playground," he said, quoting from the cover of the CPR railway schedule.

"Oh, it sounds wonderful," Kate said.

"It is a fact," he said, and he slapped the folded schedule against his knee for emphasis.

"Would you write it down for me, the name of the hotel. Please. And your name, too, would you write it here," she said, pressing an untidy piece of paper against the side of her purse, smoothing it out.

He looked at her then as if for the first time, and self-consciously she straightened her posture just a little. She was wearing a pair of brown knit gloves whose left index finger had begun to unravel; her hair was tightly curled and formed a dense halo against the brim of her hat, and above the dimples, she feared, her pale skin was flushed the most amazingly earnest pink. The man gave a sudden clipped laugh. "Here, let me see that paper," he said. And he wrote out: *Dear Sir: Allow me to introduce* . . . "Say," he said, "what's your name?"

"Kate Riley. No, Katherine Riley, say Katherine." She hesitated, adding, "If you wouldn't mind."

"*Miss Katherine Riley, who I know to be of excellent character and background.*"

Kate giggled.

"*I shall be obliged if you should give her* . . ." He paused, touching the tip of the pen to his tongue. "*every consideration in regards a position. Trusting you will be pleased with Miss Riley, I remain yours very truly, Anthony Snider.*" Then at the top of the paper he wrote: *The Langston Hotel, Thurlow Street, Vancouver, British Columbia.*

She read the paper again. "Do you really mean it, the part about my character?"

"Yeah, sure kiddo."

"You can see that right off, Mr. Snider?" (She had liked the *kiddo*; it made her feel modern.)

"Call me Tony," he said, and then he shrugged. "I'm a salesman. People are my business. I have to figure them out fast." The train was full of soldiers going home to see their people, but this young man wore a white shirt beneath a gray suit whose weave incorporated a single fine gold thread, so subtle that Kate realized only someone such as herself would have noticed it.

They talked—or she encouraged him to talk—for over two hours. When they were only one stop from Moose Jaw Kate felt a pang of urgency. She would probably never see Anthony Snider again. Almost everyone else she had encountered in her life she was sure to see again, but not Mr. Snider who had told her so much about his dreams, about how it had been during the war, the wounded and the fear, the tense boredom of the waiting, and he even told her about a girl he had met who worked in a pub. Tony had been able to see who Kate Riley was so quickly, and he was practically arranging for her to have a real job. It would be like a little taste of death, their parting, poignant and exciting. She looked intently at him, conspicuously ignoring his voice, and he stopped talking as she had hoped he would, his dark eyes eager and his mouth searching for the lost words.

They would never see each other again.

"Only fifteen more minutes," she said as if in a dream, and saying it, her heart began to beat rhythmically faster. She pushed at her curls with the flat of her hand, then dutifully, obediently, she tugged on her brown knit gloves, as if to suggest Fate was giving her no other choice.

"You're a good girl, Kate. A girl with refinements. You're going to make some fellow real happy. Yes sir, already I envy that fellow . . ."

"Tony . . ." The name felt so strangely intimate in her mouth, like an exotic new candy.

"And proud." His eyes dropped; he seemed unable to look at her face and focused instead on her knees pressed tensely together. As though he had already moved on to another subject, he repeated the word "refinements," but his voice drifted away.

"Oh Tony, I wish we had met . . . I've always felt so lonely. I wish . . ." and she let her will swoon the instant he leaned over.

A year later on a late November morning in 1949 Kate sat waiting in the Riley parlor for her friend, Jan Larsen, to come by with his father's Oldsmobile to take her to the station. She had tucked her hands under her legs and she was so excited that she could almost lift herself bodily from the chesterfield.

At first Fiona Riley refused to talk about it, and then when that seemed to have no force, she refused to listen, and finally, all words expelled from the house, she stared at her daughter, an expression of wild terror in her eyes, and simply wailed.

By the time the car rolled to a stop beside the iron fence Fiona had fallen into a deep, calculating silence. Having positioned herself beside the door with her hat and gloves already on, she would either prevent her daughter from leaving or make sure they would not try to go without her—it wasn't clear. "Dear Katy," she managed finally. Her quivering lip exposed the crooked line of her lipstick, which she had tried to apply without quitting her post, and ·it was this more than anything, this pathetic emblem of neediness, that had broken a little of Kate's heart. Her mother had been standing there for over an hour. "Dear Katy," she repeated.

Jan ducked through the front door, hoisted Kate's two suitcases, and made his escape down the walk, clearly not wanting to get between two females at parting time. He was wearing his coat and tie for the occasion. The tie brought tears to Kate's eyes, which she quickly swiped away. It would not do for her mother to witness and then to misinterpret them. Kate could see Jan leaning against the Olds, running his fingers through his thick blond hair, an act she herself had so often enjoyed that, watching him, she could feel the hair parting around her own fingers. Every now and then he gave his head a sad shake and looked down at the frozen ground, poking at it with the toe of his boot. He did not want Kate Riley to leave.

It was a bleak day, a day that offered nothing by way of compensation. A northwest wind moaned along the eaves. Two inches of old snow held wherever it had gotten soft enough during the day and then hard enough at night to resist the daily blow. The sky was mottled, the blue wan, the clouds coalescing for a vague autumn storm. Outside town the stubble fields had a picked-over, skeletal look about them, like the remains of an enormous dead animal laid flat. She couldn't wait to leave. Miriam Pettigrew had already gone on to Vancouver, and they planned to hook up. Oh, the thought of it all practically made her insides jump up and go without her.

"But how are you going to get along, dear Katy?"

It was so seldom her mother called her Katy that instinctively Kate returned the favor: "Mummy . . ."

"I was a fine mother, I was, dearie. When you were a wee tot . . ." There was a persuasive lilt in her voice, as if she actually entertained hopes of stopping this departure.

"Mum, it's all been arranged. John has let a room for me at a boarding house. The woman who runs it is his friend's sister-in-law. I've tried to tell you about it for weeks."

"I was not only a fine mother but a pal to all."

Kate inspected her fingernails, discovered a bit of dirt, and dug it out with her thumbnail. "You're a good nurse, I know," she said with cold sincerity.

"Nurse, yes, well . . . there are the bills to be paying, Kate, when Dad died there was still the keeping up. If you go off you'll have bills of your own." Then she added the single word "nurse," as if to bring herself back on topic. "Yes, always plenty of trouble about, sickness don't lay up. It was a smart profession for a widow with no one." A film of dreamy rumination spread over Fiona's expression. "I've had a little of the summer complaint," she said, and pressed the flat of her hand against her abdomen. "Before that was the cold, a humdinger, even the doctor said so. I remember it began when the farmers were finishing up the last of the combining and went on right through to middle October. That's how I remember it starting, the farmers had swathed and were just finishing the combining and I wasn't feeling quite the fiddle and . . ." Fiona's mind seemed to slide away with her voice, and into the silence the ticking parlor clock surfaced with a portentous insistence.

Kate gazed out the window at Jan; he was using his handkerchief to wipe something from the windshield.

So that I can see clearly this place for the last time, Kate thought.

When Fiona came around, she seemed surprised to find herself standing where she was, and reached up to stroke the doorjamb as if to get to know it better. "Kate," she said with a pleading voice, and her eyebrows wobbled hopefully.

"I'm sure to find work. I've a letter from the Success College. They're going to teach me to type and keep books, and that will get me a job, an office job. There's nothing left for me to learn here. Even Mr. Bowles says there's no good in my staying on through my last school term."

"You sure was a clever little cricket. Dad was always noticing how quick-like you took to things."

"And there's no work in Netherfield, not even for fellows."

"He worshipped you, he fairly glowed when he looked at you. And you had to be the famous one."

How do you know when you've had enough, she had asked Jan a month earlier.

"I've simply got to go away, Mother."

"Out there in the world, Kate, you'll have no chance to monkey up, and no mother to be taking care of you if you do, neither."

When you have to ask, she told him. *That's when.*

"You could end up on the wrong path. Your chum Miriam, always blowing about the great times she is having, is that what's got into you? But her people are here, her people are here in Netherfield."

Again, Kate glanced out the window. Jan hunched his back to the gathering wind. If she missed the train she'd have to wait two days for the next one. "I promise to visit," she said wearily.

"No word from my boys. They never write."

"Mother. They write."

"And now Kate, too," she murmured with a kind of sad ethereal wonder, as if Kate were already part of the past and the people in it who never wrote.

"I will visit."

Fiona seemed to brighten suddenly. "Christmas is coming, lickety-split. Stay until Christmas, you always liked Christmas. This is no time to travel, with all the crackpots racing around."

"What are you talking about?"

Then she seemed to fall upon another course of appeal. "Is it that you're lonely, Kate? You've got young Larsen out there, waiting on you like a little dog. He's a dandy little dog, to be sure."

What her mother said offended her, but there was a part of her that liked the analogy, that liked the idea of Jan and his dog-like devotion. It was something to be proud of—an accomplishment, though she couldn't help feeling a little embarrassed for Jan.

"But I've no one, dear Kate. Since Dad passed. It's one thing for Miriam Pettigrew to run off, with all her finery and her people, they have money. Sure, and Mrs. Pettigrew has her hubby to keep her through the winter. It's another kettle of fish. But I've no one, Kate, since Dad passed on I've had no one."

"A person can just stand so much, Mother, and I think I've tried every way I know of making you feel loved and you just never wanted it."

"Dear Kate, t'isn't the same." By now Fiona's tone had taken on an educational crispness, as if she had forgotten momentarily what they were really talking about. She worked her lower lip against the edge of her dentures with pensive superiority, removed a piece of lint from her dress, and matter-of-factly told Kate, "And after all, it was owed me, you'd agree."

"What?"

"Dad fairly worshipped you. My share, why, you took it, Kate, dear, long before he passed. It was owed me." Dipping her chin toward her right shoulder, she shot Kate a steady incontrovertible look, as if to say that she regretted having to mention this, it was awkward, bringing up such matters, but that if Kate refused to acknowledge the obvious, well, reluctantly, she'd have to.

A dull heaviness infected Kate's movements, and yet in spite of it, or perhaps because of it, because it was pulling on her the way gravity tugs everything down toward a final core, she gathered up her satchel, her coat, her scarf, she pressed out the wrinkles her body had made in the fabric of the chesterfield as her mother always insisted she do, she gave the parlor a quick, desperate, last review, then she walked past her mother and out the door.

"Well then, are you leaving now, daughter," Fiona's voice rose, "is that what you're doing now?"

At the edge of the stoop Kate stopped. "Yes," she said, not turning, "my mind's made up."

Jan had climbed into the car, and with the windows shut and the wind shoving about Kate decided—with relief—that he probably could not hear them.

"After giving you a fine bringing up and a fine standard of living."

"Yes."

"It makes one bitter."

Kate started down the stairs. She noted the tremble in her mother's voice; noted it and let it go.

"Now all my people have moved away so I guess I'll forget it. I hope you will not regret it some day."

Kate could not say *but you never loved me*; she was not ready to give up the illusion of a mother who loved, or to say aloud that life since Poppy's death had been a form of barbarism. Behind lace curtains, inside those wallpapered rooms, over steaming English tea in cups whose porcelain was as thin as sugar wafers and whose designs were as delicate as the flowers from which they were drawn and which no one in Saskatchewan had ever even seen, there in that civilized house small brutal crimes had been committed, every day. Every single day.

Fiona insisted on going to the station. She put on her black tweed coat, which was too big for her—a gift from John and Vera. (Afraid that they wouldn't turn it back for the correct size, Fiona had refused to send it to Moose Jaw.) She put on her public face, her

Netherfield's nurse façade, mouth fixed in a tight smile, eyelids at a worried half-mast. She adjusted her hat with the two black feathers that hung their curled heads out over her forehead. Then into the car she climbed, compacting herself against the door like a walloped dog. Having failed to affect Kate, she launched into a story for poor Jan's benefit, a story about a young man who had been jilted—"the experience cooked him on women for the rest of his life," she concluded with a jaunty, satisfied grimness. Otherwise, Fiona managed to behave during the ride to the station.

There was a quick cautious embrace . . . the smell of Fiona's face powder, of the closet (faintly stale) where she hung her coat; the sting of fine dust in her eyes as the wind picked it up and lashed it around the edge of the station house; and against Kate's chin, the coarse caress of tweed. That was it.

Kate Riley strode across the wooden platform to the waiting train. Jan caught up. "What say," he asked under his breath, "how about a good-bye kiss. Your Mum won't mind." But Kate would not kiss Jan Larsen in front of her mother, not with Poppy's presence eternally between them. She smiled and touched Jan's yellow hair. "You," was all she could think to say.

The single word obviously pleased him. "Us," he whispered.

She pictured Jan in the cemetery the morning her father died; watched him struggling beneath the bags and boxes of goods he delivered each week to the widow Riley and her daughter; felt him always two rows behind her in the schoolhouse, like a silent guardian; remembered him in the coulee beneath the shimmering poplars and his natural manly way with her body. They had known each other a long time; their friendship was quiet and steady and dear to her, especially at moments like these. Except that there had never been a moment like this. Did she love him? "Oh you," she said again, afraid of the answer.

"Us," he insisted.

"Take care," Fiona called out, "and do not trust any of them."

A secret smile passed between Kate and Jan.

"Bye now," her mother said. "Chin up, dear," she added, needing the illusion, too.

"Good-bye Mummy," Kate hollered from the stairs, one hand keeping her hat and the other held high and firm in the prairie wind. "Bye."

Scoop Pettigrew gave an arm signal. The train whistle blew, piercing, penetrating, filled with hurt and yearning—the right music to accompany her departure. A screech of brakes, a heavy jolt as if from behind, and they were moving. When the angle was such that she was sure they could not see her she gazed back: Jan stood beside her mother, his arms hanging straight down along his sides, his legs slightly spread and sturdy-looking—braced, she thought—and his tie flying over his shoulder like a brave little flag. Next to him, much shorter—Kate was surprised by how small her mother really was—with her head bowed into the wind, Fiona clutched her coat to her chest and peered into the distance the train laid down tie by tie. Suddenly a gust of wind caught up the edges of the great black coat and flung them madly about, and she looked exactly like a raven, yes, exactly—a raven that had been damaged in some way, that had never flown and never would fly.

Kate gasped and twisted around; she saw that her hands were shaking, as if they had just committed some terrible crime.

There were a dozen people in her car, luckily no one she recognized. She settled uneasily into her seat and to calm herself, gazed ahead out the windows. At the edge of town she noticed young Frank Hutchins (schoolhouse front row, third from the left) wearing his usual red wool cap and squatting beside a dugout. The clouds were breaking up and Frank's tin lunch pail caught some light and winked it back at the train. Frank was always forgetting his lunch, always having to run home to fetch it in the middle of the day. The land was all around him, shades of brown in slow undulations, like the hide of a great dozing beast; patches of early snow, cloud shadows, the occasional blue-gray of a dugout or coulee like faint bruises or birthmarks, the welt of a windbreak, the scratch of a road—the land was all around the boy the way it had always been around Kate, a steady and vast and unconcerned creature. Kate saw Frank push something out across the ruffled surface of the dugout water, a toy boat maybe, and with all that boundless land watching and the sky looking down, his movements were so tiny and particular, yet impelled by something that was as big as the place and that had crept inside him at birth.

Kate glanced at her watch and smiled; he had better get back to school. Then she saw that Frank had become aware of her train passing to his south, she saw him leap up, swipe off his cap and give a wild, exuberant wave, his whole body swaying and the red cap flashing like a signal light. It put her instantly into tears, the ones that she had not cried for her mother or for Jan Larsen or for her home.

It may be that that moment, that lantern that held no light but that became a light, was the last honest moment of her life. Or at least the last simple thing she would remember, and so to it she returned again and again, like fingers to a smooth and perfect pebble.

The train gathered speed and it wasn't long before all that she could see of young Frank Hutchins was the red dot of his cap against the great brown land, then even the red dot vanished and there was just the land. Off in the distance here and there, like ships at sea, grain elevators rose up; sometimes she could make out the serrated profile of the village or town huddled against them, but mostly it was just the single or double thrust of the elevators and the earth sprawling out to the horizon and the sky bigger than all of it.

As the train moved along she thought a lot about Poppy, imagining that he could see her as she started off on her life. From her purse she withdrew the note Anthony Snider had written in her behalf; it was tucked into the same envelope with the letter from Dr. Bartholemew:

To whom it may concern:

I have known Miss Kate Riley for many years.

She is a bright pleasant young lady with a pleasing appearance.

I am quite sure that her character is above reproach.

J. S. Bartholemew, MD

In a separate envelope was the letter from the Success College acknowledging her enrollment for classes in typing and bookkeeping. And next to that, wrapped in a white handkerchief . . . *oh* . . . a funny smile crossed her face—but that would have to wait until after she changed trains in Moose Jaw, *wouldn't it?*

As she chewed off pieces of bannock she had packed into her satchel, she read the letters over and over again, charmed by their formality. A letter from a doctor . . . sure they would pay her attention now, sure she would have her pick of jobs.

Poppy would have been so impressed by those letters, so proud of her.

John and Vera met her for the four-hour wait in Moose Jaw. "How was it with Mother?" John asked.

Kate shook her head.

"Never mind," he said, "never mind. She doesn't love anyone but herself." He gazed up the tracks where Kate had come from, even took a couple of steps in that direction, but then he shook his head and through clenched teeth said again, "Never mind."

They took her out for an early supper, then presented her with their gifts: a cheque for one hundred dollars "seed money," and a mouton lamb coat originally from Steen & Wrights at Regina, very dark brown. It had belonged to Vera's mother, but Mrs. Murdock had an even newer coat now. The Murdocks had done well during the war—something to do with metal sheets for airplanes.

"Now don't you look ready for the big city, Katherine," Vera declared, her arms crossed in a tidy bundle.

"It's swell," Kate said, "but don't you want it?"

"Goodness, I couldn't wear a thing like that."

Kate looked down at the coat, stroking its broad lapels.

"What Vera means, Kate, is that a lot of farmers are not able to sell their wheat, and I've been kept busy with the loans. A fancy coat like that, well, it wouldn't do, I suppose."

Around Vera, Kate always felt in need of improvement of one sort or another. This time it was a coat that she herself would not wear; last visit it had been how to hook one ankle around the other, angling them both off to the right "when a lady sits." Once there had been a problem with Kate's curls—they weren't tight enough. Still, it was hard to complain. Vera was always perfectly nice, yes, perfectly nice.

They drove her back to the station, checked to make sure that her cases had been loaded onto the CPR westbound, but no, they wouldn't see her to the compartment, they would say their good-byes on the platform.

"Do write us, Kate, let us know how you're getting on."

And now she felt it all welling up. She had never been west of Moose Jaw. From this moment on everything would be new and everything familiar would be gone. The moment struck her like a blow. She threw her arms around John and wept, "My brother," though their sixteen-year age difference meant she had grown up for the most part without him.

"Now, Kate," he stammered.

"John!" But in her mind it was Poppy who held her up, whose strong arms she felt encircling her as if for the last time. The collar of the mouton lamb had risen up around her face, and its thick softness seemed to comfort her, even to cuddle her as Poppy had when she was a child. Somehow the collar made it unbearable.

Vera touched John's forearm.

"Kate, now, what a great fuss," John said, prying her arms from around his neck.

The collar dropped. She looked at the two of them: John was still wearing his gray banker's suit, white shirt, black-rimmed glasses, no color anywhere; Vera was neatly tucked into a brown wool coat with a tie belt. She had positioned the square knot at her exact midline, and though the knot was flawless she picked at it nervously while they stood there. No, they didn't really love her, did they? It wasn't like it was with Jan or fellows. She could have no affect on these two. What would do it, what would do it, she wondered, and in spite of the hurt, she resolved to buy them a gift when she reached Vancouver. A very expensive gift.

"Thank you for the money and the coat," she said with a quiet feminine courtesy.

John smiled at her. "Ah, well, that's better Kate. Now be a good girl and chin up."

But inside Kate Riley something essential began to harden beyond repair.

She waited until the lights of Moose Jaw became lackluster flecks in her past. A humpbacked gibbous moon, just laboring up off the horizon, roused a dark gleam from the snow filling the broad hollows and creases of the Prairies. The train was making a clean straight cut, and Kate sensed its power gathering across the flats that gave no resistance, gathering for the Rocky Mountains and the silent west. Then she reached into her purse, found the folded handkerchief, and set it beside her on the plush compartment bench. When she unwrapped the brooch, she let it lie there on the white cloth for a moment or two, like a newborn in a towel. The ruby caught up the red of the seat fabric. She tipped it with her finger, this way, that, to make it sparkle. A porter and several passengers entered the car and made their way through; with a quick practiced efficiency Kate pinned the brooch to her lapel as if she had done so every day since *that* day when an invisible halfway point had been crossed.

"Care to see a menu, Miss?"

Roast loin of pork, applesauce, new potatoes in cream, asparagus on toast, dinner rolls, coffee, tea or milk—65 cents.

Though she had already had supper, she had another, just for the adventure of a solitude she alone owned and determined now. A couple of fellows said something, but she shrugged them off and finished her meal. It left them even more interested and soon she had to ask the porter to show her where her bunk was. With a magnificent thrill, Kate Riley drew shut the green curtains, snugged into the cool white linens, and fell into a sleep as deep and as indifferent as the Prairies.

Vancouver

Swift Current, Medicine Hat, Calgary, and just over the spine of the Rockies in a high, montane valley the pretty town of Banff, followed by Golden and Revelstoke with its lean, snow-bent trees, then Kamloops and Hope—and after that nothing but green. From Hope through Chilliwack and into Vancouver rain washed green past the windows of the CPR, blurring the scene, and Kate Riley was carried into a lush and dreamy state of anticipation. Never before had she seen so much green, it was like a medicine of some sort, a medicine that soothed even as it invigorated. She sat with her forehead pasted to the cool glass, her chin propped in her palm, and the tiny rivulets of rainwater racing each other across her gaze like giddy children at a picnic. Such green and it was November!

To the north across Burrard Inlet rose the Coast Mountains; to the west, English Bay and the Strait of Georgia, the Gulf Islands and Vancouver Island, a green and blue collage; and all around her as the train *clackety-clacked* along, lay the great city of Vancouver, a grid work of broad streets cluttered with automobiles, people about their business, life.

Miriam met her at the station. She was wearing a dark gold and charcoal tweed suit with a neat, black velvet collar, a pair of two-toned pumps, and a hat like a man's, wide brimmed and worn at a daring angle. To Kate, she looked positively smart, positively urban. Miriam had always been a nice-enough looking girl with faint freckles and pretty brown eyes; she had to roll up her hair in curlers every night just to achieve the faintest of waves, but she didn't seem to mind. Miriam was all sweetness and grace. During the school Christmas pageant she always played the Madonna. It was amazing how the new city clothes had changed her. *Think what might happen to me in such an outfit*, Kate thought.

In a hand-me-down jumper, perhaps one that had belonged to a friend of theirs and that Miriam might recognize, Kate felt shabby and unfashionable. Quickly she buttoned the edges of her new coat and gave her friend a hug. "Oh, Miriam, you look swell."

"Dear Kate. Where did you get the coat?"

"My brother and sister-in-law," she said, petting its thick lapels. "They bought it special from Steen & Wrights. But will I ever need it here?"

"Can you just imagine," Miriam said with a big happy smile, her hands open to the clouds overhead, as soft as eiderdown in gray satin. The rain had let up and there was even a thin yellow rupture low in the western sky that seemed to promise more than just fair weather. A new beginning.

Together they took a trolley bus from Station Street west to Granville, then turned south. It was dusk and the neon lights of the commercial district were just coming on. In the wet pavement and the great windows of the buildings the colored lights melted together like something from a dream, and Kate stared, trancelike, until her eyes began to water. Cars honked as if for no reason, and the parallel rods of the trolley bus snapped and sparked whenever they crossed an intersection, and over there was a man wearing the most beautiful camel-hair overcoat with a red scarf thrown about his neck, and on the corner a cart full of flowers, every imaginable sort of flower, and people were stopping to buy them to take home, or to give to a girl . . . Oh, she had been right, wonderfully right, to have left Netherfield, her mother, even Jan. She could never be lonely in such a place, never again that frightening loneliness. Abruptly Kate turned to Miriam. "Jan would be confounded by all this," she said, not without a certain instantaneous smugness. After all, she was here now; Kate had broken free. "There's so much just to *look* at, Miriam. Why, you can hardly see the sky for all the buildings and shop signs." And she realized then how overpowering the prairie sky had been, how explosively empty.

Miriam smiled at her. She had been living in Vancouver for over six months. "It is exciting."

And yet Kate did wish Jan were here in Vancouver with her, or at least she wished that Saskatchewan were not so far away and Jan not so impossibly content exactly where he was. She refused to take into account the Larsen family's need for his help, and considered it Jan's right—as it was her right—to set out on his own. To escape. She recalled young Frank Hutchins, a small animate shape rising from the vast dun-colored steppe that had been her home, with his toy boat in one hand and his red cap in the other, waving grandly to her train as it gathered westward speed, and at last Kate was ready to wave back, to say good-bye. *Nothing*, she told herself, *nothing will make me go back.*

They transferred to the Arbutus line, and not long after descended from the bus three streets west of Mrs. Wilmott's. A fellow passenger, a young baker in a white tunic and a bow tie, helped with the two suitcases. "Thank you, thank you *so* much," said Kate, and she held his eyes until his blush assured her that he had felt her warmth. Everyone she met that day was significant, a member of her new tribe, her People, just as every detail became a sign whose secret meaning she would eventually discern, and which would — of course! — affect her destiny. In fact, it seemed suddenly that she possessed a genuine Destiny. For on this day Kate Riley was born back into the life Poppy's death had suspended. And like birth, it was a vivid, kaleidoscopic scene she encountered.

Mrs. Wilmott's Boarding House was a large residence at the end of the block, and though the white paint was tired and ashy, the black shutters peeling, you could tell that it had been one of the finer homes of Newbury Street before the war. As they mounted the steps they saw that beyond it down the next block the houses decreased in size and dignity. Some of them were downright squalid; one looked abandoned. But in the other direction groomed gardens with old trees embraced handsome structures, and these small, outward details helped to persuade Kate that she was indeed on her way, if only by the width of one street.

The boarding house verandah held a cluttered assortment of chairs, some metal, some willow, and among them a square bin of newspapers and old magazines. There was a wheeled tray cart next to the railing, and a game table with a chessboard bearing an unfinished competition. Attached to the clapboard on either side of the door hung two kerosene lamps with smoked chimneys. As they entered the house warm garlicky air enveloped them.

"It looks friendly," Miriam whispered.

"Oh, it does," Kate agreed. "Maybe there's even a tele-vision."

Mrs. Wilmott was surprisingly young, maybe thirty, but she acted much older. "I expected you yesterday," she said, wiping her hands on her apron. She'd lost her husband in the war and it seemed the economic consequences had rapidly matured her. Her eyes were sharp with a remnant wistfulness, as if they missed an optimism that had once been their underlying expression, and when Kate shook her hand she found them as rough as her own. "Your brother wrote that you would arrive on the 18th."

"But it's the 19th," Kate offered, confused.

"Yesss."

At this point Miriam introduced herself, imperviously cheerful.

"Well," she said, "maybe John Riley was thinking of the day Kate *left* Netherfield."

Mrs. Wilmott gave her head a tired shake. "A banker. And I've lost a day's let."

"I'm sorry," Kate said. "If I had known . . ."

"There's a housing shortage, I expect you know that. Has been since the war ended. Most of my lodgers are veterans."

"Men?"

Mrs. Wilmott shot Kate a challenging look. "I run a respectable house."

"I'm sure of it, Mrs. Wilmott. My brother would never have arranged it otherwise."

This seemed to satisfy Mrs. Wilmott long enough for her to lead them up the stairs to Kate's third floor room, the last one on the right at the end of the hallway. The roofline formed half of the ceiling and it angled up over her single bed so close to the pillow that Kate would have to be careful not to bump her head, getting up in the morning. The wallpaper was of pale primroses, the wainscoting painted a glossy white, and behind the etched glass of the hanging light three yellow bulbs gave off a trio of warmth. Beneath the window stood a steam radiator, and tucked neatly into the corner, a small writing desk. Kate was already picturing herself at the desk with a new box of stationery and her very own return address, Newbury Street. There was a bureau with a framed mirror hanging over it, a narrow closet behind the bed, and a hat hook on the back of the door.

"It's charming," Miriam finally said. It was, Kate agreed. "Just super."

"Mrs. Barufaldi will be serving supper at 6:00. She is the house domestic, and she does quite a lot of the cleaning and cooking around here. I trust you'll help her as you can by tidying up after yourself in the dining room and the bathroom, and any of the other common areas." She fished a key from the pocket of her apron and handed it to her. "The bathroom is down the hall. I supply the bed linens, but the towel is your responsibility."

Kate nodded, and half-turned toward her suitcases to begin un-packing. But Mrs. Wilmott still stood framed in the doorway. "I'll need my money in advance, Miss Riley. For the month."

"I'm sorry. John didn't tell me. I have some traveler's cheques. Will they do?"

"Traveler's cheques. How modern."

"Oh, John insisted, because I was alone, you see. On the train."

Kate was not prepared to sit down to supper with a gang of vet-erans, no matter how respectable they were, at least not on her first night. And Miriam, always shy with the opposite sex, sympathized wholeheartedly. She sported Kate to a Chinese meal at a chop suey house on 14th Avenue where the food arrived in a stack of small round bamboo baskets and they, along with her new room, became the subject of her letter home later that evening. "Dear Mummy, you can't imagine . . ." it began.

The next evening her typing and bookkeeping studies com-menced at the Success College. In addition to the housing short-age, there were not enough education facilities, so many had been turned over to postwar vocational training. Some of the Success College's more popular classes with overflow enrollment were held in the basement rooms of the Shaughnessy Senior High. This in-cluded "English Conversation for New Canadians," immigrations having swelled since the war. Kate took the trolley bus over, but had to walk the last five blocks and arrived late. She could hear the typing from outside the building, strong and rhythmic. The room was brightly lit, with seven rows of six desks jammed together, and at almost every desk sat another young woman such as herself, except that they were better dressed, sleek skirts and sweater sets, hair tightly styled, lipstick dark and flawless, their backs straight as rules. Miss Romig, the instructor, waved her to a seat in the cen-ter of the room, and Kate squeezed along behind the others, of-fering apologies. Her fellow students hardly seemed to notice her, and certainly never paused in their typing, and this was even more thrilling to Kate — that one might not notice or care about the arrival of a stranger. To be unknown and independent; to be here with people she had never met and didn't grow up with, and the magnificent industry of the typewriters *tap-ta-tap-tapping* away seemed to assure exactly what the college advertised—success.

Three afternoons a week she studied bookkeeping, three evenings, typing. There were stenography lessons too. She had enough money to last the six months it would take to graduate, then they promised to assist in finding her a job. *Opportunities for employment at the conclusion of the course are surveyed*, the brochure had stated.

Mrs. Wilmott's veterans were a nice bunch of men, and treated Kate and the only other female boarder, Louise Hislop, as though they were royalty. Louise was a nurse at Vancouver General and worked irregular hours. She had seen too much during the war, had stayed on a year after to help in a London burn ward, and had lost the knack of happiness. Her firm figure and tidy hair, cropped and straight, together with her starched white uniform lent an air of masculine competency that did not, however, deter the gentlemen of Mrs. Wilmott's Boarding House. They seemed grateful simply for the opportunity to exhibit their manners. But whenever one of the fellows would bow or pull out Louise's chair, or make up a plate for her when she was late, as she inevitably was, she always looked vaguely confused, as if these were customs belonging to a foreign land. Smiling absently, she might thank them—provided the act of chivalry had been obvious enough. Of course Kate lavished them with gratitude, especially Andy, a blue-eyed lumberman from Prince Rupert.

"Was it terribly awful," Kate asked Louise one night, "over there?" Bundled up, they were sitting out on the verandah after supper, Louise smoking and Kate flipping through a fashion magazine. It would be nice, Kate thought, to have a kind of big sister; Louise was a dozen years older.

"At first," Louise said, gazing at her, but it was as though she were seeing something beyond the verandah railing.

"And then what?"

"I don't know."

"I mean, what happened to change it? You got used to . . . things?"

Louise gave a cold laugh. "The war happened. Time happened." Her voice went drifty and weak. She crushed out her cigarette, lit another, then hugged her coat.

"It still bothers you though."

"Bothers me?"

"Well, the fellows, Andy and Pat and the others, they get on all right. Even Andy with his one arm, working in the library. They came home and now they're back in the world," Kate said with an encouraging jaunt to her tone.

Despite the dark evening, the dim glow of the kerosene lanterns, Kate made out a thin smile, fading in, fading out behind the veil of smoke. "Where were you during the war, Kate? Home in Saskatchewan?"

"I was, yes."

"Lots of sky and emptiness."

Kate gave a cheery hoot, glad to be living on Newbury Street. "That's right, that's Netherfield."

"A good sort of emptiness." Louise took a deep pull on her cigarette, then exhaled abruptly and rose. "Look, what happens is you get addicted," she said, sounding cross. "The action, even the fear. You get addicted and you need more and more of it, to fill in the emptiness, and that keeps getting bigger, you see. The emptiness. Then it stops, the war stops, the patients, the blood, and you've got to go back to being in the world, as you say. Only you don't remember how. And that's what really scares you." She paused a long time, her hand on the doorknob. They could hear the fellows inside arguing in a good-natured way about a boxing match. "If you could remember why, if only you could remember the point, then maybe you could figure out how."

"Well gee," Kate murmured half to herself, half to the departing Louise. "I was only trying to be a pal."

And so the weeks unfolded. Miriam had a small flat of her own in Kitsilano, which her parents had rented her back in June. It even had a peek of English Bay from the bedroom window. She attended the University of British Columbia; *foolish*, thought Kate, *impractical*—what would Miriam Pettigrew, a woman, *do* with a degree in political science? And how long could she live off her folks? Kate had been saving up for three years, cleaning for families, helping out during canning, watching babies at harvest. One summer she had even worked on a threshing gang. John had given her the "seed money" to help her gain a foothold in Vancouver, but she knew she must repay him one day. Still, it was not Kate's business how Miriam got on, and anyway, she seemed to have already discovered a lot of fun places, clubs and such, and so the two friends chaperoned each other through the big bustling city. It was Kate's dream that they would work their way into some terribly smart set and be included in all the best outings.

Not long after her arrival a letter arrived from Jan:

Dear Kate,

Here's hoping you decided to jump off the train and return to us. Will have to say "us" for can't help but tell you how bad your mother felt as the train pulled out of the station. Even before it left she started telling me the circumstances which has taken you so far away but it wasn't until after you had gone that she started to sniffle and I could tell she was having a time holding back the tears. I did your bidding and took her home. All the way back she spoke of you and her fears and hopes. Guess she misses you an awful lot. Why don't you return and make both of us happy? And why didn't you tell me about the scholarship to the Success College?

Yesterday was the first time I actually had anything personal to do with your mother. I always used to stand a little in awe of her. Even years ago, used to wonder what she thought of our friendship and yesterday thought she might consider me an intruder in her good-byes to you. Found it was not that way, though, and see why you are the lovely person you are.

I told your mother you did not want us to stay and watch you leave but she could not take her eyes off you. I couldn't either—you looked so cute and desirable—forlorn, too. Wanted to jump on and drag you back. Just thought of something. Why not return for good? Suppose you will become tired of me asking you continuously to return? Perhaps I should wait and write some other time when I'm able to think of something else but the fact is I would like to have you back again.

Found your mother very nice after you left, but felt sorry for her as she felt so terrible after you had gone. Don't you feel like a heel?

Hope the journey was not too tiring and that you are not happy to be out in Vancouver. Am sorry. I can't write a bright letter—miss you too much already.

Jan

Communications from her mother were all the same—short, scribbled reminders of her abandonment, the penciled letters faint and irregular as if they were fading right along with Fiona. The more desperate she felt the more her Irish heritage seemed to emerge, an atavistic fantasy of family and better times. One night she even telephoned Mrs. Wilmott's Boarding House. The phone sat on a small wobbly table at the end of the hall, and seldom rang, because telephone service was so expensive, a luxury for the well-to-do. When Mrs. Barufaldi came to fetch her, Kate bolted for it, worried that there was tragic news of some sort.

"How could you 'a done this to me," her mother wailed. "A widow on her own, and Kate, sure you're me only daughter, an' everything so dear now, even sugar, I haven't but a droplet for me tea, and you might have stayed to make it up, those years since Dad passed . . . you might 'a done by me how I done by you, daughter. 'Tisn't right, leaving your old mum alone. Ah sure, not a bit sorry, not even a wee bit. I haven't a joy to meself now you're all gone. Don't you know that I'm weak in the heart, and me only daughter not even a wee bit sorry."

"But I am, Mum, I'm sorry."

"We know what you're up to, Kate Riley, laziness and boys, out there in Vancouver, all them lights. It's the boys and the lying about, it is. And my John giving you money, too, money that might 'a eased my worries some, you not staying to do your bit. Are you sorry, Kate?"

"I am."

There was a silence. At last, in a faintly conciliatory voice, Fiona asked, "Well, how are you making out, Katy? Have you work yet?"

"I don't. I've enough to last until I graduate, and then they're going to find me a job, Mum, I won't even have to look, they set me right up with employment."

"You know that I'm weak in the heart, Kate. Dr. Bartholemew has confirmed it."

"I do, Mummy. I do."

"Well have you no shame, Kate Riley, not to come home and do your bit? What do you think Dad would say to that?"

The call left Kate speechless and distraught. How to defend herself, how to live . . . each seemed to rule out the other. From her small desk in the corner by the window she had posted regular chatty notes, in each one—several times—insisting she missed her Mummy, she loved her Mummy, she would come home for a visit as soon as she could, maybe Christmas if the fares were down. But five weeks later the holidays came and went. The Pettigrews traveled out to be with Miriam and to see the city, and of course they included Kate in their festivities and even gave her a silk scarf on Christmas Day. Kate did not want to go home until she was ready, maybe when she had her degree and a real job. A career. She could send money and there wouldn't be just the old age pension and whatever Fiona made working for Dr. Bartholemew. Then Fiona would stop reproaching her, she was convinced of it.

Nevertheless, the call had some immediate effect. Kate found work in a coffeehouse four mornings a week, and she sent six dollars of her pay back to Netherfield every other Friday. She did not write to her mother about feeling sick, afraid she would insist Kate return home to be nursed. It was the first time she dreaded that kind of attention. She was just tired, that was all. Living in the city with all its noise and people everywhere was bound to take a toll. And the nausea . . . sure, Mrs. Barufaldi's meals were flavorsome, but not what Kate was used to—pastas and dried meats and strange vegetables, like eggplant. She came home from class with an overpowering desire to sleep. Several times, dozing so heavily in her small corner room at the end of the hall, she had missed supper. So she took to storing packages of zwieback in her bureau, not only for the missed meals, but to help settle her stomach. Now and then Andy brought up a plate, his kind face worried. There had been so much going on during her first month in Vancouver that she hardly noticed missing her period, shrugging it off as simply a part of getting settled into her new life. But by the third week of January, when it was clear that she had missed a second one she could not pretend any longer. In her nightgown she sat at her little desk, preparing to write another cheery note home to Jan before she was due at the coffeehouse. Outside the window a bright winter sun glared from around Mrs. Wilmott's prize red cedar, tall and perfectly straight, as if to accuse Kate of hiding from the knowledge that had been there all along. She bit some zwieback and wrote, "Dear Jan," but the sun was ruthlessly blinding, the nausea welling, the light going an unpleasant shade of green, and she lay the pen down, knowing without a doubt, and dropped her forehead onto her arms, thinking *oh god, oh god.*

"It won't be easy, Miss Riley," the doctor said. He had inspected her then with a vaguely gentle impatience. "I must insist that you decide before."

Even at that moment in her predicament, five months pregnant and all of it obvious now despite the heavy lamb coat, even then she pressed her knees together and tried to make herself appealing, for she could not escape the Irish affection for doctors and men of status. Dr. Drummond did not have a modern office with linoleum floors and stainless steel and slick prints of European places, rainy Paris or Roman ruins. His office was disconcertingly homey—wood floors, a looped area rug of pinkish brown swirls, something his wife picked out, Kate decided, and hanging from the walls, amateur paintings, mostly still lifes, his or his wife's work or perhaps a relative's, she couldn't say; the signature said only C. Drummond. The office took up the bottom floor of a large, two-story house several blocks behind the hospital in the upper-class Shaughnessy neighborhood, and contained two examination rooms, a sitting area, and a small room for his desk and files. During her first visit, a woman—his wife, Kate concluded—summoned him up for lunch. "Busy," he called back, and Kate had felt flattered by his curt dismissal of another woman. Louise had helped Kate in choosing Drummond precisely because he was not grouped with other doctors, he was off by himself on a quiet side street, minding his own business. At least on that occasion Louise had acted the older sister.

"You've been so kind to me," Kate told Dr. Drummond during the second visit. "I don't know what I would do without you. But I'm simply not sure yet what's the right thing."

"You've said that the father is dead."

"A tractor accident."

"Yes . . ."

"We were going to . . ."

"As you've said, you planned to marry, then this tractor incident."

She nodded. "We were getting married, it was all planned, and then the priest, our town priest, he had to go off for something, up to see his people in Yorkton, and Jan and I . . . oh, we should have waited, I know, I've been to confession . . ."

"Jan, that's his name?"

It was then Kate realized that Dr. Drummond might not believe her, might not accept the purity of heart she offered like a pretty wrapped package, and it angered her so intensely that she dug in further. "Oh, why do you keep asking me this, we grew up together, it was awful, he was trapped under the tractor and the blood was just gushing from him." Kate began to cough and cry simultaneously, and the doctor relented, perhaps simply to put a stop to her wild tale.

"Too bad," he said, "tragic," then excused himself, returning several minutes later with some documents. "It will be difficult to raise the child on your own. You might want to consider the possibility of adoption. So far the baby seems normal. You're a strong healthy girl, your whole life ahead of you. With no father to help you, no support . . ."

"I don't know, I don't know," she moaned, "if my mother found out, or my brothers . . . gosh, if John found out . . ."

"Miss Riley, I assure you, these matters are entirely confidential."

"But there will be a record, somewhere, *here*," she said, throwing out her hands with a majestic dismay. "If there's any record, anything written down, Dr. Drummond, I'd rather just . . . I don't know, I don't know."

He leaned against the examining table and crossed his arms, considering her. She was wearing scuffed saddle shoes, a knee-length skirt and a faded, oversized plaid shirt that had once belonged to Colin — not the smart suits and pumps she had envisioned adorning her new self in her new life. The way he looked at her . . . it made her feel shabby; she returned his gaze, letting her eyes rove conspicuously over his form.

Drummond was a short fit man, just beginning to bald but not so much that you couldn't tell he had been nice looking not very long ago, even handsome. On the desk in his office stood a picture of his wife, a plain woman with shiny glum eyes, like a toy dog's; she seemed older than the doctor. There were the usual framed degrees and certificates; a large photo of Dr. Drummond, his wife, and a collie taken on a rocky beach. "Do you have children of your own?" she asked.

Drummond smiled. "No," he said, "no children. Tell me, was the father of your child healthy?"

"Jan? Oh, yes, why, strong as an ox . . . before the accident, of course."

"Of course." He removed his glasses and cleaned them on his lab coat, then gazed at her again, this time his eyes lit strangely and a dark furrow developing between them. "I might know a couple," he said, and again removed his glasses to polish them, "a childless couple with whom an arrangement might be made."

"A couple?" Kate repeated, spellbound.

"They are Europeans," he said, "still refugees, you might say."

"Refugees?"

"That's right."

"Why wouldn't they go to an adoption agency? I don't mean to be nosy . . ."

"They have no permanent papers as yet. It takes months, this sort of thing, now, with the war over and people piling up in the ports . . ." With some irritation, he sniffed abruptly. "We haven't much time, Miss Riley."

Kate gnawed at the skin alongside her thumbnail. In its way it was a grand solution, simply grand, but it struck her that it wouldn't do to appear too eager. She told him that she would think about it, but because she had in fact made up her mind she forgot all about telling him. During the next visit when he pressed her again to make a decision there was an odd strain in his voice that brought to mind boys who wanted it awfully. So she put off telling him. On her fourth visit the doctor's wife opened the door. She stared at Kate without apology and with what was perhaps a vague hostility—but then Kate often thought women regarded her thus. Finally, seeming to come round to the present, Mrs. Drummond told her that Doctor would be with her shortly.

From the sitting area Kate could hear them in the back office; Mrs. Drummond crying, then a minute or two of recovery, his voice firm, hers in retreat, a door closing discretely, then Dr. Drummond waved her in.

"Well, well," he said, "two more weeks by my calendar."

She smiled. "I'll be glad to get my body back."

"Of course you will, yes," he drifted over behind the examining table and gave it a pat, "everyone wants a figure again." Then he began to chat idly about a return to dances and parties and pretty dresses, and Kate reveled in his happy imaginings throughout the examination.

He listened through her swollen belly, he felt her abdomen, he had her lie back so that he could check her opening. "The baby's dropped."

"Is that good?"

He rose, drawing the sheet down from her waist, and offered an especially warm smile. "Miss Riley, your pregnancy has proceeded with admirable ease and health. A flawless gestation. Well done."

In spite of the circumstances, she blushed and thanked him. She had tried to take good care of herself, to eat well and get plenty of rest, to walk to the park each morning where the geese kept her company. The compliment meant everything to her—she had done well in spite of circumstances. She had been Irish tough.

Dr. Drummond soaked a white towel in warm water and instead of handing it to her and leaving the room as he had on previous visits, he cleaned her up himself, an act that she regarded as one of the kindest things a man had ever done, and which did not fail to remind her of the hot wet towels her father used in the barbershop. It seemed to her then that Dr. Drummond, at some point in their association, must have discerned her worth, must have understood, perhaps from the very first visit, that this was all a terrible mistake, that Kate was not an ordinary young woman with a predictable future, that, on the contrary, hers would be bright, the sort of future that oughtn't be hindered by this unlucky accident, this . . . little case of bad luck. She almost laughed out loud. The idea of it. A little piece of plain old bad luck might have wrecked her life.

"I've been thinking," she said as they returned to his office adjacent to the examination room, "I've been thinking about, well, you know, the couple you mentioned."

Drummond was facing the back wall of his office where the files were kept in alphabetical order; he tucked in one, withdrew another, glanced through it, slid it back in place. She wondered how he could read them so fast, or even if he was reading them, if perhaps he wasn't in reality trying not to look at her so that it would easier for her to say what needed to be said that day.

"I think you know that . . . well, you've been so kind to me and generous with your time, and you've kept things so private. I know now that it was to protect me and my future. Really, I'm so grateful . . ."

He dropped his arms and rotated slowly, taking stock of her as he might a patient he had only just met, the small muscles of his face softly anguished. "Miss Riley . . . Kate, it doesn't do . . . that is, it isn't a good idea to be so grateful."

"Oh, I'm sorry, and here you are being kind again, and thinking of me, when I've been so confused."

He had to turn away then, back to the wall of files. "People generally have their own reasons for doing things," he remarked, and then, almost harshly, "People always have their own motives. Do you understand that?"

She said, "Well . . . ," without knowing at the moment what else to say, and when it occurred to her to tell him that she wanted his European couple to have her baby, she watched the doctor's shoulders drop, and she heard his breath release, and she knew she had lifted some great tension from him and given him relief. "There," she added, clapping her hands once, "I've decided."

"Yes," he said, turning toward her. "At last you've decided."

On the way out of the office Dr. Drummond placed his arm on her shoulder; she was surprised just how short he was. "We'll get you through this, my dear girl, don't worry."

She could feel the tears coming, and turned to look directly, bravely, at him, and she said simply, "You." At that moment she longed for her body to be shrunk back down to its former size, so that her words had force again; pregnant, she felt herself noticed for all the wrong reasons, and invisible in all the ways that meant anything to her or—she was convinced—to anyone else.

Give the baby up for adoption . . . she thought about it all the way back to Miriam's, unaware now of the bright lights, the bright elegant people, the dizzy whirl of opportunity. But what else was there to do? She had had to surrender her room at the Boarding House when she was three months along, in order that Mrs. Wilmott wouldn't know what had happened, couldn't tell her brother, John or, god forbid, her mother. It had been a bitter winter, the coldest on record for southern British Columbia, snow piled up along the sidewalks and everyone complaining about the road conditions and the stopped trains and the downed lines; and though it was certainly better than a Netherfield winter, Kate had to admit she was disappointed. Even the weather seemed to be against her.

She had been sleeping on Miriam's chesterfield, eating in cafeterias, and now, toward the end of it all when she felt too ashamed to go out, she spent hours crouched over cups of cold tea in the back of Miriam's kitchen after she had gone off to school. One night she had walked fourteen blocks to the chicken dinner for the benefit of the Chinese Catholic School, just to avoid meeting anyone she might later want to know. After. The manager of the coffeehouse had given her the sack, and there would be no future work either—on that score they had made things painfully clear. "We don't want your sort," Mr. Hansen had said. "This is a family establishment." From behind the kitchen door she could hear the busboy with his dirty fingernails sniggering. The Success College insisted that she could not graduate without meeting their requirements, that they had a reputation that apparently mattered more to them than Kate's reputation did to her, and that she could not make up the last six weeks, she would simply have to begin again when she was "prepared to see it through." And just yesterday a letter arrived from Colin, the only one of her people she dared tell.

Dear Katy,

Well, what can I say? Ever since I guessed, and I did guess for awhile before your first letter came, I thought that would be the only thing you couldn't discuss over the phone — well anyway, ever since then my memory has taken me back to when you were born, when we were kids, and it was my job to baby-sit. You know, times have changed, I guess, but babysitting with a kid sister at that time was just the worst, I took an awful ribbing from the other kids, but for all that I loved you an awful lot and I was very happy to have a little sister. I'm afraid I was never really very good to you being a kid sister and all, and I guess I haven't changed a bit, or maybe this would never have happened. One thing I always remember about you Katy and I was always flattered, was how you brought your troubles to me large and small. I don't suppose I was a very willing helper but I remember fixing your doll and a little trike you had and sewing the strap on a shoe when we thought Mother would be cross. Then we grew apart and I went off to the War and you grew up. Through the years I've wondered from time to time what effect Mother's attempted dominance over you would have. I say 'attempted' because it was apparent that you had a mind of your own, but all the same she is pretty insistent. When you left and went to Vancouver I worried about you, wondered whether Mother would follow you and interfere with your life. I've wondered what your aim was, worried about the kind of life you would make for yourself in a big city so far away and hoped that you would find yourself a good mate someday.

There are many things in life that we cannot plan for, although we should keep control of the basic pattern. Sometimes, somewhere along the line things seem to go wrong. I often give thanks that in spite of disappointments my main interest in life is most satisfactory. I have a good wife and 2 good kids. I'm amazed when I think back over the last 4 years to when I first fell in love with Mary that I could have been so sure—how could I possibly have been so right and yet I was. These are the things that have been going through my mind, wondering how you can bear the strain you've been under and how things are going to be for you in the years to come. I wish we could lighten your load and I don't know how. I do know that you'll have to work things out for yourself for the most part. It's too late now for advice, not that there ever is a time for advice to be followed, no one could have advised me—I was just lucky. At any rate, all I can say now is that my heart is with you, and I'll always be here thinking of you and praying. I do so want to help you and the baby. You know of course that you have done wrong and God will forgive you only after how much, I don't know, anguish, in seeing your child suffer, again, how much I don't know. We can only hope that He will be lenient and that these things will soon be resolved along happier lines. But I can't help but think how nice this would have been under conventional circumstances. I promise I won't mention this side of it again.

Your time will come soon. I do wish you well.

Love every day,
Colin

Colin had never before scolded her. If there were no baby, there would be no wrong. People would simply forget. Forgetting was all that mattered. Not forgiveness. Kate had never been interested in forgiveness. She could simply put it from her mind and take up the life that was to have been hers, and still could be. So she had lost, what, six months? No one noticed anything during the first three, so that time did not count. Half a year, that was all. She would simply start over. *After*. God, it seemed she was always having to wait for something disagreeable to end.

Drummond arranged for her to deliver the baby in the examining room next to his office, because there weren't any legal documents associated with the birth. His wife was a registered nurse. If there were any serious problem, the hospital was close; otherwise, Kate would stay in the second examination room, which had a bed and a window that looked out over a garden.

When the July day came the sun shone, the rhododendrons were in full bloom, and all the way to the doctor's office Miriam, who accompanied her, whispered her pleas, the cab driver oblivious to all but the impending birth and his brief critical role in the event. He took the corners with magnificent speed, and even leaned on the horn through two intersections as if it had become a siren, while Miriam suggested in hurried undertones that Jan was the handsomest fellow in Netherfield, and that she herself had fancied him, and wouldn't Kate like to have a family, didn't all girls want finally to have a family?

Inside her purse Kate kept the letter Jan had written her the day after she left. She slipped it out and looked at her name written in his familiar steady hand—*Miss Kate Riley*—across the baby blue paper. Then another contraction reduced her world momentarily to the backseat of the cab, to the smell of stale cigarettes and worn leather, to smeared windows, the want-ad page from the *Vancouver Sun* jammed in the crease between the seat and back, and rattling around the floor, an empty bottle of Felix Ginger Ale. Her new life. When the pain passed she gazed again at the little envelope, so blue, so pure, so filled with foolish longing.

By the time Kate wobbled out of the car, she was missing him, his quiet devotion, the persistent innocence of his hands as they wandered her body, and the emotional easiness that a life with Jan offered. He adored her—it would always be so. Maybe she could persuade him to move to Moose Jaw, at least; they could rent a little place in town near the movie house.

So Kate told Dr. Drummond that she had changed her mind.

It even surprised her.

The labor went smoothly, though most of the time she was lost inside the chaos of pain. Occasionally she was aware of the nurse, coming, going, her glum eyes sharpened, apparently, by the drama of the delivery. Whenever Dr. Drummond checked in he seemed beleaguered, but Kate took this to mean he was sympathizing with her pain. My pain, she thought, with a queer sort of pride, for it seemed to be directing the course of events. Within ten hours she was pushing. She could not hang onto thoughts any longer, the urge to expel it was overwhelming, and her muscles bundled together reflexively, while her mind went empty and collapsed like a tired balloon. It was not a baby, not even an It, it was a big need filled with momentum inside her body wanting out. When at last it slid from her, the relief was so pure and complete that it was several minutes before Kate realized that there had been a point to the whole matter, and that it wasn't in her or even in the room any longer, the nurse had taken the baby away. When she listened Kate could not even hear it crying.

"Some more pushing to do, Kate," the doctor said. "Placenta."

And when that was finished he sewed up the little tear in her perineum.

She could not say how much time had passed, though it must have been longer than she could admit, but at last she did ask, "What about the baby?" Perhaps she knew then that she didn't really want it and all that it would mean, all that it would subtract from her dreams; she knew it because of the delay. That was all.

"A girl," he said.

"A girl."

"Yes."

"I don't hear anything, any crying."

"Nurse is cleaning her up."

"Why don't I hear it?"

The doctor made no answer.

Deep inside Kate Riley, so deep that it could not be articulated, a savage struggle went on; all that she seemed to know of it was that the longer she waited to hear the creature cry out, the more desperate she became not to hear it.

Finally she managed to ask, "Should I have it now?"

"If you still want her." Something beyond the literal words . . . his voice . . . a terrible uncertainty. She saw him glance to the side through the open door, as if to confirm something, or perhaps—she later thought, and much, much, later realized when it was entirely too late—perhaps to solicit encouragement from the nurse, his wife, for what he was about to say.

"What do you mean?"

He leapt up from the chair that had been situated between her legs, leapt up so violently that the chair knocked into her foot, he looked fiercely at her, then dropped his head, shook it once, hard, as if to fling something away, something clawing at his head.

"What? What have I done?" Kate cried, trying to rise up now, to see.

"She's blind," he said, and with that he threw down the towel he had been using to wipe his hands. She saw that it was covered with her blood. "Blind," he shouted, his disgust worse than his anger, oh yes, far worse for Kate Riley, young and lovely Kate with the Irish green eyes, for how could she have produced damaged goods, a flawed thing, a mistake, he seemed to ask. And how could she and Jan live such a future together, she wondered frantically? Perhaps even he would not want her then. It was a shocking idea.

And imagine, she thought at rapid speed, the Prairies without eyes, a girl without the ability to know a place that was all vision, all space and color and distance, sky lording it over land and the land not resisting, not caring, the land laid out flat and endless. And the pity, there was nothing more monstrous than small-town pity, full of fear, self-congratulation, relief, silent mockery. *Boys*, she thought, there would never *ever* be boys for this girl—oh, it was hopeless, hopeless!

No, she decided then that this shame could not be hers. It really was a mistake but not one she had made; this was a large mistake that found its origins in vast forces; it had nothing to do with her and nothing to do with bad luck either, for even bad luck, finally, was personal.

She felt a hard interior cold form instantly, like ice crystals spreading throughout her body, swift and perfect and perfectly executed. "Your couple, they expect a baby."

"Of course, you didn't change your mind until . . ."

"Yes, I know," she said, cutting him off. He was standing at the sink, washing his hands, and when she spoke, when she said, "It's theirs then, they agreed to it," she watched him reach methodically to the faucet and shut the valve, his hands clean at last. "They don't have papers, documents, they can't complain."

"I suppose not." He gazed at her then with a hard pity, but she would have none of that, and closed her eyes and felt the tears.

"Beggars can't be choosers," Kate said, swallowing a stone of regret and laying back down on the bed.

In the year and a half since she had met Anthony Snider on the train to Moose Jaw the Langston Hotel seemed to have changed hands, or perhaps Snider had never really known Gregor Vancleve, for Kate watched the big man rise from behind his desk with an elegant priestly confidence, while Snider's letter of introduction landed at the edge of the desk, its tidy creases and enchanting formality having cast no spell whatsoever over the interview.

"You are staying where, Miss Riley?"

"I was at the Wilmott's Boarding House, and then I moved to a friend's in Kitsilano near the park," Kate replied, and without thinking she told him how the geese huddled around her whenever she went out for a walk.

With a small smile Vancleve interrupted her: "And you wish employment." He ran his fingers through white hair as stiff and thick as dried grass.

"Yes, I do, Mr. Vancleve," she said, remembering now to be quiet, even aloof as the tellers in the bank were when she went in to withdraw her money each week. Oh, she would have given anything to be like those tellers, up there on their six-inch ledge, dispensing money or receiving it, counting out tidy bundles, while the men in their dark overcoats and the shop-girls with their belted narrow waists stood expectantly.

He stared openly, gently at her shoes, a pair of brown pumps well broken in, and at the introductory curve of her ankles that seemed to gesture upward, away from the scuffed shoes, toward ever greater curves.

Kate shifted from one foot to the other. "I've been learning to type and keep books. In less than a month I will graduate from business college. My diploma . . ."

Vancleve waved his hand, not interested in office skills and credentials, false or otherwise. "I don't need a bookkeeper, Miss Riley, but I could use a chambermaid." Adjusting his heavy black glasses, he shuffled a stack of correspondence on his desk and glanced at the envelope second from the top. He seemed uncomfortable with her reaction, for her disappointment was as plain as her ignorance, she realized.

"A chambermaid?"

"Perhaps something else will come up later. It's the best I can do at present." Vancleve held her eyes as if to convince her. *Trust me*, he seemed to say.

From her purse she removed a handkerchief, peering at him as she dabbed her nose, trying not to cry. At that moment she longed for the interview to be over so that she could hate him completely. A chambermaid. She had spent her childhood, it seemed, in that capacity.

A heaviness settled into her legs; she longed to sit down. Her throat tightened painfully. So, a chambermaid. She was going to be a bookkeeper, or a secretary to someone important; she would wear smart suits and lovely little hats that hugged her head, and she would take a trolley bus to work each morning, and the driver would tip his cap the same way each time she entered, and at noon she would meet a friend in the luncheonette at the Hudson's Bay Company downtown. And after work, after she'd gone home to freshen up, a fellow would come around for her and they would go to one of the new clubs that were springing up everywhere now that the war was over, and there would be a band and dancing and spinning lights. That was where she belonged, that was the world she dreamed of entering, not making beds and cleaning bathrooms.

Without warning, Gregor Vancleve dropped into his chair with a great sigh. Too much time had passed without a response.

"I'm sorry," she began, snapping shut her purse and assuming a prim attention.

"I see," he murmured with an odd bitterness, "yes, yes, it's always the same thing, always . . . ," and he shuffled papers without seeming to care how they ended up.

"I beg your pardon, sir?"

"I see that you are wondering if I am German."

She told him no, but did not fail to notice that he had revealed something about himself, an anxiety she might later turn to advantage, if only because she now knew of it.

"I am Dutch." Vancleve gave a sharp laugh. "Canadians cannot hear the difference."

"Oh Mr. Vancleve, I'm sorry, I grew up with families from all over, Swedes and Norwegians, French, Polish, we even had a Hungarian couple in Netherfield. I do need the job, Mr. Vancleve," she insisted. "I accept your offer."

Vaguely, wearily, he said, "Tomorrow then."

What else am I to do? And how many times had she asked that question? The thought of going back to Netherfield a failure . . . and if she were to go back, then giving up the baby would have been for nothing, no fancy new life, no career, no fellow. And it was only ten days since . . . well, she still wasn't feeling that chipper. It was unfair, all of it. Everything. What had she done to deserve this?

The following day at 7:00 a.m. she arrived for work at the Langston Hotel. It was July but the air was cool and fragrant and the summer rain that had fallen throughout the night had quit with the dawn as if to cheer her up, to urge a fresh start. There seemed to be water everywhere, the enormity of the winter of '49–'50 still present in the brooks and rivulets that rushed about and finally committed themselves to the Fraser River or Elliott Bay or to the Pacific. The rain had shined up the glossy leaves of the Arbutus trees; under the porte-cochere each car left its own puddle. The doorman, a Mr. Slattery, had had to drag long red mats up the marble stairs that led to the lobby. Kate did enjoy the regal mats, and mounted them with the air of a hotel guest who had paid for privileges, but Slattery stopped her with a jerk of his finger: "Service entrance." How could he know? she wondered. A young couple waiting for their car glanced at her; the woman's hands were tucked inside a fur muff that matched the trim of her car coat, and when Kate passed she withdrew one hand and discretely extracted something from her nose. Kate was so close that she could smell the man's after-shave cologne.

No refinement, none at all; it's her that ought to go round the back door, not me, Kate thought. It's me that ought to be standing there with a man like that, who wears cologne at 7:00 in the a.m.

The service entrance led directly into the kitchen, a cavernous room smelling of dish detergent, an amalgam of spices, and at that hour, coffee and breakfast meats.

"You want Mrs. Kim." Kate gazed past the wash-boy to the tall Negro man dressed in white, jiggling rashers of bacon on a vast griddle. She had never seen a Negro in the flesh.

"Down the hall," the boy said, "and quit staring, Miss," he added under his breath.

In the laundry room the old Chinese woman known as Mrs.

Kim was tugging towels from a dryer; she was so ugly and yet so impeccably quaffed and so ceaseless in her labor that Kate understood instantly—and with some disappointment—Mr. Vancleve's priorities. Looks didn't matter. He was just a nice man, a gentleman. She would never have any influence with him; she would be a chambermaid as long as this old hag had been.

Mrs. Kim fit her for the brown dress and crisp white apron, gave her a set of keys and a cart, towels tipping from its uppermost shelf, and bade her follow. They cleaned half a dozen rooms together. The Chinese woman kept saying, "See, like this, Miss Wiley," each time she accomplished the least intervening act, like making a corner in the sheet, or setting the matchbook, tentlike, in the ashtray, and when it was all apparently finished she stood in the doorway of the room and said, "Now, look-see with the eyes," clasping Kate's hand and bringing it up to her face, "the eyes see what not done." There was never anything Mrs. Kim left undone, and Kate was relieved when she was at last released to the fifth floor to clean on her own.

Room 503: one night; a businessman—the newspaper stock page folded near the telephone; ashtray full; cocktail napkin on which was written "75 at 6% discount." The wet towels were hung over the shower rod and the bed had been roughly tidied. Married, she concluded.

Room 508, one night; another businessman—breakfast tray with coffee and pastry remains; used razor blade; loose change on the dresser; one black sock.

Room 512: three nights, a family—everything used, even the second roll of toilet paper; wastebasket overflowing, empty box of brittle, a finished coloring book, one drained half pint bottle of Crown Royal *for mum and dad*; roll-away bed near the window and both doubles slept in; one bath towel tied to make what looked to be a cape.

Room 519: a couple, still in residence. *The* couple. His cologne stood open on the bathroom counter, the scent familiar, recent, filling the room. A bottle of Vitalis. The woman had left several outfits strewn on the bed; it was clear she had had fun deciding which to wear. In order to change the sheets, Kate would have to hang up every article of clothing—the tweed Evan Picone suit, the narrow, dark blue skirt with its white middy blouse, the dove-gray jumper, a pair of Orient nylons, a creamy, lacy brassiere that must have cost over five dollars. She held it to her chest and looked in the mirror. Too small, especially now; small and beautiful and pure, still new probably, it hadn't even been washed yet because it hadn't been soiled yet. In fact, all of this woman's clothing looked pristine, as if nothing bad had ever happened to her and she herself had never gotten into any sort of trouble.

Kate sat down on the edge of the bed. The spread was white with a pale yellow and green chenille pattern, flowery and inno-cent; at the headboard the big white down pillows lay side-by-side in tender disarray. It was even imaginable that they had not yet made love, or if they had, that it was innocent, sibling pups explor-ing the earliest of possibilities. The ticking sounds of the radiator seemed to assure the guests' happy return. Their room would be clean and tidy, spotlessly clean, and they would enter in a playful burst of laughter and perhaps hardly register the change. Because it was what they deserved; they were good and right and had never done anything wrong, and they would not even notice a world that approvingly prepared their way. The white middy blouse still lay across the foot of the bed—it was the kind of blouse that was popular among women who were expecting, roomy and long with a sailor bow. Perhaps Kate might have worn such a blouse, perhaps she and Jan might have stood on the red carpet waiting for a car and Mr. Slattery would have opened a door for her . . . she gave her head a single sad shake, drew in one corner of her mouth . . . *no*. It could not have been that way, not with Jan Larsen. He would never leave the Prairies, and Kate did not belong in Saskatchewan, that was definite. Here, this city, this green wet place with mountains and big ships moving as if in a distant dream under the Lions' Gate Bridge, the secret blued light of downtown where the sun had but a brief say in matters, and the tall gray stone buildings with their big glass windows, beautiful mannequins in frozen gestures of temptation beckoning to passersby, the Alexandrite ring at Grauman's whose colors changed with the light, and which she tried to visit each day as if it had been promised her, and the men, so handsome, so important, striding along. She was here, but none of it would ever be hers. Not even the ring at Grauman's.

She looked around the room at the clothes, the cologne, the two white pillows . . . it all made her feel cheap, without resources. Alone. Even Miriam was disappointed in her, but then Miriam believed in things—God, love, gifts that were homemade.

Forcing herself to rise, Kate hung up the clothes, stripped and remade the bed, dusted. When she opened the window to air the room, she paused for a long time to listen to the rushing brook that fell behind the hotel in a series of pools and drops. It was a comforting sound, like the prairie wind that took things away in long clean sweeps. In the bathroom the mirror exposed her pale skin, her red hair thinning, the curls out of order and frayed—Dr. Drummond had said to expect hair loss for a while. Under her eyes faint shadows like smeared mascara seemed to suggest that she should have cried more; she should have offered some resistance. She was so tired.

But she should have cried. It was only a poor, damaged thing not even its own mum wanted, because its own mum was a poor, damaged thing too, only worse, my god, worse, because she could see and would not. She could see and fled.

She touched the skin under her eyes, warm and moist. Above, two cool green eyes stared candidly back. In the Langston Hotel mirror Kate saw the young woman she was—just a glimpse—but it was a glimpse as naked and as frank as a door thrown open on a scene that was to have remained hidden forever. What was in that room? The baby? No. Not the abandoned baby. Only Kate. The machinery of Kate's identity. What drove her, the cold hard workings grinding ceaselessly along. And in the far window stood the ghostly image of Poppy.

She could go back to Netherfield. To Jan. Her mother. *I could always do that*, she told the mirror.

Sure, and here you come, tail between your legs, but I'll forgive you Kate, dear, put the kettle on and give me feet a rub, and we'll put things right, eh?

The green eyes went stark.

As Kate left the couple's room, she noted the middy blouse hanging in the closet, so confidently white. The elevator was slow, impossibly slow, but it didn't matter now, and she hung her wrists through the triangular metal of the cage door until the little room bobbed to a stop and she was obliged to move. Outside, the garden paths were deserted and damp; the table umbrellas were folded like the wings of sea birds wet from a dawn feeding, the tulips were loosely closed and waiting for stronger sun, and atop an old willow stump a squirrel sat puffed against the morning air. Through the formal gardens the path was paved, but beyond the last stone wall it was gravel, then mud, and as such, led through untamed brambles and trees to the brook. The brook was full, the size of a river. Kate marveled at the mud working its way up the sides of her saddle shoes, and it was this—the mud on her shoes and getting it off—that crowded out any other thoughts she might have had as she entered the water.

She felt first the weight of the water against her left hip; its heaviness surprised her, like a sack of grain swinging into her. Then she noticed the second deeper cadence of her heart's beat. The water's surface was smooth and swollen, and when she looked down into it she could see through the jade-green darkness to the rocks rounded by the river's work, all their jagged edges subdued. She could see, too, the mud from her shoes trailing off. At once and quite easily, as though they had agreed in advance, the current pushed her over. Her breasts were still full and the buoyancy was a relief. The brink was near, she could see space beyond it, and she thought to turn about in order to go feet-first, but there wasn't time, and anyway, the water was heavy and tight about her body, moving with a swift, massing force, as if about to give birth to her as she had given birth to the blinded girl. Just above the brink a small faded rainbow hung in the confluence of mist and light. In her head she could hear the rush; it was like the airy call of distance inside a seashell that was only the white noise of her own life calling back. She saw the rocks at the bottom of the fall, docile as the ones flashing beneath her. She thought about the little faded rainbow lifting up and away from her. It was not a long fall; at the bottom she felt nothing.

There was a man in the water . . . trousers, a pale shirt; whether he had just waded in or had been there all along she did not know. His hair was white, his glasses awry, and she wanted to help, perhaps because he was old, she wanted to set right his glasses, but it was nice, after all, floating down, it was painless and in her head the rush like the inside of the shell seemed to protect her, to keep her apart from the individual sounds of a world that had asked so much and for which she had had, it seemed, all the wrong answers.

Blind or not, she would have got rid of that baby.

"Grab on!" he called. His voice came to her as from a great distance, from across the Prairies on the wind. "Please," he cried out.

Really, she did not have to pay attention. What she was doing was at least honest, perhaps her last honest act.

"For god's sake, child . . ."

And she could not go back to Netherfield.

"Take my hand!"

Kate flicked her eyes upstream, saw Gregor Vancleve struggling through the water toward her, his glasses cock-eyed, his old hand shaking. The way Poppy's had at the end. *But it doesn't have to be the last thing I do*, she thought, almost absently, as though her life had broken off, broken free, like a weak branch in the wind.

And with that, her head exploded with pain.

That was the beginning and the end of Kate Riley's career as a chambermaid. From the hospital Gregor Vancleve took her to his home on the other side of the Lions' Gate Bridge in West Vancouver, and there she recovered from the head injury, and eventually from all that had lead up to it. A young priest, Father Deneau, from the local church came to see her regularly. She couldn't bear to confess to him about the pregnancy, so she showed him her mother's letters of recrimination and told him about her childhood and about Poppy dying. She did not want him to leave without giving him a reason for what she had tried to do that morning behind the Langston Hotel. She did not want to do without his beautiful sympathy. He came to her bedroom and laid one hand atop hers, and in the other he held a silver cross, which he kissed now and then. She talked for hours, the tears coming and going, Vancleve at the hotel, the house as quiet as the house of God. His black garments smelled of the iron and of incense and faintly, of the oiled walnut pews that filled St. Raymond's Church. He brought her a vial of holy water from Lourdes. She touched his arm, as if unconsciously, whenever her own enthusiasms might appear to carry her away, for the seduction emanating from a person of uncertain or concealed sexuality was powerful.

Two weeks into their visits a letter arrived from Father Deneau:

Dear Kate:

It has certainly been very nice talking with you. I wish that things were such that we could carry on a real conversation without worrying about other angles. Well Kate, sorry to know that you are so unsettled in mind re what you should do, you have no good clear logical reason for thinking as you do, as I told you before. You possess many outstanding assets, personality is certainly one of them and you are definitely liked by people, it seems, which definitely is a great help when one is down. Being dull or blue is a common denominator of mankind here below but behind it all there is a silver lining, some days we do not feel as good as other days, that again is part of God's plan for it was decreed by God that mans' life in this world would consist of many crosses no matter who you are, crosses and thorns are yours, despite all that each and every one of us have an individuality all our own, in other words we are all different people and possess good points as well as imperfections and as such we move about this world and contribute our little part in order to make it a little brighter for ourselves and others. You are too young to let thoughts like that invade your thoughts and stay there, you can rest assured and be certain in your mind that I have a very high regard for you, also Father LaPorte and no doubt Father MacFarland would if they met you. Once you get what you want to do, that is, in the line of work, I think you will be alright—at least you will feel happier that you are doing your little part in life. Perhaps the condition of your mother has something to do with the way you feel at times, but once again Kate those feelings are absolutely unfounded. You can do your duty to your Mother as a daughter by writing frequently and assure her that you always remember her and pray for her health and welfare. She should know and understand that you have a life to live. Perhaps it would be different if your mother was physically sick, but under the circumstances continual contact would not be good for you. Send me her address and I will write her a letter, no doubt it will do some good.

Remember that I care a great deal for you, Kate.

As ever,
Fr. Russ Deneau

She sent back a thank you note, and there was another visit, then another. And several more notes along the lines of the first. But the sixth note read:

Dear Kate,

There is no doubt about the fact that I have a true and sincere liking for you so much so that it would not be good to see you so often. You know as well as I do that I am quite human coupled with the high regard that I hold you would make it extremely hard on both of us. We could grow to like each other more and more as time goes on and I am sure my Dear Kate would not want matters that way in view of who I am. I appreciate your love for me, if you do not object to me using that word. Words are inadequate to express how happy I am in your company. You look so nice, refined and upright, even in bandages.

I think this letter should be brought to a close not that I am getting tired of writing but you might become bored.

> *God bless you and*
> *pray for me,*
> Russ

With every letter, perhaps more so than the visits, Kate felt better. She read them and smiled and held the linen pages to her nose, inhaling their ecclesiastical scent. In her mind the young priest wrote them sitting at a bare table, dusty morning light streaming through a window somewhere high up. In her mind he missed breakfast in order to write her, and posted it before others would note his absence. Confused, he spoke of her only to God.

Vancleve cooked and cared for Kate each evening, and during the days—not every day, but many—the priest stood in her doorway. "May I enter, Miss Riley," he always said with a wink, and thereafter used her Christian name. His face was pale as an anemic, his eyes dark and burning; she liked his Quebecois accent, the way he used his hands to talk, the purple mark on his cheek. At the base of his neck the pure white square seemed to support, like a little pedestal, his good intentions. She wanted to believe all the nice things he said about her, she wanted to believe everything. But it wasn't until later, until *I really feel tops while in your company* and *you know Kate, I hope that I will not like you too much;* then letter #11 which concluded, *I think I had better bring this epistle to a close, otherwise I might shock you if I keep on writing. When we meet again I think we will have plenty of things to talk about,* and its cryptic postscript, *please destroy, Kate, when finished* — it wasn't until he had begun to debauch his own vows that Kate Riley began to feel strong again.

Several days before his last note he happened to arrive as Vancleve was leaving. She heard them talking downstairs; it was friendly, even jocular, as if they might have known each other, and when Father Deneau appeared in her doorway she felt that Gregor had blessed him in some way. It made Deneau slightly less attractive. His usually pale skin was flushed, the purple mark like a fiery brush stroke.

"Father, hello," she exclaimed as if surprised. To cheer Kate up Miriam had sent her a charm for her bracelet, a tiny, gold-plated replica of the Lions' Gate Bridge, and Kate retrieved it now from her bedside table, slowly twiddling it among her fingertips as she studied Father Deneau.

He drew his chair — it had long ago become *his* chair — to her bedside and leaned to kiss her forehead. From his pocket he withdrew the silver cross, then he kissed it too — his ritual.

She was aware of the exposed curve of her breast above the gathers of her nightgown, for she had earlier turned the radiator up to the point that covers would not be warranted.

"You are lucky, Kate, to have Gregor Vancleve as your benefactor."

"Well yes," she said, and noticing his still-flushed face she heard herself ask, "but why?"

Deneau gave a small laugh, avoiding her eyes. "He won't . . . that is, he is honorable." Then he added, "And look how radiant you have become. Soon you'll be painting the town, or giving it a little color," he added with a wink. But his pleasure did not seem connected to his observation; it was leftover from Deneau's encounter with Gregor, she was sure of it.

He did not stay long that last visit. His hands were in his lap and despite the awkwardness of the cross he kept wrapping one hand over the other, then reversing it, as if each had been charged with keeping the other in check, yet neither was quite subdued.

He wants to touch me, she thought. But he can't.

Finally, the young priest leapt up and said that he had better go, that he was scheduled to hear confession that day.

"Hear mine," she said, "please." She made her voice both ebullient and throaty as if to convey a lustiness that no one had yet explored and of which not even Kate was wholly aware.

"Oh God, Kate . . ." He was halfway to the door, facing away from her. "I'm just as human as anyone, Kate, perhaps a little more so."

"I like you so much. I trust you, I only trust you." She did, it seemed.

"Our liking is mutual."

"Then don't leave. Please come back, sit next to me."

Still, he had not turned toward her; he spoke as if to another human being who stood beyond the doorway, outside the room. "The laws of nature, forces of attraction and of emotion are at times unexplainable. The fact that one is a priest does not alter the realism that he is a man first, although he is not supposed to show externally what is going on internally."

"Father . . . Russ, isn't there a special feeling between us? With you I am alive as I've never felt before. You've saved me," she said in a childlike voice, and even to Kate it seemed that he had, indeed, saved her in some manner that was inexpressible, and that she did not want expressed ever, that would be undone if words were applied. She touched her brow with a kind of wonder, and dropped the little gold-plated charm to the floor. Deneau rushed to recover it for her and in so doing the cross slipped from his hands and clattered under her bed.

"Jesus," he muttered, groping about for it in the darkness, and when he had located it he snatched it up and fled to the door.

"You're going, really?"

He was shaking his head slowly; something was driving him, driving him, and he couldn't stop it or make it go away. "Constantly living with men . . . it's not good," he said. Then he turned abruptly and stared at her with a strange and devouring attention, taking his fill as though taking a draught of curative waters. "No, I should not be thinking this way." As he ran from the room she saw that his fists were clenched. "This house, this house . . ."

The last note arrived five days later; Gregor himself delivered it to her room, laying it on her bedside table with a cup of tea and a soft silent smile. She waited until he left for the hotel, then tore it open. There was no date, no *My dear Kate*, only a single typed sentence at the top of the page—*Time hangs heavy on my hands*. Below, in an inky scrawl, the word *destroyed*, then again, but this time almost illegible, the letters sliding wildly down the page—*destroyed*.

But where was the first page? And what was she to destroy? He had forgotten to include the first page, and now she could only imagine the pretty words that he had written about her, the confessions of true feelings, how it might have been with them, how she made him feel.

Her hand with the letter fell to the coverlet. Never mind, she thought, abruptly chipper, full of *esprit*. "I'm feeling better," she announced to the room, "oh, much much better. Ayah, dandy," she added in her best Irish accent. And she tucked Deneau's final letter in her bureau with the others, and at last arose from bed. For it wasn't until then, until she was certain that in Fr. Deneau's chaste heart Kate Riley had surpassed God, that she was finally convinced of her worth.

Within a month she was working as a teller-in-training at the Royal Bank. Gregor knew the manager—Joe Willoughby—for he kept a number of large accounts with the West Vancouver branch of the Royal Bank, including the hotel's. It had been a simple matter, making arrangements. "Good morning, Miss Riley," Mr. Willoughby said on her first day; she seemed to have honored him with her very presence.

She wore narrow, belted dresses and little hats that hugged her head, her hair swept up in a French roll, and when she gazed down from her six-inch ledge customers caught, like bright coins, flashes of the giddy enchantment Kate Riley had at last found. Her customers — mostly men — seemed eager to encounter her at the end of a day, deposits in hand.

Kate expected Vancleve to exact some sort of payment for the time she spent recovering in his home, as well as for the job. But he did not press her, would not press her. He bought her clothes, standing like a guard outside the dressing room curtains; he rubbed her calves at the end of a day of standing; he roasted fine meats brought home from the hotel kitchen; he changed his will, though he never told her — a letter arrived one day and her curiosity had got the better of her. Late at night when the world would not have seen, he never once knocked on her door.

At first she was intrigued. Anything about him, his kindness, his wealth, the basic fact of his maleness, even, merely, his proximity, could have aroused her, but it was this — his restraint — that seized her completely. At the same time it sowed a vague unease. How could she hope to keep this man without giving herself to him? It had been a long time since she had been with a man . . . maybe she had lost something, an ineffable knack. Finally one morning at the breakfast table she took his hand and slid it inside her sweater, her nipple propped like a berry between his unmoving fingers.

"Don't you want me?" she cried when too much time had passed.

"Kate," he said, "I adore you."

"But my body, don't you want it, don't you want me? Haven't you ever wanted me?"

Again he gazed at her, his eyes bright, his hand resting exactly where she had placed it. "I am honored by this breast."

The longer his hand remained immobile the more knotted up her thoughts became. She had tried to be a lady; it had always been easy to wait and then to succumb when the inevitable appeal careened inevitably out of control. But she had never ever had to ask for it. It was always their desire followed by her gift; their gratitude, her power — a natural order.

The August sun streamed through the kitchen window, firing off the stainless steel counters. On her plate the scrambled eggs were a cold counterfeit yellow, the ham glistening and pinkly suggestive. She dropped her eyes; his hand was like an enormous growth she had just discovered and that seemed to have been there all along. Everything felt exposed. She longed for darkness, for his hand to be back where she had found it, resting with peaceful dignity in his lap. From her open sweater she could smell her own skin faintly, like a food, maybe warm bread pudding . . . could he smell her, too? Was it a bad smell?

It was unbearably awkward, his inert hand on her breast and his arm reaching between them like a great tree root. "Gregor, please . . ." (Oh, she hated him for that.)

Then, only then, he rose. In silence he took her to his room. When the door was closed he walked her backwards to the wall and there let her feel his desire angling up across her abdomen. She was surprised by his hardness, sudden and complete, as strong as a young man's. It was a moment she never forgot, not for the success she could now claim — no, not at all — but for a vague and baffling disappointment. Somewhere in the back of her mind she heard a soft, sad, definitive *click*, as a door latched shut forever and a vast emptiness seeking to envelop her; she could almost feel it tugging her foot from below. But however vague, however distant, it was nevertheless unendurable; Kate turned instantly from the feeling and gave herself over to the thing itself.

He kissed her. She heard herself moan, a strange animal. Now the bed lay beneath her. Piece by piece he undressed her, his face expressionless. He had not closed the drapes and the room was awash in dusty light, but she didn't care, it didn't matter. To someone, somewhere one had at last to surrender all, and he was at least a gentleman. Father Deneau had said so. She had never wanted it so much; it was nothing like Jan or the others, it was the paradigm, as if she and Gregor Vancleve were the first to have ever lain together, and at the same time, it seemed she had arrived at the future moment that all her life had predicted, all her life had pursued with a deep, unacknowledged intensity.

From his old shallow hips he thrust with a steady formality. Nothing wild corrupted his bearing, nothing that did not lack a full measure of confidence. It was mesmerizing. He was precise, thorough, generous. She took her cues from him. She agreed, without having to be asked, to do things for him that she had never done, and that she would never do again. When it was over, she felt raw, scoured clean of Kate Riley, of personality and past, of rules and qualms, of society.

And each time was the same. He came through the door at the end of the day and without speaking, pressed her against a wall, his hand smoothing her hair from her forehead, his blue eyes searching her face for anything he might have missed. "Why do you look at me like that?" she asked one day, and hid her face against his herringbone jacket.

"I look for shadows, a change."

"Nothing is going to change," she quipped, burying her face deeper in the rich gray herringbone.

He kissed the nape of her neck. "Ah, Katrina."

"It won't," she insisted.

She was awed by his technique—there was no other word—but she began to notice that it did not leave her warm, it left her razed, like a country that had been taken and purged of its distinguishing features. Kate could not say that Gregor Vancleve loved her, only that he adored her with a clinical and all-encompassing exactitude. One day in a drawer she discovered pieces of herself—a lock of hair, a pair of soiled underclothes, a glass from which she had drunk, the pink lipstick impression of her mouth flawless, even a tooth she had had to have pulled, its root brown with blood. Still, it would be hard to walk away from Gregor Vancleve, to leave his house and give up his money. He bought her the Alexandrite at Grauman's, though he thought it too big, too gaudy, for sweet Kate. And the clothes . . . how Kate loved clothes.

When she found herself pregnant again, they were married at once. It was not the big wedding she had dreamed of; Gregor was not that kind of man, no pomp and circumstance. It took place in a pea-green office in the basement of the courthouse, Miriam and Vancleve's assistant from the Langston Hotel, a sallow bookkeeper named Mr. Prible, witnesses. But Gregor did arrange for a four-day honeymoon to California and Kate thought the pregnancy well-worth the sights of Frisco (as she referred to it with a cool pride among her fellow tellers), at least during the month following their honeymoon.

Her mother thought the marriage "a fine match," which vaguely disappointed Kate. Shouldn't a mother want someone, well, more appropriate for her daughter? Or maybe Vancleve only confirmed Fiona's notions about Kate, and that was what recommended the match to the widow Riley. But Kate accepted her good wishes, they were so rare. The rest of the time her mother wrote about her abandonment, her ailments, her loneliness, her sacrifices.

Her brother and sister-in-law sent a card with money in it, to be put toward some "domestic necessity." If they had any opinion about Vancleve's age or money, they kept it to themselves—as, of course, they would. Colin sent flowers with a note; he wanted only for her to be happy and if this was where she had found it, well then, bravo.

When her time came—exactly one year after the first erased birth—Vancleve hired a nurse who came to the house. Renée was a stocky Basque girl with dark curls and a flat, honest face the color of caramel. There was no doubt that Vancleve was aware of his young wife's limitations. Perhaps the attempted suicide still whispered to him. So Renée would take care of everything. Renée was waiting at the door when they arrived home from the hospital, her white nurse's cap wedged in her hair like the prow of a good ship, awaiting orders.

Instantly Kate found her irritating—she did not want another female in the house. At the same time she realized how important a live-in might be to a smooth transition back to femininity. Nothing about motherhood was compelling. She put her clothes away and hid in the bathroom, examining her breasts, swollen and elongated, like melons left too long in the patch. Her fair skin was blotchy and even it brought to mind burned fruit. In the hospital when they had brought the baby in at regular intervals for her to nurse, his tiny pinched face disappeared beneath the bulbous curve of her breast. She found it embarrassing, as if she were forcing her prodigious self, distorted by pregnancy, on a little old man who, each time, almost choked on the gush, burped and spit up. How long could this go on? And what would she look like when all was said and done? What would this creature do to her once round and creamy breasts, so symmetrical, so firm, and who would want to look at her, to hold them, after? It was then, standing before the mirror the day she and the baby came home from the hospital that Kate knew there would be other men. In fact, she realized with a quizzical half-smile, that even as she had married Gregor Vancleve, even as he took possession of her night after night, secured his claim and made her pregnant and paid her keep, she was assuming that there would be other men. Whenever they happen to come up.

"It's your loving nature," she told the mirror, quoting a cadet she had dated once.

Outside, beyond their big bedroom in the nursery, the baby cried out. Her breasts began to itch. The hospital staff had been efficient about whisking the baby away whenever the feeding was complete, the howling over. It had been a difficult labor, a lot of transfusions, and Mrs. Vancleve was to rest. Doctor's orders. Each time they brought the baby in, Kate half-expected an apology for what she had been put through, but each time it arrived in an oblivious squall of hunger, utterly unable to make things right between them. As much to shut it up, she pressed her nipple into the frantic pink hole and waited for the baby to drain her. When it was over, she rang for them to take it away, even when it was sleeping soundly. "I'm so tired," she kept saying. She lay in the hospital bed trying

to imagine life with a baby, trying to assess the outcome of this
… *incident* was the word that appeared. Beyond the obvious—that
she would no longer be able to come and go freely—it was frankly
unimaginable. There was no reason why she should have to behave like everyone else; she wasn't *like* everyone else, that much
was clear. So why pretend? Where was the dignity in lying about
who one was? Other women were cowed by babies, reduced to calf-
eyed worship; at least her own mother had kept herself above that.
Kate had even witnessed grown men breaking into falsetto cooing
around their own new offspring.

But it was the sudden recollection of the baby's fingers, fat and
grasping, kneading her breast as if all at once Kate belonged to him
and to no one else, that convinced her the costs were too high. A
form of bondage. In a way, the whole thing brought to mind living
with her mother—someone else needing her, someone else defining her duties, someone else driving her to a back corner of life.
Well, Kate had no intention of giving up her life for this; Kate was
in charge of Kate. And after all this baby had put her through! He
would simply have to wait to be forgiven like any ordinary, decent
person, then perhaps she might allow him to earn her love.

In the meantime, the breast-feeding had to end. Queen Elizabeth and Prince Philip were making their first visit to Canada in
October and Kate was hoping that her husband's status in the hos-
pitality business might get them into some posh affairs.

It happened that flu was passing among the service personnel at
the Langston Hotel, and Kate made certain she caught it, visiting
the kitchen, the washroom, and the grimy lunch corner behind the
office on a surprise visit to Gregor. She even gave the dishwasher a
sudden kiss—he had let his admiration be known months earlier.

"What are you doing here?" Gregor said, bolting up from his
desk. "You must go home, my darling."

"Oh, Gregor," she pleaded, "I can't stand being home all the
time. I miss the bank," and then she added, "I miss you so. And
Renée is cold-hearted. One little peep and off she goes. I've had to

fetch things for myself. And I'm still recovering. She's supposed to be helping me with the sitting baths. It was slippery in the bathroom, I almost fell."

"You must go home, Kate. Now. I will talk to Renée." Vancleve was so upset that there were little flecks of white forming at the corners of his mouth.

He led her out to the porte-cochere where Mr. Slattery bowed obsequiously. It was worth the bus ride across the bridge, Mr. Slattery's great bow, and it didn't matter one whit that he didn't mean it at all.

The flu lasted six days — fever, nausea, aches, diarrhea. Her milk dried up and the baby took happily to the bottle and to Renée's arms that held him like a soft cinnamon cloud, the sun of her smiling face beaming down from above.

"There's no point in going back to it, Gregor," Kate told him. She walked into the bathroom, found her lipstick and returned, talking as she moved about the bedroom, as if to convey how easy and simple this all was. "The baby is perfectly fine on the bottle."

"But you must miss it," he said a little desperately, and gazed through the half-open door into the nursery where Renée was walking the baby about, trying to get him to sleep.

"I have to think what's best for . . . ," here she stumbled, the baby's name unnatural in her mouth, "for Brendan, for the baby. It's cruel to make him adjust again."

Vancleve ran a hand through his white hair. A gentle man, even his gestures seemed infected with a slow, uncanny grace, as though he moved through his own private sea. They could hear the nurse cooing comfort. Gregor gazed at his boy's head resting on Renée's shoulder. He was a big healthy baby with strawberry blond hair and he looked, he told Kate, like "*mein eigen liez moeder*," gone thirty years. "But you'll hold him, won't you, you will be his *moeder* still?"

She pressed her palm to the side of his face. "You," she said, knowing that she had won, and won easily. Leaning in, she added in a confident whisper, "I want to be beautiful again for you, Gregor. I want these," she said, cupping her breasts, "to be nice and compact and yours, again. You understand that, don't you?"

The upper half of Vancleve's body jerked backwards as if a wintry gust had caught him off guard. "I have work to do," he said, and as he left the room he gave his head a single slow shake, but really, it did not bother Kate, his disappointment in her.

She told herself that Gregor was an older man, a busy man. Gregor's devotion to the baby could only be maintained by his attraction to her, which meant that she must take care of herself, she must reclaim her figure, her beauty, her breasts, her charm. She must be happy again, a part of the busy world. It was all for the baby's future benefit.

Anyway, after all she had been through, all she had endured, she simply would not be cheated by a mere baby. He would have to pay his own dues, just as she had.

A year passed, then half of another. Renée lived in rooms behind the kitchen, though on Wednesday afternoons and weekends she went home to her parents who had a bulb farm southeast of Vancouver. Cooking and cleaning were added to her childcare duties, and Kate learned to tolerate her presence by regarding it simply as yet another accoutrement to her new life. "The girl," as Kate referred to her was there to tend to "the baby" or to "the chores," although "the girl" was in actuality older than Kate by several years. The Langston Hotel was booming, along with all the other hotels of Vancouver, part of the postwar prosperity that offered a brand of glamour so innocent, so new, it was tawdry. They did not need more money, the Vancleves. Gregor tried half a dozen times to persuade Kate to quit her job at the bank. Joe Willoughby had moved her from the teller's cage to the clearing room, then from the clearing room to a position as a current accounts clerk for their best businesses, because Kate had proved adept with numbers, with the mathematical formulas that had to be applied hundreds of times a day. But having to balance to the cent, sometimes two or three times a day, with each ledger containing hundreds of accounts sometimes meant that Kate worked nights looking for a nickel's worth of error. The statement sheets held dozens of transactions, and had to be letter-perfect, too. Once she spent an entire Saturday retyping statements. There was no overtime pay.

One Wednesday night, Renée gone off to her parents and the baby asleep, Gregor pleaded with Kate to quit.

"But I want to be a part of *things*, Gregor." They had just finished supper, a rump roast Kate had managed—it was the only real dish she knew how to prepare, rump roast with carrots, new potatoes, and onions—and she was gazing at her own reflection in the side of the chrome toaster, reapplying her lipstick. "To make a contribution," she added.

"As a mother, as my wife you make the contribution."

She peered at him over the top of the toaster, and rose abruptly. "That's not enough, don't you understand, Gregor?"

"Not enough?" he said, a helpless note in his voice.

She turned away from him and ran hot water into the kitchen sink; above, through the window, she could see across First Narrows, across the dark opening to the sea, all the way to the lights of downtown. The lights seemed to embolden her. "Someday I'll need to take care of myself. Out there," she added dreamily.

She could not see him but heard him shift in his chair against the dining room table. "What are you saying?"

"Gregor. Darling." Turning to study him, she tipped her head ever so slightly, and offered a small, almost amused smile as though she couldn't quite believe she had to say the words. "Your age."

He began to nod vigorously. "Yes, yes, I know this, I've taken care of this, long ago."

"What about them."

"Katrina."

"They're your children too. They must have rights, don't they? Legal rights."

Gregor Vancleve was old world and old-fashioned; he did not like to talk about money, especially with a woman. He had not discussed such matters with his first wife, and after she died and he immigrated to Canada, he refused to discuss them with his two grown children still living in the Netherlands. "I have taken care of this, Kate," he said, pacing out the words, like stone steps he himself had laid and that only he might safely tread.

She knew he was angry but lately she took pleasure in seeing how far she could push him. In fact, she had already seen an earlier, pre-baby version of his will in which he had, as he insisted, taken care of her. But she wanted him to trust her, to offer her his most secret self, which for Gregor resided in his papers; to do things for her that he had never done for any other woman. She was not interested in ordinary devotion—it meant nothing, nothing. Couldn't he understand that? And after all, there had always been something special about Kate, hadn't there? Dr. Drummond had seen it right off; why, even strangers on trains, like Anthony Snider, noticed it; and of course Poppy had been the first to perceive her rarity, even though, in recognizing it, he incensed his wife and jeopardized the marital relationship. That had been the measure of Poppy's love; that was why the brooch belonged to Kate—by all that was just in the world—because in Hugh Riley's heart his daughter had surpassed his wife.

But what about Gregor, what had he done, really, to demonstrate his ardor? Had he turned from wife, from God, from his stuffy, Victorian code? No, he had only to accept one sunny morning what a young and beautiful woman offered him, free. He ought to at least break his silly rule about his papers, she thought, if he really loved her.

They had been married over two years and she was beginning to notice things—the puffy folds under his eyes, his old-man breath, faintly sweet, the way his derriere had begun to flatten—and to wonder if being taken care of was really worth marriage to Gregor Vancleve.

"I worry about the baby, Gregor," she said, "the baby and me and what will become of us. Why, in a month you'll be seventy. Seventy years old," she repeated, and the far-off lights of downtown seemed to blink in sad accord.

She heard him sigh, exasperated. "It is taken care of."

"I'm Head Accounts Clerk now, they let me handle all sorts of important documents, private things, and you don't trust me with our own papers."

"Trust?"

She turned and pulled a pouty face—a miniature charade that was usually successful. "Well, it does hurt my feelings just a little."

He slammed the flats of his hands down on the table so hard that the silverware jumped. "It is taken care of. Do you understand? It is done."

Later that evening Kate developed a stomachache fierce enough for Gregor to telephone the doctor; there was a frantic exchange—food poisoning, appendicitis, ulceration? He was to bring her down the next morning, provided she could bear up through the night. But the next morning Kate seemed to have forgotten about her stomach. She bathed and dressed the baby, gave him a bottle, and left him in the playpen while she began her own ablutions. Brendan did not like being abandoned to the pen, especially when his bottle went empty, so it was not long before he advanced from mild whining to ever-frantic spasms of desire, rattling the bars, throwing toys. "You've had your turn," Kate told him firmly. "You're a lucky thing, very lucky, you've no idea. You could end up like those two babes in the woods over in Stanley Park, just skeletons." For the longest moment she stared through the doorway at the baby boy, at his fat legs and his cheeks pinked with thwarted greed. "Just a skeleton in the dirt," she murmured, then she leaned over and shut the nursery door, frightened by her own thoughts. "Be quiet," she said. When he heard the voice of his mother, her tone, the baby seemed to know that he would get nowhere, for presently his whining ceased. Kate grinned at the mirror and danced her head side to side. "You," she intoned, her voice brimming with a sudden husky sensuality.

"We must take you to see Doctor Stone," Gregor was saying as he entered the bathroom, though even as he spoke his confusion was plain. He stood behind his wife, watching her as she brushed and patted her curls into place, using an ornamental comb of tortoise shell to hold it back on one side. "You are better, my Katrina?"

"I don't know about *that*," she said, and visibly winced as she touched her stomach. "I'm going to work, that's all there is to it."

"Good God."

"I've got to be able to take care of myself. Someday." She penciled her eyebrows into severe arches, dark as coal. "And the baby, of course. Our adorable little house dog," she added in a voice as sweet as a child's.

"I understand this was finished."

Swiveling about, she gazed at him with mock surprise. "But how? You haven't told me a thing, darling."

In silence Vancleve left.

It was 1953 and Kate's confidence was as brassy as Vancouver's, as the whole country's. The war was over, her prairie past gone along with the region's founding dreams. More and more of the farmers were moving into the larger towns and cities, paying only seasonal visits to their land in order to plant the wheat, to combine and thresh, and living in auto trailers or abandoned cabins during the work times. Her mother had gone to Winnipeg where she found a room in a residential hotel, and secured a position in the hospital working with the elderly; it served to distract her from futile family resentments. Even Jan had departed Netherfield for a job in the burgeoning auto-parts business on the outskirts of Toronto, sister city to Detroit. Vancouver was known to be a magnet for unemployed young men from the Prairies, and at first Kate thought it curious that Jan Larsen would go east instead of west. Later she decided that he did not want to be near her because she was now unavailable and proximity would be too painful. In spite of this they wrote to each other regularly, for Kate could not bear to lose a man entirely. In fact, it was a point of some pride that all her former beaus still liked her, still desired her. They were like deposits in a bank account, there to draw upon when she found herself at a loss.

The times were good, people starting out fresh, making money, making babies. Kate felt that she could do anything she wanted; she could do no wrong; no one, not even her husband, could stop her. She strolled across the marble-floored bank as if it belonged to her, the fabric of her tight skirt sharply percussive, snapping forward, snapping back, and her heels *tap-tapping*, and her arms swinging, everything about her presence, her personal-kinesis utterly synchronized to the unstoppable beat of the times. Joe Willoughby, the manager, had given her a lot of free rein—a lot—she was so "effective," as he put it, with the business crowd. Often after work she hooked up with Miriam or with some other friend, Margaret McCauley—Scottie as she was known—or Phyllis Lane, two of the tellers at the bank, and together they attended dances that the reserve military bases put on, or they went as a group to a dinner club where there would be floor shows imported from the States, or they would dance to popular bands—Ralph Flanagan, Louis Armstrong, Russ Morgan, even Guy Lombardo. She was making $182 each month, all of which she spent exactly as she pleased, thanks to Gregor Vancleve.

There was nothing for him to do but accept these evenings out; after all, she was nearly fifty years his junior. The privilege of youth, he called it, energy that one could take for granted with an associated lack of manners that was dimly excusable, like young love, perhaps only because it seemed largely irrepressible. The Langston was often booked solid, which meant he might be called in to address problems at any time of the day or night. He was a reasonable man—how could he insist she stay home? So long as it was to his bed she returned, Kate knew that much.

In early April Scottie moved to Seattle. She was dating a cook in the U.S. Navy, George Smithers, and it was getting serious; she decided to relocate to his home port. The National Bank of Commerce gave her a job, and a month after she left, Scottie invited Kate, Phyllis, and Miriam down for a weekend of fun. By now Miriam had a car—a birthday gift from her parents—a '53 Buick Super Riviera with lots of chrome and wide whites, so they were smartly outfitted for the trip to the States. Mr. Willoughby agreed to the Friday off; Renée offered to stay through the weekend with the baby; Gregor would be busy with a convention of French travel agents—Kate was free.

The big red car slid up to the curb on Chartwell Place at dawn, glinting chrome and emitting a subtle rhythmic vibration; the window flew open and Johnny Maddox's new version of "In the Mood" prowled about the sleepy neighborhood ... *who's the lovin' daddy with the beautiful eyes* ... The young women were determined to have most of Friday, as well as the weekend, to see the sights of Seattle, to fling their youth against a strange background and see just what turned up. Gregor leaned against the doorjamb, hands resting in his pockets, half-in, half-out, watching as frail Phyllis hoisted Kate's overnight bag, and demure, level-headed Miriam waved with shameless gusto from the driver-side window. He offered an elegant nod. *So, I said politely "Darlin' may I intrude ...,"* he said *"Don't keep me waitin' when I'm in the mood."* At the last second Kate remembered to trip back up the steps to say good-bye properly to her husband. He was dressed in his robe, a pale gray shapeless woolen he refused to exchange for something more spirited and tailored, a royal blue Pendleton perhaps; his long feet burrowed into a pair of leather slippers that looked as though they'd been run over by Miriam's big Buick. The night of sleep had pasted his hair out into several small stiff flags, which he failed to subdue despite the public occasion or the fact that there were ladies about. He seemed vaguely resigned, Kate thought as she mounted the steps, to some cheerless demand that Fate was making upon him. "It's just the weekend," she called in merry defense.

The house sat high on its lot, the lawn sloping steeply down and contained by a stone wall whose height from the sidewalk was almost five feet. Parting the lawn was a sequence of three flights of six steps, with short landings between each. When Kate reached the last flight Gregor twisted around, as if he'd heard something, probably Renée with the baby to whom Kate had not remembered to say good-bye. It was then she noticed what she had been noticing of late—faint, brownish spots. The first time she couldn't bring herself to mention them; she simply had Renée scrub the slacks and put it out of her mind. But after three or four incidents, she told him he was "leaking." No other word came to mind.

"Ah," he said in his graceful, almost judicial manner, "dear Kate, how difficult this must have been for you."

She couldn't help staring at him. "Well, what is it? I mean, what's happening?"

A small smile composed itself, so small she was not sure it had actually happened. "Now and then an older man passes more than he intends."

"Oh," she said, not having the faintest idea what to say. It was all just a little too much like those last weeks with Poppy, wasn't it? It was all part of a world and a time that she did not want to hear about or become intimate with, clinical things concerning people and their various workings, what really happened behind doors and under coats, behind handsome smiles. Plus, he was not apologizing—that was evident. And why not? Here she was, a young woman, a young *innocent* woman, she said to herself, in a pretty spring dress, and it was only morning, the start of things, and it just wasn't fair that she had to see something like that, something that might very easily spoil her holiday, and she was sure, absolutely positive that Miriam and Phyl hadn't had to come across anything like that . . .

Gregor turned toward her as she reached the doorway, his arms extended so tenderly it was as if they might collapse from the weight of the feeling they bore. A kiss on the cheek, an embrace she swiftly escaped. "My makeup," she said, aware of badly concealed irritation.

Instantly Gregor released her.

She fled halfway down the steps, spun about, fanning her skirt not only to make up for her manner, but to somehow obliterate the memory, the very presence of the brown spots. "You didn't say you liked my new dress. You didn't even notice it."

He looked at her, a frank appraisal. Just then the sun broke above the roofline, and Kate had trouble making out his expression, but she heard him say in a ringing voice, so bold it gave her a start, "Charming."

"Oh . . . ," she stammered, "oh, I'm so happy you like it. Because this is my little holiday and I won't let anything spoil it. Not anything, Darling."

And to that end, as the Buick rounded the corner and headed down toward Marine Drive she instructed Miriam and Phyllis not to mention that she happened to be a married woman. "I don't know why," she said with a gay shrug, "just for the fun of it."

Phyllis ticked her head: *okay*, she seemed to say, it made no difference to her. But a frown crept across Miriam's smooth Catholic brow, and not wanting to start things off with one of Miss Pettigrew's morality lessons, Kate leapt back in: "Oh, never mind, I'm being silly, aren't I, worrying that no one will dance with me."

"Gosh, Kate, that really is silly," Miriam laughed, her relief unmistakable.

There were other functions—or malfunctions—Kate would have preferred not acknowledging . . . Gregor was having trouble in the bedroom maintaining "his vigor"—a verbal delicacy introduced by Gregor and that some old part of her, the intransigent naturalist, the prairie girl who had seen her share of barn births and backseat groping—refused to appreciate, and in fact, found slightly foolish. For months they had not entirely, or *really*, as she thought of it, made love. It did not bother Kate, for she found that she was less involved in the act than in the desire—she wanted him to desire her, to keep desiring her—that was all. Sometimes she would lie naked among the tousled covers, caressing herself, while Gregor observed from the foot of the bed, or sometimes simply from the burgundy club chair in the corner, his manner relaxed, self-possessed, his eyes clinical in their attentiveness, like a surgeon seeking hidden conditions. If it made him sad not to participate she did not notice. Often he thanked her and after awhile, Kate thought his gratitude entirely appropriate. She was putting on a kind of show for him, wasn't she? One night, afterward, when he simply slid under the covers and switched off the light, she lay in uneasy silence, smoothing her belly, propping up her ample breasts. Finally, unable to endure what she took to be his indifference, she said, "Do you still find me attractive?"

He rolled over in the dark toward her. "Pardon?"

"You didn't seem to like it this time."

"But that's ridiculous."

"You didn't say thank you."

"Now Kate . . ." He stroked her hair.

"Is it because I've put on some weight?"

"I don't care how you look, I adore you."

"Then you do think I've gained weight."

"I think you look wonderful. This is nonsense."

"That's it," she said, as if to punish him, "I'm going on a diet."

His age, too, had begun to embarrass her. It was no longer a minor fact hidden behind status and money, dignity and gentlemanly grace. Somewhere along the way the balance had begun to shift, and all that had never been hers, or part of her meager prairie life now seemed as standard as tea at 4:00, not an enviable novelty. What might now compensate for his age? she wondered as they sped down Highway 99 toward Seattle. In her mind she reviewed the lines in his face, his hurried shuffling walk, the broken blood vessels behind his left knee, the way he picked at skin anomalies, bumps and rough spots whenever he was reading—exposed, exposed like the debris at the bottom of the river in late summer, the smooth and flowing blueness gone, and the power gone too, the clear sense of forward motion, of going places . . . stopped, dried up, gone.

Something, she decided, would have to make up for it. An old familiar feeling, foul vapor, wafted up from a fissure in the past, a feeling that, without quite realizing it, without knowing exactly who was doing it and least of all *why*, a feeling that she was being swindled.

And for the first time it occurred to her to question what her girlfriends thought of her marriage to Gregor Vancleve. She had always assumed that they envied her—the status and money, his standing in Vancouver business circles. Could it be that they *felt sorry* for her? That they didn't think him grand and distinguished? A catch? *Oh*, that would be impossible to bear.

Phyllis sat in the front seat, filing her nails, chattering on about Mr. Delaney in accounting who wouldn't raise her. She was a slight blond girl with skin so pale that in certain lighting it became vaguely transparent, and wonderful lips, Kate thought, lips to envy, red and plump, as if all the blood from her complexion had rushed into them. Hardly taller than a broomstick, the fellows liked to show off with Phyllis, sweeping her about the dance floor, but it was to Kate they came when the music slowed and the lights dimmed, red-headed Kate with the curving curves and the legs that wouldn't quit, not ever.

They reached Seattle by noon, owing to a stop in the Skagit River Valley to walk among the tulips, broad bands of reds and oranges and pinks, each supple goblet opening to the ascending sun. Never had Kate seen anything like it, thousands and thousands of flowers, happy brilliant flowers bobbing their fat little heads against her calves, the petals so cool and soft. She heard herself giggle, and the others laughed at her.

"Kate, you sensuous creature," Phyllis quipped.

A playful shimmy sent her flouncing down another row of tulips, then back up to her two friends, her efforts against sinking into the dark, newly turned soil further exaggerating her swaying hips, her bouncing bosoms. Miriam put her arms out and spun around. The scene was like a child's drawing of a dream land. At the eastern limits of the tulip fields Mount Baker soared in volcanic perfection, Douglas fir foaming up to a quintessential cap of snow, and the sun like a great yellow bubble escaping a picture-perfect cone. The three looked at each other, and then laughed again. If any one had made mention of something they ought to do, a duty or obligation, a phone call home, it would have been utterly unenforceable.

Of the group Phyllis was the smartest; she would go far, Kate guessed, farther than Miriam with her college degree. Phyllis would marry well and preside over fancy dinner parties, she would keep her figure, and travel, lots of travel—Las Vegas or Florida, or even some place abroad, like Rome. She would set money aside and never be without. Yes, Phyllis had one tough head on her shoulders, and it wasn't about to give her heart much quarter.

From a distant greenhouse the man who owned the fields wandered toward the three ladies, a pair of clippers in his hand; now and then he bent to cut a tulip, and by the time he reached them, he had one of each color for each young lady—full endorsement. Naturally, Kate took it as a sign; this would be a *perfect* holiday, no question about it.

Further south they visited the Marysville Pie Place, a diner just off the highway; Scottie had insisted they simply had to, the meringue was as high as a hat. The small white building sat beside tracks so long abandoned that grass and blackberry bushes had grown up between the rails, but Kate managed to climb up onto them and gaze east toward the mountains, then she swung around and faced west toward an ocean she could not see but whose presence she felt with the same vast-reaching familiarity the Prairies had bred in her. "I used to stand on the tracks," she said with a trace of sadness, "and watch them leave Netherfield." She couldn't help thinking of Jan.

"It won't be long before even the town's gone," Miriam said as she gave the Buick's door a nudge, and Kate listened to its solid closure, so pampering, so protective. There had never been any question about the Pettigrews's only daughter, about her future and where she might go, where she could go with all her "advantages," as Fiona called them.

"Don't say that," Kate murmured.

"I only mean that everything's changing."

"It's home."

But Miriam would not quit. In two months she would earn her bachelor's degree in political science, and as far as Kate was concerned, Miriam was always alert to cracks in conversations through which she might insert some obscure shred of her newfangled knowledge. She spoke fluent French, thanks to her mother, Celeste, and a national society that included the Canadiennes of Quebec. One day she hoped to get a job as an aid at the Canadian consulate in Paris. "People are finally realizing that it was too hard a place to build a whole new civilization. It just wasn't worth the effort."

"Don't say that. I've got family buried there. My father, twin sisters." She reached into a bush and tugged off a handful of hard green nubs. "There are six churches," she tossed an unripe berry toward Miriam, "a school and a train station," two more berries, "shops and two hotels, a library," one, two, three berries—Miriam was staring at her in astonishment, trying to dodge the hard little berries—"a chemist, the bank and post office, there was the farmer's local . . . what's missing, Miriam? Tell me that."

"Gee, Kate, I only meant that when you see a place like London you realize how . . . ," (it was obvious that she was searching for a word that might not offend), "how unlikely it is that Netherfield will ever be anything like that."

"London."

"Come on," Phyllis said, "let's cut the gab and eat."

Kate made her way down off the tracks and followed them in. "London," she repeated under her breath.

The coconut cream was just about the most wonderful thing she'd ever tasted, and Kate was willing to forget Miriam's high-headed ways. They promised each other a return engagement on Sunday, because of course the Marysville Pie Place had instantly become a ritual they must now rigorously observe.

"What about our waistlines, girls?" Miriam said.

A slow satisfied smile opened across Kate's face. "We're on holiday."

"Right." Phyllis snapped shut her purse. "On holiday. Our battle cry."

It was grueling, holding her weight down, but that Friday in April Kate felt that she was celebrating something, a decision—not one that she had made, but one that was being made by the *clackety-clack* of events rushing down the line. That momentum and the spontaneity it drove through Kate and the other passengers made it all seem so easy, and so right because of the easiness; she hadn't to struggle against anything, she hadn't even to try, it was as natural as tulips opening to the sun.

Scottie's new apartment occupied the southwest corner on the eighth floor of a high-rise that featured a swimming pool and its own laundry room—very swank. They unloaded their bags, then bustled back into the Buick and headed downtown to Pioneer Place, and from there they ambled about. It was a clear spring day, almost warm, and Seattlites seemed electrified by the changing season, smiling at the capricious foursome whose obviously aimless itinerary took them from a shoe store across the street to the milliner, then to the edge of a fountain where they did not fail to toss in a few pennies, eyes pinched shut and wishes wished, then on to a soda shop for root beer floats, Miriam posing them whenever she could persuade them to stop and snapping pics with her Brownie. And throughout they indulged in what was becoming prolonged foreplay—a deliberation about which of the clubs to go to that evening.

"What about the Trianon?" Miriam had been to the Trianon

once with her parents on a holiday junket, and felt a special loyalty to it.

"The 4 Spot's supposed to be fun."

"Yes, but if we got an early start we could get in at the Magic Inn, and that club is tops. We'd just have to get there early for seats or we won't have a good time," Scottie said. A good time meant dancing, that was all there was to that.

Back at the apartment after an hour of preparation Scottie opened a bottle of Canadian Club, and they made four CC-Sevens, to start the ball rolling.

George, Scottie's fellow, arranged for several of his shipmates to join him with the young women, so that each would have an escort. But it was understood that once in, they were free to mix it up, as George put it, and pour it out. He was a funny man, full of one-liners, a talent it seemed he had had to develop as a Navy cook, but George was not good looking, to Kate's thinking, big-eared and wedge-faced, thin blond hair he was already losing. Still, he was just as nice as could be. He took her hands, held her out and gave a whistle. "What a hunk of love," he announced, waving one of his buddies forward, "yessir, Nick, this is Kate-your-date, and it is your privilege to walk in with this babe, dine and disappear, like magic." He snapped his fingers, having dispatched his duty to Kate, and fixed his attention on Phyllis, hooking her up with John Nielsen, a machinist mate, second class, not much taller than Phyllis, lean and quick-eyed, who acted as if he had several plans going at once, and all of them, abruptly, had something to do with Phyllis Lane. Carlos Bandura strolled over to Miriam; "I don't need no help, fry boy." Without a word he took Miriam's arm and wove it onto his, placed his other hand atop hers, then led her through the tufted red door of the Magic Inn, his back arched with Latin pride. A tiny spasm of jealousy zapped Kate's heart.

She offered Nick Bowie a guilty smile. "You don't have to disappear," she said.

"Thank you," Seaman Bowie replied. "I would enjoy a dance or two."

"You're from the American South?"

"Yes'm." Then he gave his head a half swirl, examined his shoes, black and bulbous and shiny enough to pass the most rigorous inspection, and blushed. There were already mottled ruddy marks on both cheeks, as if he'd been slapped twice, and the blush only served to pinkify the background. "Right on down to sweet potato pie," he added. Despite his muscular development and the blond military butch, there was something stubbornly innocent about Nick Bowie; perhaps it was only the way he drew in one corner of his mouth before speaking, as if soliciting advance mercy, or perhaps it was the way his blue eyes flicked upward in shy appreciation of her looks. But it disappointed Kate; she was used to someone experienced, someone—well, masterful—and this fellow, Nick, with his excruciating manners and what she decided was outmoded naïveté at once warned of several potentially disagreeable aspects to the evening, not the least of which was that Kate might have to teach this boy something, not be swept away by him. Suddenly a pause inserted itself within the *clackety-clack* of events driving forward, driving on, a pause in which she might have to stop and think and actually decide something. And then be responsible for whatever transpired.

They were early enough to get a large, semi-circular booth on the first tier bordering the dance floor. The dinner show ran until 9:00 p.m., then the stage would open to dancing. The couples sat side by side, Kate and Phyllis the last ones in on opposite ends, an arrangement the two had planned in advance so as to have express access to the floor. Nick shook out her white napkin and laid it across her lap. She smiled back at him; he did have wonderful manners.

Right away a cocktail waitress arrived. She was wearing a black chiffon skirt not much longer than a tutu, white peasant blouse and black silk vest, and net stockings with dark deliberate seams that leant an artificial quality to her legs, like a mannequin's. All the waitresses, in fact, looked like models, their perfect figures notice-ably on display. The men had to give her the twice-over, then smile sheepishly at their dates as if they had been simultaneously wound up to perform this rite in unison, and at last, with a gravity born of their youth and relative inexperience, they ordered the drinks.

"A CC-Seven," she told Nick.

"CC-Seven for the lady and I'd like a Bourbon doubled, on the rocks, Miss."

The size of his drink, his apparent expertise with waitresses, im-pressed Kate. "How long have you been in the navy?" she asked.

Nick cleared his throat. "Most all my life. I was what they call a navy junior. My father was stationed in Richmond, Virginia and my mother's family come from Georgia. We moved a lot during my youth—Corpus Christi, Boston, Baltimore, San Diego, even Hono-lulu. By the time we came here, I was old enough to join up." He offered a penitent shrug, as if joining up was something he couldn't avoid.

"Honolulu," she said, imagining herself under swaying palm trees.

Nick Bowie smiled. It was soft and poignant, like a portrait of a child who had died. "Beaches and sunburn."

"You must be a wonderful swimmer. That's something I never learned, growing up on the Prairies. We waded in the coulees, sometimes in the river late spring, but there never was anything we could swim across, and anyway, the water was always shallow and full of mud. I usually ended up with the itch."

"I could teach you," he said so quietly she wondered if he thought it somehow embarrassing that she didn't know how. "I do swim well enough." His drawl was so pleasant, so easy to listen to, like ly-ing about on a hot summer night and it not mattering what anyone said or did. "And dive."

George, who had caught this last word, flung the back of his hand toward Nick, like a circus barker. "Dive? This guy flies. Almost made the Olympic team."

"I guess that explains the muscles," Kate said, trailing her hand along his biceps.

Miriam glanced away, always uncomfortable with Kate's fast familiarity, but it was none of her business, was it? She didn't know what Kate put up with at home.

The waiter wore a modified tux and addressed them with deference so profound that one of the fellows got angry and took offense. "What's up his nose," Bandura said, and he sniffed and cocked his head forward aggressively.

"Ah, leave it alone, Carlos," George said. "Have another beer."

Kate turned to her partner. "I don't understand."

"It's the uniform," Nick said calmly. "A bunch of uniforms in a classy joint like this, why, they think it's bad for business."

Reflexively, Kate inspected the four dress blues around the table, their gold braid, their raised creases as sharp as a blade. She had always been enchanted by uniforms, by the attention to strict standards, their precise fit and exact creases combining to suggest a masculinity so uncompromising that sometimes when a soldier asked her to dance she hesitated touching the fabric, as if it might transmit a powerful jolt. Now here came this idea that a uniform was somehow low or objectionable, that it tarnished the shine of a place like the Magic Inn.

"A guy in a monkey suit," John Nielsen said as he poured Phyllis another glass of wine, "what's that worth? Nothing, that's what." Then he stretched out his arms, clasped his hands and pressed the palms out until they could hear knuckles cracking. "When I'm rich that guy'll still be shuffling plates, what you want to bet?"

No one took John's bet. At age twenty-three he was a ranking machinist, two stripes and a future; everyone was already convinced Nielsen would go far.

The waiter brought their salads on a large round tray, which he set atop a portable stand, delivering to the ladies first, one arm keeping the edges of his black jacket tidy against his torso, while his gaze drifted down Kate's yawning décolletage. When he turned to leave, Carlos emitted a curt whistle. Kate shrank against the booth. "Pepper here," he said, jabbing his thumb at his plate. The entire table went silent. The waiter—a dapper, middle-aged man with a wintry smile—hung the grinder over Bandura's salad, let it swing pendulously back, forth, then he gave it an effeminate twist as he whisked it away. It was doubtful any pepper managed to land where it was requested, though the waiter had left a distinct trail of black specks across the white cloth. Bandura shot up. Across the table from Kate, past Phyllis, past two more tiers of booths Kate noticed a dark man in a dark suit leaning against the bar. Something shiny glinted from his hand—a ring, a small glass? In the next instant the man was at her side.

"Mr. Leonard," he said to the waiter, "the chef wants a word."

Leonard gave a small bow and departed with his tray and stand.

A busboy appeared, a Chinaman in a white jacket carrying a bottle and a small tray of stemware.

"Champagne," the dark man said, "to honor our forces."

"Well that's swell. Bubbly!" George said.

Bandura eased back down into the booth between Scottie and Miriam, and in short order Miriam had her mouth to his ear, whispering fervent pleadings.

"But who are you?" Kate said, dumbfounded by the entire near-incident.

"Max Wyman." He looked at her then as if discovering her for the first time, but Kate was sure that she had already seen him appraising her from the bar, a view she hoped he appreciated. She was wearing a deep turquoise dress that swung in and back out, following the gentle curvature of bust to waist to hips, concluding in a filmy fling just below the knees. The dress had cost almost thirty dollars.

"He owns the place," Scottie laughed. "Thanks, Mr. Wyman," she added, "we'll keep this sailor on a short line."

Bandura ducked his head and focused intently on the salad before him.

Max Wyman worked the wire and foil off, then tipping the bottle at an angle, he twisted not the cork but the bottle itself until they heard a tiny exhalation. "Mr. Wong, the glasses," he said, and the obedient Chinaman placed one before each diner. With ritualistic style, Wyman poured champagne into each glass, just a little, then around the table he poured again, his pinkie slightly extended, yet still the glasses were not full, so once more he began his journey, arriving at last at Kate's into which the remaining golden liquid abandoned itself.

"Gentlemen," he said to the four sailors, and he lifted his hand in a careless salute. "Ladies," he said, and the polite glance he bounced from each of the others concluded precisely with Kate, as if he had instructed his eyes to form a visual exclamation mark just above her red head.

Who could say what it was that captured young Kate Riley's heart, and more than her heart, her soul? Such things resist definition, resist dissection and analysis — they are as smooth and as irreducible as the elements from which the planet evolved. Perhaps it was his size, strong and generous, unashamed — he wore his body with the unconscious pride of an animal, custom-made and so beyond question. Or his hands, broad and powerful, as if at one time they had handled great slabs of stone, though the skin was now groomed for a woman. And the ring, a wide band, white gold, with a single square diamond centered between several inferior stones, the ring enhanced the hint of femininity in his gestures. He was barrel-chested, narrow-hipped, oddly disproportionate, everything impressive and overlarge above, and below, quietly understated. His head was big, but somehow not grotesque, his nose too, bold with a rebellious curve in it. Had someone broken it once? It was as if he belonged to a superior species whose physicality was driven not by visual standards or fashion, but by the nature of the man himself. His body refused to lie about who he was, and Kate Riley had never encountered anything so sexy. He had the darkest eyes she had ever seen and from them, she was convinced, he saw more than most, he felt more than most, because something had hurt him deeply and now he could not hide it, even if he had wanted to. And Kate could see it, and it touched her heart.

Miriam was watching her as Max Wyman left. "There's a French expression," Miriam said, "*beau-laid.*"

"What?" Kate murmured, hardly listening.

"Handsome-ugly."

"Yes," she said dreamily.

Their dinners arrived—prime rib, potatoes au gratin, cooked beans with pearl onions. The floor show commenced before they had finished eating, a stand-up named Larry Katz who did several bits on the subject of women and shopping, then he switched to men who repair their own cars to make it up to the ladies, he told the audience. Kate saw Max Wyman move to a small corner table between the lounge and the stage; the same Chinese busboy delivered a highball. After the comedian came Dee-Dee Adoré, pronounced *Adoray*, who did a slow sashay to center stage, her tight blue gown designed to suggest a mermaid. Undulating before the microphone she sang *à la* Marlene Dietrich, "Taking a Chance on Love." She was short and shapely with a hard, well-appointed face, striking but not pretty, her black hair crashing in waves over her shoulders, and even her Spanish accent helped conjure up Dietrich's foreign sensuality. A couple of much younger guys appeared for the last few numbers, dancing around Dee-Dee in a snappy choreography of male competition, some sort of fishing theme. At the very end, instead of choosing one of the dancers, she swam across the stage to Max Wyman's table and planted a long stagy kiss on his lips. To get her to stop, Wyman had to give her derrière a fake slap, and off she reeled like the wrong fish thrown back. Everyone laughed. The band slid into "Bensonality" and the floor filled with couples.

Nick kept drinking double bourbons. He was a terrific dancer, "the real McCoy," as Scottie said. "Mama insisted on lessons," Nick drawled as he placed his left hand with expert pressure upon Kate's hip and executed a quick pivot that shot them to the center of the floor. "But Madame Tudorovich did not shine as you do, Kate of the Prairies." By 11:00 Nick Bowie had all but drowned his expertise in the bourbon, and Kate was actively encouraging other men from other tables to invite her to dance. There were at least six to choose from, not including their own table-full of sailors. Still, she kept track of Max Wyman, hoping he might be tempted, as she spun about the dance floor. But each time she managed to locate him in the smoky crowded club, he was occupied—emerging from the kitchen, still chewing something the chef had given him, she imagined, a sample of some Magic Inn delicacy; sitting with a table of four apparent regulars; at the register counting out money, some of which he bundled and stuffed into a canvas envelope for the bartender to deal with, and the rest, a small neat wad he slid into his pocket; she even spotted him back by the coat check room, lighting a cigarette for Dee-Dee Adoré as she left in her mink stole; and now he stood at the far end of the bar, talking to a businessman who kept pulling sheets of paper from a briefcase and nervously rattling the ice in his glass.

Wanting to put herself squarely in Wyman's path she went up to the bar to order something, she didn't know what exactly, maybe she'd ask him for a recommendation, yes, that was it. Advice. Men were always flattered by that.

"Mr. Wyman," she said.

He turned and squinted at her. If there was recognition he concealed it entirely.

"I didn't thank you for the champagne. I mean properly."

"No need." He turned back to the businessman who seemed to be making a sales presentation.

"I wonder if you might suggest an after-dinner drink," she said.

"Your boyfriend knows enough about booze."

"Nick?" Ah, so that was it, Wyman thought she was already taken; that explained his aloofness. "Nick's just an escort. We only met right outside your club, just tonight," she added, with a giddy appreciation of the possibilities opening like so many doors before her very eyes. Her marriage to Gregor Vancleve did not count. If anyone had asked her why, she could not have put it into words, but she sensed both the certainty and the logic of the situation the way one breathes the surrounding air without ever having to analyze how or why it happens.

Again he gazed at her, not squinting now, his eyes heavy and inert, his expression missing. "Brandy Alexander," he said quietly.

But he was talking to the bartender. "Right away, Mr. Wyman," the bartender replied.

And then it was the bartender who told her that Sheila would deliver it, because Max Wyman was examining the salesman's papers, leaning in to discuss them, oblivious to her green eyes, her red hair, her breasts so full, her new turquoise dress, her legs that wouldn't quit, not ever.

Around midnight Kate was dancing with a lawyer from Bellevue. When he had maneuvered her around the floor once and was approaching the edge of the lounge Kate slipped. The lawyer bent over her; a waiter showed up. "My ankle," she said. The band took a ten-minute break. Max Wyman appeared.

"What is your name?" he said.

"Kate Riley."

"Let's get you to the booth . . ." She saw him skim the many eyes of his patrons. "Or maybe your friends should take you home now, Miss Riley." Then he smiled warmly, softly as if he had always known her. "That brandy Alexander," he said in a teasing, scolding voice. There was something so personal in his eyes, so intimate, that she practically swooned.

The lawyer bristled. "This had nothing to do with liquor, if that's what you're insinuating. Maybe there's too much chalk on the floor. Is this your place? Because if this is your place . . ."

"No, it's all right," Kate said, gazing up at Max Wyman. "I was having a gay ole time, that's all, and I slipped." Wyman's dark eyes deepened with appreciation. "Into your arms," she murmured. That was when—she was sure of it—their secret communication began.

They helped her to the front door where the others awaited Miriam's Super Riviera. The lawyer returned to his own table, but not without sliding one of his cards into Kate's pocketbook. Max held Kate up on one side, his big hand devouring an amazing portion of her waist. Now and then she winced, but she made a point of being discreet, never crying out, or at least burying her face against Max Wyman's enormous shoulder whenever her ankle conjured up too great a pain. His cologne was still strong, even at that late hour.

Back at Scottie's it was decided by vaguely democratic means that Kate should soak her ankle in cool water, and in order for that prescription to include everyone, the party resumed poolside. Bandura sat at a patio table, one leg crossed over the other, smoking Cuban cigars, while Miriam made another attempt to explain the nature of political science; whenever she finished a sentence, he fixed his eyes upon her, their message fierce and uncompromising, but utterly indecipherable.

"What a mismatch," Kate whispered to Phyllis.

"I'll say." Phyllis kicked off her pumps and thrust her feet into the water. "May as well join you."

The rest of the fellows had stripped down to boxers and were horsing around in the water, despite the cool sixty-five degree temperature. Scottie had gone up to her apartment to put her suit on, and was now proposing chicken fights with George as her partner, and John atop Nick's substantial shoulders.

"Say, how's the ankle?" Phyllis said.

"I think it's swelling up." She lifted her foot from the water and turned it about for Phyllis's evaluation.

"Doesn't look bad. There's no bruising."

"No."

"So you like that guy, Max Wyman."

"Why not? It was sweet of him, to help me, you know."

"He had to. It's his place."

"Well, the champagne, that was awfully generous. He didn't have to do that."

Phyllis sat in silence for a few minutes, glancing sideways at Kate as if trying to resolve a private question, then she said, "You think he and The Star are an item?"

Kate watched Scottie give John Nielsen a big shove; a moment later she toppled him amid hoots and splashing. "That was just an act."

"Maybe."

"No, it was," Kate insisted, turning to look directly at Phyllis. "Anyone could see that."

Phyllis kicked little plumes of water out toward the center of the pool, her calves lean and taut, her toes pointed delicately. Sometimes the fact that Phyllis was effortlessly petite annoyed Kate. "Have you ever thought about other men? I mean, romantically?" Phyllis asked.

Kate leaned back and stretched. "Yes. And I'm not ashamed, if that's what you're thinking."

"What about your holy state of matrimony?"

"We don't . . ." With a fingertip Kate wrote her name in the turquoise surface of the water and watched the confused rings collide outward. "That is, Gregor can't exactly . . . he can't perform."

"Gee, Kate."

"Yeah."

"Gee, I'm sorry. I didn't know."

John climbed back up on Nick's shoulders, but Nick was so drunk that he kept staggering back into the water, John back-flopping into the deep end. More whoops and laughter. Someone in the apartment building slid open their balcony door and hollered at them to keep it down.

Nick pushed up out of the water and stood motionless at the edge of the pool. In the next instant and despite his state of inebriation, he executed a sleek arching dive, his entry as clean as a dart finding a small, well-marked circle. There was enthusiastic applause from his fellow swimmers. Again, he pushed up from the water and this time he stepped up onto the board, positioning himself sideways, and the dive peeled off backwards in something that resembled a human comma. Miriam and Carlos joined in the ovation.

"I'm only twenty-one," Kate said.

"What about divorce? You think he'd understand. A reasonable man would understand."

Kate said, "My family. My mother," and rolled her eyes.

There was a third dive, a mini swan, but this time Nick stayed under, swimming the length of the pool to surface before Kate's dangling feet. "Kate of the Prairies," he burbled.

"Seaman Bowie. I believe you're drunk." She pointed her toe and flicked the lobe of his left ear.

"Those were for you," he said, jerking his head back toward the board.

She smiled vaguely, then turned to Phyllis. "Well, how long can he live?"

Phyllis stared at her. "Years."

Kate looked back at Nick. His body was beautiful, the skin tanned and wet, his muscular contours seeming as fluid as the surrounding water, swellings flowing into shadowed vales, then up again and over his shoulder, down in a series of broad tributaries to the long shallow canyon of his spine. Not far beneath the surface she saw his wavering boxers, and now and then through the opening a hint of secret flesh. "They were nice," she said to him. Faintly she desired him. It was like food when you weren't really hungry anymore, but if it looked tasty enough . . . Then she thought of Max Wyman, his big hand on her waist; she thought of Dee-Dee Adoré and the assembly line of beautiful waitresses and pictured Wyman interviewing them, frankly examining their figures. What would he think of hers?

Without taking his eyes from her, Nick Bowie kicked slowly away on his back. "High dive's my specialty," he drawled.

"Specialty?"

"Yes, ma'am."

Kate threw up her arms as if to challenge the world, and let loose a gay laugh. "Well am I special or what?" she demanded, the sound of her voice strange in her ears, husky and aimless, full of a knowledge she had no words for yet but which was forming inexorably, inexorably, the words gathering in the shadows like a chorus that one day would step forward and be heard.

Suddenly Nick rolled over and shot off into the deep end. George was treading water, Scottie sitting on the edge of the pool, wrapped in a towel, mesmerized by a sea story he was narrating—"Then a very healthy typhoon came along and really raised hell with the Philippines . . ." John was hanging from the end of the diving board, counting off pull-ups. Just past the board stood a small building, a two-story annex to the apartment tower that attached perpendicularly. The apartment building had been positioned on a slight slope, so that the second floor of the annex containing the mail and laundry rooms joined the first floor of the apartment complex, while the bottom floor at pool level was used for storing chaise longues, umbrellas, buoy lines, etc. They watched Nick enter the pool house and then quickly exit, making for the gate that led out of the patio.

"What will you do?" Phyllis asked.

"I'm only twenty-one," Kate repeated. "It isn't fair. It isn't natural," she added with increasing confidence in a position that she realized had begun developing months earlier but for which she had not articulated justifications. Not until that night.

"Whoa, wait a minute," George yelled. Everyone followed his gaze. "You just wait a minute."

Atop the annex a dim shape formed. "Kate," Nick called out.

"Why, Nick," she smiled. "There you are, up there."

"I am 'tending to prove how special you are."

"Nickie, come down now," John said in a steady, coaxing tone.

Miriam had leapt to her feet. "This is not a good idea," she was saying, "this is really not a good idea."

"That's an order," John Nielsen said.

"Kate of the Prairies," Nick sang full volume. The building was flat-topped, and he had worked his way to the edge, curling his toes over as if it were a diving board.

"Seaman Bowie," George called.

"Kate?" Phyllis whispered, frozen in place, her hands gripping the cement lip of the pool, her knees tensed together.

"Well, what am *I* supposed to do?" Kate shrugged. Out of the corner of her eye she saw Scottie slip through the patio gate and scurry into the apartment building, Carlos close behind her. "Anyway, he says it's his specialty, he must know what he's doing."

"He's drunk."

"Nick," she called out, "they don't think you can make it . . ."

Nick had already left the roof, arms outstretched. There was no moon, and it was dark up there, but lower down when he passed through the outdoor patio light, just for an instant, as if someone were snapping a picture with a flash, they could see all of him, his perfect young body taut with potential, with the sweetness of too much pride, outrageous intemperance, then there was only the sound, like a slab of raw meat hitting a kitchen floor—the sound of Nick Bowie not quite reaching the water.

Down the long shallow canyon of his spine a rivulet of blood trickled; otherwise, from the back, he looked unchanged. But he had changed forever. People stood around, strangers from other apartments, clutching extra towels, waiting for the ambulance.

"We tried to stop him," Kate told the little man from 2A, and then she collapsed onto her knees beside Nick Bowie, sobbing, pressing the side of her face to the pool deck, trying to see into his closed eyes. When the ambulance came they had to pull her away. She kept crying, "He did it for me, he was just showing off for me, oh god . . ."

Nick Bowie had indeed proved her special.

The next day Miriam and Phyllis drove back to Vancouver, but Kate stayed on. Her friends were apparently so subdued that they forgot to say good-bye to her. It hurt her feelings. Scottie went with George to the hospital; Nick had broken his back in several places, the doctors said. No one expected him to walk again. Kate could not bear to see what she had done, or even to think about it, so she took a cab down to the Magic Inn to find Max Wyman. Maybe it was better that her friends had gone home, for now she could pursue this other thing alone. No one could see what she was doing, so she could do anything. She hadn't figured out what to say to Wyman, but that had never mattered to Kate—the words would come spontaneously, and for that very reason they would be the right words. From a block away she could see the door, tall and red against a wash of gray stone, and it seemed to beckon the way a summer prairie sun sinking from the sky draws the eyes and spirit down with it to the bright side of the world. *What if he isn't there,* she thought. *I'll leave a note, something short and mysterious.* The heavy door swung open and the noonday light flashed in; a lone busboy, his white jacket rumpled, sat on a milk crate next to the kitchen entrance, eating a candy bar. He gaped blindly in her direction. The room smelled of stale cigarettes, liquor, ammonia. A distant vacuum cleaner moaned. Suddenly she wasn't sure she wanted to encounter Max Wyman—*like this,* she thought.

The busboy bit off a corner of his candy bar. "Mr. Wyman not here," he said. (Which was funny, because she hadn't even asked.) He was the Chinaman from last night who had seemed more than a busboy—like Wyman's valet—but he looked older today, much older, his facial skin loose and as mottled as blue cheese.

"When will he be back?"

"Not today. Today Mrs. Wyman."

"Mrs. Wyman."

"You want me get her?"

"No."

"No," the Chinaman echoed and gave a laugh, a single *hah* that popped his head up.

Later Kate bought a ticket on the Greyhound bus to Vancouver. It was just past dusk and when she peered out the window she met only a shadowed transparency of herself and the woman beside her, the mostly full interior of the bus overlaid on a murky landscape of brick buildings giving way to opposing walls of Douglas fir. The woman's name was Clara—going to see her son in Burnaby. Kate pressed her face to the window and tunneled her hands about her cheeks, but all she could see were the tall, baleful trees lining up and the highway streaking north between them. Her cheeks were damp and she realized that she was crying. Clara supplied a handkerchief. Turning, Kate assessed the woman beside her, the soft jowls beginning to drape, the penciled brows, the depthless gray eyes—a face you could not remember even if you had wanted to, a face so ordinary it seemed altogether reliable. So Kate told her about Nick, "my boyfriend," she said, who had broken his back and who would never make the Olympic team now, never dance with her, never walk beside the sea at sunset, and there could be no babies, of course. Clara put her arm around Kate's shoulder and offered dried apricots from the Yakima Valley in a box she carefully unwrapped, never mind, she could get another one for her son in Burnaby, folding the shiny paper and tucking it into her purse.

Kate was not unaware of taking minor detours from the truth, but after all, she was feeling bad. She had been thinking about that nasty Chinaman, about the Magic Inn, how rich and thrilling it had been the night before—the champagne, the show, the dancing, Max Wyman's big hand on her waist—yet how empty and exposed it had seemed that day . . . how empty and exposed she felt. But how did you explain to a stranger something you did not understand yourself? How did you obtain solace when nothing had been promised and nothing lost exactly, or lost so long ago that you could no more say what it was you had had before than say what it was—really—you wanted now? To get the comfort she needed, to get it right away without a snaggle of details that might delay or even qualify the comfort, it was so much easier to come up with a simple, straightforward matter that anyone, even a fellow passenger on a night bus, could wrap her heart around. This woman would not want to be burdened with long stories, complicated explanations, to hear about the other babies, not the ones she couldn't have with the overstated Nick but the ones she had already had, about Gregor, a man who was probably Clara's age, about Poppy and the wind on the Prairies, and how it had been after, after, *ever-after*; she would not choose to stumble into unsolvable mysteries that in the end might not lead to anything nice, like sympathy. It was too risky. Did anyone really want to see what had fallen to the mud beneath the water's surface? Could anyone bear to know that it wasn't all, quite beautifully simply, blue and cool and pretty? Who was ever on the side of the damned?

Kate ate an apricot and tried to smile; Clara gave her hand a pat. "You're a lovely girl. Think of your future."

"You've been so kind to me, so much kinder than my own mother."

"You're upset."

"No, it's true."

"Have another apricot, dear."

Perhaps that was why Fiona had become a nurse — to be free to give the love and comfort that Poppy's death had closed off. In its way, nursing provided a starkly pure medium of exchange for Fiona. Sick people deserved her attention, her comfort: it went without saying. Even a naughty girl like Kate.

At 9:50 p.m. the bus pulled into the station lot and she could see Gregor in the brightly lit waiting room rise and head for the arrival door, his head shifted forward, pointing the way, and the hem of his trench coat comically hiked up in back. She hoped he would discover it before she had to greet him publicly. *At least don't embarrass me*, she thought with a fierce stab of anger. Now that Kate had met Max Wyman how could she ever recuperate her feelings for Gregor? And what were those feelings? She couldn't seem to remember. *Max, Max Wyman* . . . oh, it was easy to feel around him! Just to *feel*. And the feeling was like a drug. That she and Wyman were both married evened things up some, and in fact at that moment offered the sole mitigation to her marital state but provided no solution. He lived in another city, another country! He was married to another woman.

A dull rain fell insignificantly, not enough to wash the grime from the sidewalks of Vancouver. Or the grime Kate felt clinging to her heart; the thoughts of Nick Bowie and the life he might have lived, if he had not met her.

The driver shoved open the door and warmish diesel fumes rushed in around the passengers already rising to gather coats, bags, food wrappers. Kate checked her makeup but decided there was no point in touching it up, there might in fact never again be a point in makeup, in watching her weight and wearing smart clothes and looking pretty. Tugging on her gloves, she remembered to present a grateful smile to the woman beside her.

"Someone meeting you?" Clara asked.

Kate glanced out the window at the tall old man, his white hair shocking in the rainy gloom. If Nick was supposed to be her boyfriend, then who was this? "My father," she replied.

Years passed; two, then three. Kate struggled against the sameness of the days, time rolling out like a bolt of patterned silk that threatened to go on forever. She was sick of seeing and doing and feeling the same thing, and finally feeling nothing, a blankness. Occasional liaisons with men relieved some of the dullness, but even the liaisons themselves — how they began, how they proceeded, their inevitable conclusions — began to acquire a scripted quality. She would tell them that her husband was elderly *and, and not interested, if they knew what she meant,* her manner as poignant as a little bird quivering in a cage, her voice sweetly faintly embarrassed by the topic and by the predicament Fate had dropped her in, and then she would let go a tear or two, but not so much that they couldn't think her brave or not bucking up as Mummy was always advising, not willing to accept her lot. "Gosh, what a waste," he might say, or "it's a darned crime," and off they went, he to rescue her self-esteem, she to rescue, ironically, the exact same thing. But she never forgot

Max Wyman. In Kate's mind he grew to occupy a steady peripheral place, yet whenever she tried to gaze in his direction, to plan an active strategy, he—or what he meant or might mean to her—darted away. Max Wyman would not be one of these afternoon fellows with whom she killed time, a filler, a throwaway. More importantly, she felt increasingly certain that he not only remembered her but that like Kate, he'd had a premonition of the two of them together, the intense rightness, so right that anything less would be a crime against the natural order.

And so she learned to drive; Gregor bought her a car, a black Oldsmobile "88" sedan, and down she drove to Seattle once a month, visiting Scottie.

"What is the purpose of your visit, business or pleasure?" the boarder guard always asked.

"Pleasure," she always answered.

After Nick's accident, George—Scottie's husband now—wasn't so keen on hooking Kate up with any of his other shipmates, but she managed quite well on her own, *thank you very much*, sometimes going down a day early to attend an ROTC dance (Scottie had got her on the invitation list), then arranging an escort for the next evening at the Magic Inn. With Mrs. Wyman drifting in and out, Max could not buy her a drink or spend any more time greeting her than he did other women—Kate could see that. But it was clear, *so obvious*, she told Scottie one Saturday afternoon, *that he was sweet on her*. Anyway, all you had to do was have *one wee glim*, as her mother used to say, of the wife—Dot Wyman—to understand the misery in Wyman's face. "Did you see her bum? And those piggy eyes, and the way she practically waddles . . . I could hear her all the way back in the kitchen, shrieking about something, and I was in the lounge, why, it's absolutely shameful, poor man, poor poor man, and him with a fancy club to run and all."

"That was funny," Scottie said into the silence that followed.

"What?"

"The way you sounded just then, like one of your mother's letters."

"My mother? Impossible."

Sunday and back to Vancouver, to the machine of her life droning along, but in her head a one-line melody went round and round, as if by repeating again and again the part she knew, what had happened during that first visit to the Magic Inn, she might one day chance upon the rest of the song. And it would be their song, and it would make up for all the years of suffering. It would.

Very often upon her return she fell ill. *Travel*, Gregor told her, *it's not good, this to and fro all the time.* She'd even had a heart attack, and at age twenty-four—it was incredible. There is a picture of Kate Riley Vancleve lying on an elevated pallet, dozens of elegantly dressed people posed in a loose circle around her, glasses lifted. Gregor had received the annual Hotel Association *hotelier* award. The ceremony had been planned to coincide with the Canadian Innkeepers' Conference, but the day before, Kate complained of pains in her chest. Her pulse raced; there was a tingly sensation in her hands and around her nose and mouth; her breathing went shallow. Doctor Stone wasn't sure, perhaps a mild heart attack, though at her age . . . "Strictly speaking," he said, "we can't detect pain in our patients, we must, ah, as it were, take their word for it. Perhaps . . . well," he concluded, "your wife *is* high-strung, Gregor." But the patient, having dressed and returned to the consultation office, had heard everything and argued that there *were* pains in her chest, "like lightning." In the car driving home she insisted that Dr. Stone was no good, he was too old, he wasn't up on modern diagnosis, which pretty much made him a quack nowadays—"Well doesn't it, Gregor, doesn't that make him just a quack, when he hasn't kept up with modern things?" A specialist from Vancouver General was called in, Dr. Belavance. He seemed more willing to accept the unlikely, or at least not willing to distress Mrs. Vancleve any further, or perhaps it was only that he could not bear to disappoint the lovely and most impressive young lady lying in his examination room, asserting her pain. The treatment would be the same—rest. At Kate's insistence, the award ceremony proceeded—"I wouldn't have it any other way"—but it was not Gregor in his tuxedo with his handsome plaque who stood at the center of the photograph that appeared in *The Sun* the next day, it was his lovely delicate wife atop her pallet, which someone had thoughtfully padded with down-filled satin and ornamental pillows. In the background next to the doorjamb stood the honoree, the plaque tucked under his arm and an expression of modest contemplation arranged upon his face.

One day when Brendan was five she picked him up from a chum's, and driving along 12th up toward British Properties and Chartwell Place where the Vancleves resided, she found herself behind an automobile whose bumper she recognized—it bore the words, "Make a date before it's too late/Raimer Insurance." A new customer, Don Raimer had visited the bank less than a dozen times. Management considered it part of Kate's job to make new business *feel welcome*, as they put it, so she never failed to swing out from under her bookkeeper's lamp and glide slowly toward him, her hand extended languidly, her smile playing hard to get. He was not a particularly imposing man, not tall, his features neither fine nor disagreeable, but he carried himself as if nothing could hope to succeed in hindering his pursuit of goals. The minor speech impediment served to put people at ease, and Kate had even wondered whether or not he had affected it in order to sell more policies. After all, Raimer owned his own agency, he had to be a smart fellow.

Instead of continuing on up into the Properties she discovered that she was following him around this corner, then another, and then apparently home to a nice-enough split-level on Mathers Avenue—yellow with gray trim, ornamental yew tree in the yard, an unruly mass of nasturtiums growing about the front stoop suggesting, indirectly, that Don Raimer was not as disciplined as he appeared. Kate rolled to a stop next to the curb, shifted into park, and let her idle. She made a casual effort to find out what was in her own mind, but nothing came forward, nothing revealed itself. Her thoughts were like naughty children hiding in the back of the classroom. In fact, all she seemed to know of herself at that point was a sense of drifty restlessness, as if her life had become a little boat that lacked a rudder or oars, that welcomed even bad weather for the action it would provide, the surprise destination.

After two days of hovering offshore a cold front had finally shoved in that morning, clearing out the fog and triggering dramatic rainsqualls around Burrard Inlet; in between, sunshine poured through temporary rifts in the cloud cover, only to be sealed off by another squadron of rain-laden billows plying inland. Shivering, she switched on the heat and watched Raimer climb out of his automobile, collect his hat, some papers, and a couple of laundered shirts, which he carried like a brace of pheasant. It would have been nicer if in fact they had been wild fowl, something he had just killed. At the front door he glanced down at the quart of milk waiting beside the threshold, but his hands were full, he would have to go in first, he seemed to decide, then return for the milk. A sudden blade of light sliced down through the clouds and glared against the windshield; Kate flinched and turned away. In the backseat sat Brendan—she'd forgotten about him—humming almost inaudibly to himself amid a litter of Tinkertoys, picture books, a box of Cracker Jacks, a Zorro lunch bucket. At least he had grown into a mild boy, the sort of child you could do practically anything to without meeting resistance. "I'll be right back," she said. It was chilly out, so she left the engine running, the heat on, windows shut. "Stay put," she told him. A pair of wide-awake blue eyes stared back at her, asking nothing, saying nothing. "I'll be right back," she said again, not liking his expression, which wasn't really an expression at all but what was left after you had erased one.

She picked her way through the tangle of nasturtiums, lifted the cool bottle, then knocked on the door. After several minutes Raimer appeared. "Your milk," she said, extending the bottle.

He raised his eyebrows and smiled carefully. "Well, this is service."

She said, "I read your bumper," realizing as the words emerged that they had nothing to do with the milk. "I was just tooling along, a round of errands after work. There was a meeting this afternoon, at the bank, new benefits for business account holders. Like you." She tossed off a gay laugh. "It's silly, isn't it . . . it's just that I was driving along with the meeting still in my head, and I read your bumper."

"Yeah," he said, gesturing her inside, "everyone does." The room was thinly furnished—two captain's chairs, a coffee table, brown chesterfield, one lamp stand—the only wall decoration an un-framed canvas depicting Santa Claus, except it wasn't jolly St. Nick, it was a haggard, ugly old fellow, a bum in a Santa suit with bags under his eyes and a burned-down cigarette hanging from the cor-ner of his mouth. Kate gave a nervous laugh; the painting made her vaguely uncomfortable.

"I dabble in the arts," Don Raimer said as he went into the kitchen, put the milk in the icebox—it was practically empty—and then opened a cupboard. "What do you want? I've got gin . . . ah, here's some rye. Plus what's left of some crème de menthe."

"I hadn't meant to intrude."

"No?"

"Of course not."

"Have a drink," he said, his voice strong, even authoritative in a sexy way. She noticed that his speech impediment was absent. To Kate it was alarming to have been entirely right about that sort of thing. People were usually better than she expected.

"I'll have some rye, if you've got anything like Seven-Up or gin-ger ale to go with it."

"Ice." Without waiting for her response he opened the icebox and removed a tray of cubes, which he slammed once, firmly, on the countertop, the sudden *crack* of the metal tray possessing a vio-lence all its own, as if in its little inanimate way the object meant to protect its master. Raimer rattled a couple of cubes into a water glass and poured the rye glug by glug, releasing a series of addi-tional crude, faintly aggressive sounds, until the ice was floating a full inch from the bottom.

With a slow formal nod of courtesy, for she wanted to teach him something about manners and ladies, Kate accepted the drink, took a sip, and again noticed over the rim of the glass how bare the place seemed. "Are you some kind of ascetic?"

Raimer grinned broadly and she saw that his teeth were bad; one was missing—a bicuspid. How was it that she had never spotted it? Her own teeth, though attractive now, were not healthy, the result of prairie town living where the dentist wandered through every few months, and sold and repaired copperware on the side, and where it was considered all but vain to pay much attention to oral hygiene. Over the last five years Gregor had arranged for the gradual restoration of her smile, including substantial gold and three caps.

"Ascetic? Never been accused of that," Don Raimer said as he poured himself some rye, neat. Then he led her back to the living room where she placed herself on the edge of the chesterfield, her ankles crossed primly, legs canted to the side. Raimer went over to the wall and adjusted the thermostat, then he dropped into one of the captain's chairs opposite her, the derelict Santa peering over his shoulder.

"That guy is funny," she said, "really funny."

"Think so?"

"It's supposed to be a joke, isn't it?"

Raimer shrugged, put his drink on the coffee table and leaned into a stretch, his slacks pulling tautly over his groin so that she could view plainly a longish ridge with a knob at one end pointing at her. "It's up for interpretation."

"Oh, you," she said, trying to feel amused. The room began to warm and to smell distinctly of heating oil.

After they had each had two drinks she said, "You know I'm married."

Raimer stared at her, sucking air through the gap in his teeth. He had the eyes of a dog you didn't know and weren't sure you could trust yet.

She glanced away, up at the wretch in the Santa suit, and thought better of trudging through the usual narrative about her elderly husband and his lack of interest, his various inabilities, her sad and lonely predicament. There was something about Raimer . . . The other fellows she spent afternoons with, why, they made her feel better, they were warm and fun and grateful, yes, that was it, they seemed grateful that she had bestowed herself upon them, so grateful that quite often she went away feeling that she had done some sort of good deed. But Raimer with that hole in his mouth, and his stark house, and that disgusting mockery hanging on his wall . . .

"Let's get naked," Raimer said, lifting his chin once.

She was hot, the acrid smell of the heating oil was making her queasy, and she was not sure, not sure at all that she wanted to go through with this, and at the same time it seemed that the only thing that might make her feel even the tiniest bit better, even faintly worthwhile, was to follow Don Raimer into his bedroom and do what he knew—*oh, that was obvious, he was making that quite rudely clear*—she had come to do. "It's late," she murmured, rubbing the small white face of her wristwatch with her thumb.

A gelid smile formed beneath his strange eyes.

"I am married," she repeated, but even she could hear the tinny note of surrender.

Raimer stood, locked the front door, and headed for the bedroom. "Now, none of that."

If she had remembered Brendan, if she had thought about the four-inch gash she put in the rocker panel of the Olds high-siding on a stone out at Fisherman's Cove, a spring downpour having exposed underlying debris and bedrock, if she had listened to Gregor who insisted she get it repaired as soon as possible, if she'd considered the engine still idling at the curb, the boy waiting, she might have easily extricated herself, even from Raimer's rough grip. But the instant the insurance man had invited her in she forgot everything.

A double bed took up most of the room; the window was small, too, the glass dirty and cracked across the upper left corner, and the gray light all but blotted out by some sort of vine that was out of control and prowling freely up from below the sill. The door had been shut, so the heat had not been able to enter. On the bedside table she beheld the missing tooth, gleamy and perfect, white as milk, a human fang bound up in some sort of wire contraption, and she understood then that his impediment resulted from having to wear this thing, and that without it his speech was as natural as the next man's.

She took off her clothes and quickly bundled under the covers, fixing her gaze on the pale mottled light of the window as she listened to his belt buckle clink to the floor. She could not remember ever feeling so self-conscious; this guy had a way of making nakedness somehow more naked, as if he could see through skin into parts of her even she had never come upon.

Don Raimer took time to enjoy himself thoroughly. Besides the fact that he was clearly a man of opportunity, he realized no doubt that this was a one-shot deal, that the filly was spooked and skittish, and once released, would bolt. Someone knocked on the door and he ignored it. The telephone rang and he was deaf to its pleadings. When he had finished sampling more conventional positions, he rolled her onto her hands and knees, greased himself up with something clear from a tube using slow, two-handed strokes, his eyes drifting leftward just out of focus and a mini spasm quivering his lower lip, Raimer sidetracked briefly in masturbatory ardor and not caring at all that Kate saw, and then without even asking or warning her he swung around behind and drove himself like a piston rod between the halves of her rump. She let out a yelp, in pain and deeply affronted, tears instantaneous. "Quiet. Don't distract me," he said, and there was not the slightest hint of feeling in his voice. Against the windowpanes she could hear another rainsquall let loose as the smell of her own bowels tinged the cold air of the cold little room.

It was dusk when she left finally, *three hours*, she thought, hurrying down the walk, *with that bastard, that . . . wretch. What an ingrate.* At the same time she felt profoundly wounded by his indifference to her charms, to her pleasure, by the rye without ginger ale, by the shabby emptiness of his house, which he seemed to think was just fine, perfectly suitable. *The nerve.*

Over the years Kate had grown careless about the afternoon men. This one lived along one of several main routes that wound up to British Properties and when Gregor Vancleve had recognized his wife's Oldsmobile, the engine running, he had stopped. There in the back was his blond-haired boy lying on the floor, his knees draped over the axel hump and the Cracker Jacks box clutched to his chest, and he looked simply asleep, but Gregor could not rouse the boy, banging on the glass; no, he seemed terribly soundly asleep, and no one came to the door of the yellow house when he knocked and knocked, behind him the engine still reliably droning along, a good car, the Oldsmobile, solid and safe, the salesman had told them, dependable, he had said, gazing pointedly at Mrs. Vancleve, *you'll never break down in an Oldsmobile*, and Gregor raced home for the extra key, the engine still purring like a black lynx, its breath poison, scentless and unseeable, a dark lynx that had swallowed up his blue-eyed boy. Fumbling the key into the lock, throwing open the door, he snatched his son away and held him up into the driving rain, his brow pale as pale stone but the cheeks flushed bright, a glaucous shadow about the mouth as though moss were already gathering in the stillness, the rain dancing upon his face until at last the eyelids twitched. Not dead, *God zy dank*, not dead. When Brendan had finished emptying his stomach beside his mother's car, Gregor rushed him to the doctor, and it was while the boy was being treated for carbon monoxide poisoning, cradled in the arms of a matronly nurse, breathing from a tank of pure oxygen, that Gregor Vancleve telephoned his attorney. About the same time Kate discovered her car door open,

the engine off, the boy gone. It had all come out in the legal documents, every abject detail.

"You will not leave me, Gregor, oh no, not after all I've been through,
how long I've put up with . . ."

"With what?"

"Your age."

He seemed to be having a hard time looking at her, perhaps, she
decided, because he understood that he would miss her beauty, that
he would be giving up a lot if he went ahead with this divorce. Knowing that there would be a row that morning-after, Kate had gone to
extra lengths to be particularly arresting—a dark green taffeta dress
with a matching, velvet-trimmed bolero, a plumed toque, her hair
curled loosely beneath it, a new pair of black kids. Gregor walked over
to the picture window and gazed south across the Narrows to Stanley
Park and to the hazy band of serration beyond that was downtown
Vancouver. The sun was only just established, still laboring up from
the rim of the world, but yesterday's clouds had all but vanished,
and he put his palms to the glass as if catching the new light. "This
yearning," he said, "inside you deep, it is impossible." About his torso
a crisp white shirt planed sculpturally, and indeed he seemed like a
living statue, someone venerated and prized, backlit by a dazzling
world, and for a good long minute she wanted to touch him again, to
feel the fabric warm from his body heat, the strong subtle sinews beneath. His jacket, a Crofter-made Harris Tweed still faintly redolent
of peat, hung over the back of the wing chair where he sat reading
poetry most mornings before work, and if she had had the courage
she would have pressed it to her face to feel its soft elegance, to smell
its fine quiet history, the smallest bit of which had included her.

Instead, she tugged on the black kid gloves, fanning her fingers
to admire their sleek fit, and said, "I haven't the faintest idea what
you're talking about."

His hands slid from the glass. "Poor love, I know," he murmured
as he picked up his jacket. "This I know."

"Wait . . ."

He fixed his eyes upon her, eyes she trusted completely, eyes that once held the glow of adoration, extinguished now, the light gone, the love worn out; still, even at what seemed final moments she felt undressed by these eyes as by a confessor who would forgive all. It was in its way a gloriously liberating sensation, and from around a last corner it managed to coax a frail waif of hope.

"You . . . you can't mean this, Darling."

He was making his way toward the front door, drawing on his jacket, gathering attaché case, umbrella.

"I'll change. I will."

"It is impossible."

"But you still want me, don't you?"

Turning, he regarded her as he had that first day when she stood in his office at the Langston Hotel, desiring employment for which she was not in the least qualified. The light was not behind him now, but she felt it peripherally flooding into the room.

"You still want me," she repeated, only this time she was aware of a desperate fury. Her hands were shaking, her breath came fast. "Say it. Because I won't let you beat me to the punch, do you hear, I simply won't let this happen, not after all I've put up with, all I've given you." She paused, watching him watch her, and suddenly she felt like some kind of specimen, a newly discovered animal displayed in an overly lit room. "You know, Gregor, I was the one who wanted a divorce, not you. I resisted it for your sake, because I knew you still wanted me. You do, don't you? Just say it," she screamed, the tears coming in a rush now, "say it once! That's all you have to do, damn it to hell, is want me, still want me . . ."

"Want you?" He gave a sad sort of laugh that instantly disintegrated. "Poor Kate, but I have had you quite enough."

Eight months later in January 1957 the Vancleves were divorced, the court granting Brendan's father custody, in part because of the damning incident in the automobile, and in part because (curiously) the mother made no petition and put forth not a single claim with regard to her son. She wrote in her statement that the divorce would leave her destitute and that she could not afford to properly care for the boy, though the record indicates that Vancleve settled a handsome sum upon his young wife, including a monthly stipend that would continue two full years. Until all of the legal matters had been concluded Kate stayed in their home up on Chartwell, occupying her first quarters, the sickroom where Father Deneau had come to visit her, where Gregor brought her meals and her mail after the suicide attempt. He had saved her once, but he could not save her twice. When the last documents were signed Kate let a two-room suite in North Van on the edge of the somewhat seedy commercial district. She hung a brown woolen blanket over its sole window and lay in bed surrounded by magazines, eating jelly on bread, Neapolitan ice cream, Spam and Beefaroni, licorice candies. When every one of the dishes she owned had been used and not washed, she ate off long-playing records, then the glossy covers of the magazines, and finally, straight from the food packages. She bought a television and put it atop the dinette table and let it run from test pattern to test pattern, the light flickering over there in the corner, the sound down low, voices smothered. Sometimes she draped an old tea towel over the screen and watched the obscured lives struggle on beneath a print of faded violets. Her father loved violets . . . *Hugh Fergal Riley*, her mind whispered—she was always buying up things with violets on them.

It came as a mild surprise that she missed Gregor, his silent restraint, which always seemed to tell her that he considered himself remarkably lucky simply to be with her and wouldn't bother her with any of the rest, no matter his rightful claim, his abilities or inabilities. Her new situation inexorably led her to wonder if there had been anything wrong with Gregor's competence in the bedroom, or if at some unnoticed point in their six years together he had frankly had his fill. The idea provoked a crazy sorrow so deep inside her that it scared her almost as much as late night thoughts of death, which, if she followed them too far down the path before sleep could snatch her safely away, stirred up a terrible and viperous panic.

She even missed the boy, "our adorable little house dog," was how she often referred to him. She missed his crawling about on his knees, pretending to be her puppy, and his small doting hand on the back of her head as he brushed out her hair at the end of the day. It had been an accident, after all; she hadn't meant to be gone so long. The boy was fine, just fine—*everyone seemed to forget that, even Miriam—what a pious witch. And as for Raimer and the others, well, my goodness, what was she supposed to have done? Twenty-five and married and no young life, no one to love her in a normal, natural way, how God meant it should be, and all sorts of proposals, people had no idea how much temptation she resisted all the time, it was unfair to judge her like other women, why, she was positively swamped with letters and calls from fellows, and easily a dozen proposals, two of them "standing." It wasn't her fault that she was pretty, that there was something about her, a magnetism that excited men, even women. If people could just consider all the temptation she was exposed to, all the times she had resisted, the additions and subtractions, if they could just take into account her loyalty to the marriage, and her not wanting to abandon Gregor Vancleve at his age, then they would see that she was a good girl at heart, just a good girl trying to make the best of things.*

Joe Willoughby had consented to a lengthy leave, but when at last Kate showed up for work in late February he extended it by another month, directing Phyllis to explain to (the now) Miss Riley that "in business a worthy appearance is key" and that "her seniority alone required that she admit no personal matters in her comportment and in her wardrobe," and that "a flowered housedress" would not do, "not at all" and neither would "unclothed legs." Kate told Phyllis that she could not fit into any of her separates, her tweedy ensembles, she had gained some weight, it seemed, and that nylons were tight and uncomfortable, and after months of padding about barefoot the snappy, two-toned, sling-back pumps made her feet hurt, and that at any rate she couldn't bear to run into Gregor who still banked in the West Van branch, and how was it that Joe Willoughby could insult her after all she had been through? So she quit. Went back to her flat, wrote her mother, turned out the lights.

In March a letter from Fiona arrived, postmarked #239 Hotel York, York Street, Winnipeg, Manitoba.

My Dear Kate

Your letter received, and so very sorry to get the news, I just don't know what to say I never thought he would do such a thing, it must be very hard on you, you must make the best of things. There are many girls in the world have had a worse deal and thank god he will support you for a while. I wish I was real near you and could try to cheer you up, pop in and have a wee chat. I wonder what brought on the change of mind. Would you consider coming back home, or even to Winnipeg and I could see you now and then? Kate, I am very heart broken that you are so far from me and never thought such a thing would happen. I do wish I could help in some way. Well dear, I want to tell you to chin up and think of all our blessings so many people have troubles too, but in spite of it all we have to carry on and hold our heads high and play the game of feeling fine.

I myself not too well with sore throat and headache and not sleeping very well my nerves are not good either. I hope you folks did not get the mumps, I have never had them, neither have you so maybe you are safe. The boys never had them either. The Drs. and I are looking after myself, I'm back to eating good food, no more starvation for me. They said they might put me in a mental if I didn't eat. The pain killing pills cost a fortune, so it will take good common sense to keep my money from wasting away. The whole thing boils down to starvation diet. You can't run a car without gas. Still, wish I'd had the guts to have done it 3 years ago, finish things, if you take my meaning. I'd like to see all my relatives real quick.

We have a bunch of queer women here now, I've no notion of wanting their company. I used to go out and have some eats and a beer with Mrs. Dodds, but she has a new steady and eats out all the time. He sure keeps himself neat, but is a real crank, bangs the elevator door every time I don't want to hear it. She don't ask me to go with her anymore I sure would. She bought me some chops today. Norma Roswell took her dress-making sign down they say she did not have a license. And her with new glasses to pay for. My grandma in Ireland bathed her eyes two or three times with tea, also my mother, and never wore glasses. As I write this I have my feet in a pail of water with Epsom salts in it, two toenails and a third are in growing the pain is near to unbearable. I pray that I get well again. I may have to make a change, Kate, as I do not like the new neighbors, they have come from Puerto Rico. I am rather nervous everything is changed now and they brag that they are going to Rule the world. They are filthy and curse and swear and they are very rough. I do not open my door to anyone and carry my umbrella at all times and I've made up my mind anyone who tries to get my purse will get a good crack of the umbrella. Well, I'm my own boss so will give the change some thought. The Hotel is under new management, he is quite handsome.

How is the wee tot? You are a smart girl not to put the burden on yourself as he has the money, you with a new husband to attract. I always wanted more kiddies but you had to be the famous one anyone saw that. Well then time went on and Dad had to go to Rochester came home in a month after removal of the kidney. And then there were the other trips to the Mayo Clinic, but I had no regrets, as I sure did my utmost to make him happy and comfortable in his time of suffering. I know this that I will never get so nice care. I had to go and get the coffin all fixed up, then on the Sunday was the funeral my son Colin looked sad and said it should have been him. Colin was the good one John too busy to write so I better just forget about it.

There is no heat on half the time so would have had to move long ago if I didn't have the heater you folks sent Xmas, I haven't told anyone I have it we are not supposed to have hot-plates either, so put it on and don't answer the door and keep it locked. Well, Kate, will soon be my birthday, so don't go getting me anything, only if you feel you want to get something a cou-ple of pair of nylons would be alright size 10. I will be 67 and no one to turn to, the boys are married and no room for me.

Well dear I'll close for now I am very lonely and blue. I'll have a cup of tea and a smoke.

> *Bye now*
> *Loads of love,*
> Mother

PS The world is in a terrible state and could smash up any mo-ment, so I have decided to live one day at a time.

Kate would not have a phone put in, so Miriam left several calls with the manager downstairs, all of them unanswered. One night Phyllis tried to persuade her to come out for dinner, but Kate would not release the lock and in the end, Phyllis slid two notes under the door, one from Padraig Delaney in accounting and the other from Scottie.

Paddy Delaney had been with the Royal Bank for almost twenty years and knew how to keep just the right distance, to do a fine job but not an ambitious job, not one that might bump him into re-sponsibilities that latched on at the end of each day, never to let go. He'd come over from the *auld sod*, as he liked to call it, Oughterard, County Galway, a Hurling star in his youth. Paddy's sense of the West Vancouver Branch of the Royal Bank had everything to do with his nostalgia for his Hurling team, supporting "our local lads," doing one's bit. She knew there could be nothing genuinely per-sonal inside the small envelope addressed to Miss Kate Riley, that it would consist of something that he or any one of the teammates might say when a lad—or lassie—went off. For Kate's Irish heritage inspired him, and she in turn had always liked the reminder that there was a deep vein of Rileys over there, and that if things ever got bad for her here in Canada, she might always go back, way back, to her *true* home in Carrick-on-Shannon where Hugh Fergal Riley had been born.

Inside Paddy's envelope she found a neatly typed poem:

See Katy, begorra and why are yez leaving us
Can't yez be see'n that the thought it is grieving us?
Sure and we've all got to liking your ways—
And even if sometimes you seemed in a daze
As if quite unconscious of labor and summaries,
But thought—so yez did—of your lipstick and flummeries
Yet still you've been part of the banking—and so
Your leaving is really upsetting poor Joe;
Bedad and his appetite's starting to fail
It won't be so long 'til he's thin as a rail.

But never you worry, young Katy colleen,
Just laugh and be happy—but sometimes between,
Think back to the Royal and your first little job
And shed a small tear drop and sob a wee sob.

It was signed Paddy, and there was a postscript:

ps A boil on the elbow would be hard to beat,
But you could do better with one on the seat.

She gazed at the light straining through the brown blanket still draped over her window, and felt a smile tug into shape. It was so ridiculous, so unrelated to anything, the boil on the seat, old Joe who didn't give a tinker's damn, *oh, she knew that*, yet Paddy's lyric had invoked that haloing impression of an all-forgiving Home over there, of her father's boundless devotion to her, and somehow it served to wrench her from the deep mire in which she had sunk since Gregor's rejection. She read the poem again, then picked up the second note from Scottie:

Dear Kate—

Listen, George's orders have materialized. His new destination is New Orleans. He hasn't received them officially but it's pretty definite. I'm leaving here May 1st, and have already given notice at the bank. I told them that I had a friend who might be interested in a position, but didn't give them your name or tell them where you were. All I told him was that you had about 5 years experience and could assume a head bookkeeper's job. This is a good time for you to get out of Van. The States are wide open. Think about it and let me know.

We were at the Magic Inn last Sat nite with a bunch from the bank. We had some good dancers in the crowd so I had a marvelous time. George did too. M.W. was there, natch. I think the wife is headed out of the picture.

Mardi Gras day is simply out of this world I hear. One of the fellows here now had a ball there while he was stationed in N.O. I'm really looking forward to it. You have a standing invite when we get settled. I'd love to have you even if you didn't feel like doing anything. Phyl says you're holed up in some dive. Don't throw it in like this, Riley, pull yourself together and come down here. You can have the apartment too. Write.

Love,
Scottie

In one of the glossy magazines strewn about the bed Kate found a diet plan. She cut out pictures of movie stars, Elizabeth Taylor, Kim Novak, Shelley Winters, and taped them to the front of the icebox. A month passed before she removed the tea towel from the bathroom mirror and resumed daily makeup applications. A month and fifteen pounds. In a three-day fury of action she cleaned the flat, washed and pressed what of her clothing permitted, took the rest to the dry cleaners, and gave notice. Since she had stopped combing her hair weeks earlier, tying a scarf around her head whenever she needed to make a foray to the store, now she had to wash it, and wash it again, then spend hours gently working apart the mats; in the end some of them had to be cut out by the hair stylist.

"There was a death in the family," Kate explained to the woman, because that was exactly how it felt—that someone had died. "I have been in mourning."

"Of course, dearie, of course. We'll get you all prettied up again, you'll see. Ready to face the world."

Then Kate Riley of Netherfield, Saskatchewan became an American citizen, a landed immigrant, and took over the Head Bookkeeper's position at the Central Branch of the National Bank of Commerce in Seattle where, as it turned out, the Magic Inn maintained its accounts, a little secret Scottie meant as a pleasant parting surprise.

Seattle

"What kind of friend are you?"

Scottie went silent.

"This isn't the way I am," Kate screamed into the phone. "I've got sixteen pounds to go. And here he came, Scottie, picture it? I want you to picture it. In his camelhair overcoat and his red tie and that envelope filled with money. And no wife, it was you who told me, no more wife. And there I was with sixteen pounds to go. You knew about the diet and you deliberately set me up. I have half a mind to tell George something . . ."

Scottie gave a derisive snort. "There isn't anything to tell him."

"What difference does that make?"

"Tell him about your mean streak, Kate. Except he knows about that already. Some of us defended you, that business with Nick Bowie. Or have you forgotten? Now I know what that was all about, what it's always been about—you."

If Max Wyman noticed the extra weight he revealed neither disappointment nor abrupt disinterest. Kate tucked herself into her desk and propped up an open ledger book, which left only her head fully exposed, though that alone would have been sufficient evidence for any man whose powers of observation had been heightened by love, as they so often are. For Kate possessed a head as round as a model globe, and it was only the subtle shadowed planes created by cheekbones and eyebrows, the angles, however broad, defined by the jaw, the tidy elevation of nose, that served to weaken and even disguise the globular effect. With the extra weight, the flesh puffed out to meet perimeter structures, the shadows and angles all but disappeared, and Kate's was a remarkably round face, a moon face, freckled and (to Kate) quite possibly hideous. In the mornings when she applied her makeup, she pretended the face did not belong to her but to some hapless stepsister temporarily assigned to her care, like that sinister bum dressed up in a Santa suit. *We'll fix you right up, Ramona Moon*—the name she gave this pathetic creature—*and I promise, some nice fellow will ask you to dance, nice and kind who will love you, who will positively adore you no matter how you look or what you've done or where you come from.* One morning it struck her that Jan Larsen had been such a fellow, but it was Kate he had loved, *not you*, she told Ramona Moon.

Poor Ramona stared back, her fat round mug flushed with envy, the newly applied makeup a farcical dream.

No, Max Wyman made no effort to notice her and for Kate's part, she merely offered a vague gesture of greeting, allowing the teller to complete his deposit, then she picked up the phone as if an important call had just come in, and Wyman shoved through the big glass doors out onto Westlake Avenue where the crowds of Seattle swept him away like a dream she was not worthy to dream. A presence, then a nonpresence, the bank suddenly as coldly cavernous as the space opening up in her heart. Slowly she returned the phone to its black cradle and stared through teary magnification at the numbers pacing up and down the long white ledger sheet.

Maybe he had perceived the weight gain and meant to spare her the embarrassment of his official recognition until she had got rid of the interloper, Ramona Moon, maybe that was why he seemed not even to recognize her.

The weight would come off, nothing would stop her.

Under the desk, she took hold of a roll of tummy fat and pinched it as hard as she could.

From that moment on, Kate Riley's weight became a second self far worse than any specter or nightmare phantasm, either of which would have constituted at the very least a separate entity. An Other. But this *fat* . . . (she refused to be lenient with the language, and in fact, there was an old part of her that reveled in sadistic condemnation of the Kate she could not abide, the Kate her mother had found so loveless) . . . this fat inhabited and distorted her own lovely body, at times a fifty pound incubus, so that she did not even recognize herself in the mirror. It was Ramona Moon again, Ramona who did not deserve even one dance now, let alone a man in her life. Spiteful, pathetic Ramona who was more than willing—eager!—to cast herself down to the bottom of life and to drag Kate Riley down with her.

She lost the sixteen pounds. She captured Max Wyman's attention—more easily than she had ever imagined possible. One night at the club, passing him in a slow conspicuous swag, she lobbed a bawdy tidbit, he caught it with a wink and outdid her, something that featured the word "dame" or "dish," and later in a back office amid a rush of zippers and bunched clothing, invoices seesawing to the floor like tired petals from the last apple tree, he had her. She felt a little wounded—only a little—by his celerity, as if he had decided to have the dessert after all but had no intention of lingering over or even officially appreciating something that wasn't on his diet; nevertheless, Kate was immensely relieved as if by a puzzle solved or a baffling illness finally diagnosed, that Max Wyman had been tempted at last. He had failed to fall for so long. Since she had come to Seattle to start a new life, she had regarded Wyman as an answer, *the* answer, to a need that she alone could not begin to fill. The longer she had to go without it, the more anxious she felt, and the harder it became not to eat, so that there were evenings when, passing the refrigerator, its hulking huddled whiteness there in the corner like a rejected lover, she felt almost bullied into releasing the stainless steel lever and accepting the comfort it offered inside, the yellow glow of the little interior bulb backlighting the food, arranged randomly, like ugly girls waiting to be asked and not wishing to associate with one another. She was even beginning to have health problems of her own, headaches sometimes, or abdominal pains, a feeling of tightness in her chest usually in the wee hours of the morning. The doctor had suggested she keep a record — when different things occurred and in what circumstances — just in case they were related. But it would all end now, she was sure of it. There was nothing like a man to brace oneself up for another serving of Life.

Afterward, when Max had locked the office door and walked her out to the street, his big hand piloting her through the small of her back, when he had tucked her into her Oldsmobile and she drove slowly back to the apartment, the night seemed a cool simple place, the stars friendly, vivid flecks of light, there as if to please her alone, the whole world was an easy smooth pleasing phenomenon across whose surface she glided nymph-like, belonging entirely. Never mind what he had said at the end, "Wonderful to meet you, Kate," it was a joke, a naughty joke. Oh, he was a devil, Max Wyman was, there was no doubting that. A deliciously exciting devil.

The wife was not exactly out of the picture as Scottie had implied, but she was out of town quite a lot, owing to a diabetic mother in Port Angeles with declining health, and widowed six years. Less than one month into their affair — there could be no other word — Kate was feeling grand. On top of the world, she told her mother. Seldom could she summon the courage to call unless she was doing well, unless she was thin and loveable and safely with a man whose very presence in the foreground of her day might deflect whatever sharp words Fiona shot her direction.

Yes, she felt simply wonderful. She even hired a portrait photographer who spent several days memorializing her triumphant figure. They were in themselves remarkable photographs, tangible testimonies to the special plot of narcissism she managed to fence off from the encroaching emptiness; remarkable too for the fierce sexual confidence Kate emits, like a strong and steady drumbeat in the night, and simultaneously the barely audible melody there in the very nature of the photographs, the sad song of her need, helplessly recklessly exposed through the black-and-white, the yin and yang of her psyche. In one a steamer trunk has been upended, a zebra hide draped artfully over it, and upon it Kate poses, her angular legs sheathed in black net stockings, her fulsome torso in a white peasant blouse that is all soft curves mimicking the soft bare shoulders, the doppelganger swellings of décolletage. The attitude of the body is one of casual assurance—left leg up and crossed, right leg swung down to the point of a black pump, torso leaning forward, one arm on her waist, fingers feathered, the other propped on the crossed leg, chin resting upon the hand which folds away from the viewer as if to conceal a secret. And yet the attitude is preposterously a pose, invoked or invented. It is all pose. The eyebrows contain almost no arch; they are dark sudden strokes executed in high temper, or as if she is irritated by their necessity. The eyes look directly at the viewer, the lips are firm and full, and something in their set—matter-of-fact, unemotional—suggests a curious inconsistency, a single note that pipes back to her Canadian past, to her prairie culture where the object was to endure, to have a shrewd sense of the possible, to be determined but not dreamy. The expression is less inviting than challenging, and seems to say, "This is who I am, all yours, if you dare," but timorous, too, whispering behind that folded hand, "*oh please, please dare.*"

There are two other photographs of note: Kate in a toga-like gown leaning against a stage prop Greek column. Her hands are crossed loosely behind her back, her hair flowing across her shoulders, her feet bare. Into an imaginary distance she gazes, like a Delphic virgin longing to be possessed. The last shot offers up a sadly glamorous Kate enveloped in fur, heavily made up, her hair a tightly coiffed knot of curls, and again, she casts her attention away from the viewer, up into the sky as if somewhere up there is a guardian angel.

The photographs, their very existence, announce Kate Riley's fatal miscalculation, for they fail to honestly assess the viewer in the same way that she failed to accurately size-up Max Wyman, to hear the things he did not say, to see what was not even hidden but only casually disguised, as if she was hardly worth the effort to lie convincingly. No, he could not get his divorce yet—*financially ruinous*, he told her. Of course he no longer loved his wife (*Dot*—how Kate hated to hear her named; in its mere utterance Max Wyman married her anew, *Dot, I do*), but they had been together since high school, and it was a long and complicated relationship; Dot's mother, Ethel Lincoln, actually owned a percentage of the Magic Inn, and until her death, which was imminent he promised her, (*imminent*, such a high, satiny word, so deserving of its import) an intact marriage was essential, in terms of the disposition of assets. In the next breath, he would tell Kate that he wanted to buy his mother-in-law out, that it was a matter of pride; that he wanted to come to Kate as a whole man in full possession of his future, and by extension, her future. And there was something else he was involved in, he wouldn't tell her yet, but if it panned out then he would have the "funds"—a word he was especially enamored of—to make the club his own. If he wanted he could sell it, realize a sizable profit; they could move to New York, he'd already had promising dealings with a man in New York. She assumed he meant to marry her, though (understandably) it was a word he was shy of using as he faced down a costly divorce. She assumed the mother-in-law would in fact die soon, judging by the wife's many extended trips to Port Angeles. She assumed that by New York, he meant Manhattan, Broadway shows, glamorous restaurants, haute couture, beautiful people admiring her beauty, so raw, so authentic, a living work of art—*from the Prairies, you say?* It was a dance of delusion, easier to understand when considered in the light of Kate's previous relationships with men: except for Don Raimer, she had never before known a man who was not essentially good, or at least making regular efforts to be so. More than that, she needed to believe this man, this particular man for whom in a way she had already abandoned so much; her very identity depended upon believing in him. Because from the moment she had given up that girl child seven years earlier, she had become a fugitive fleeing the woman she could have been, the life that might have been hers, even to a certain extent the life she had not had the courage to reclaim with Gregor Vancleve's help.

A year into the affair the excitement of secrecy began to fade like breath from a mirror. Kate took a good long look at herself at age twenty-six; she was ready for the next step. She wanted people to know that she and Max were together, to kiss in public or at least dine in one of the nicer restaurants, maybe even Rosellini's 410 in the White-Henry-Stuart Building downtown, instead of out of the city or in its seedy fringes, or sometimes on roundtrip ferry boat rides, the two of them in the backseat of his Imperial on the car deck, drinking CC-Sevens, or in a corner booth on one of the upper decks. But Max would not permit disclosure.

On one such trip in early June of '58, a damp morning ferry out to Bainbridge Island, she became aware of an urgency that she realized had everything to do with her sense of momentum, vast and overarching and perhaps even preordained, and of it having been somehow impeded; and of the forces that governed her progress in the world and the quick, confident fanning out of a future that had been hers, lying there across the pink palm of her hand, hers since the day she left Netherfield where you could sift tomorrow through a pile of broken dreams and end up with the same dusty, moribund towns, the same monster wheat farms owned by corporations faraway; where the future had been run off with the young men from the war who had blown like seeds before the winds of opportunity, and who would never go back; the future run off or run down or simply marooned in the past like a sapling out in a torrent; Netherfield where the future *was*, and never would be, not according to any dream dreamed up by man. They had bogged down, Kate Riley and this man, Max Wyman. She could *feel* it through the soles of her feet as surely as she had felt the spring mud walking barefoot out to the cemetery the day Poppy died.

It was the onset of tourist season, and Max had boosted the level of attention he paid the club as well as his pre-existent life—the last Kate perceived as a particularly bad omen. The Wymans's adolescent girls, off in a Connecticut prep school, had come home for the summer holiday, and both Ronna and Jody were making claims Max seemed powerless to resist. Kate had spotted them together the day before, shopping at *Frederick and Nelson* downtown, Ronna, the dark-haired younger of the two, leaping about her Daddy like a teenaged pup, and tall Jody hooking Max's arm, an expression of charmed disdain maturing her beyond her sixteen years. There was something about them . . . the little shopping expedition, so wholesome, Daddy's fat wallet blissfully shrinking, and the girls oblivious of their own confidence and of its power, their greedy giddiness . . . there was something about the tableau that sent a heat wave of disgust through Kate Riley. And the way he seemed to let himself be carried away by their fawning antics, not realizing that his passivity encouraged it. In many ways he is such an innocent, he should not have had girls, thought Kate, who had ducked behind a rack of fur coats. I know girls, she told Ramona Moon.

At all times now Ramona could be found against the back wall of Kate's mind, slouched in a rickety ladder-backed chair, mostly in silent observation though occasionally asleep, a faint white smear of slaver at the corner of her mouth, or with one leg splayed, her limp hand dangling down, idly masturbating. Ramona never left, even when Kate was on the thin side of matters. Ramona had started out a playful invention and had become more and more convenient as the perfect recipient, the embodiment of things ugly or unseemly that Kate discovered within herself—a bad temper, a pound or ten of flesh, an act of gratuitous cruelty aimed at a fellow worker. Ramona was a figment, except that sometimes it seemed to Kate that it was she herself who was the figment and Ramona the literal woman.

Kate gave her head a single sensible yank as she slid from behind the rack of fur and headed for the elevator. The wife, the deficient wife, *Dot* (how perfect, how stunted her name, and yet obligatory as a punctuating period), Dot was entirely responsible for the state of affairs.

The elevator tones sang their song and the doors began to slide shut. At the last instant a woman with several parcels and a young boy bustled in. The boy twisted around to stare at Kate; she waggled her fingers at him and he waggled back, a curled pink exploration of a pretty stranger, and then, afraid of their impromptu conspiracy, perhaps guilty, he pressed up close to the backside of Mama's wool coat while Kate looked away to spare him the humiliation of his retreat.

A boy? A boy . . . yes. Max was the sort of man, because he was *all* man, who needed a boy.

The following morning the fog was thick. The ferry run to Bainbridge employed one of the smaller older boats, and at that hour—7:20 a.m.—there were only a dozen other vehicles on the car deck deliberately scattered to provide nautical balance. The ferryman had motioned for them to pull up along the port side in a single lane flanking the structure containing the stairwell. A rough gray sea blinked at her through a string of oval openings as Max drove forward, cut the engine and set the parking brake. He gave her thigh an affectionate pat, his hand warm. She stared out her window at the rust forming around the big, one-inch rivets that held the sections of green- and white-painted steel together. What would it take to break this thing apart? she wondered. How wild a storm? The ferry shifted and jerked inside the pilings, like a restless animal in a chute. Several car-lengths behind them a turquoise pickup came to a stop and a bantam, red-headed man popped out and made for the stairs, a new cigarette wagging from his mouth, ready to be lit the instant he reached one of the upper decks where smoking was permitted. Then they could hear the men hollering to each other, and the sound of the heavy chain dragged across the deck, and finally the buffoonish blast of the ferry horn sending its one-note ultimatum out across the empty sea.

She turned and looked at Max, as if he had shouted at her.

Up? he pointed.

In answer, she opened the passenger door and wobbled out. She should have worn flats; if she and Max were really together, officially a couple, she wouldn't always have to dress up for him. The wind grabbed her coat and she yanked it back around her front, ashamed of the tummy she was developing.

On the passenger deck in the stern they slid across the last green vinyl bench and watched the others scatter throughout the deck, settling in for the ride. She realized that Max was making sure that there was no one on board he knew. The fog was so thick that passengers walking forward on the promenade disappeared before they reached the bow into a white dream of the future.

She thought about the day before, Max with his daughters, and wondered if the fact of children rendered him more malleable.

Beneath them a deep erratic throb accelerated until she could feel through her body the steady vibration of movement, and then the pilings slid backwards past the wide, double-paned windows and it was just the swirling fog and the quality of Max beside her, the only man in the world for Kate, the only option she could bear to consider, the only choice, period.

"Max, I want us to be married."

"It's too soon, honey."

"A year?"

"I have to get everything in place, financial and legal matters.

Ethel is . . ." He paused and she saw a wincing tug about his mouth that for more than just a moment she refused to believe. "Well, the truth of it is, she's at death's door," he finished with a solemn drop in his voice. "We have to be patient."

She gazed up at the ceiling at the hanging wooden cages filled with orange life vests, one for each passenger — what if there weren't enough, she wondered as she turned to consider Max. "I have been patient, all this time, all these long months. Don't we have rights, too? What about our future? They are not the only ones with a future," she added in primly imperious tones.

"They?"

"Your wife and your daughters. Who are almost grown, in case you haven't noticed. I saw you with them yesterday."

She sensed him inspecting the side of her face, as if she had threatened him and he was suddenly obliged to gauge just how dangerous she was, this preternatural innocent. Then he stood up and ambled over to the counter where they sold pastries and pack-aged sandwiches, and returned with two coffees, milk in hers. She was so relieved to see him coming back toward her, that slightly crooked amble of his, so confidently masculine, that she smiled foolishly, a Ramona Moon sort of smile, pathetic and begging.

"I feel very hopeful of our future, Kate," he said, passing her the coffee. His voice was as cool and smooth as sherbet sliding down a sore throat. "We can't let anything stand in the way of eventually having everything right."

She stared out the window. The little red-haired man from the pickup was leaning against the railing, smoking. His blue jeans were faded and frayed; his jacket, a misshapen quilted thing with a greasy stain down one arm, was sloppy on him, probably second-hand from a relative or the Salvation Army. A farmer, Kate guessed: he had the keyed-up wiry build of someone who worked nonstop, like all the farmers she had known in Netherfield. She remembered Jan . . . at least he had avoided farming. Kate had been determined to avoid it all, not just the miserable nonexistence of a prairie life, but whatever it had predicted for the poor, ill-equipped souls who managed to get out. What was Jan? A car parts dealer, last she heard. Beth married an assistant undertaker in Virden, and Corine was styling hair in Winnipeg—Fiona had run into her last November. Benny managed a fish camp up north, but it shut down in the winter and then he was pretty much on the dole. None of them had done anything important so far—gone to college or started a business. None but Miriam who was living in Paris, working in the Canadian Consulate's office, exactly as she had dreamed, though of course, Miriam didn't count—her family had money and connections.

But Kate Riley would make it, make it big. "Happiness is the best revenge," her mother liked to say. And happiness meant Max Wyman. As for the revenge, what it was for, what prompted the need for it, she wasn't sure exactly, though it seemed to be all wrapped up with her father's death and the bad times after, what was owed her.

Peripherally she sensed his head. Max had a big head; sometimes it seemed he was all head and that the rest of him was an afterthought intended somehow to compensate for the intimidating presence perched on his shoulders. His body was easy, a welcoming place, the skin nut-brown and smooth, the muscles in clear evidence but conveying benignity, the torso too long, the legs too short but remarkably beautiful. Yes, she felt at home with his body. But in a conversation, in a fight especially, his head seemed to loom like the bow of a great ship plowing toward her, and there she was, just a girl in a life preserver out of her depths.

"I have my reputation to think of," she said as if to the farmer outside, or to the farmers of her past where such things like reputations mattered. She had been loyal to Max. A year was a long time, long enough to encourage if not total amnesia, at least a favorable amendment to the reputation she had gained in Vancouver. Marriage to an old man like Vancleve could not help but sponsor supplementary conduct. It was only natural, she told herself.

"I have my reputation," she repeated.

Max made no reply.

"I do," she insisted, plumping the collar of her coat up around her chin. It was a dove-gray wool coat trimmed with silver fox—the collar was especially showy. Max had given it to her for Christmas, or rather, he had given her the money for it, because it would not do for him to be seen purchasing items in a women's department for anyone but his wife.

"Help keep me proud, honey—it's my life blood, you know."

His words were always so high-minded, so *elevated*, and they almost never failed to inspire Kate with a sense of her own importance to Max, of the essential role she must—and would—play in his entrepreneurial success. He was always telling her how smart she was, smarter than Dot, smart in a business sense, and he even implied that they might be partners some day, not just lovers who were married.

"Max," she said, huddling her hand beneath his, thinking about pride and happiness, but mostly about how long she had waited and how much she wanted this man with his vision, this man's man, "I'm going to have your child."

"What?" He twisted toward her, slopping hot coffee on his slacks.

"A son."

"How can you know this?"

He was excited, clearly excited, but not necessarily angry ... there was a chance she could hold her own, make it work, this dangerous ruse. "The doctor says he can always tell."

"You've been to a doctor? What doctor?"

"Someone out of town, in Everett." A choking sound escaped her throat. "Don't worry," she added, feeling hurt and faintly sickened, and making sure he could hear all of it, "I was careful."

Wyman looked out the window as if searching for the responsible party. Wispy veils of fog drifted by, and now and then seagulls swung down or popped up, trying to keep pace with the ferry. Beneath his crooked nose a sheen of perspiration had developed despite the cold drafty lounge. His head seemed smaller now, a buoy in rough seas. "Well, what do you intend to do, Riley?" She knew that he called her Riley whenever he wanted to invoke the prairie pragmatist in her, which he regarded the source of her natural business acumen. There was something in his voice, too, a suppressed quality, as if he had had to wrestle a part of himself to the floor and clamp a hand over his own mouth.

Get pregnant, was what she thought. What she said was, "I intend to give you a son."

In not too noticeably more than nine months, Ethel Lincoln was still alive, and Max Wyman was still married, and the New York venture had been cut loose by overly cautious investors and, now unmoored, was drifting into open seas. Nevertheless, it was difficult for Kate Riley, having been raised an Irish Catholic, to have a child out of wedlock, and it was only Max's vague assurances, the fierce prohibition against abortion, and her theory about Max Wyman's susceptibility to a boy child, that persuaded her to let the pregnancy run its course. After all, she had brought it about. And so once again, she listened to a doctor urge her to give up her baby for adoption, but this time there was no question that she would keep it, not exactly *with* her but within her purview, because one day soon she and Max Wyman and the baby would be a real family.

The delivery went badly—a breach. Kate had driven herself up to Everett, the contractions gaining with each mile beyond Seattle. The emergency room staff put her on a gurney and wheeled her in. There was a lot of blood loss; four transfusions; shadowy figures scurrying about the delivery room, smells that made her afraid. Doctor Fallon had had to yank the baby out by one foot, the other foot wedged up by the head, further jamming the birth canal. Phyllis had come down from Vancouver and was with her for the twenty-seven hour ordeal, but Max didn't show up until it was all over because he'd gotten into a fight with one of his chefs who retaliated by quitting one hour into a Saturday night shift, and Max had had to throw on an apron and work the stove himself.

"We almost lost her," Fallon told Max as the two of them stood at the foot of Kate's bed, arms crossed, each defensive for utterly different but wholly male reasons. Kate was groggy, but she could hear them. Opening her eyes, she made out two blurry shapes, black for Max's suit and white for the doctor in his lab coat, and she managed to raise her forearm, the one with the blue tag tied around the wrist, blue for boy, and jiggle her wrist, displaying her new trinket. Later when they were alone, Max sat on the edge of her bed, fingering one of the tubes attached to her arm and gazing out the windows at the lesser lights of Everett where his mistress had had to come to bear his child. Maybe it had gotten a lot more serious than he ever imagined; maybe he had let things slip away from him. This unmeant affair had produced a baby, and a baby could complicate into a promise, and more than that, this girl had nearly died and that in itself cast into the sea of his future a debt, a hook, he would be hard put to escape—or so were the thoughts Kate made up for Max as he sat in ponderous silence. A disagreeable blend of cooking odors clung to the fabric of his suit, but it only made her glad for the silent testimony it offered—that he had come directly from the club, that he loved her. There were tears in his eyes, and it was this she took as irrevocable proof that he would be hers. It made nearly dying worth it—and nearly dying became that day, and for all the days and men to come, an unexpected and surprisingly effective weapon in the mêlée of love.

"Mum always said I was a survivor," she murmured, at last able to relax.

Kate named her second son David, after Max's father, a beautiful infant with dark hair like Max's, dark blue soulful eyes, and the ruddy cheeks of an Irish ancestry. He was so beautiful that people stopped to say things to her in the market, or in the out-of-town restaurants—the Marysville Pie Place, the Clamdigger

Café in Mukilteo, the Snoqualmie Falls Diner—where she and Max Wyman and the baby met secretly as a little family. But the baby did not live with her in the apartment, or even later in the bungalow Kate purchased on a 3 percent loan up in Montlake, one of the tonier districts. Father O'Driscoll—another priest, another country, another celibate charmed by Kate's strange mix of sensuous narcissistic ferocity and blind gullibility—helped her place the infant with a couple.

The Wheatons took in children for money, but it was obvious that the work was not work at all, it was a way of requiting some of their oversized longing for children, for they could have none of their own. They were caring for seven when David arrived, the eldest being five years old, and the youngest—David—six weeks. In a spacious sunny room on the second floor of their big brick house, five cribs and three cots lined up four to a side, and at the foot of each stood a doll's cradle, blue for the boys and pink for the girls, each one made and painted by Dick Wheaton. When David came to live with them, Mrs. Wheaton cut out his name in gold letters from a fancy lettering book and applied them to the cradle employing a process she seemed fond of pronouncing—découpage. The Wheatons were simple people who had come into a modest sum when the elder Wheaton passed on. Now Dick did not need to work the counter at the family's hardware business off 34th; he could hire managers and spend most of his days with the children.

There was another feature of David's prettiness, a secret consequence of which only Kate had knowledge, and this was the way in which it served to affirm, even to (obliquely) commend the decision she had made nine years earlier, to give up the girl child whose blindness practically assured homeliness. If David's charms and good looks embodied all that was right about Kate and Max and their future, then that first baby by contrast came to represent a sort of cosmic gaffe, the memory, with the baby herself, more properly abandoned as swiftly as possible.

Kate brought the new baby home on weekends, not every weekend, but enough, she hoped, to remind Max that he had an obligation, that they had a future, that it was marriage and legitimization she desired, not just good times, as good as they were she was quick to avow. For at last Kate had found a man to whom she believed she would be faithful, though it was not something he mentioned, or ironically, seemed to require, and Kate's conclusion blurred into yet another assumption—that he took it for granted that she was his and his alone. Still, she found herself waiting again for Max Wyman, this time in closer proximity than Vancouver and the stuffy confines of her first marriage, but nevertheless, still waiting—for a death, a divorce, a deal to pan out.

Whenever she was with the baby she introduced herself as Mrs. Riley, and she insisted on the same veneer of courtesy even with the Wheatons, despite the fact that they were well aware of the circumstances. She was already counting on the wished-for future, assigning it both weight and credence, while the present kept cropping up like an inconvenient chore she must simply slog through.

Kate decided that she rather liked this new boy, this David; he was so pretty to look at, and—as her mother used to say—he cleaned up nice. At the Bon Marché she found darling little sailor suits, tiny camel's hair coats with leather buttons, doll-sized suspenders and perfectly dear bow ties that, when she clipped them under his chin, brought Christmas and presents instantly to mind. She used bobby pins to create a curl that lay against his pale forehead like a detached talon, and sometimes for effect, she painted his bow-shaped mouth with pink lipstick. One of the professional photographers to whom she had taken the baby asked if he might use David's image in his advertisements, but Kate had had to refuse, owing to the circumstances. "We are private people," she told the man, almost oblivious now to the lies she traded in, and went on to intimate that there was a considerable fortune in the family and that they had to be careful, if he understood what she meant. The man gazed at David with fresh interest, perhaps images of the Lindbergh baby coming to mind.

The baby bubbled and gurgled and laughed freely, a magical creature, and once he had learned to wave, he waved at one and all. The Wheatons came to adore him and several times had discreetly inquired of Father O'Driscoll about the mother's plans and the likelihood of their success. O'Driscoll, thinking Kate might be interested, even relieved, conveyed their "willingness" to raise the child themselves. Kate threatened to take the boy away entirely if they didn't stop "sniffing around like stray dogs," anticipating her failure. Because that was how she thought of it—failure. If Wyman did not leave his wife and marry her and give her the life her dreams described and that everything about him seemed to forecast, the travel and shows, the fancy people with money and influence, the big wide world, why, it would be the end, that was all there was to it. The end of everything. Sometimes she felt as if she had drifted into some backwater off life's expanse like a wooden decoy, trying to keep Max attracted, dreaming of being real, of flying off into a widening sky . . .

As for Kate's everyday ideals, the things she dreamed of, the objects she craved, the stuff that gave shape and definition to her new American identity, they no longer belonged to her prairie past or even to the long arm of her Irish heritage, except in cherished bits of nostalgia; they were lashed entirely to the bow of a booming, fast-paced, and largely directionless modern culture plying through time like a gassed-up cutter. Seattle was a blue-collar town with white collar ambitions in a nation making up for the denials of war, and before that, the shortages of the Great Depression, a nation not only hungry for glitter and gleam, but self-righteously demanding it, never mind the moral detractions, the acquisitiveness. It promoted advertisement from seedy back pages to canonical, glossy spreads depicting not merely what one should want, but the very image and embodiment of dream. Even Kate's femininity was constructed of prescribed fancies and incoming purchases—lacy nighties, mink stoles, the bright chunky glass of costume jewelry, Dior perfume and a Hamilton watch, patent leather pumps, cashmere sweater sets—whose allure was defined by the same unruly and unexamined cultural momentum. A shifting mosaic of magazines occupied the foot of her bed, pages torn out or their corners turned down, a dress or a pair of strappy shoes having caught her eye, or quite often merely the expression of pouty authority worn by some billowy-chested model with a waistline Kate could only yearn for retrospectively, after two pregnancies. Three, she reminded herself, not without a trace of surprise even, but only to strengthen her excuse. Otherwise, her mind flinched reflexively at the memory of that time, of Jan and what might have been, of the girl she used to be and would never again be. It was all part of a life that was worthy of nothing less than total rejection.

This waiting for Max Wyman, though, was not exactly the good life. Each morning she went to the bank. The others—the tellers, the assistant managers—they had surmised, with Kate's subtle collaboration, that she was involved with a married man. As for her reputation, Kate thought being with Max Wyman, a man admired in Chamber of Commerce circles as an entrepreneur, to some extent made up for the fact that he happened to be married. So while she didn't flaunt it, she also undertook only minimally to conceal the relationship. Sometimes at lunch they met in a restaurant, small and shabby, south of downtown, which no one he knew frequented, where her arms stuck to the oilcloth and her hair acquired the smell of a deep fryer. Or he came by her bungalow in the late afternoon before the dinner hour at the Magic Inn commenced. She was usually tired from the day's work, already bracing not for his arrival, which was as easy as a daydream, but for his looming departure, which came so quickly and left her feeling so empty, the door clicking shut, the hum of the refrigerator expanding into the silence like a slow alarm to which she must respond. And he was always entirely sober then, politely authoritative, almost effeminate in his way, teaching her how to touch him, the small place underneath made for the tip of her tongue, the soapy play afterward in the shower. It was better late at night after the club had closed, when he had had perhaps a drink too many, when he was rough and pawing at her, when he might tie her hands behind her back and inspect her leisurely, a boy who has cornered some lesser creature, and something in the feel of his belt cinched about her wrists, and his greedy fingers thrusting inside to determine her state of readiness and then the stumbling ursine accuracy of his entrance, erection gliding instantly to the deep, matched exactly an unnamed need of her own to be possessed not by an animal, but by a man who has let himself become one in her presence.

One day Janis Wheaton stopped referring to David's age in months. Kate had just arrived, wearing a tailored tweed suit and a silk scarf tied about her red hair, ready to take the baby home and dress him up for Max, who had said he would come over. It was the baby's birthday—April fifth. After trying the front door she found Janis with the children in the Wheaton's unruly backyard, the sweet April grass not mowed in order to enhance games of hide-and-seek. David sat at Janis's feet with another child, Hilary, a year older, and the two were tugging petals from daisies, one at a time, approximating "loves me, loves me not" in the grave voices of tots putting love to the test for the first time. Janis told one of the older children to watch the others, then she rose from the back porch, carrying David. "He's three years old," Janis said simply on their way out to the drive. And suddenly the baby was not a baby, not a newish contingency, an open question, but a three-year-old fact occupying real space and taking up real time in Kate's life. "We have to return him, Mrs. Riley. At the end of the summer."

"No," Kate replied as if there were an option and practically dazed by the news that this outsider, this glorified babysitter, dared to deliver.

Janis Wheaton held David on her hip, and he in turn clung to her like a playful monkey, tangling his fingers in her long hair until she jiggled them free and kissed his naughty fist. She was a real plain Jane, her face a mass of freckles and her voice so soft Kate wondered how she always managed to keep the eight children in line. David grabbed her hair again, and again Janis teased his curious hand away. It did not bother Kate to see her son in another woman's arms, for she felt flattered by his attractiveness to others, and the love this barren couple were willing to waste on her child was another measure of Kate's worth, another feather in her cap. "Dick and I, we're very fond of Davy," Janis said, squeezing his pale thigh gently, the skin revealing a bluish map of tender veins, the baby fat lingering, reluctant to abandon the job of protection. "Too fond," she murmured, as if to chastise herself.

"But we are not ready," Kate said, employing an imperious tone and futuristic "we" intended as usual to keep the Wheatons in their place, to remind them that they were, in effect, employees of the future Mr. and Mrs. Max Wyman.

"Mrs. Riley . . . Kate," the woman began, "we are so awfully fond of your Davy."

"He is darling," Kate admitted, and she blew him a big kiss, marveling at the boy's superiority and the fat sweet way it embodied her assessment and her vision of life with Max Wyman — its *rightness.*

"We've considered the boy, all along." With obvious unwillingness, Janis held David out for his mother to take. "We've got to think of ourselves now. We've feelings, too, Mrs. Riley."

"That's all you have," Kate said, suddenly intensely furious, blind with fury, the place between her eyes going red, her hand shaking as she shoved the boy into the backseat and slammed the door. David began to whimper. "We had a deal." She flung herself into the driver's seat and started up the engine.

"Wait, wait . . ." In Janis Wheaton's eyes great tears welled so that even Kate could not help but see through the watery magnification how beautifully and unequivocally blue they were. A pale hand flew up, swiping the tears away.

"I'll send for his things," Kate said, staring straight ahead, now not deigning to observe Janis Wheaton in her diminished state.

"But the end of the summer, the end of summer will be fine . . ."

"You had your chance," Kate spat out. She twisted round to David and her voice, straining to sound soft and sad, betrayed a fierce tension: "She doesn't want you anymore, David. Do you understand? She loves you not." The child gave himself over to anarchic wailing as his mother shifted into reverse and let the heavy black Oldsmobile glide like a loaded hearse back down the Wheaton's drive and onto the dark asphalt slick with rain water. Kate glanced up toward the brick house where Janis Wheaton still stood, one bare arm thrust out and her fingers darting forth, as if to catch hold of Davy before he sank from sight.

Kate drove along the tree-lined streets listening to the baby's lament, to the comforting *shush* of the tires through rain water, and inside, something warm twisted up from her past, frightening and close, tangled with odors, like an embrace one longs for but that threatens to undo once it has been attained, or perhaps only the first false breath of spring across a numbed winter landscape; there had been so many on the Prairies, Chinooks come whispering down off the eastern slopes of the Rockies, pretending to a season and a mood that could not be sustained; still it had been welcome, the dream, the illusion, and she pulled to the curb, turned and placed her open palm against the child's warm wet cheek. He had lain down on the seat, curled into his grief, and the undersides of his white booties faced her like two supplicant hands warding off a blow. With hardly any hesitation he nuzzled against her fingers, snot smearing, but the closeness was too close for Kate, the snot unappealingly slimy, and she remembered that he was probably crying not for her but for Janis Wheaton. "Stop it," she told him, "you're only feeling sorry for yourself. What about me? What am I going to do with you now? This could ruin everything, do you realize? Everything."

At home just before Max arrived she developed abdominal pains, which, it occurred to her, might at least soften the news. But he was angry, particularly because Kate hadn't optimized (his word) the child's time with the Wheatons. "You could have had until September. Four more months. What were you thinking, Riley?"

In silence she sliced Max a piece of the birthday cake. Worn out from his crying, David had already fallen asleep on the living room rug among his new Lincoln Logs and a coloring book. In the background an episode of *Romper Room* was showing on the television. "She insulted us."

"Us?"

"She implied we weren't going to be married."

"Look," he said, forking cake into his mouth, "that's not important. You've got to find someone to take the kid."

"The baby."

"Kid, baby, he's got to go somewhere. What're you going to do Monday morning when they expect you at the bank? And what about the fair? It opens on the twenty-first. You're a part of that now, I need you there. Did you think of that when Janis Wheaton insulted you?"

"Us." She had been clearing dishes, but she returned to the table, sat down opposite him and candidly regarded Max Wyman and the life he portended for her, for them. Maybe he's lying, she thought. Maybe he's been lying all along. "You're right," she said. "He's a kid now. Three years old. Your son."

Max threw down his fork. Afraid to look at him, afraid of his temper, his enormous hands, his face like a boulder coming eerily alive, she watched the fork skitter across the table and onto the floor. "Is this just another excuse to push me or did she really insult you, Riley? And since when did you become so thin-skinned?" He went and stood over the child who had fallen asleep so instantly that there were several Lincoln Logs trapped under his face. Squatting beside him, Max used his finger to wiggle the pieces out, the other hand, large and tender, about the boy's head, lifting it slightly, as if testing a melon for ripeness. "At any rate," he said, straightening, his voice muted by the small dark-haired presence slumbering at his feet, "it's done. Call the priest."

"Father O'Driscoll?"

"Use your Irish charm again. Maybe he knows someone else. There's too much at stake right now. I've got half my net worth invested in this Century 21 deal. It's only a six-month fair; it'll be over in October. I thought you wanted to be a part of it, the World's Fair, the restaurant. I made you a part of it. This is what you said you wanted. Your timing couldn't be worse, Kate. You know I love you and David, and I have every hope that we can be together one day, but it can't be rushed. I wish things were different . . . maybe after this project it will be. There is too much at stake. Why can't you understand that? What will it take for you to understand?"

As if to punish him, to preclude the intimacy she longed for, Max wanting her, Max needing her, and her briefly and rapturously in power, she hurried to the bathroom, suffering a sudden bout of diarrhea. Wyman had never been much of a nurse, she knew, certainly nothing like Gregor who had always been so caring, so attentive to her physical needs, but Max did get her into bed, and he found some aspirin, insisting that four were what he took for pain of any sort. Then he left — an hour before he even needed to leave. The front door clicked shut and the sudden silence of the house exploded around her. She unfolded herself from the bed and padded out to the front hall to throw the latch, and then on the way back she stopped in the bathroom to examine herself in the mirror. It had been a long day, Friday balances due at the bank, Janis Wheaton's announcement, the argument with Max. Her eyeliner looked positively neon, her eyes stark and staring, and from her pale skin they seemed to protrude with a chilling insistence, though it wasn't clear what they demanded. "Well no wonder," she told the mirror as she rummaged for her brush in the cabinet drawer. "No wonder he was so impatient." She tidied and pinned her hair, squeezed her cheeks to rouse some color; she tried out a few saucy expressions, but none of it undid the way she appeared to herself, none of it chased off the apparition gazing back at her. "You," she finally said under her breath, tears coming now, at last, tears she had wanted to shed since Janis Wheaton had had to tell her how old her own son was. "You bitch."

Ramona Moon stared with spiteful satisfaction, having usurped the lovely sprightly Kate long enough to have alienated Max. He would not have left if it hadn't been for Ramona peeking through the curtains, Kate was sure of that.

In the cabinet she found some Pepto-Bismol and took the recommended dose, even though the diarrhea seemed to have passed. Back in her bedroom she dug the notebook out from under her lingerie in the top dresser drawer and, noting the date and time as the doctor had suggested, she recorded the abdominal pains, the diarrhea, the four aspirins, and the two teaspoonfuls of Pepto-Bismol, and at the conclusion of the entry she wrote, *I may not have a bowel movement tomorrow morning because of this, maybe pick up some Metamucil?*

Monsignor O'Driscoll was not happy about the Wheatons. "Frankly, Kate, this fellow of yours had better fish or cut bait." O'Driscoll was a big easy man who had come to the priesthood late enough to have had a hefty serving of life in the real world beforehand, and in fact had been married and widowed. He treated Kate like an inexperienced niece requiring extra firm avuncular guidance—exactly the quality of concern she'd had in mind.

"I never told you," Kate said, pausing, letting her hands drape delicately over the arms of the chair in which she sat opposite his desk. The chair was like something out of a museum where they staged the rooms of royalty, dark walnut and massive, each arm ending in a broad carved curling feather that created an ample resting place for the palm of a hand, and in its palatial embrace Kate felt herself to be more than she actually was, more important, more lovely. She caressed the wood as she conjured a dramatic pause to rise and fill up the space between them.

"Told me what?"

"His wife is sick. Very sick. She's been dying all this time. He doesn't want to abandon her."

O'Driscoll sighed heavily and squeezed his jowls. His fingernails were pinkly clean and looking at them, Kate experienced a sudden and complete relief—this man would help her. And in fact what he said was, "Ah, I suppose that does change matters some."

Occasionally Kate noticed that she was practically oblivious to the commerce of lies that funded her needs, whatever they may be. Did it matter whether it was the wife or the wife's mother who was sick, so long as a vague mist of factuality emerged, enough to lend strength to her tone of voice, a steadiness to her gaze as she delivered it? "She has a disease, a rare disease . . ."

He stopped her with a gesture, his hand open, his eyes shut. "No, no, don't tell me. I have enough to be praying for." Then he was scribbling on a pad. "There is a place, Sacred Heart Villa, west side of the lake . . ." He slid the piece of paper across his desk and stood. "I'll have Louise draft a letter."

Kate stood, too, feathering her fingers against her chest. She had on a pair of white gloves, the kind girls wore to church and teas—one of several measures she had enlisted that morning in the hope of encouraging paternal leniency. Because there was more and more she simply could not admit aloud to herself and which she blamed on Ramona Moon sitting in her chair at the back of the room, always there now, it seemed, watching, watching. "Father, I have to be at work on Monday morning. A letter won't arrive in time."

It was then that he regarded her with genuine dismay, his head assuming a slow admonitory tilt as he searched for words. "This child is your son, Kate Riley. You have a maternal responsibility. Your employer will understand, sure he will."

"They don't know. I can't tell them. You see, I just can't. I know you understand. My reputation . . . and the shame, Father. The shame."

Now it was Father O'Driscoll who seemed to be cultivating silence. Finally he lumbered over to his office door and opened it for her. He had bad knees and preferred to sit, but he never failed to rise to the occasion of door-opening for Kate. "The Wheatons are good people," he told her before she left. "Think about it, Kate. For the sake of the lad."

Her feathered fingers contracted in a spasm of utter fear, her hands dropped like two dead birds caught by the same load of shot. "Without David, without a son . . . well, he might not marry me then."

Again O'Driscoll regarded her, this time with impatience and pity.

She could not stand pity.

"He might not ever marry you," said the priest.

In his official letter to the nuns, a copy of which Kate received by post, O'Driscoll implied that Sacred Heart would be a temporary solution to a temporary situation, that the young lady, Miss Kate Riley, had slipped on Life's path and needed now a helping hand and "our prayers." Early on the following Wednesday morning—she'd had the boy for four days straight and was exhausted—Kate bundled up David in his camel's hair coat with its matching cap, a white shirt and a red bow tie, and found her way to Sacred Heart Villa. It was located atop a hill that ran down to Lake Washington through several hundred acres of untended land, much of it choked with blackberry bushes or impenetrable thickets of young Douglas fir and underbrush, though here and there a narrow, well-trodden path offered some relief, a reminder that civilization roared on beyond the iron gates and stone walls. The paths were used by the nuns for walking contemplation and prayer and, when weather permitted, by the children who raced down to the lake to wade about of an afternoon, and then wandered back slowly, picking blackberries that Mrs. Binkley, the cook, served up with heavy cream. There were two structures, a five-story brick main building and an L-shaped addition that housed the nuns, some of them in cloister, as well as the kitchen and cafeteria, winter playrooms, and classrooms for the older students. Sacred Heart served as a nunnery, a day school for kindergarten through grade six, and on a minimal basis, as an orphanage. There were a dozen or so female orphans, all ages, and fewer males, around eight. The dormitories for the orphans were separated by gender and building, the boys living on the fifth floor of the old brick building, and the girls on the bottom far end of the L-addition.

Kate followed the drive that wound up toward the imposing brick edifice of Sacred Heart, looming atop its solitary hill, overshadowing even the great old monkey tail trees that milled about the sloping lawns, waggling their boughs in the breeze. Toward the top of the drive the hedge that lined both sides had gone so long untrimmed that it had joined its other half to form an arching green tunnel hardly wide enough to accommodate Kate's Oldsmobile. When it emerged and drew to a stop before the steps she felt anxious, her hands trembling, as if the tunnel might prevent her from returning to the real world. Upward again, mounting the steps that led to yet another daunting structure—the double doors of Sacred Heart, carved and painted a glossy black with an enormous brass knob centering each—she squeezed David's hand, afraid for him, afraid of what she was about to do, afraid of her temper that had deprived him of the Wheatons. But he was hers, after all, an innocent, a pretty boy. And now, possibly her best bet, so far as Max Wyman was concerned. But what could he want from her that he did not already possess? I have nothing left to offer, she thought with creeping panic. And the possibility that she might fail to capture Max worked its way into her brain until she could feel its presence like an iron wedge driven by Fate itself and rending her even more completely into Kate Riley and Ramona Moon.

Mother Statnekov was in charge of the orphan boys, a tall, dour woman in a black habit from whose fabric the smell of wax emanated—one of her jobs was to light and snuff the candles for mass. Beneath Mother Statnekov's gray eyes, like smears of soft brown dirt, lay permanent shadows, a pinched nose, and a long lower lip that wavered unnaturally and that brought to mind earth worms some boy's shovel had exposed to light. It was impossible to guess how old she was, but everything about her seemed ashen and half-lit, as if she were only reluctantly present in her own life and too much had been required of her already. In her mind Kate tried to piece together a line that might amuse Max later on, something about blushing brides of Christ—she was always trying to make him laugh—but in the somber surroundings her usually quick wit stumbled into submission.

She set the boy's suitcase down in the black marble foyer and actually mustered the courage to pause and to consider its small packed solitude. It wasn't even a new suitcase; one of the tellers at the bank had offered it around and Kate had snatched it up. She introduced herself. Mother Statnekov nodded and tucked her pale hands inside the tunnels of her great sleeves—to prevent contact with a practicing woman of the world, Kate thought. The room was cold and silent, the ceiling a high carved affair from which an enormous cyclopean globe hung down, inserting itself. It seemed as if the world did not exist or could not exist, that simply by stepping through those two black doors the world had wheeled off and away, never to reappear. Kate was desperate to hurry things along. To get it over with.

"Did, did you receive a letter?"

"Monsignor O'Driscoll has informed us of the boy's circumstances. And yours," Mother Statnekov added, lifting a scant eyebrow, a mere cinereal wisp of smoke.

The color rose to Kate's cheeks. "I'm grateful for your help."

There were two sets of stairs that climbed from opposite sides of the foyer, a grand white marble staircase, its polished oaken banister winding gracefully around the first landing and on up, and a second narrower stairway constructed of pine or fir, the finish worn to gray, a simple iron banister. It was these from which Mother Statnekov had descended, Kate supposed, because the nun stood with her back to them, guarding against intrusion. Maybe up those stairs were the rest of the nuns, hiding from the public, from parents of children, from the unkept promises of ripening fruit and morning light and handsome smiles. Nothing lasted, nothing could hope to last, not in this world. Being a nun was a pretty safe bet; at least you knew that what you waited for would eventually arrive. Or if it didn't, if was all just nothing and nothingness, you wouldn't be in any position to know how wrong you'd been anyway.

Between the two staircases stood a life-sized statue of Jesus, the drapes of His robes open at the chest where in His left hand He held His own heart, as though He Himself had plucked it from its fleshy niche. The heart was not only larger than it ought to have been and alarmingly realistic in form, but painted a deep burgundy and dripping plaster droplets of blood down the unyielding fabric. A gilt cross bound up the organ, as if to contain it or prevent it from sloshing apart. His other hand was raised in blessing, His eyes were dewy, His long chestnut hair as sweetly disheveled as a young woman just awakening.

The boy was staring with obvious horror.

"Do you plan to visit?" Mother Statnekov was inquiring.

"I hadn't thought about it, but yes, of course," she said, and she fingered David's hair. "He'll come home now and then, on week-ends." Thrusting his hand in his mother's, David began to twist up his face and whimper. Finally he swung around her body in order to keep his mother between the bloody heart and himself. Kate considered asking to see where David would sleep, maybe even the playrooms, the cafeteria, but she hoped to get to the bank on time, after missing two days, and she did not think it prudent to drag out the good-byes—as it was, the boy was about to blubber.

"You will telephone us, Miss Riley, and we will have him ready after matins." Then she reached across the marble foyer and took David's hand, adjusting his body so that he stood to her side, his arm angling sharply up, like a rag doll jerked up off the floor and left hanging. "Wave good-bye to your mother, child."

And he did, his little pink fist like a heart itself, open and beating in the still air.

It was June before she returned to Sacred Heart Villa to bring David home for a weekend. Two months. School had already let out and, if it could be said, it was even quieter in the foyer as she awaited her son. The boy was quieter, too, and thinner.

"Is he eating?" she asked Mother Statnekov.

"He does not always eat lunch."

"No?"

"Tomato sandwiches."

"I'm not fond of them," David said into his mother's skirt, almost in a whisper.

Kate was delighted with this word, *fond*, so adult, so high class, and when she bent down to peer into David's blue eyes, she said, "But you're learning such nice words, Davy," then, genuinely happy with the education her son was receiving, so happy that she thought without really thinking that she could make actual requests on behalf of the child, she glanced up at the nun. "Can't he have something else, peanut butter or Spam, something easy?"

"Mrs. Binkley serves tomato sandwiches or pea soup to our orphans. That is lunch. He sees what the day-students bring and wants what they have. We do not reward envy, Miss Riley."

"No, of course not."

"There is greater variety at dinner."

"Oh, that's good then, that's nice." Wanting to move on, away from her son's transgressions, it occurred to Kate that now might be a good time to see where David slept and played, since she would be taking him home, not leaving him off. And so Mother led them up the white marble stairs to the fifth floor and down a hallway of white walls and dark wainscoting. On the east side of the hall, almost at the end, the door to the boy's dormitory stood open, a room containing a dozen or so iron beds painted a robin's egg blue, each with a white coverlet and a bedside dresser. In one corner of the room there was an alcove formed by two false walls, about ten foot high and not reaching the high ceilings—this was where Mother Statnekov slept. Along the east wall ran a bank of windows which looked down on one of the playgrounds—a cement area for ball games, a grassy bank, two swings, a sand pit—and beyond the playground, descending to the lake were the wild acres of berry bushes and fir woods. Next to the dormitory was a cavernous green lavatory smelling of ammonia, plus a narrow dressing area lined with cubbies. Both rooms were cold and impeccably tidy.

She asked David which bed was his and he went over to the one in the corner by Mother's alcove and patted its pillow. "But I'm still ascared of the leeches," he announced without apology, his voice so clear, so pure that Kate was reminded of harp music.

"Leeches?"

"We had to move him," Mother Statnekov said. "He was by the door but the nightmares . . ."

"He has nightmares?"

"It is not uncommon, Miss Riley, for children his age."

"He dreams about leeches?"

A great sigh departed Mother Statnekov. She rolled her pale hands up inside the draping sleeves of her habit and glided toward the door, meaning for them to follow. It was strange how she managed to conceal her feet even when she walked, how inside her habit her shape all but disappeared so that she was like a shadow entire that slid about, a shadow without a body to cast itself, that had been lost perhaps or rejected, and her gray face was a worn patch in the fabric of the shadow and her eyes two peep-holes to nowhere. It was only her hands that kept posing problems, that needed to be drawn back in the way one might call back wayward children. "Mrs. Binkley pulled a leech from the boy's leg several weeks ago," she said. "They had been down at the lake. There was no infection."

On the way back to the foyer they stopped to look into one of the upper playrooms, a large hollow brightly-lit space of white walls and wood floors and the same bank of windows staring down on the playground, the same cold inert air. In the center of the room stood three dollhouses—that was it. From each, one exterior wall was missing so that the interior rooms sat exposed to the imaginations of children enacting the lives of the little dolls. David ran to the middle house where apparently he had been occupied when his mother arrived, in order to show her how he had arranged the furniture and the family inside. While Mother stood in the doorway practicing patience, Kate admired his efforts—the wee chairs and tables, the blazing miniature fire of painted cardboard, the tiny terrier with its plaid collar sleeping at the foot of the boy doll's bed. On his knees, making adjustments in the postures and poses of the family, David seemed to hope that his mother might stay to play with him.

"You play with your friends here, not your mummy."

"I don't have any friends, not any," he said, not bothering even to look at her, busy with his make-believe family.

Kate rose, acutely aware of her fitted skirt, her high heels, her bare legs scissoring about in the empty room. "Doesn't he have friends? The other boys and girls?"

"Boys do not play with girls, Miss Riley. That is our rule."

"Other boys then. Where are the other boys?"

Mother Statnekov fixed her eyes on some spot down the hall as if she were speaking to someone else, an underling who had just arrived with an idiotic question. "School concluded two weeks ago. The preschoolers and kindergarteners do not return until September. Our male residents . . ." Here she paused to study Kate, and something in Kate's expression prompted a revision. "The younger orphans are favored for adoption. David is not available for adoption. Because of your circumstances. Though we have had inquiries, Miss Riley, from respectable families, yes, we have had inquiries. As for the boys that remain, they are all at least five years older than David. This time of year we encourage them to take their recreation outside. They prefer it." After a moment she added, "Naturally they are not interested in dollhouses and other indoor divertissement."

The boy was listening, humming a song, maybe "Twinkle, twinkle . . . ," Kate wasn't sure, nursery tunes and rhymes had always annoyed her. She was feeling dizzy, even remotely queasy. The room was so bare, so cold. Mother Statnekov's formality was making her feel very bad somehow, everything was so tidy and smooth and perfectly sorted out, perfectly explainable. She did not belong here, not in a place like this, not even for the few minutes it took to gather her son, even though there were strong hands still reaching up from her Irish Catholic past, grabbing hold of a foot now and then and tugging her down into the ancient bog of shame. It was all on account of Kate needing to be a woman in full measure. This nun—why, she wasn't a woman and she didn't want to be a woman; she had renounced all that, the animal side, and Kate, too, what she represented, normal natural interactions, beauty, femininity, love. Could it be that she was jealous, that around a woman like Kate, Mother Statnekov regretted what she had forsaken? Or was it only that she had been an ugly girl who had suffered a *disappointment* long ago, as Kate's mother liked to say? *The lass had a disappointment.* And how was this nun, this self-neutered creature, with boys, if she had turned from what they were as potential, what they must become some day? Of course she would be kind, of course she would do the right thing, but there was none of Janis Wheaton's foolish adoration. "Come on, Davy," she said, thrusting out a trembling hand, "it's time to go."

"Minute," he said, making several final adjustments in the dollhouse characters. "It's breakfast and they have to all go to the kitchen because they said matins and washed behind their ears and now they can have Cheerios." He brought the father down the stairs, tapping his rigid plastic feet on each tread, then the daughter and son, followed by the terrier who rocked from step to step, barking through David. Mother doll was already in the kitchen, propped against the toy stove. Once he had them composed in a happy circle about the dining room table David clambered to his feet and fled the room.

Out on the brick steps that led down to the drive and through the shadowed green tunnel that was the untamed hedge, Mother Statnekov removed her hands from the caves of her great sleeves and clasped them just below her waist. They were colorless hands, waxen as a figure in a museum. "You did not tell us that he was sinistral."

"Pardon me?"

"Left-handed. Sinistral," she said, but the sound of the word and the casualness with which she had released it into the air set Kate's heart to pounding.

"I guess I hadn't noticed."

A premonitory smile grazed Mother's face, vanishing before it could fulfill itself. "Well. He is learning to use the other."

"With Sally," David piped. "She has freckles. Sally and me practice stuff after lunch with our good hands and not the naughty ones, not ever the naughty ones." And he actually slapped his own anarchic hand, the left one he had been born to use.

Mother Statnekov said, "Sally and I." Then she turned to Kate. "They are allowed to work together, the boys and the girls, and Sally is close to David in age. Also a sinistral."

Kate did not know quite how to respond. She had never heard that being left-handed was bad or undesirable, and she felt vaguely embarrassed that David, her perfect product of a perfect and destined relationship, had exposed a flaw, particularly to Mother Statnekov. "Thank you," she said, still at a loss, "I'm so grateful for your help."

But by Monday morning, in spite of her vague concerns about the boy and his nightmares, the lack of friends, the empty room with its eerie dollhouses and doll characters waiting for some orphan's sad little commonplace dreams; in spite of Mother Statnekov's funereal ways, the other nuns who only ever nodded in passing, never spoke except to each other and then in some sort of coded Latin, she drove David back to Sacred Heart and then saw him only twice over the summer until his illness in the fall. She was busy nights and weekends working with Max at the fair, and she had naturally kept her position at the bank since the fair was only a six-month proposition, but David had to have his tonsils out. It became one of the rare occasions on which her maternal duties could not but be invoked and even required, for there was no one else legally allowed to check him into a hospital or sign off on the surgery. By then Sally was gone, adopted by a family from Moses Lake. David was quiet and reclusive. They had to search for him when she arrived. One of the novices who had not yet completely abandoned youthful intrigue or proclivities thought to lug open the bomb cellar door where she found him sitting in the dark down on the lowest step with a handful of pill bugs and a fugicle subsiding down his other arm. Mrs. Binkley had specially bought the fugicles to ease the boy's pain. "You have an owie in your throat," Kate told him in her coddling voice. He was always distressed when his mother left, but now not necessarily comforted by her return, and when she tried to kiss him he looked worried. They went directly to the pediatric ward at St. Mary's. A jolly old nurse scooped him up while Kate filled out all the forms, lying about her marital status and grilling the registrar about the cost. "Does he have to stay four days?"

Every bed in the pediatric ward was occupied. They had tucked David into the corner that had no window and when she spotted him he was staring at the wall as if to make the outside magically appear. A girl with a shaved head and enormous brown eyes followed Kate as she made her way to David's bed.

"I have to go to work," Kate told him. "You know I love you. Tomorrow after it's all over I'll visit."

"Roy Rogers is coming," the boy informed her. Again he regarded the blank wall, and with his right hand pretended to inscribe his name in large letters on the plaster.

"Aren't you lucky," Kate said, patting his leg through the covers.

Century 21 Seattle World's Fair closed at sunset on October twenty-first in a grand potpourri of music and speeches and mass maneuvers. At the end, when the ceremony was supposed to have concluded, the band began tinkering softly "Auld Lang Syne" with Patrice Munsel, the opera star, sending in her voice, and then the entire audience piled on, and even Kate and Max had tears in their eyes. It had been one hell of a run. And they had done it together, she and Max, and in public, too; after all, Kate was an official employee. Wyman called his restaurant and piano bar the Domino Club, everything done in black and white, a swank affair at the edge of Show Street, which was the adult entertainment section of the fair. It did so well that he thought he could buy out Dot's mother in the Magic Inn, provided he could keep the appraisal dipping down the low side of the ledger. Wyman worked up some black tie theme, and had Kate (twelve pounds leaner) dress up in a curvy tuxedo number that cinched in at the waist and exposed her stellar legs, and it was she who ran the piano bar, a favorite drop-in joint for Chamber of Commerce types. The Domino Club was a setting in which Kate Riley shone — the music, the dim lights, the predominantly male clientele, the interchangeable and faceless female companions, the Rob Roys and Manhattans and dry martinis like large liquid jewels gleaming about the curvaceous perimeter of the piano bar. She pulled her red hair back in a French roll, and applied a decorative mole next to her upper lip, and the fact that she had already labored most of the day at the bank, that she had blisters from wearing pumps all night, and bilious breath from the sometimes desperate measures she had to take to hold her weight down, that they often had sex on a sagging couch in the back office among cases of booze and crates of vegetables not quite spoiled enough yet to be thrown out, didn't seem to matter; she thrilled at being the Domino's grand dame and Max Wyman's right hand gal.

But when it was all over Max did not take the money and buy Ethel Lincoln out. Mrs. Lincoln, in fact, was doing well, in fact, well enough not to need her daughter's regular visits. And now it was Christmastime. Kate was still at the bank. David was up at Sacred Heart, not budging on the tomato sandwiches, not talking much at all now, a quiet introspective boy with a penchant for little live things, turtles and bugs and such, and who mostly preferred the outside now, according to Mrs. Binkley watching him from her perch on the back kitchen steps as she strung beans or peeled apples, the boy picking through the jungled ivy in the grotto of the Virgin Mary, for what he never said, never seemed to know, beetles or a nice glossy leaf, maybe a salamander, or something lost by another child, a shiny bit of toy . . . or twirling, his face skyward, beneath the apple trees with their golden fruit bobbing on the autumn gusts and overhead the heavens a savage blue.

It was Christmastime and Kate had put on a good thirty pounds and was calling in sick whenever she thought she could get away with it, holing up in her bungalow, the curtains drawn, the heat high, and the refrigerator watching with its cold and somehow malicious indifference, waiting for Kate to succumb. Again and again, as she did, as she would, as she must. Waiting for Ramona Moon to succeed, to rise as did her namesake and cast her lurid glow across the now gloaming landscape of Kate's life. She could not seem to stop thinking about herself, her plight, and at the same time she felt powerless to do anything about any of it; she was so far down that nothing seemed to warrant the least effort even to think about scratching her way back up, what she might have to do to begin the task, the first deep shudder of faith that preceded a reclamation of any sort. Whenever she had to go out she was convinced that others, even strangers, especially strangers, watched her, and that a cursory study of her face and her form communicated the dire straits in which her life had drifted, and that these people who watched and who could see were not just embarrassed for her, they were repelled. Waitresses were the worst. One day in the luncheonette at the Bon Marché around the corner from the bank she ordered a piece of banana cream pie from the petite blonde working the counter. Shirley, her nametag read. Shirley plucked the heavy restaurant crockery off her forearm where it had occupied the upper tier in a tripartite system of balance, and let the plate skid onto the Formica with a kind of bored superiority that Kate understood to be scornful of her menu choice. The slice was deliberately enormous, Kate was sure of it, intended to mock her, its custard quivering ever so abjectly from the trauma of the delivery, and the meringue slinking off the edge of the cream bed like a one-night lover escaping at dawn. She demanded to speak with the manager. Shirley scurried off, wiping her hands on her white apron. Soon, from the kitchen, Mr. Warren emerged, a lean, middle-aged low-level professional from whose pocked face small eyes peered with the weary forbearance of someone for whom there was no escape — wife, two kids, thirty-year mortgage, difficult customers.

"This girl has been very rude, very . . ." she hunted for a word that might impress the manager, "insolent. Insolent and disrespectful."

"Shirley?"

"I didn't do nothing," Shirley protested, in hiding and in tears behind Mr. Warren. "I got her pie. It was the last one so it was nice and big too."

Despite the plausible explanation, the girl had uttered the word *big*, and that was more than enough to extinguish any flicker of clemency sputtering in Kate's heart. "A big piece for a big lady? Is that what you were thinking? How dare you!"

Abruptly the manager gave a subtle nod, sending the nubile Shirley away. "Ma'am, the pie's on the house. I'll see to Shirley."

"The customer's always right," Kate murmured as she hoisted back atop the stool and snatched up her fork. Her hands were trembling, and in her chest a tight fist of emotion clenched, but by the time she had finished the banana cream pie the tension had opened out and flattened, and she walked back to the bank with a dull sense of triumph. Maybe Warren had fired the insulting bitch. Maybe she could lose the weight by New Year's. Maybe Max would not leave her.

But a strange dichotomy began to open up inside her, and in the breach she could feel a steady draft arrive from someplace distant, someplace chilly and unpleasant, issuing from a time that was lost to her. From Max, from the unrelenting situation, she was simply not getting enough; the whole thing seemed to be breaking down, the ground she had relied upon was giving way and she kept slipping, slipping. The only thing she could think of that might ward off an ultimate collapse was the attention of another man, someone who could help her hang on until Max was ready to come to her. Someone who didn't and couldn't really mean anything but who would make her feel better about herself, prettier maybe, and not so abject.

He was talking about another fair, the one coming up in New York scheduled for '63–'64. After all, he had made a killing on the Seattle fair. Fairs were the deal, he said, quick easy gold mines. He didn't have to be chained to them the way he was at the Magic Inn, despite two fairly reliable managers. "At any rate," he said, "I'm good and tired of the place, I've had bellyful of moody chefs and waitresses with their gossip and cliques, liquor orders that never show up—the whole heck of it."

So he went to New York for two weeks in order to scope things out, properties on the fairgrounds, investors, liquor laws and licenses, short-term staff, apartments. Her birthday fell during his absence, but he had penciled on some scrap paper next to the kitchen phone a schedule intended to soften the abrupt turn in events and the bad timing.

Dec. 1—whoopee—got rid of old man
Dec. 2—too tired to go any place
Dec. 3—shop for Christmas snowie suit, go see little one
Dec. 4—go to church
Dec. 5—work hard all day—mess around house all nite
Dec. 6—go to a show
Dec. 7—watch the fights for me
Dec. 8—take a bath
Dec. 9—eat fish
Dec. 10—a nite on the town
Dec. 11—better go to confession
Dec. 12—one year older—should be wiser—change to winter
        undies

Dec. 13 — damned old man returns — shouldn't have spent
      birthday that way — head feels terrible — must be the
      Asiatic flu — no?

A birthday by oneself isn't the most to be desired, dear, but
maybe it will be the last time you'll be alone — other than the
child I mean — take care of yourself.

Yes, fairs had a beginning and an end, and in between, why, the
chance to create something exciting and not have to wait around
for the excitement to die, for the deal to go stale. Plus, loads of
dough. What did she think about a Polynesian theme this time?
Palm fronds over the entrance and dresses of batik and rum drinks
with tiny umbrellas? What did it matter what she thought? It was
physically painful even to hear about his plans, the restaurant, the
exotic dresses she would never get to wear. Because, no, she could
not come with him this time. Dot would accompany him. New
York was so close to Connecticut, the girls were still in school there.
No, he would have to do this without her, it couldn't be avoided.
But he would be back. And she could visit. He would arrange for
a hotel when his wife was off with the girls, he would take her to
Lutèce, a Broadway show, the top of the Empire State Building. Of
course it would be ludicrous for Kate to give up her position at the
bank. "At any rate," he said (Max was always beginning sentences
with *at any rate*), "it's not forever."

"It's not forever," she said aloud into the bedroom gloom. The
sheets of her bed were white with a lavender rose print, but in the
late twilight the roses were almost black and ominous in their insistence, cropping up everywhere she looked, her head on the pillow, the blackish-purple roses like an infection of boils or lesions,
of love gone rotten. Their sheets, their bed, their home, their future. On the bureau a dull mist of dust had gathered. The morning
following his departure she had cut her finger with the discarded
blade to his razor just to watch the blood, red and insistent, blooming on her skin until finally it let go and fell to the bureau top. Now

the small lump of clotted blood was itself dusty, the color having vanished like the color of the roses into the murk of the room.

"I'm sick," she had told him.

"Go to a doctor," he had said.

It was one of the things that had never worked with Max Wyman, getting sick. It had elicited attention, concern, time from Gregor Vancleve, and before that from Jan, and usually, because Fiona had been a nurse, from her mother, and always, always from Poppy whose love was true. But Max was only receptive to her body's charms, not its problems — her stomach pains and headaches and intestinal ragings, which he regarded as so many impractical blunders, slip-ups that were best papered over, even (*oh*, she could tell, she could see it) as annoying and inconvenient impositions, subtractions from his gift of time to her. Of which he had so little, he seldom failed to remind her. The only thing that had ever worked with him had been the baby and almost dying at his birth — that had got his attention. Having a baby couldn't work again, though, of that she was more than convinced.

During his absence a letter arrived:

Dear Kate,

It's been little over a week but my thoughts have been of us. I still believe there is a chance for us if you can wait. This is an awful lot to expect or ask, but it must be this way — maybe I must prove something — that I can exist on my own in business — maybe that I'm really loved (for me alone).

What do you think about moving back to Canada? You need family and friends.

The time I've asked for is necessary — win or lose. I wish I'd never experienced doubts — things and thoughts would be so much easier to analyze.

I do love you and the boy.

All my love,
Max

Doubts. It was the first time he had used this word, and reading it again, and then again, she felt a queasy weight form in the bottom of her stomach.

The manager at the Bank of Commerce was given to understand that Kate had the Asiatic flu, and after several days she began to feel as though she did in fact have the flu, or something similar. Frequently in the mornings she wrote in the notebook, because she was worried about herself, because there was no one else who worried now, not her mother, not Jan, not Gregor, not even the afternoon men who used to summon enough concern to earn the tacitly promised favors in return.

> Dec. 2 — 2 bowel movements — normal — got up 6 or 7 times
>   at night to urinate (?)
> Dec. 5 — strong pains in legs and calves — 4 aspirin — bad
>   diarrhea
> Dec. 6 — explosive diarrhea — saw Dr. Ignatius
> Dec. 9 — fast pulse 115+, then down to 90's — is this normal?
> Dec. 11 — saw Dr. Kaye about sore hands — took x-rays
> Dec. 12 — bladder attack
> Dec. 13 — jumpy and throbbing over breast bone

Yes, it was Christmastime and again she was alone. Even Gregor had given up trying to interest her in visits with Brendan, eleven years old now and accustomed to a motherless world. Fiona was still living at the Hotel York in Winnipeg and seemed at last to have abandoned trading on the old guilt, or trying to lure Kate back to Canada in order to resuscitate the illusion of familial love. Her communications, usually written on the free stationery provided by the Ladies' Lounges of department stores, Eaton's or The Bay, were brisk penciled laments that seemed to presume a wider audience, the others who peopled life-in-general and who had, as a group, profoundly disappointed Fiona Riley. Colin and his family had moved to Edmonton because his wife had been diagnosed with multiple sclerosis and needed to be close to more advanced treatment centers. Kate sent them money and goods now and then, but it seemed to bother her sister-in-law and to mystify Colin.

I can't for the life of me see why you are always so concerned about me, *he wrote in his last letter*. I've never been especially kind or thoughtful of you, always too busy or some other thing and it just makes me ashamed to see how wonderful you have been to us. But after all, Kate, you're young and you won't always be. For goodness sake, take a little time to enjoy yourself and live! Of course I know what your answer will be before I even write this down, you'll say that this is your enjoyment, and Oh, Kate, I can't tell you how we love you for your pure unselfish self. I remember a lot of things that you don't remember, when you were a very little girl. I remember how Dad worshipped you, and yet there was never any jealousy, I knew that this was quite normal, that after all you were a little girl. Our Dad was the best, Kate, I don't know whether you can understand that, you were very young, and of course I was young enough too. I have many regrets that I could have shown him, I could have really let him know how well I understood and loved him. When I think of then and now, I feel very unhappy and I wonder if some day I'll regret not being more understanding and patient with Mother. But you know Kate, as much as my heart aches and as much as I worry for Mother, I don't think I'll ever have any regrets. I've tried to love her but she just doesn't want it. She doesn't care about anyone but herself. Pretty harsh words but I'm afraid that's the truth.

It was a mystery to Kate as well, why she kept posting goods to Colin and his family, but something in her wanted to overwhelm them with fancy stuff from the states and her new life. She'd wrap each item elaborately so that it was easy to imagine a great fanfare upon their unwrapping, Colin and Mary and the two wee ones—well, they weren't little any more, were they? They had to be in their teens—gathered in their modest parlor, a special time having been set aside to open the big box from Aunt Kate in America, a couple of glasses of sherry perhaps, and cocoa for the kids, and outside the snow blowing across the oil fields, bleak and barren. Once she even sent them silk sheets, but it was the one gift they never mentioned, and the sheets had been dear, as Fiona used to say, yes, quite dear. Sending cheques wasn't as fun or as exhilarating, unless she could put together a conspicuously lavish amount, and then it usually took a while before the cheque cleared, because Colin and his wife would have to think about it, maybe pick it up now and then and stare at the figure, and then it might require several prompts—the fourteen-year-old's shoes that pinched, or a second notice on the heating bill, or one afternoon Mary's hand dropping and the teacup shattering and the unknowable future with MS flooding in around them with a cold implacable authority.

Colin still resembled their father, though he wasn't quite as handsome; something about the eyes . . .

But Kate never sent gifts or money to John and Vera. They had three children now, were still living in Moose Jaw, though they had moved to a larger house where each morning Vera made cinnamon buns and each night after dinner she washed and he dried, and the monthly newsletter they sent to each member of the family lay unanswered and recriminating in the kitchen drawer beneath the bills.

Christmastime and no family and no friends close enough to have extended invitations, and no man, none of the peripheral ones, either, who she used to keep just out there in the fringes, beyond deed but not necessarily beyond summon.

When Max returned from New York he arranged to spend an entire day and evening and most of the next day with Kate. Dot had taken the girls—home from school for the holidays—out to Port Angeles to visit their grandmother, and Max had invoked his two-week absence from the Magic Inn as excuse to remain in Seattle and clean up whatever disasters had developed. It was the Saturday before Christmas, bustling and festive downtown, people crushing about with packages and ruddy cheeks, kids in tow. Kate hadn't lost the weight she had gained but she had at least managed to hold it in check, enough so that she could still fit, albeit snuggly, into some of her nicer outfits. She bought a pink babydoll nightie to conceal the fat, and early in the afternoon when they were together in bed, she kept it on, so that it was only her broad peasant shoulders and her flawless legs that were fully exposed. Max said something about the weight but it was funny how she couldn't remember what it had been when they went downtown later, her arm in his and the shoeshine man looking at them the way people do at lovers, and the snow on the ground still white, still fresh. The winter light was just as bright and shiny as could be, and Max had that sexy glint of power lingering there in his dark, dark eyes. She connived—coyly —for clothes, shoes, a gold ring with a smoky topaz, but Max was entertained or at least not surprised by her vanities, her desires, which must have seemed beyond innocent in their willingness to remain untamed and naked. Swept up in the moment whose very publicness ratified the composition of each and every detail, the whole picture, she gazed at him beside her on the busy sidewalk. "You," she said with a thrill of pride.

That night after dinner at the club, the place overflowing with holiday crowds, the mood high, Kate waited outside the tall red door that had once seemed to her a trail of setting sun full of prospect on its way to the dazzling side of the world; she waited for Max to tie up the evening's loose ends and join her. It was a clear night, the stars white and hard and scattered like chips of enamel across tarred paper. The moon was not up yet, but it had waned to a mere trimming of itself and would have little effect on the starlight whose night it must be, though even their radiance was trite finally, mere bits in a patternless backdrop of cosmic monotony above the city's festive luminescence. They would go back to her bungalow, make love again if he wanted. They would sleep together—a commonplace usually denied them and perhaps appealing to Kate alone, for on the dozen or so occasions on which it had occurred, he slept almost immediately while she noted the layer of heat between his skin and hers, the discreet vibration of his breathing moving in unseeable waves across the bed, the intimate access to his breath going stale—all of it with a tenderness so acute it kept her awake hours into the night. To have this man beside her, to own him for the eight hours that he slept, vulnerable and abandoned to her, his palm lying open upon the scrambled sheets—oh, it was like a drug craved by her entire being. Perhaps she might drop her breast gently onto that oblivious palm and wait for his fingers to stir with dreamy admiration . . .

Wintry air off Puget Sound scuttled through the maze of downtown buildings, throwing up scraps of litter and bullying along the sidewalks. She hugged the fox collar of her coat to her cheeks and slung one shapely calf over another, leaning against the wall of the Magic Inn. There was a group of young people in their twenties, arms draped over shoulders, their expressions free of trouble, singing Christmas carols in a sort of stumbling unison. She was not that much older than these revelers, yet their world seemed as distant as the stars—distant and somehow trivial, and for that, amusing, a light divertissement, a skit performed solely to fill a few of Kate's moments. Diners leaving the club paused to smile; some even joined in. There was a man in a gray suit moving among them, handing out cards, but she couldn't see what they were. The red door opened and Max stepped out, pausing to tug down his cuffs and to wrap a scarf about his neck. He jerked his head, meaning for her to come over beside him, that it was safe, the red door had closed. But what did it matter? Long ago the staff had blinded itself to Max's affairs.

"Good for business," he said, nodding toward the carolers. And indeed, from the small crowd that had gathered, couples peeled off now and then, entering the club for a drink to warm themselves up.

The man with the cards approached them. Now Kate could see that he was older, maybe in his mid-seventies, his chin grizzled, his gray eyes agleam with rheum. The suit and vest were of an old style, obviously not clean, an unguinous stain down the vest front, and the jacket ashen-white along the lapels and cuff edges where it was worn, but she could see that it had once been a good proper suit, and something about its tidy narrow cut and the way the man fit inside it, comfortably and with a cute sort of pride, reminded her of Poppy and the suit he kept for special occasions and in which he had been buried. The man's smile was nice, despite the infirm air, the vague quality of weakness that hovered about the corners of his eyes, and the way his lower lip skewed down in a continuous act of remorse. Beneath all of it, deeper and stronger and conveyed in part even by his shabby appearance she sensed a bygone dignity, perhaps a scrabbling dignity but dignity, sure. Kate watched Max accept one of the small cards and read it. And then she saw his shoulders collapse slightly—the carolers were singing "Joy to the World" and there was a considerable hamming it up, with arms flung out and laughter burbling behind the lyrics—she saw and felt peripherally the collapse of his shoulders; it was so subtle and concentrated a motion that it seemed to occur within an altogether separate medium, like a viscous liquid; his broad shoulders huddling inward and his upper back dropping, as if he were accommodating a coat offered by a thoughtful host at departure. Then the slow heavy medium evaporated and there was nothing suddenly between Max and the man with the cards, not air, not space, not time. His big hands clutched him about the collar of the suit that had once been fine, and he was shaking him with animalian violence, shoving him back into the crowd of young people, who kept singing, their awareness lagging, the song—"Joy to the World"—perhaps extending the incomprehension, encouraging continued disbelief. The old man was down on the sidewalk now. Max had driven him through the group of carolers, rending them into two uneven lines. Banjo-eyed and slack-jawed, they watched with Kate, the night air gone eerie with a sickening wonder. Down on the sidewalk, crumpled up against a miniature range of dirty snow left by the city plow, the old man kept his hands up before his face. His mouth worked itself around a series of frantic shapes that might have been words, but not a sound emerged. Nothing. Max was not interested in the man's face though. He was using the tops of his wingtips, the force of his short, muscular legs, to try to dislodge him, and when some of the young people began grabbing at Max, he shrugged them off, bent down and rolled the old man out into the street. A taxi careened past the small mound of humanity, sending up a spew of liver-colored slush that seemed to hang in space, time lugged down, before splattering. Max was yelling, something about "my place" or "not in front of my place," but there was a great commotion now. At her feet the small white cards lay in a terrible configuration of lost order. She picked one up and staggered backwards to the wall, feeling through her hose the rough stone against her calves, and in her heart, something very like the shock of rough stone. The card said: "I am deaf and mute. Can you help me?"

It did not take Max long to get over the deaf mendicant. Such was the nature of both his arrogance and his fierce, almost maternal protectiveness of business. He was not bothered by the rush of young carolers who came at him, hollering, and in fact he ducked quite handily and with clear amusement the empty Fanta soda can a coed hurled his direction, her cheeks crimsoned with outrage. But it bothered Kate. Maybe she and Max were more alike than she realized, except that he had been smarter about things. Shrewder. He had cared about that deaf old beggar about as much as she had about her own baby, blind and by the very helplessness of her presence in the world, begging. Bad for business. Brendan, too, had been bad for business finally. Kate's business. Even David had not, so far, panned out as an investment. And for the first time in her life she wondered what exactly that business was—not the getting married and having a fine house and flashing about with a smart crowd—but what she was after *through* all of that, the **true** business, the final business.

Kate followed him into the bungalow and with a respectful tentativeness of which she was detachedly aware, and that suggested she was the guest, not Max, she placed her coat and pocketbook neatly in the rocker by the front door. He had flipped on the kitchen light and was rummaging for the bologna and bread, a favorite late-night snack. After the dark neighborhood streets of Montlake, the light was harshly revealing, his skin pale and where his beard was making its vain nightly appeal, bruised-looking. In the small suburban room, his head seemed even bigger than usual. Max's head was beginning to trouble her. The night before she'd had dream, a bad dream, of carrying it about—just his head, alive—under her arm and then of taking a shower and of turning the head as it sat on the tile floor away so that his eyes could not see her. The Vitalis he used each morning to form a double wave diagonally across his crown had been worn out by the day and then blown apart by the wind off the Sound, and now his hair, dyed, was almost savage in its fuliginous disorder. She remembered what Miriam had said the evening they met Max Wyman—*beau-laid*—handsome-ugly. Now what Kate saw had nothing to do with handsomeness or ugliness. Max Wyman was a presence, and that presence constituted merely a moment in the force of his momentum, a point on a long fast line. Because Max was always on his way, going somewhere, and it was the excitement of the contact with that force, that powerful trajectory, that had led Miriam and Kate and many others no doubt to mistake it for a visual impact, a look. In a man, there was something commonplace, even facile, about appearance; it was beside the point. No, the point was power, and Max had it, and Kate knew it, had always known it, obliquely and now directly, and that night desperately more than ever, which itself struck her as unwholesome, she wanted a part of it for herself, to possess.

On the Formica countertop he laid the tube of meat and cut several thick slabs, peeling the plastic skin from each using the tip of the butcher knife. Then he tore off several hunks of French bread, dropped them atop the plate of bologna, and with a weird, engorged sort of authority, collapsed into one of the leather chairs, big and black and squared at the end of the living room facing the marble fireplace. Kate had purchased the chairs because they echoed something about his character, which only now was beginning to frighten her.

Events had a way of making other events inevitable. So it was that Kate Riley discovered herself on her knees beside the black leather chair, her arms wound around his calf, her cheek pressed to the side of his shoe, still wet from the winter slush, still perhaps recalling in scuff or diminished shine the too-heavy, too-silent presence of the old man, and she heard a voice that was hers, but the words belonged entirely to Ramona Moon swelling inside her like another bad moon rising. "Please Max, please don't make me wait any longer, leave her—please. I've waited so long, I've done what you said, everything you wanted. It's my turn now. You've got to marry me, you've just got to."

Max leaned forward and set the plate of bologna and bread on the ottoman. Then he untied her arms from around his leg and carefully drew his foot away, whereupon she straightened and waddled to him on her knees, throwing her face in his lap, her hands groping blindly for a hold about his torso and finding purchase only in the loose fabric of his gabardine suit. His suits were always overly capacious, as if he were planning ahead to be larger than his life had thus far achieved. Her sobbing was utterly undisciplined, ragged and mixed up with bestial moans, but when he spoke, when he said under his breath, "For Christ's sake," she lifted her face, her misery instantly gone and something else rushing in.

He had his arms up, palms open, as if he were waiting out the attentions of a slavish dog and it was then she felt the wood hard beneath her knees. "You owe me," she said with a bolt of fury, clambering to wobbly pumps, steadying herself against the mantle.

She heard an amused, curt exhalation, a puff of derision or disgust, as he reached for the plate, one enormous hand dropping over the food, and with an uncanny gestural grace that brought to mind a grizzly delicately working the red flesh from a sockeye, still alive, still wriggling, the great hand assembled a round of bologna upon a chunk of bread. That morning, in anticipation of their night together, she had bought the items, along with a bottle of Canadian Club and some Seven-Up, and it galled her now to see that the food was more compelling than their future together. "You owe me," she said again. But he wasn't looking at her face, he was staring with bored fixity at her breasts, even when she changed her position his dark eyes followed and kept their focus, and there was something so intimidating, so insulting about it that the words were out before she could tame them, the threat bristling between them. "I'll tell your wife, your daughters," she said coolly, drawing out the word *daaaughters*, why, she could never had said, not in a dozen lifetimes.

And then the plate and ottoman were over on their sides and he was lunging at her, but Kate managed somehow, in a running, traipsing sort of scramble, to maneuver beyond his grasp through the kitchen to the basement stairs. She clattered down, flinging off the shoes, the beige, patent leather sling-backs newly acquired to grace his return from New York, and then where to hide? The basement was a dark, cavernous, cement-floored space in which were stored her old steamer trunks, abandoned household items, toys for the boy when he was home on the odd weekend—a rocking horse and a trike, an inflatable standup clown as tall as the boy and weighted at its bottom so that never in a thousand years would it stay down after a punch, a holstered pair of toy Colt-.45s, and a blue wagon the boy wished had been red like the neighbor's Radio Flyer. The toys were ominous in their silent innocence and in the absence to which they could not help but testify. David's absence. There were unfinished walls disgorging useless insulation and a shower where a rec. room had once been planned by a former owner. She was already in the shower, and he was already crashing down the stairs. Neither, for wholly contradictory reasons, had flipped the switch that would have illuminated one of the two bare bulbs spaced unevenly and attached to the joists overhead, the second bulb having burned out months earlier and the boy's play not motivation enough to have replaced it. But clerestory windows through which Kate on tiptoes could see the backyard weeds growing in spring, the empty quadrangle of grassy domestic possibility running out to thicket and fence, allowed the desultory moon glow of the night to stray in. And it was enough for her to see the unmitigated blackness that was Max fast approaching and the basement behind him, so cinereal, so gravely lit that it was this, this waning background, this dying hope, that held her attention as he loomed up to the shower door.

"Get away," she whimpered, "get away from me."

Though his face was a lightless void she could make out the silhouette of his arms and at the ends, his fists clenched into stones. From his chest a sound, or a jam of different sounds, was trying to get out or to become something more than raw sound, and almost as if to assist him, to introduce language, she cried again, "Get away, leave me alone!" But he didn't move, and the sounds ceased, and it was worse without the words, more ominous without the sounds, and she felt herself suffocating in a press of shades of shape and space and darkness. Abruptly her mind drained of thought. It seemed an act of self-protection, not to be exposed at that moment with its particular configuration to thoughts. And if it were possible for the body to remember its own birth, the dark heat of compression and release, the menace of death everywhere in the passage, the passage itself a death of one world for another, the momentum away from it that could be and was so easily lost, so readily surrendered, the panic marvelous in its purity, it was this Kate's body experienced in those moments absent of thought. Max was still there on the other side of the glass shower door, but he shifted slightly, and with amazement, as if she did not expect ever again to see, she could make out the elongated teardrop figure of the tippy clown that no punch could keep down, and it was this that emboldened her. This and a picture that was less image than a vast memorial sensation of the Prairies radiating around and away from her with the same rhythmic throb of the passage, only freed now, free, the wind clean and the sky brassy.

The shower stall was so small, so close, so like a coffin.

She clenched her hands together, she threw her arms against the shower door, the glass shattering, the huge dark shape beyond jerking back and shrinking to a manageable size. The broken glass did not surprise her. It was part of a plan to which her thoughts had not had access. She remembered light then, the jagged place underneath near her wrist where the deepest cut was, and the blood just flowing.

"I'm going home," she told Max in a tired voice, ready to die.

He said, "You're going to the hospital," and tied towels around her arms.

In the car, in his Imperial with the electric windows and leather seats, nausea welled up from deep down. Too much blood had been lost. Dropping her head between her knees, her forearms bundled and propped on her thighs, she gagged and coughed.

"For God's sake, not in my car," he said. And beside her she heard the whirr of the little electric motor letting down the window, felt the rush and sting of cold December air. *Another Christmas alone,* she thought, hanging her head over the rim of the door, *another year without a man, without a home . . .*

The emergency room doctor asked a lot of questions. It was Kate who fabricated the story—of slipping in the basement, the burned out lights, the glass door. Listening to her bald prevarications and perhaps even more alertly to Max's silence, the doctor made no effort to stitch up the three worst wounds neatly or with any consideration to surgical aesthetics. An angry crosshatch of black thread angled across her right forearm just below the wrist, and two lesser cuts, one on each arm, were almost comically ugly, like staged wounds for a theatrical production. Then he bound up her forearms with great wads of white bandages and told her to keep them clean and dry for two weeks.

This presented Kate with certain unanticipated problems the next morning. How to wash her hair. She could fill the tub and bathe, holding her arms up and out of the water, but how could she wash her hair?

Max, who had gone home after delivering her to the bungalow, stopped by that same morning, perhaps because he cared, perhaps because he felt badly about the whole thing—or so she hoped, faintly, when she heard his key in the lock. But when she asked him to wash her hair for her in the kitchen sink, he gazed at her with a kind of indifferent disgust, which she understood was not just an improvement on last night's blind fury but now the very best he could muster. "You got yourself into this," he said with a shrug. And she realized then that he had come by solely to establish some insurance against her threat to tell his wife. On the table, conspicuously at its exact center, he left a clipped stack of new bills—three thousand dollars—"for expenses," he said, giving his head a light tip. "Go back to Canada, Riley," he added. "It looks like you need relatives."

"Is it over?" she asked quietly.

He was standing by the front door, his overcoat still buttoned, sucking a tooth. "Well Riley, what do you think?" As he spoke he worked the brim of his hat, then eased it onto his head in such a way that it canted sharply, concealing all but the strength of his jaw, the soft plundering lips.

And so she could not see completely what was not there, what had never been there. "I'm leaving you, Max," she said, the words riding a sigh that seemed to have no end.

A silence followed but not a long one, not one that might have dulled some of her anguish, or muted the awareness of waste howling like the wind inside her head. His hand was on the doorknob, the door was opening, there was a sudden lash of wintry light that, as the door swung wide, yawned into an oblivion of gray. He murmured, "At any rate . . ." And as he passed out into the world, his enormous hand flicked toward her, not exactly in a farewell wave but to refer back maybe to the good times he hadn't yet forgotten but would forget, sooner than she could stand to imagine.

So it was that, at least in Kate's own mind, at least technically, it was she who left Max Wyman.

That afternoon she rode the ferry out to Bainbridge Island and back, not disembarking, not moving from that last green vinyl bench they had often shared, she and Max, not even when the ferry began the return run so that through the window she was obliged to view where she had just been. There was no wind, not even a breeze, nothing, and the fecal smell of the pulp mills along the Sound hung in the air. The sea was flat and listless. Later it began to rain, a chill, unforgiving assault that made quick dents in the water.

Her hair was dirty, her body shapeless beneath a brown winter coat and announcing at full volume the weight she had gained; her shoes were sensibly flat and broken down along the outside of the heels where overpronation made itself known. The long night, the tears, the lack of sleep had taken an inevitable toll that makeup would not have reversed—so she hadn't bothered. She could see where she had been. She could see, too, in the thick nautical glass a frail transparency of herself. A switch had occurred. On the outside now she looked exactly as she envisioned Ramona Moon, a fattish slattern doomed to solitude. But inside she felt like Katy Riley, Poppy's best girl, wounded and sweet and sad beyond words.

San Francisco

The California coast gave up in light and wind and space, a vast gesture back to the Prairies that had been, in so many ways, Kate Riley's last home. She had made the drive in two days, stopping at a Travel Lodge in Grants Pass, Oregon for the overnight, and then, after crossing into California, stopping along the way at a half dozen juice stands shaped as monster oranges. It was June and hot, and oranges having been the definitive and paramount Christmas treat on the Prairies, the stands could not be easily passed up. She drank from the white plastic containers, too big for one female hand, and heard herself weep, for it seemed that perhaps, at last, she had arrived in a place and time that might make up for all the other places and times.

It had taken six months to sell the bungalow, to resign her position at the National Bank of Commerce in a manner that would assure recommendation to subsequent employers, and to make arrangements for the boy. David had turned four in April, which made it over a year since Janis Wheaton had offered up her pleadings to keep him, over a year since Kate had first left the boy at the orphanage. He was not the same. He would probably never be the same bubbly cherub, the damage done, a heart broken, a soul erased, and Kate unable or more likely not interested enough to make repairs. The Wheatons, making no effort to conceal their moral revulsion with her, agreed to adopt the boy on condition that his mother had no future contact. And so on a cool morning in May, a month before Kate had planned to leave Seattle and so a month before she actually had to relinquish him, the meeting was set. Once the decision had been made, her feelings for the boy quickly hardened over. She could hardly bring herself to look at him, even though he was still terribly cute and Kate would always be susceptible to a pretty thing. He had been home from Sacred Heart going on a week. For his part, David did not often try to engage his mother. When she entered his bedroom that morning she found him dressed, his back to the door, standing at the window pressing his tongue to the glass as though to taste the world outside. At the top of the glass the snowy cone of Mt. Rainier had been cut off from its massive lower reaches by a halo of cumuli so brilliantly white it was painful to gaze at, but when she came around from behind the boy she saw that he was doing just that—staring hypnotically, dreamily at the disembodied peak, as if up there were all the answers to all the questions of the morning.

"Are you ready?" she asked him, though it was clear he had been ready for some time. Much earlier he had slicked back his hair with tap water and when she touched it she found it as dry and stiff as straw. The bed, with its green and pink chenille spread had been roughly made. That morning, before the sun was up even, she had heard him jumping up and down on the bed, the springs bleating like some lost lamb trapped in its own desolation, or the way dogs do when their owners have gone off to work, dogs who are yet too young to have learned to give up. She had decided to leave him be—it was his last chance, after all, to disobey her, and she herself at that age had known the pleasure of breaking rules. Atop the two little suitcases sat the stuffed elephant Kate had given David when he had had his tonsils out, its legs worn limp and splayed over the grip and its trunk flopping off to one side. She thought again how funny it was that he had given the animal a girl name. Ellie. The suitcases had been packed for two days, his toys and knickknacks already sent on in pasteboard boxes, and except for Ellie-the-elephant the room had a dusty untenanted look. In fact, she rarely cleaned the room because he was rarely home. They might have just moved into a house that had sat vacant for months.

"Ready," he replied. His voice was soft and grave, but then it had been that way for some time now. Kate blamed the nuns at the orphanage for imbuing the child with somber abstract notions, like sin and redemption, and for leaving him to play alone so much of the time with those awful dollhouses.

Something in her, some desperate need for his blessing combined with a perverse desire to punish him for his part in the last and most cherished of failed dreams, prompted her to say, "You must be excited, going back to the Wheatons." She put her hands on his small shoulders and turned him firmly about. There were tongue blots all over the window, more transparent than the surrounding glass, that gave back the outside view in a loose mosaic of vivid color and slightly skewed form. "The wonderful Wheatons," she added, making no effort to hide the sarcasm or her jealousy. The jealousy was vague and shallow, but it suited her to feel it just then, to feel the moment alive that way. He was her son, after all.

He clumped over to the suitcases in his brown lace-up boots, gathered the elephant under his arm, and did not look at her but at the floor instead. "Can't I stay, Mummy? I wanna stay."

"Look, I have to go away," she said.

"I prefer to stay. I do," he said, still not daring to even glance up at her, instead, tracing a length of the blond hardwood flooring with the toe of his boot. He must have known, this boy of four, the way any child seems to know what particulars please his own mother, that she liked the fancier words.

"Oh, well, of course," she said, making a grand flourish of her arms, as though the dusty bare bedroom were a richly appointed chamber. "You prefer this, you're not fond of that, tomato sandwiches and scribbling with your right hand. There are lots of things, lots and lots of things I *pree-fer*, too." He was looking so pathetic there with the elephant squished under his arm and his nose running; he was making it inordinately hard on her. "I have to earn a living, David. Don't you understand? I don't have anyone to take care of me." She thought she might cry, but what would be the point? The boy couldn't understand what it was like, being alone in the world, no one who cared if she lived or died.

David ran a finger under his nose and peered up at her through a fringe of dark lashes.

"Handkerchief," she said. But he ignored her, was already walking out the door, so that when she hoisted his two bags and followed she felt so much like a bellhop trotting after some wealthy guest, some Napoleon putting on airs, that she didn't make any effort to talk with him all the way over to the Wheatons. She thought about Brendan and how he had been a kind of miniature tyrant as well. Children, truly, were merciless; you couldn't ever satisfy them. You brought them one thing and five minutes later they were whining for another thing. Bottomless pits of need.

Kate was not to exit the car or even to pull to the top of the Wheatons's gravel drive, former scene of her dismissal of Janis's affections, of Kate's intemperate temper, of the boy's last best hope. Dick Wheaton marched down to the curb and Kate, staring straight ahead, thrust her hand out the open driver's window to pass him the key to the trunk. When the two bags had been extracted, the trunk slammed shut, she reached behind and jerked the handle on the backseat door and then pushed it open. The boy climbed out, trailing Dick Wheaton up the drive in silence. She listened to the crunch of his tiny boots, to the small weight they sought to carry, and then she could not resist calling out with perky encouragement, "Bye bye, Davy. Be a good boy." For he was her boy, after all, in which she had reposited so many of her own dreams, broken though they seemed to be, broken though he must be, could not finally help being.

But her son made no reply.

I suppose I can't blame him, she managed to think. *Still, it's a good home he'll have; I've provided that, and more, too. He might at least say good-bye . . . I'm his mother, after all.* In her mind she heard a distant echo, Gregor in the bedroom, their baby son, Brendan, in the next room in the arms of the au pair—*but you'll hold him, won't you, you will be his* moeder *still?* It had been with a sense of triumph that she had received those words a dozen years earlier, releasing her from the liabilities of breast-feeding. But now, watching her second son in his shorts and his doll-sized suspenders and his pale chubby calves, the muscles undeveloped but not untried, nothing about the boy untried and all of it tried too early, she was not feeling that she had won, only that she had cut her losses and rather deeply at that.

Then a shocking thing happened: Janis Wheaton had been at the top of the drive past the place where it curved away from the road and slipped behind several hazel shrubs, taller than she. Her pale pink dress made itself known, even behind the heavy foliage. Suddenly the dress, and Janis bound up in it, the bodice snug across her minikin bust and cinched with a matching belt, and the skirt a fan of perfect pressed pleats, appeared from behind the hazel, and down she came in brisk steps, an advancing specter of virtue, passing Dick Wheaton with the suitcases, Davy behind him, his head down, the curly dark Irish hair all that could be seen, and strangely, all that Kate could remember at that moment of her father. Then Janis was at the driver's window, her mouth inches from Kate's ear. "Why don't you go get yourself sterilized?" She rapped the palm of her hand twice on the sill, discharging two sharp judicial reports to settle the matter, and headed back up the drive without waiting for a response Kate had no capacity to make.

Before he reached the hazel, David rotated about and something mechanical in his movements suggested to Kate a soldier preparing to salute a superior. But he kept his hands at his sides, and his eyes, which were as dark as Max's but bigger, enormously round and unblinking, his eyes stared down at her with an all-encompassing emptiness, devoid of impurities, and around her a clear black light lowered and set her right hand to shaking as she turned the key in the ignition and shoved the Plymouth into gear.

Yes, the California coast with its westward reach of sea rolled off into the infinite periphery as the prairie sea had, and when she crossed the Golden Gate Bridge, so tall, so grand against a sky as blue and blank as heaven had to be, those two orange towers presenting a visual fanfare that announced her entrance, she unfurled a tatter of hope for the occasion that hastened her descent into the city of San Francisco. She had done well on the bungalow, had realized a nice profit. With the three thousand in cash that Max had left on the kitchen table, she had purchased a showroom Plymouth—turquoise, white vinyl seats, and a grill that flashed a gleaming smile of chromium confidence she longed to emulate. Her stay at the Holiday Inn amounted to less than two weeks. In the seaward flats west of 19th Avenue she found a place, the second floor of a row house on Quintara Street. And not much later a job as a receptionist in a fledgling law firm near the Embarcadero where they could not afford to be picky, and where Kate's bookkeeping experience might serve in a fix.

So commenced Kate Riley's fourth and penultimate incarnation.

She was only thirty-two years old, yet in San Francisco she became aware of a delayed rhythm, a syncopation driving beneath her life. Women and men her own age seemed younger, dressed differently, more casually, wildly even, and were wrapped up in things like rock music and poetry jams and Eastern philosophy for which she had no aptitude let alone curiosity. It was as if she had been marooned in a past whose dreams were not keeping up with the times, or which were leftovers or castoffs from other lives, other generations. These hippies who loitered in parks, who had taken over the Haight-Ashbury district, who talked politics as easily as the businessmen she had known in Seattle had talked profits and losses, and who used drugs and never worked, never married — they were impossible to fathom. Everything magnetizing to Kate's longings was somehow slightly passé once it had been obtained. If it had to do with the older men, there had been younger men, too, in the odd afternoons, or even for weeks, months at a time, and yet they too were somehow old-fashioned — there was no other word for it. Something vital had passed her by, some living scintillation at the center of things had blinked out, not her youth exactly but who she might have been as a youth, susceptible to the beat and swing of the times. A careless immediacy, natural to the young, might have landed her who knew where. That would have been perhaps the best part of it, not knowing the where or even the what. But she had missed out on that too. That was the thing: fixing on certain desires, longing with so much force and stamina that the longing itself had enameled over what might have been a life lived, one that was not impervious to accident or whim. She had wanted to be original, but instead felt herself enslaved to some unnamable need that could not be original but ancient instead.

At Slokum, Merritt & Smith the young gents wore suits with vests and kept their hair short, sideburns tidy margins, lane lines defining expressions of assured providence and clear direction and broad straight thoroughfares, and they carried their briefcases like vestigial shields. And the partners, too, especially Mr. Robert Slokum, round-headed and stern, followed his own great chest into the office each morning as though it were a battering ram. Estate planning constituted his field of expertise.

Nelson Burke's mother was one of Mr. Slokum's new clients. Constance Howerton Burke. Near death and mostly muddled by pain and pain medications, Mrs. Burke nevertheless had enough

wit left to make certain revisions in her will favoring her youngest son over his older sister who had married well and so required
less, by way of inheritance. It seemed a nice family all in all—considerate to the last. Even the older sister was not objecting. Kate
glanced over Mr. Slokum's notes scrawled on a yellow legal pad
before rolling a clean sheet of Eaton paper into the typewriter and
casting them into the standard initial consultation format. A lot
of money was at stake. A lot of money was always nice, but not at
the top of the list of desirable characteristics, not as far as Kate was
concerned. On that Monday morning in July when Nelson Burke,
representing his mother, was to have a second appointment, the
fog was a heavy and indifferent shroud, there for the duration, and
Kate, feeling that she had wound up in some dead-end alleyway off
the sunny boulevard of life, made an extra effort to be attractive.
Monday came and you had to get up and make your way through
the hours that led down to the brink of sleep. You had to hold your
head up and survey your prospects among what was available, and
even if much of it seemed to be debris from old ships that had run
aground, something passable might be salvaged, patched together,
made to work again. You had to survive, as Fiona insisted.

Now Kate was resolutely stout, but at least the weight distrib-
uted itself evenly, so that there was no single conspicuous aberra-
tion of flesh that required disguise, like a pot belly or pear-shaped
thighs; there was only a generalized sense of heaviness that would
still submit to summer weaves and linen shifts with matching blaz-
ers. She smoothed her hair into a chignon, curled her eyelashes
with the wee Draconian device of the times, and before exiting the
bathroom used the atomizer about her décolletage. Christian Dior.
Max's favorite.

Burke himself was a large man, but not as Max had been, not
muscular and solid. In fact, there was something altogether soft
about Nelson, even his flat broad face possessed a baby-like quality. And his derrière, as Kate mentally referred to it, was notice-
able. The rest of him, though nicely proportioned, seemed curi-

ously unused, his hands as smooth as a woman's, neither large nor small, and when he removed his jacket, she saw that his arms lacked contour and color. He did not spend enough time outdoors, that was plain.

In response to her instruction, "Please wait while I let Mr. Slokum know you're here," Burke offered a gentle smile, the sort a country doctor might use with a new patient. It was early, the office was quiet, but the way he was looking at her did not bother her. From the start, Nelson Burke was easy to be around.

"Red hair," he murmured from his chair in the waiting room. On his lap a slim file rested; he had hung his beige windbreaker neatly across the chair back. His black penny loafers stood side by side, perfectly parallel and so beautifully polished that the lamplight scudded across their tops. "You have beautiful red hair," he added for the record, tapping his finger once for each word, like the bouncing white ball at the bottom of the TV screen that kept syllabic time to the lyrics of jingles and simple songs. But Nelson Burke did not turn out to be so simple a song as that.

She smiled and bent her head forward, as if to invite supplementary praise. "Irish."

He gave a sage nod. "Ah, Irish."

"Yes."

"Does that mean you have a temper then, lass?" he asked in a badly forged Irish accent.

In playful contradiction Kate lifted a single eyebrow. "Perhaps a wee one."

From a pocket in the windbreaker Nelson Burke found a tube of chapstick and carried out the application in two liberal passes, smiling throughout the task. His lips were large, cherry-red, and shaped according to acknowledged standards; his eyes, too, were large and drawn to ideals. In fact, sneaking peeks over the typewriter, Kate noticed something funny about him, a representational quality, like a picture designed to help children identify parts of a man's face, the features simplified and blunt and slightly outsized so that it would not be easy to make a mistake. Nice and comfy. Kate's response to Nelson Burke possessed a similar quality, as though she were acting out an idea of romantic interest rather than experiencing the thing itself. Even what they went on to do seemed to stand for something you would know some day when you grew up and it *really* happened, or perhaps had known years ago but would never know again, all of that over now, the heat and thrashing about, the necessary information—about love and falling in love—found in a tidy little brochure you kept at the back of a bedside drawer.

Lunch at Alioto's later that week, and a follow-up phone call; dinner at Vanessi's; an afternoon at the Palace of the Legion of Honor; a black dress purchased from Macy's; lovemaking at his mother's elegantly appointed house on Scott Street, Nelson so thoughtful, so considerate that Kate worried if she didn't make an effort of some sort, she might lose interest. She found herself wishing he could be just a little greedy about it all, just a little rough, if only to persuade her that he wanted her beyond politeness, outside the exigency of manners. She wanted to know that in the end he would hurt her to satisfy his desire, that the hurting would deepen his lust, and hers in turn.

Then it was fall and the fog had retreated offshore, the same distance every morning, not daring to roll inland now that the weather had cooled, and the skies were a pale, worn-out blue waiting incuriously for another turn of season. Nelson Burke was no Max Wyman, no one to fall irredeemably in love with, but he was a steady companion. A new man, a new season. When his mother passed in October, he was a gentleman of some wealth, too. Still, Kate felt that she had traded down, not up, that perhaps every man after Max would be a concession in a contest she was losing to Destiny.

For reasons that he never really offered, Nelson had had a number of jobs, some of which could be called actual careers, though he was only forty-one. He had managed a fine wine shop downtown, taught music theory at the Conservatory, he had even worked as a male nurse in the burn ward at the UCSF Medical Center until it got to him. "Burns are extremely painful," he explained. It was this perhaps more than anything else, his medical experience, his compassion for physical disorders, that was uniquely compelling to Kate. One day as if she were revealing the naughty secrets of a former love affair, she showed Nelson her health journals. At that time they filled three 8 ½ x 11 spiral notebooks, the entries meticulously dated, the report kept up even when—she was proud to point out—she was in some distress, "in pain," as she put it.

They were sitting in the living room of the Scott Street Victorian, the baby grand behind Nelson draped with one of his mother's crisp linen runners and setting off a silver candelabra that reached toward the high white plaster ceiling, ornately molded, late afternoon light filtering through chiffon panels, and the casements themselves substantial, tall and deep and of oiled, darkly grained oak, everything about the room with its furnishings so quiet and elegant that it could not be questioned or argued with. Anything she might reveal would have legitimacy here, she felt, and not only legitimacy but elevation as well. Two martini glasses, full, outward opening, waited on a low table to provide further pleasure, further guarantees. She reached and sipped, uncrossed her long legs, then passed him the notebooks. There was a knot in her throat the size of a walnut and her breathing shoaled with anticipation.

Nelson began to read, starting with the first page, but within minutes he had abandoned the chronology and was flipping randomly ahead, snatching up the next notebook, and then the third where he ran his open hand down the pages, his eyes jumping about, his attention seeming to stagger from one entry to another. She thought she heard him gasp, and then she was glad she had given them to him, for it was always desirable to be one who could provide dramatic effect, a skill she and her playmates practiced during the slow prairie days of summer.

—very sore joint—third finger left hand
—yeast infection in the gut

—sputum clear—after 12 hours without ampicillan it was yellow again
—bad sleep
—bowel movement slightly looser
—explosive bowel movement probably from corn on the cob
—cramps in calf
—saw Dr. Ignatius—come back in 6 months
—saw Dr. Levenson. Says no worry about loose bowels if they do not continue during the day. 2 or 3 in morning no problem.
—eyes very scratchy—Dr. Hittand says might be a low grade staff infection—cleansing the eye lashes with Johnson's baby soap maybe once a week may help—glaucoma test ok.
—bladder attack
—saw Dr. Kaye—does not think aspirin is causing the bladder trouble
—saw Dr. Linde—says blood pressure low—take more salt. Did a pelvic exam and all is ok. Nice doctor

Leaning forward, staring at the floor, Nelson pinched his brow as though he had momentarily lost purpose, then he straightened with a jerk and resumed reading.

—sitter hurting again
—report from tests—stool culture normal
—feel better about Dr. Heckman now that *he* called
—explosive diarrhea
—saw Dr. Dawson—given up trying to see Heckman
—saw Dr. Bertleson in desperation—other treatments simply did not help the diarrhea—prescribed sulpha twice daily—no milk products—wants a fresh sample of feces
—saw Dr. Deborah Speer—she gave me a thorough exam waist up. Wax in ears. No taste test. Discussed my whole history
—one week later—no candida—she thinks I need pancreatic

enzyme because of my scalloped tongue, my coated tongue, and my tainted breath. Dad died of pancreatic cancer—me?

Nelson paused and spread his fingers out upon the open page, his breath making a slow controlled exodus. He looked across the coffee table, over the two martini glasses, which he stopped to stare at and, as if prompted by the reminder that a drink waited there for him, was waiting and would keep waiting unless he did something about it, he lifted his glass and swallowed deeply. "Kate," he said. The way he said her name sparked the memory of an answer, or a part of one, to a question she hadn't asked for years, and she could feel the sting of tears.

"You didn't read it all," she said, and her silent request—that he keep reading, never stop reading, never cease loving her or attending to the secret details of Kate—sent the heat of blood into her cheeks. She felt exposed, but the exposure was as thrilling as sexual excitement.

"No." He gazed down at his hand on the page, his eyes glassy and fixed. "There's so much."

"I know."

"I'm not sure I understand . . . why you want . . ."

"Just keep reading," she insisted. "You'll see . . . what it's been like."

Half an hour later, closing the third notebook, he lay his hands, palms down, atop it, as if to keep it from bursting open of its own accord, like some Pandora's box. He said her name, but his expression was unreadable and she didn't know yet how to prepare her response. In the room the light had yellowed with the dying day and was drifting toward the shadow line across which came the night. She looked at his hands, so soft and unused-seeming, like the hands of royalty, not grubby or common or calloused over by the crude demands of a scrabbling life, demands with which she had had to contend, and she was glad that it was hands such as these, clean and pale and pure, the scent of soap trapped under neatly clipped nails, that held the record of her inmost worries and the duties they had imposed upon her over the years. "Kate," he said again, drawing in a corner of his large mouth, cocking his head so slightly, so delicately, she thought he might be trying to hear something that was coming from very far away, bits of a private conversation never meant for public consumption. There were in fact muffled fragments of sentences reaching them from the house next door with which the Burke's home shared a wall. But these were not the utterances his ears sought to decipher, for his head canted toward the window, not the wall, the window soaring up to his right in tall ecclesiastical splendor, and whatever it was he meant to hear and perhaps to comprehend was outside in the gathering night. His big animal eyes conveyed a weary but willing kindness, and she pictured him in the burn ward peeling away the old dressings, pus-encrusted and rank, preparing the new, the patient wincing, embarrassed by the pain, by the foulness of his own emanations of mortality, but grateful. And full of trust—yes, Nelson was a man she could trust, at least and at last.

"Yes," she said, wanting to know, to hear him speak, to receive the news. "Yes?"

He brought himself back, tapped the notebook with his index finger and frowned as a doctor might, puzzling over symptoms. "It says here you had a cold last week. November 8th."

"A bad one."

"I don't remember this cold."

"Very juicy," she added with a snuffle.

He picked up the other two notebooks and held the three together in his hands as if they were the original drafts of a master working in deepest isolation over years. "Remarkable," he said finally with a frank assessment of her face.

"Really?"

"Remarkable," he murmured again, only this time the word showed up on its own without any apparent effort on his part. "So many problems . . ."

With a nod, a pensive study of the transparent puddle lingering in her martini glass, Kate had to agree. She finished her drink, uncrossed her legs, and tucked her hands under her knees with a childlike timidity.

"So many doctors."

"Specialists."

"Yes, of course," he said, lifting his eyebrows, an almost comedic assent. And then, "Indeed."

She shrugged. "Everyone specializes nowadays." It couldn't be helped.

"You've never said anything to me. We've been together since July, four months, and you never mentioned . . . this," he said, lifting the notebooks an inch or two with renewed wonder, patting the tattered red cover of the oldest and earliest. She had written her name on it so that it looked like an old school assignment, though on the last and most recent she had brutally lined out Kate Riley and had scribbled beneath it *Ramona Moon*. He asked her about the unfamiliar name and she dismissed his question. "A joke. Private joke."

Nelson tried to smile but he was obviously distracted by the larger matter of the notebooks themselves, their very existence. They seemed to constitute another entirely separate being there in the room between them, someone she had asked him to meet, like a relative or a childhood friend.

Yet overall, the occasion was immensely gratifying to Kate, borne into the room on the soft ceaseless wind of the past, the hours, the quiet lonely bedside interludes beneath a cone of lamplight during which she'd had to note with religious devotion the conditions of her body, to care for it because there was no one else who cared enough or properly. How sad they had been, those moments, and impassioned, too, a form of monastic practice.

"You never said anything," Nelson Burke said again. He was having trouble moving on. It was this pause that led beautifully, perfectly to what was for Kate Riley a kind of *coup de grâce*, a small expensive gift of time, circumstance and culmination set upon a satin pillow as it were, and carried to her by an invisible servant, *amé damnée* of the Past who must serve, and serve to remind, citizens of the Present; the moment, the way it had worked its way around and was placed respectfully there in her lap, could not have been imagined—perhaps fantasized—but never imagined. Because now she could say, "Dad was a bit of a stoic too," brushing a strand of red hair from her forehead. "I guess I . . . well, I try not to trouble others." And the knot in her throat came undone in a wrenching sob. "You can't imagine how it's been, Nelson," she wept, "you simply can't imagine."

It was a measure of Nelson Burke's kindheartedness and his sensitivity to the matter, and perhaps also of his bafflement that he said nothing more, merely rose to comfort her, his soft hand squeezing her shoulder; to mix them another two martinis, to order a cab to take them down to Jack's for their 7:00 p.m. dinner reservations. When a week later he brought up the health journals, wondering if Kate was not, "well, too concerned," with her body's functions, perhaps "too meticulous" in her observations, she burst into a rage so sudden and total that he retreated from the subject forevermore—which, after all, did not amount to so very much time.

Less than a month later, a crisp, clear fall day, November 22 in a pub on O'Farrell where they sat nursing black and tans and waiting for cheeseburgers, the dimmed-down roar of a sporting event on the TV was interrupted by the news that President John F. Kennedy had been shot. With a collective compulsion, the patrons rose to their feet as if it had all been rehearsed, and gathered around the set in silence to watch the events flicker by, the replay indisputable in its black-and-white candor. Some of the huddled—two men, an older woman—were unwilling to forgive Mrs. Kennedy's scramble over the seat back. But Kate found it understandable, "poor frightened thing." The assassination seemed to affect Kate more profoundly than others, if such calibrations could be made, an entire nation in mourning and the rest of the world extending sympathy. The Kennedy family—Irish, Catholic, beautiful—embodied so much of what had eluded Kate. If they could not be allowed to thrive on, what chance had anyone? Had she?

A creeping desperation began to claw its way up the back stairs of Kate's new life. Nelson hadn't proposed marriage. In fact, except for his volunteer work at the opera and the occasional substitute teaching at the Conservatory, a tennis game now and then, he wasn't doing much of anything except living his days from beginning to end. Following nights when she stayed over, he brought her coffee in bed, lingered long over his ablutions in the pink- and black-tiled bathroom, before taking his two Dalmatians on their morning constitutional, as he liked in ritual fashion to say. "Time for our constitutional, boys." Kate would have gone off to work before his return. It was always a mystery how he filled the rest of the day. If he mentioned tennis, or the market, an editorial he happened to have read in the *Chronicle*, lunch with a friend, there was still something uncomfortably motionless about Nelson Burke's life. It was not going anywhere that she could see. It was like a rudderless ship on some peaceful backwater that might shift and creak and even drift a short way here or there, but never far and never to any purpose. And it seemed to Kate that the inertia was so innocuously pleasant that he accepted it without really noticing it, the way a temperature-controlled room provided warmth in continuous undetectable increments. She began to wonder if he were not somehow too contented.

Max had always liked work, not for the money so much as the challenge. But Nelson seemed decidedly uninterested in proving anything. All that money, she concluded, was undermining his ambition.

At Christmas, after a great many hints, he took her to Paris for a week. Paris represented the apotheosis of love, and though she did not feel exactly that way about Nelson Burke, where they went and what they did seemed at least to impersonate the advertised package of ideal love. But it wasn't the sort of love these young people down in the park were swaying in each other's arms about, hippies, flower children, long-hairs. Kate and Nelson—theirs was the brand you saw in the movies, or in magazine spreads or on the decks of Caribbean cruise ships, fully codified and bearing the stamp of approval that only money and circumstance could provide. It seemed she had loved Max, or at least she had felt something fierce and undeniable for him. The antagonism between them had always been a form of affinity, hadn't it? As for Jan . . . he may have been the only man, young though he had been, and she, too—the only man except for Poppy whom she had loved with a recalcitrant innocence, and that seemed to suggest that she had loved him truly.

In Paris it was Max Kate often thought of. She liked to imagine him knowing she was there, catching just a glimpse of her in some sidewalk café, shy and effervescent beneath an Audrey Hepburn sort of hat. It rained most of the time, so there were few meals spent in sidewalk cafés. The French were kind, because of Kennedy's death; it seemed to mean more—the kindness—because they really didn't want to have to like Americans. Despite his size with its predictive inelegance, Nelson ambled along the Rue de Rivoli with the soft swinging confidence of American apathy born of American money. It was easy to persuade him into clothing shops where he stood complacently for the chalk measurements and voluntarily felt the fabrics and draped a languorous finger upon the perfectly layered cravats; and even easier to lure him into the polished-silk chairs of dress shops from which he could view her prospective outfits in the muted light of haute couture. The French women were all so thin, so svelte, that Kate tried to conceal the sizes from Nelson. The clerk was a petite brunette with narrow eyes and a smile she had practiced to such unvarying solicitude that her disdain was palpable. She brought the dresses in one at a time, carrying them over her extended arms like bodiless brides across the threshold, or like virgins to a sacrifice not of taste, for the dresses were lovely, but of suitability, she implied as she helped Kate pull and tug the last garment down over the impedimentary waist.

"Katherine," Nelson said—he always used her full name whenever he wished to soundly make a point, "you're *zaftig*."

Kate repeated the word—*zaftig*—as he tried to define it with another word, *pneumatic*, which she had likewise never encountered. Among other things, she took genuine pleasure in Nelson's refined vocabulary. Of course as a Burke he had had the finest of educations—a Jesuit prep school followed by a degree in musicology from Boston University. They were seated in the backseat of the taxi amid the packages and parcels, and she was trying to see out her window to the Paris streets, the colored lights collecting in the rain puddles and streaking along the gutters, and no one in too great a hurry, as they seemed to always be in the States. But it was a pouty, puffy Ramona Moon who gazed with dull eyes back at her from the glass.

"It's womanly, don't you understand?"

"Really?"

"Yes," he insisted. "I've been with slender . . . individuals. It's wonderful to have so much under my hands," and he turned his palms upward as though remembering the weight of her breasts.

"You," she said and looked out the window again. Through the glass front of a café she could see an older man in a beret standing alone at the bar, his hand resting on the base of a wineglass and an air of sovereign pride in his bearing. And further along the street a coiffed young woman leaned down to her daughter and spoke in her ear, the girl's eyes bright beneath squared bangs, and whatever it was her mother was saying, perhaps the promise of some longed-for treat, raised an eager smile. It would be nice to have a daughter like that, Kate thought idly, with bright eyes. The rain had let up during their time in *les magasins*. The city lights grew so brilliant with the onrushing night that it was too easy to think herself into a dream of reality. Simply to be where she was constituted an achievement. Even Fiona thought so, and had said as much in her holiday card, though it was of course tainted by the usual guilt-mongering—"You'll be having a gay time in Paris, I expect. And what of your mum, the heat gone again and no proper coat, and the old boy down the hall with his cough won't stop, and there's no sleep to be had, even in the stone dead of night. You have a great way with the men, Kate, I'll give that to you. Sure, and this one with the means too, but no job, you say? What sort of man has no job, hasn't he any pride?"

Nelson bought Kate's mother a wool and cashmere coat for Christmas and that put a stop to the question of employment.

After that day in Paris Kate moved into the fullness of her body with the courage of a woman who knows at last that she is loved, that nothing can shake it. Nothing. For Christmas he gave her a pair of opera glasses, mother-of-pearl and brass fitted into an exquisite embroidered case. From the balcony seats of Opéra Garnier for *Così Fan Tutte* she held the glasses before her eyes, thrilled to be where she was and trying not to cry for having finally landed in a soft safe place. And without Max. Without her parents, or even her fantasies. One afternoon they met up in a café, Deux Magots, with Miriam who had laddered her way up at the Canadian Consulate—flourishing was the word she used. She had married a doctor—*of course*, Kate thought—and they had two girls and a three-story *maison* on the right bank in Passy, a tony quarter of the Sixteenth, plus a summer place in the hilltop village of Rousillon in Provence. About Netherfield they talked only briefly, because Miriam had been right years earlier and again that day in Paris, in saying that the prairie towns must die, that the hodgepodge of imported cultures and ethnicities encountering bouts of ungovernable aridity and the postwar development of the corporate agrarian model would swiftly and inevitably forestall what might have someday been called a civilization. That was the way Miriam talked now, at least around people she didn't know. Nelson was impressed and Kate was glad they had phoned her, the ancient jealousies in retreat and their childhood camaraderie once again a thing to value.

When Nelson slipped off for *les toilettes* Miriam leaned across the table. "You've heard about Jan."

"No," Kate said, affecting disinterest. "What?"

"Finally married. An actress from Toronto. Ginger something."

"I don't believe it."

"C'est vrai."

Kate stared out the window at passersby bundled against the inclement weather. "I can't believe it."

Miriam tore off a piece of baguette, then spread a generous slab of paté, embedding the thinly sliced, fanning cornichons in the pinkish meat with a practiced assurance. "Frankly, I never thought he'd get over you."

A small puff of breath escaped Kate as she reached for the bottle of Côtes du Rhône and poured herself a second glassful. "No," she murmured, suddenly at a loss, and feeling just as suddenly and strangely unmoored, as though some vital unseen line of her identity had come loose and she discovered herself plying shoreless waters toward what, she could not have said. The direction of her life went unaccountably blurry, now that where she had been — Jan, Netherfield, her native country of Canada, her past or *the* past — was dropping entirely from view. Jan's unspoken loyalty to her over the years, as she had always thought of it, had at last worn out, and now he too had entered the wavering light of the future and they had become, all of them, these sequent fugitives of European poverty, these children of the Prairies, orphans of both an old and a new world.

"I haven't heard from him for over a year," Kate said. "Everything is changing so fast, and I feel pretty much the same. Or I want to. Isn't that funny?"

"But Nelson . . . ," Miriam tried, by way of compensation, "he's so nice."

They could see him wending his way toward them between the closely arranged tables.

"Yes, he is. He's what I've always wanted. I guess."

Eyeing her steadily, Miriam produced an odd little frown and then shrugged the way the French liked to, as if to say, what does it matter, one makes do. "*Bienfaisant*," she sighed. "In the long run that's what counts."

The next day Kate bought Nelson a very expensive watch, diamonds encircling its face and a chunky band. He extended his arm the way a woman might with a stunning new bracelet, and together they laughed at the gesture, so ridiculously feminine. When they returned to the States it was with a plan to marry in the spring.

One afternoon in March, during her lunch hour, Mr. Slokum summoned her. His was a spacious corner office on the third floor with six foot windows from which could be seen the sedate tonnage of the shipping traffic plying a surreal bay, their progress nearly imperceptible. A stiff wind chafed the surface of the water, and the blue was so dark and raw it hurt the eye. She preferred her own windowless cubby off the waiting room. As much as the relentless space of the Prairies had bred in her senses certain abstract requirements, like independence and freedom, there was nothing like the solace of a small dim enclosure.

Having taken several courses at San Francisco State, Kate had been promoted to legal secretary, which paid twice the wage of receptionist. She did not like Slokum, not at all. He was stern and pop-eyed, his face pitted from the havoc of adolescence, and he was always licking his lips.

"Sit, please," he said, indicating, with a faintly oblique jerk of his head, the leather and chrome chair opposite his desk.

Kate sat and made an obvious point of glancing at the clock on the wall. It was her lunch hour, after all; he was the boss, he could eat whenever he wanted.

"Miss Riley." The glare from the windows behind him converted Mr. Slokum to a diffuse silhouette, but she could still see his wet red lips, the whites of his eyes above the white, overly starched shirt, and his general shape—a small ball atop a very large ball bobbing above the plain of his executive oaken desk. "Miss Riley. Your wardrobe."

She tipped her head ever so slightly to register surreptitiously her dress, a flowered knee-length shift gathered under the bust-line in the peasant style of the day, and that accommodated the bit of extra weight she had gained during the winter. They were sometimes called mumus, after the Hawaiian model. She'd had to purchase several in different colors in order to vary her outfit throughout the workweek. The French dresses no longer fit, but she enjoyed seeing them in her closet and conjuring up the day when they would once again contain her figure. She did not care quite the way she used to about her weight because Nelson loved her with the bit of extra, the way Poppy had and would now if he were alive. But exactly how much weight had she gained?

Mr. Slokum's hand flew up in a gesture of muffled exasperation. Kate had failed to answer promptly enough.

"My wardrobe?"

"This, this is a . . . my wife wears these at home," he said, using that same exasperated hand, flicking the air. "On weekends. It's a housedress, Miss Riley. Hardly appropriate."

She felt her cheeks flush with embarrassment so violent she wanted to scream it out of her very body. *It couldn't have been much more than fifteen pounds, could it?* She thought of her freckles, and how the deep flush would fill in behind them and how horrid she must appear, and how, at that moment, it suited her just fine—to be Ramona Moon with a vengeance.

Slokum snatched up a yellow legal tablet and gave the notations a cursory review while he licked his lips. It was obvious he was having trouble, but equally obvious that he was determined to deal with the matter thoroughly and finally. "The other girls brought it to my attention. Naturally. It's hardly my business," he stammered. "But, you see, well of course it *is* my business, Miss Riley. That's the thing. We have clients come in here and they expect professionalism. How a man—or a woman . . . ," he jabbed the tip of his pencil into the air between them, "how she dresses says so much, you have to agree."

She nodded, looking at the beige Berber carpeting. Something at the center of her was freezing solid as an icicle in a north wind. At the same time she felt that she could leap across the desk and shove him through the plate glass into the raw blue of the bay.

When she left it was not for her place on Quintara Street but for Scott Street and Nelson's. Her hands were shaking with anger as she came up the steps and used her own key. Nelson always kept the door locked, there were so many solicitors in the wealthier neighborhoods, and transients, too, or hippies from the perpetual encampment in the park down the street. He owned a BMW but often took cabs because of the parking, so the fact that his car was in the garage did not necessarily mean that he was home. But as it happened he was, and he had company. A young man, lean, blond, wearing a straw yellow shirt with a Brooks Brothers insignia on the breast pocket, and a pair of white chinos with a navy blazer. He was sitting on the arm of the couch, one leg crossed over the other, resting one hand on the couch back. Nelson was beside him and slightly below on the cushions. There were two cups of tea on the low table and a plate of cookies. And even in her rattled frame of mind, her distracted entrance into the room, she did not fail to register the funny, vague, and finally unidentifiable mood created by their configuration, and to which the innocuous tea and cookies seemed to obscurely contribute a significant, if elusive, clue.

Nelson rose. "Kate," he said. "You're here." It was an odd thing for him to have said, but she didn't think about it until much later. The young man shot up, too, fingering the brass buttons of his blazer. "This is Rudy. Rudy Sonnenberg."

Kate nodded at him, still distracted and wishing Nelson were alone so that she could tell him about Slokum. "Hello," she said coolly and took Rudy's extended hand.

"I'm glad to have finally met you. Nelson has told me so much."

Nelson said, "Tennis pal," by way of identification, and cleared his throat.

"Yes," Rudy agreed. "Nelson has a formidable backhand." There was a lapidary brilliance in his blue eyes, as if he had in fact just walked off the court with the sun still cutting through the irises, and it, together with his taut posture, elaborated an edgy, high-strung quality about him.

"Tennis, right," she murmured. Though it was only just after lunch, she went to the bar in the corner behind the piano and poured herself a shot of Canadian Club. "Bad morning. Terrible morning. My boss . . . ," she broke off, not wanting to venture further into the subject of her clothes with this nicely turned out young man.

Rudy smiled. He had a pleasant smile, gentle and solicitous, like a younger brother still uncertain about his interpersonal duties. "Poor girl," he said, and seemed genuinely to mean it.

It was satisfying, being referred to as a girl still, and she decided to flop onto the couch next to Nelson, who had resumed his seat, and accept the fact that there was a stranger in the room. With some hesitation, Rudy settled into an opposite chair and lifted his teacup.

"I myself have had some trouble with a superior. The department chair."

"What do you do?" Kate asked. She had downed the whiskey and was reaching for one of the cookies.

"Assistant professor of art at San Francisco State," he said with mocking self-importance. "But only just. I started in September and there's the usual pecking order."

"The pecking order," Kate repeated, appreciating the term. She liked clever summations of that sort.

"Lowest in the food chain," Rudy said with a look of cheerful acceptance. "That's me."

"Isn't *that* the story?"

"Maybe it's human nature, to need hierarchies. I don't know," he shrugged.

"Yes," she agreed, and added, "Even in a democracy." The conversation with its intelligent and subtle scorn of people like Slokum who lorded it over underlings or newcomers, was having a calming effect.

Nelson raised a single brow and examined his right hand as if it bore a large dinner ring. "As Twain said, some of us are more equal than others." And they laughed, the three of them, at his false pomposity.

Leaning into his shoulder, Kate dusted the cookie crumbs from the front of her dress, sighed and murmured, "You."

It was Rudy who asked her what had happened, not Nelson. Nelson stroked her heavy red hair and waited. Nelson knew how to be silent, a talent that, at many moments in the past, had suited her well, for she often launched into verbal riffs that supplied their own sort of high, as though she were the performer and he the audience. High—that was a popular word of the day. Everyone was getting high. And at that moment, with the midday light swarming through the tall windows, dust particles in a glittery swirl over the grand piano, she yearned for some sort of high, some elevation that might free her from the strange burden of the past with its impossible and increasingly leaden claims.

Kate relayed the interview, watching Nelson's large exemplary lips nip the edge of the teacup, and Rudy Sonnenberg's fingers, which were clean and beautifully tanned, but with the nails bitten down to the quicks so that there were only eye-shaped remnants at each base and the skin of the nail beds had shrunk into calluses and begun to curl backward over the retreating nail. Poor fellow, she thought; he must have a lot of worries, what with his new job.

At the end of her story Rudy brought both palms down on the tops of his knees with a crisp and sudden resolve. "We're going shopping."

Then they were downtown in Union Square, bursting in and out of department stores and shoe shops, leaning elbows on the glass accessory cases, putting pocketbooks to test of arms bent or shoulders lax, primping collars and smoothing hems, and laughing, the three of them laughing at the brave turnabout they had made of Mr. Slokum's nasty complaint. Rudy was much more involved in the selection of clothing, Nelson loitering in the margins, amused. "Miss Riley," he kept calling her with sweet formality, one, finely-drawn eyebrow arched as he stepped back from her to properly regard each ensemble, his two hands flung open in gesture of approval. And once with charming playfulness, "Bring me the Auerbach brief, if you've the time, Miss Riley." But he didn't like every outfit, not at all, and it was this that lent absolute credibility to his taste and counsel. And he wasn't afraid to be frank, even intimate, in his opinion. "Too much going on up here," he said, dashing the air above her ample breasts. "These embroidered pockets . . . *no*." Two pantsuits, one vented black gabardine skirt, several coordinating blouses, a tweed Evan Picone blazer, black pumps and a matching handbag, three silk scarves, a stunning gold-plated brooch in the form of a unicorn, one navy blue dress, simple and A-lined, with white, pin-sized polka dots, and everything in sizes that actually fit. By late afternoon she was feeling restored. Ramona Moon in her flowered mumu, was wadded up in the bottom of one of the shopping bags. The three strolled up Sutter, pausing at the flower vender on the corner to sniff the narcissus and hyacinth, to admire the almost plastic perfection of the daffodils, blooming everywhere, setting off the grass of the domed Square over the parking garage, bobbing from third-story boxes. Kate wore the blue dress and black pumps and swung along between the two men whose kindness about broke her heart even while it seemed to repair the day's damage, and to some but finally cureless extent, the damage done that day in 1942 when Poppy left her for another world.

"Hey, let's have a drink," she said. "I'm buying."

L'Obélisque was off Union Square, two blocks up Post. Rudy knew the owner, he said. College roommate, he added, by way of identification. The former roommate, a tidy little fellow in a pair of bookish pince-nez, twinkled and led them to a small table near the front. "Not so smoky," he explained. The place hadn't filled up yet, it being only 5:30, and most of the clientele were men just off work, judging by the suits. It was beautifully elegant, L'Obélisque, with deep red crushed velvet chairs and wallpaper that featured a black and gold fleur de lis pattern, the bar itself a great carved affair capped with polished copper, and a vast mirror behind that doubled the room's opulence. On the sound system jazz was playing, some late-night strolling sax that seemed to presume more promise than the early hour had yet made good on but probably would. Rudy ordered a single-malt Scotch and Nelson and Kate had gin martinis. The young man talked about his work, not the teaching but the painting. Watercolors. He talked about The Light, as if it were some sort of god. He had studied in France where he felt understood. A gallery in Carmel had agreed to handle his work. The department chair, a sixty-something man who had never "practiced"—that was the word Rudy used—took Professor Sonnenberg's incipient artistic success as pedagogic betrayal, and that was what had started the trouble between the two. It seemed terribly unfair to Kate, and she looked again at the young man's fingernails, gnawed down and desperate in their appeal for validity.

"You have to follow your heart," she said. "You just have to."

He set down his glass and smiled softly at her. "Thank you."

"You just have to," she repeated.

Rudy glanced at Nelson across the white tablecloth. At its center a thin, curvaceous vase offered a pink rose in a pointillist cloud of baby's breath. He was staring fixedly at the rose, as though not seeing it, seeing instead something from the past living on in his mind, when he said, "Sometimes you haven't any choice in the matter." And he drew in one corner of his mouth, delicate and bruised-looking, to indicate that like Kate, like all of them, he had had disappointments, regrets, certain things that could not ever be got around.

Beside her she could feel Nelson moving his knee gently in time with the music, contentment in the moment and in Kate and Rudy's new friendship marked by the placid intimation of a smile.

Sipping his scotch, Rudy gave a single lazy salute to someone in the smoky nether reaches of L'Obélisque. "Of course I have to make a living, too."

"Like most of us," she said, delivering Nelson a playful nudge.

"What? I'm here to provide contrast."

"Oh you," she said, and again they laughed, the three of them.

Yes, she had indeed landed in a soft place. California was more than all right. California had been waiting for her like the answer to the question she had been asking that night on the CPR rolling westward across the night prairies to the sea.

Their wedding could hardly have been called an elopement, but it had elements in common with that impromptu venture. Nelson chartered a plane and the three of them flew down to Santa Barbara one weekend where Rudy's older sister lived with her husband who was a landscape architect. They arrived in the late afternoon, following a winding road up one of several canyons that opened between plunging foothills, briefly green during winter and early spring but already in late March fading to a soft celery viridescence. The shaggy eucalyptus trees along the road gave over to canyon oak, bay, and bigcone Douglas-fir where the canyon tightened and the fog could tuck in and hold well past noon, and then rounding the base of a squat sunlit knob the ravine abruptly widened into a secret valley at the east end of which stood the house. It was a two-story stucco built decades earlier in the style of a Spanish grandee's villa, with terra cotta tiles and lots of wrought iron and a vast por-tale under which a burgundy-hued patchwork of rugs had been laid. Rudy and his sister, Dawn, had inherited the estate from their parents, but because he had found employment in San Francisco it was she who had taken up residence. Around the house, foresight-edly placed, were immense live oaks, the biggest Kate had ever seen, taller even than the dwelling they seemed desirous of protecting, with great branches as thick as a man's thigh that reached in sinu-ous multiplicity out from the trunks, easily four feet in diameter. Beneath them an even dappling of light and shade evoked a dreamy mood as of a scene from childhood long forgotten, or of a painting done by someone humbled by what he sought to capture. It was truly paradisiacal, the Sonnenberg estate. And for Kate it had the unanticipated effect of promoting Rudy up some other pecking order that everyone took for granted but no one liked to mention, though in truth such distinctions had never bothered her. This was exactly the sort of place where her wedding reception ought to be held. She felt giddy as a schoolgirl.

Rudy popped from the backseat and opened the passenger door for Kate before Nelson could quite make his way around the front end of the car, the two of them making a funny show of fighting over the honor. She smiled down at the small elliptical leaves of the oaks, fallen and faded from glossy green to sallow gold, and lying everywhere atop the pea gravel, their barbs like tiny claws digging in, hanging on to the literal earth. It seemed the right thing to do, to hang onto this moment, to what was exactly underfoot. To be living here in California after so many lost places and lost times. She could smell wood smoke, and bay, and something else, too, a weedy pungency. The air was warm and dry, compared to San Francisco; there was a good chance she could wear the sleeveless white linen shift without its matching jacket tomorrow, and show off her arms, still young, still round.

Suddenly from around the house two children burst, one in pursuit of the other.

"God damn it, Jake," the girl hollered, "it isn't fair, you're not playing fair." She was a scrawny thing, maybe seven or eight, with greasy yellow ropes of hair flying aside a sharp, purposeful face.

The boy stooped, grabbed a handful of pea gravel and launched a salvo over his shoulder as he took up his getaway.

"Shit," the girl said.

"Shit yourself," he cried as he tore past the three of them, breaking into a smile made more feral, more gleaming by the patina of surrounding dirt. "Who're you?" he called back. Then, "Whyn't you fucks take a picture?"

It was true, they had been standing there staring at the twosome, the car doors flung open almost as wide as their mouths.

Rudy made a face and looked at his topsiders. "I neglected to tell you about my niece and nephew. Dawn . . . ,"—Dawn was the older sister—"she subscribes to the progressive school of childrearing."

Nelson gave a chuckle, but Kate, still dazed, said, "Their language. And they're just children."

The two men began hoisting bags. "It's the scene," Rudy said. "You know, hippies, free love, marijuana?"

She tried to see where the children had gone off to, but they had vanished just as two yellow labs waddled up, pressing their wet noses to her calves and wagging with irrepressible and obviously random ardor.

"Hippies? But I thought he was a landscape architect, her husband."

"Well, he's a gardener. This is the age of euphemism, among other things. Come on, let's find some grownups."

Despite the size of the house and the expanse of its grounds, finding grownups proved far easier than Kate could have imagined, for the place was strewn with alleged adults. They located Dawn in the kitchen hovering over a pot of thick brownish soup—"Hey," she said gesturing with a wooden spoon. Then, "Little Bro," with dull enthusiasm, as though she were on the verge of falling asleep. She was a healthy young woman, round at every turn, with big frizzy hair and a smile that was clearly something one had to earn. Like her brother's, her gemlike blue eyes hinted at a sharpness of wit and intelligence.

Introductions seemed to have occurred, but it was all so casual, so relaxed, so much as if they'd already covered the territory that Kate found herself wishing for the clean impersonal delineations of a hotel room, the bed smooth as a tablecloth and the glasses wrapped in crispy tissue and the toilet sealed to assure a sanitary start to business. "Meet my friends," Dawn said, waving the spoon ambiguously outward, beyond the kitchen. Her "friends," in twos and threes, lounged, loitered and lingered in the shadowy corners of rooms, on a bench outside the so-called greenhouse, in a close circle on big orange floor cushions in the living room where the throb of music could be felt, the Rolling Stones turned down so low it was reduced to rhythmic racket, and on a dirt path behind the house that found its way through the tall green meadow grass of the valley. One fellow wearing a pair of Levis patched with what appeared to be scraps of purple lingerie touched his chest and talked about their souls and about how much he wanted to experience them. "It's going to be groovy," he added as he drifted off along the path that disappeared into the meadow.

Behind the house on a cement pad sat a potter's wheel with an attached stool; next to it adjacent to the house, a brick patio offered a wooden picnic table, wobbly and splinter-stricken, along whose center line paced several candles that had over countless evenings generated layered, multi-colored buttresses of dripped wax. A half dozen director's chairs with faded green canvas sprawled about the table. This was where Nelson, Kate, Rudy and his sister and brother-in-law, Jake senior, ate dinner, the soup Dawn had made, which was some kind of bean and vegetable brew, with loaves of coarse bread and jugs of D'Agostini red wine. Dawn seemed unconcerned about the whereabouts of her children, probably dining with some of the other residents who were evidently happy to function as associate parents. On the small potter's stool where she worked in the afternoons, Dawn sat facing Kate and the others while at her back the sun ducked behind a smooth run of western hills and the sky went from cameo pink to that dark peacock blue typical at the coastal edge of California where the ocean and heavens came together and swapped vast things, like color and mood. They were surprisingly well-educated, Rudy's relatives. They had made, they said, "certain choices" rejecting the "socio-political paradigm."

Normally, to Kate's Irish way of thinking, a good education and high-toned talk bought considerable leeway, but not this time. "Well you have this place," she remarked with a dry smile, opening one palm.

"Yes," Jake said, then he nodded as if to agree. "That made it harder."

"Harder? But it gives you options that most people don't have. You can actually have preferences. You can indulge them."

Jake dropped his head and inspected the bricks between his boots. He was a red-faced, muscular fellow with a full beard and a pair of overalls that, though obviously new, could not help but recall the farmers of Kate's childhood, come into town to the Farmers' Local where there was always company to be had around a boilerful of coffee, their cuffs tattered and caked with greenish manure or the white-gray mud of Saskatchewan. They were not difficult to take seriously, those men. They worked hard. They meant what they said, and said little.

"Of course," Dawn allowed, her voice hinting at impatience. "We do have too much. That's why we share it."

Nelson gave Kate's leg a pat, meaning to communicate that he understood her, but that they were guests here. And in silence Kate found herself wondering whether or not she would deliberately give up comfort or wealth in order to follow some distant philosophical star. It was all right here, wasn't it? Life. You had to milk it for what it was worth, without questioning good fortune or even worse, renouncing it.

She said, "Well, I don't know." She noticed how irritated she felt both by idealistic freeloaders and by Nelson's passivity. The times, it seemed, were saturated with people who in one way or another were maddeningly passive, hippies or young scrubbed families colonizing tract neighborhoods with postage stamp front lawns, having block parties, living clockwork lives, growing their children twelve Wonder bread ways. She was so tired of lassitude—it made it impossible to fall in love and it made people so boring. She was thirty-three years old and though Dawn and Jake were not that much younger they behaved like coddled children, piously giving away this, rejecting that, *sharing*. The luxury of doing good. They had convictions, but where was the urgency? Rudy wasn't anything like them. He was a young gentleman, a professor. An artist. There were real things that meant something to him. "Maybe if you start out with nothing it makes a difference," she said. "If you have to work all your life and take care of yourself . . ."

Nelson whispered, "Kate."

"We have different value systems," Jake shrugged, undaunted. "That's all." He pushed himself up from the chair with a lazy forbearance, as though he had had this debate many times before, dug thumb and finger into the chest pocket of his overalls, and fished up a pack of matches with a joint. "Different strokes," he added, his voice pinching off as he inhaled through the flame and gazed off toward the west. Holding in the smoke, he flashed a set of perfect vulpine teeth and so meant to insist upon his chosen state of sublime complacency. Jake and Dawn's way of life was impervious to such as Kate, to a past, and perhaps receding, culture that defined who she was and what she desired. She felt as conventional as the marriage she was about to enter into, and at the same time unable to want anything else. She was also, she vaguely understood, trapped into a continuous defense of it as a lifestyle.

Rudy said, "Kate has had a hard life," despite having heard only the barest outline of her story. For the first time since she had known him she actually witnessed him nibbling at a fingernail, and realized with stupid surprise that it was something he tried to hide. Again her heart flew out to him, so privileged, so sincere, and yet so terribly unsure of himself. He was beginning to remind her of Jan, of the little tics that used to give away his shyness, like the way he flicked his hair from his forehead only to let it fall back down over upward searching eyes.

With a faint nod Dawn received her younger brother's words, then she peered benevolently through the cool air that in California kept its clarity even at night, and told Kate to stay as long as she liked. "With the rest of our family," she added, arms languidly opening, a gesture that was like a slap in the face and almost as shocking as the language used by her feral children.

On Saturday Nelson Burke and Kate Riley were married. She had wanted the ceremony to take place in the old Mission on Laguna Street, but her marriage to Gregor Vancleve—and subsequent divorce—barred her from a Church wedding. Instead, they had a small, quiet affair on a sun-shot bluff overlooking the sea. It formed the westerly corner of a backyard owned by one Dr. Merlan who was an old friend of Nelson's, a Jungian psychologist with an additional degree from a dubious school of divinity that allowed him—at least in California—to legally officiate. A three-sided wall of Plexiglas provided shelter from the elements, but in fact the day was warm, almost eighty degrees, and the air along the shoreline hung unusually still, as if waiting for something it had yet to conceive of. The sky-dyed ocean was a pale milky blue, the slow viscous motion of the water evident only where the kelp beds floated in ambiguous lengths, rising, shifting, and then wavering upon the deep obscurity of the swells as they rolled underneath and broke open at last in clean white-crested lines, the waves poised and quivering like long green blades before sinking to the sand. The last wave was exactly like the next, and the one that would follow it, and so long as the weather held, the ones that would keep coming in. Kate stood for several minutes, watching in spellbound isolation, her hands on the Plexiglas. She thought about Nelson, and the ones before him, and believed that there would be none following. So long as the fair weather held. It came as an immense relief, knowing that some deep obscure search had come to an end.

She wore the white linen shift without its jacket. Nelson was tall and impeccable in a pale gray swallow-tailed morning suit, and Rudy, who stood up for the groom, appeared wearing his father's beige seersucker, discovered, along with his mother's minks and wool capes and evening gowns from a bygone era, in a cedar-lined closet upstairs at the Sonnenberg's house. The girl with the straw hair known as Izzy begged to be the flower girl, and once she had promised not to swear, was allowed to carry a basket of rose petals that were scattered before the bride, then to stand behind her, pressing a miniature bouquet to her sternum with prim delight. Having neglected to consider a maid of honor, it was Dawn in a paisley smock and with the heads of wild daisies floating in her enormous hair, who flanked Kate. Though Kate had suggested something by Dean Martin, she had also known that Nelson's taste would prevail because he *had* taste, and a Haydn String Quartet played on the portable, and the fine notes strained through the soft salt air, and the ring was a band of fair-sized diamonds not equal to the hueless glare of noon but that nevertheless glittered sweetly across her finger.

Back at the house the family, as Kate was encouraged to deem them, had prepared a touching array of vegetarian dishes for the reception. There was a lot of wine and marijuana and more potent substances as well. "Psychedelics," Nelson told her at one point. They were seated in one of the living rooms where everyone had let her play her Dean Martin LPs, one cut repeatedly, "You're nobody 'til somebody loves you," because it was her wedding day, after all; plus, she had had quite a lot to drink. At around 1:00 a.m. no one cared what was playing, even Kate, who was valiantly trying to solve the words to "Time Is on My Side," a clear Rolling Stones favorite among the younger members of the party. With some satisfaction and a certain measure of sympathetic feelings acquired from a young man claiming to be Cajun and to have had a friend whose father worked in the Storyville district of New Orleans, she understood what "The House of the Rising Sun" was all about, how it had ruined many; and they had actually chuckled at themselves, Kate and the young man named Monte, because, as he put it, they were both pretty "fucked up" themselves. Dancing was spontaneous, random, and sometimes unaccompanied by music. A woman from Montana doused in patchouli oil began telling Kate about her childhood, but it was sounding too much like Kate's own childhood only slightly more recent and a lot less premeditated, the woman having hitchhiked out to the coast with a cute guy from Billings who called himself Chance. "Here's your Chance," he was said to have cried over the rumble of his Harley, and aboard she climbed.

Kate said, "The past is the past," and stood up.

"Right on."

"I have to find my husband," Kate said, and repeated, "My husband." For some reason they both grinned with the kind of sudden found joy that only two strangers can share on a train perhaps, or late at a crazy, amorphic party.

And so Kate wandered from room to room. Everyone was nice. Everyone waved or smiled. The guy with the patched jeans offered her a toke on his joint. The girl Izzy was still clutching her little bouquet from the wedding as she and her brother sat cross-legged before a TV in the family room behind the kitchen. There was a Hitchcock film showing and Jake was making fun of his sister's fright. In the dining room Monte was necking with a brunette; they had apparently returned for more of the wedding cake, which spread in deconstructed profusion across a great silver tray at the center of the table. A handful of the revelers seemed to have fallen asleep or passed out on the big orange cushions in the main living room. Dawn was draped on the couch with a book. "The bride," she announced not without proper appreciation as Kate, barefoot and still sheathed in the white linen dress, picked her way through the room. And even though it was not her "scene" as Rudy had called it, Kate felt welcome and at home, a part of the nowness of it all. Monday morning she and Nelson would go back to San Francisco to the Burkes's beautiful house on Scott Street and look back on their funny offbeat wedding with charmed amusement. Rudy would be a part of their lives, and there would be other new friends, dinner parties, trips to Europe, and the past would stay where it belonged—in the past.

She was tired, ready for bed. Nelson, she guessed, had already turned in. It was that kind of party, nothing to take offense about. But he wasn't upstairs in their room at the south end of the house. And then she began to worry just a little. It was a cool night, everyone had come inside hours earlier when the fire on the portale had smoldered down to bits of charcoaled oak. Down the hall she went, peeking in bedrooms — there were at least seven, eight if you counted the closet-sized chamber behind the staircase. One of the yellow labs struggled up from his slumber at the threshold to a small sitting room, and waddled and wagged along behind her as if she were leading him on a capricious late-night adventure. She bent to pet him, comforted by his simple-minded optimism. From the central bathroom soapy steam emerged; people did things at the oddest hours at the Sonnenberg's. It was not a way of life she could ever get used to, but she was nevertheless pleased by her own newfound tolerance. If Nelson could be progressive, if Rudy could shrug it off with liberal grace, why couldn't she? The idea of being modern, of being *cool* welled up inside her, and it seemed she was being given a chance to be young and spontaneous again. Or perhaps, in some ways, for the first time. Maybe when she got back home she would take a pottery class at S.F. State. Dawn had let her sit at the wheel, and the spinning wet clay had felt alive inside her hands, like a small animal forming itself. Something unexpected might be made from the things she didn't know about herself, secret untapped talents.

The door to Rudy's childhood room, a cheery yellow suite at the opposite end of the hallway, was closed, but she thought that, even if he were asleep, he wouldn't mind her knocking. And when he didn't answer, he wouldn't really object to her nudging open the door whose raised panels and glossy paint affirmed something sound and impeccable about his upbringing and the young man he had become. Inside she saw a small couch, a loveseat, upholstered in a light fabric with a fine dark stripe. A single lamplight was dimmed to a cone of murky amber at the far corner of the room, and the curtains were drawn. But she could see both of them. Nelson and Rudy — Rudy bending over the back of the couch and Nelson behind him, his pants puddled about his ankles, his groin pressed against Rudy's buttocks, which in the slant-lit tenebrity of the room were shockingly pure and white. And for the first time ever she found what had always been missing in Nelson's expression—ambition.

In her ears a strange ringing took up that somehow became the wail of a distant train, not the CPR, never again the CPR but the Southern Pacific heading south to Los Angeles or north to San Francisco, and for half a second she wished with the purity of panic to be on that train or any train headed somewhere else. The dog dug his nose into Nelson's piled slacks, but Nelson was jerking them up his legs, trying to tuck in a glossy erection. Rudy's exposed rump disappeared inside a pair of boxers. And she heard herself saying, "I don't understand, I don't understand . . ." But of course she did.

To Kate Riley nothing, *nothing*, not Gregor, not Max, not even men like Raimer with their cold ravening ways, had ever been as mortally insulting.

She staggered back, unable to make sense of the words he spoke, they spoke, not wanting to hear them or even to recognize them as being part of her life, or that moment as having happened, this place, this strange house of anarchy booming like an explosion around her, silent and remorseless, and she running down the hallway whose many doors hung slightly ajar because she had made the mistake of opening each one, the inside obscurities peering out at her now in shadowed shafts of darkness as she flew back to the room that had been and never again would be their room, their bed, nor any room or bed, theirs. Locked the door, locked out the light, crumpled into a corner, cried. And then Dawn coming with a key and using her stout arms to lift Kate from the floor and help her into bed. "We thought you knew about Rudy."

"No."

"He's always been gay. Since childhood."

"I don't care about Rudy."

"Nelson loves you. He was only experimenting. It doesn't mean he's bisexual."

"I don't want to hear this." She clapped her hands to her head. "I don't want these words inside my ears."

Dawn sat on the edge of the bed and smoothed the comforter about her. Kate could smell her unalloyed body odor, and from her great stormy nimbus of hair the sharp scent of marijuana. The wedding daisies were still entangled and even in the grainy dark, the small white rounds were visible. "It's merely a form of physical play," Dawn murmured with a maternal—and to Kate, condescending—singsong.

"Please . . ."

"Nothing's changed."

"No," Kate cried, shoving Rudy's sister away. "It's all changed. It's over. Everything."

Now Dawn rose and Kate could see the shadowy action of her arms as she straightened her smock. "Rudy wants me to tell you . . ."

"I said, I don't give a damn about Rudy. He's a freak."

This seemed to have at last piqued Dawn's otherwise tame new-age temper. "Only a blind woman could have managed not to see the affection between . . ."

"Get out! Get out!" She was screaming so loud that in seconds someone was knocking on the door.

"It's cool," Dawn called out. "Bad trip." Then she leaned in toward Kate and in steely undertones told her, "You get out. Tomorrow. Make it early, too. Before I'm up. I don't want my day polluted by your selfish, narrow-minded vanities. Are we clear?"

"Yes," Kate whispered in utter defeat.

The next morning she called a cab to take her to the small, regional airport at the north edge of Santa Barbara. Desperate to leave town and oblivious to the rest of humanity, she climbed atop the duffel bag belonging to the young man who stood waiting at the head of the line, in order to usurp him at the ticket counter. He put on a look of amused outrage even while he indicated to the ticket agent with a stagy lurch to the side, his hands up in helpless surrender, that being first wasn't worth wrangling with this redhead.

There was a flight out in the late afternoon, so Kate had most of the day to kill. The cab dropped her off downtown where she spent a couple of hours wandering in and out of the tourist shops, trying not to think about what had happened. But the image of Nelson and Rudy together, *like dogs*, she thought, was seared into the back screen of her mind. The courts were closed, it being Sunday, but as soon as she got back to San Francisco, she would have the marriage annulled. That was definite. And she was thinking seriously about placing a call to the chair of Rudy's department, letting them know just what sort of man — *man* — he was. There was nothing she could do to Nelson, to hurt him as he had hurt her, except never see him, never speak to him again.

She decided to keep the ring — *damages*, she thought.

Around noon she found her way to a sprawling beachside restaurant, with a patio that descended in wooden decks to the white gleaming sand. There were a dozen or so tables, each with a canvas umbrella. It was another sunny day, but the wind was up, the palm fronds along Cabrillo Boulevard swishing about, and there was enough surf to attract the body-boarders while confining the little kids with their plastic pails and shovels to the shallow froth spilling lace up the sand. Kate took a small table on the lowest terrace furthest from the hub of restaurant and bar activity, and when the waiter came by she ordered a glass of white wine and a French dip sandwich, not the calamari he had recommended. Beyond the breakers the sea was electric blue, the noon brilliance scattered like bits of broken glass across its surface. The waiter brought her wine and set it atop a bar felt with the outline of a sailboat pressed into its center. Then she gazed out to the sea again, farther out this time, where she found the skewed white wedges of actual sailboats beating south and west against the wind. Behind the boats across the Channel the green blur of Santa Cruz Island rose up from the water like a ghost of a place she would never know. There were a lot of places like that, a lot of things she would never know. Life seemed very short suddenly, almost over. Here and there, at first almost imperceptible but gaining credibility the longer she looked, were the oil platforms, and though their squared shape brought to mind beamy masted ships at last coming home to port, it was the space between them, flat and unkind, as if it was meant to keep them everlastingly apart, that took her back to the Prairies, to the grain elevators statically plying a land sea, town to town, port to port.

The waiter brought the sandwich, tucking one corner of the napkin beneath the plate to keep it from blowing away. She ordered another glass of the white wine. "Too much breeze?" he asked.

"No, it's fine."

"It always picks up in the afternoon."

"I don't mind it," she said.

The waiter took the empty glass and came back with a full one. This time she didn't glance up at him, not wanting to see the faces of young men. But she had felt his spectral white-jacketed presence come and go. She thought about the wind on the Prairies, lonely and ceaseless. The Qu'Appelle River had been named for it—*who calls? Who calls?* It was always calling, it was always searching for someone it had lost. She thought about Poppy. And then Jan. It seemed to her that the ocean was a lot like the Prairies, the wind lost and wounded, and that strange tautology of importance and utter insignificance, and that she had not come so very far, that it had been useless to grow older. It was all just one wind, one sea, one time.

Above her the valance of the canvas umbrella luffed and flapped. Piping gulls littered the sky and there were signs at the bottom edge of the terrace advising diners not to feed them. But here they came anyway, the gulls, in their wheeling and unappeasable hunger.

She finished her sandwich and thought about dessert. What did it matter? The restaurant had filled up and she was having a time, getting the waiter's attention. Tables were cleared and new parties arrived, tourists, couples, an old woman with a sunhat lashed beneath her chin. Then she saw Rudy, still blond, still boyish in a pair of shorts and a red polo shirt, weaving through the tables, descending the last two steps to where she sat.

"Kate."

"You. What do you want?"

"We've been looking everywhere."

"Here I am."

"He's worried. *I* was worried."

"What's the point?" she said, staring down at the blistered planks of the terrace deck. She didn't want to recognize him but she was glad, if it had to be one of them, that it was he, this younger one who somehow stirred up memories of Jan Larsen.

"May I sit?"

She shrugged. "Suit yourself."

The young man leaned in, crumpling his hands before his face so that she could not see the beautiful wounded lips she had in the past found occasion to admire. "He loves you."

"He loves me."

"Yes. He does."

The waiter stopped by and offered Rudy a menu, but he shook his head and asked for a scotch rocks instead.

"It's a little early," she said when the waiter had gone away.

"I should have told you. At the beginning. It's my fault."

"No. He should have. Now it's too late. It's all too late."

Rudy did not say anything. The waiter brought the scotch and said, "Same check?" and then Rudy said, "Let me have it, will you?" and Kate would not look at his hand with its gnawed fingernails covering the piece of paper in order that the wind would not carry it away.

She picked up her napkin and along its edge tore a single strip, rolling it between her thumb and index finger until she had made a small limp spindle of it. Then she tore off another strip and began again, tossing the spindles to the gulls. They swept down and landed in a flurry of bent wings and snapping orange beaks, lifting off once they discovered the hoax. "Trying to buy my silence?" she asked.

"No." He raised his glass and sipped. "But if you mean to make more of this . . ." He put the glass down. "More than it means, than it's really worth . . ."

"Worth?"

"He loves you. What happened was just, uh . . . an anomaly."

"Words," she said and turned toward the sea where she marked, one by one, the oil platforms, the sailboats, the vaporous island far off, and then the purple line of the horizon. "Words. Oh, those fancy words. You think, both of you do, that's all it takes to deal with someone like me. I don't have the education, I'm not sophisticated enough to understand. It's the times. He was just experimenting. Words, words, words."

"It's the truth. He was just experimenting."

"It was just my wedding night," she said too loudly and feeling a small fist clench in her throat. The old woman in the sunhat was watching them now.

On the table Rudy spread both hands palms down. "This is who I am." He lowered his voice. "I can't help it. You said once that we have to follow our hearts. It's been hard, it's been unbearable sometimes. The secrecy. The names. But it's not who *he* is. It really was an exception."

"My god."

They sat in silence for a while. Finally the young man said, "That's all." And she could hear the disappointment in his voice.

She said his word: "Exception."

"Yes." Vaguely he surveyed the nearby tables, and then the gulls, and then he looked back at her. "That's all it was."

"It was my wedding night," she said, "my wedding night."

Rudy pointed to her empty glass, and she dipped her chin to accept, then he went up to the bar to order two more drinks for them, paying with a single bill and walking away from the change. The sun was making its way down from the high hovering daze of noon into the golden depths of the west where it went faster but felt hotter, and her stomach had gone queasy from the wine and wind, and the long night before that could not now be undone, no matter the words. When he had resumed his seat, Rudy stared into the bright new scotch, amber and prismatic, stroking the condensation with his thumb from the rim of the glass to the tabletop, turning the glass a notch, then stroking down another swath until the glass was clear. In the afternoon glow the red of his polo shirt had intensified and she found it difficult to see in his direction and began to register him slightly off to her side as a gory shadow she wished would go away.

"What are you going to do?" the red shadow said.

It would have been better if he had not asked the question. Things would have been different. Everything. But she glanced over at his blond hair, his crystalline eyes in the blue shade of the umbrella, and then the bright stain of red below, his shirt, his torso hidden beneath it, and she thought about Jan, leaving him at the station that raw November day in 1949 with his brave tie flying in the wind, and his last word, *us*, the baby that had been theirs but that only she would ever know about; she thought of Poppy and his long infirmity, his endless dying with its medical particulars delivered each day in words that were fancy and terrible and impossible to erase, and of her undying love for him, keeping it alive, herself alive, even when it meant inventing problems she must triumph over—as he had not—the particulars of her own life dying, and of the health journals that were like a long love letter to him that could never be finished; she thought about Nelson choosing this young man in his red shirt over her on their wedding night, how it really said nothing about her, meant nothing about them—or did it? And she said, "What am I going to do?" downing the last of the wine. "I'm going to get it annulled. Tomorrow. Then I am going to deliver a letter to the chair of the Department of Art at San Francisco State about a certain assistant professor."

Across the table she heard the young man sigh. The sigh seemed to belong to both of them, or to have come from the wind itself, but in either case, to have been something vastly held that was at last released. He stood without a word and walked past her down to the beach, and she did not turn to watch him go. After a while she picked up his glass and drank the rest of the scotch. The old woman at the next table shot an ugly look at her, and Kate stared steadily back until she felt she had won that, too.

Most of the tables had emptied. Despite the slow declination of sunlight, the wind off the sea felt cold, with fine grains of sand sharpening it. It was then she turned toward the water, sensing a new secret that must enter it; she saw the long ranks of breakers that had been pounding in all day, and she noticed down the beach a spot of red that might have been Rudy, but that brought to mind young Frank Hutchins waving his red cap as her train pulled away from Netherfield fifteen years earlier. *Jan*, she thought. Or *Rudy*. Or perhaps even, *mo chuisle*, my pulse, my blood. The girl child. What did it matter? They had all been her victims. And she stood up, dropping her sandals as she trudged across the sand and into the surf, the waves clubbing her knees and then further out, the heavier surf crashing against her stomach, finally plunging in a muted roar behind her as the sand fell away from the soles of her feet and she found herself in open sea. *I can't swim*, she thought, without any feeling. Each day in some capacity, in some measure she had encountered the same choice—to act either heroically or cravenly—and probably, without exception, she had chosen the latter.

The salt water washed over her face and she paddled her hands and popped back up into the air. She thought: *one must be a good swimmer, to go out this far alone.* But the thought was only the merest tatter of something like a dream she knew she could not possibly retrieve. *I'm strong*, she thought, even while she understood that it was her weakness that had driven her out. There was such a big space, a great prairie distance between what seemed real and what was. Then the water swarmed over her face again, but there was more of it this time, enough so that it bore a greenish hue with the light above and beyond it dirty and uncertain, and her chest felt as though it were clamping down inward on a mystery it could not ever let out. Kicking and paddling, she broke the surface once more and took in a ragged lungful of air as she jerked her head about, peering directly into the sun that seemed to have halted in its path downward. She called out, "Jan," and smiled fractionally at her confusion as she dropped under, not caring about the going under, only about how everything was all the same now, and that there was some comfort in that at least, the sameness, the oneness. But still she wiggled back up in order to correct her mistake, back up enough so that her mouth cleared the cold skin of the sea, and she called out in a wrenching burble the young man's name, "Rudy." But like the others, he seemed to be gone, too. What to do but try? It was exhilarating, the trying—she understood that now. She said his name again, though it could have been Jan's—what did it matter? It was only her voice, only a sound lost on the wind. *Qu'appelle, qu'appelle*? And then a different voice told her to relax, an arm encircled her chest, and she felt sunlight cutting her eyes. Not Rudy, not Jan, not Nelson, certainly not Max who had been most like her. Not Gregor Vancleve who would have if he could have. Saved her. Or Poppy. Who was gone. But a stranger. Maybe the waiter? Yes, the waiter, his white jacket undulating like a ghost under the surface, the waiter whose face she had tried not to witness.

"You," she said. Then she told him very calmly: "They're out there."

"Just relax."

"But they are," she said.

"Don't struggle."

"They are."

Brendan

My father, Gregor Vancleve, once referred to her maternal heart of darkness. It was unlike him, to say something of that sort. He was a kind man, a good man. But even if you had wanted to, even if you really tried to see all of her, the complete life, and be understanding and maybe forgiving, at some point you heard yourself saying things or thinking things, no matter how hard you tried to dodge them. Judgments.

Dad was in his eighties, not doing well, and at age thirteen, I was staring down another parental loss. News of my mother's life was like a bad dream I kept having, one of those narratives that somehow ends up feeling ominous because you can't figure it out. It starts out ordinary, you're in your own room maybe, and it's sunny, and then it shifts subtly, goes dark and sloppy, and you don't know why anything is happening or how to break out of it.

Nelson Burke disappeared into her past with the rest of us. Oh sure, she saw me now and then, whenever she made it up to Vancouver—not often—and of course it wasn't to visit me, it was mainly her two brothers and their families. She never gave up those old prairie connections; I suppose she couldn't even if she had wanted to. They were her lifeline. They were like that sunny room your dream starts out in before it goes wobbly and out of focus. The fun house mirrors—like that. Next thing you know, you're scared to death and beating a retreat. In fact, there was definitely something about my mother's life, careless and headlong, that brought to mind a fugitive. But what she was running from is hard to say. Some kind of miserable knowledge, maybe. Her dad's death, or giving up Marie . . . who knows?

About those six years in San Francisco none of us knows much. My brother, Eamon, was born in 1965. Father: none listed. She had a mix of jobs, each one less promising, less successful, less permanent, than the last. There was a string of increasingly meaningless relationships, triggering ever more desperate illnesses. Once she pretended to have cancer, did her research at the UCSF medical library to get it right, the symptoms, the details, the treatments, all because some fellow she was dating had cancer himself and she thought she was losing him, that sharing the same deadly disease would help her hang on to him. When he found out that it was all a sham he was so offended or repulsed that he left town, no forwarding address. So she gained weight, and sometimes signed her holiday cards to me, *Ramona*. It was supposed to be a joke, I guess. She could lose the weight, too; then I knew there was a new man. And new clothes, and another manic mood on the rise. And so she went, pendulating from fat to slim, from Ramona to Kate, from self-hatred to self-worship.

I knew Marie, who was a year older, Marie Drummond; and David, eight years my junior, living with the Wheatons in Seattle; and we all kept track of young Eamon Riley, once she confessed his existence, which wasn't until she packed him off to a boarding school in the Napa Valley. The four of us were scattered like flotsam in her wake, across time, across the whole continent, for that matter. It was a sad way to be, as a family or as what might have been a family. But we managed to stitch something together, her children.

Somehow she ended up in Monterey working at a textbook publishing house. Then in 1970 there was the brain tumor—alleged, faked—and something really did change then. She went into seclusion, bought a little cottage on the coast, made an effort to improve herself. Inside, I mean. Heart and soul.

We had hopes, all of us.

Eamon

Kate Riley was living in a white cottage by the sea, just north of the city of San Francisco when I went finally to see her for the first time at the end of my official youth. Everything was white . . . the house, the walls, even her clothes, white cotton pants, loose with a drawstring, and a white tunic, the kind of outfit people meditate in. From the kitchen I could smell tea, the non-smell of really fine green tea. Outside, it was just the white noise of wind and sea, a midday sun muted behind fog that would not quite burn off. Hers was the last little cottage on a ragged half-sand, half-dirt road that ran along the bluff. On the windward side the paint was peeling down to a gray that was so weathered it had achieved an under-stated, canescent sheen. Crowding around the front porch were ice plant and other native succulents, some sea grasses . . . she hadn't tried to import anything. Odd pieces of driftwood that, when they had been growing had twisted against the wind, lay about, or stood, like small abstract statues in a garden of Japanese simplicity and spacing. It was all very natural.

At that time I knew her to have two other sons. There's the one she might have finished raising—Brendan. You could call that lucky, maybe, that he had a few early years with her. He's in the fruit business, small community north of Penticton. The decent dependent type. But after all, who could blame him?

There was David, named for the statue, I understand. I met David; he *was* beautiful—curly dark hair, straight nose, a blocky, muscular shape. Once I gave him money. I liked him best, though in a way half brothers are worse than strangers. Even if you have the opportunity to know them and be close, the way our culture says you ought, something in you doesn't really want to, something in you wants them just gone, erased from the playing field, no longer a factor in the wakeful consciousness of the world. David had a drug habit, and since I knew we wouldn't be visiting each other much, I didn't see any good reason to play the reformer. By the time I went to see her he had already killed himself, or at least they thought it was suicide, though it was hard to imagine quite how he managed it. Mysterious circumstances. She wouldn't believe it. Our mother.

Then there was me, or *is* me, son number three. Eamon. After six weeks of my squalling, she farmed me out to a Mexican family down the street from her place in the city. Nice people, about five feet tall, every one of them. There were a lot, too—aunts, uncles, *niñas* and *niños*, and the *abuelos*, of course. My mother gave them money once a month, and I spent the early years of life speaking Spanish. Which nowadays will get you a job just about anywhere in the West. The western U.S., that is. When I was around five she took me back for maybe six months before a new lover distracted her, and off I went to boarding school and then college, graduation, and on a mild day in June of 1990, I found myself motoring west to start a career in the tech industry making more money in my first year than my entire education had cost.

And to see her. *Mother.*

Why not? I thought. Over the years she had become a phenomenon, something I had to mentally manage, not a human being.

I had called ahead. Surprise can be a mean thing. Plus, there are always things you don't want to stumble into. The door was open, but I knocked anyway, and here she came, all white, even her hair, which for so many years had been long and red; here she came walking in her bare feet toward me, and it seemed as if she was awfully relaxed. Right away I wished I hadn't come. I found all the white annoying . . . who was she trying to kid? And I wanted her to be the nervous one.

"Eamon here," I said, sticking out my hand. Strange greeting . . . I must have been wishing I were telephoning, not standing in her house.

"You," she murmured. What a voice. What . . . a . . . voice. "Oh *you*," she said again, really rubbing the Y up against her palate, as if I had just said something terrifically clever and funny, and maybe even slightly bawdy. I know I smiled; it was so . . . seductive, to turn the attention where it wanted to be, with permission, with encouragement, on *you*. At the same time I felt she owed it to me, of course.

You.

Some habits, I was to learn, were not shakable, even after twenty years, even after her reformation, like the indiscreet way she said the word *you*, instead of hello, or you don't say, or that's an interesting thought. She just said *you* the way she said it, and you didn't really care what it was supposed to mean. She absolved her male companions of the need for verbal acrobatics, delicate revelations of recent successes, back-door explorations of themselves — the full guided tour. She said you, and *presto*, she was there with you, beside you, home, at home, and you were admired simply for that. For being you. The other thing about the *you* was that you had the feeling it meant she knew you, even when it was not possible. It nevertheless seemed she understood something deep and inexpressible that all of your life you had longed to confess. And if you didn't have it to confess, you were willing suddenly, right then and there, to do something that would require some sort of confession—just so you could give her that gift.

My mother found me a beer from a full six pack, expensive, micro-brewery stuff, which I could tell she had gone out and bought in the time I had allowed her between my call from the pay phone in Boulder, Colorado and the California coast. Enough time to pull it together.

"I am living now in a time of silence," she said.

I had been there maybe fifteen minutes.

"The silence," she went on, as if I had specifically asked her about this *silence*, "began at the end of my life in 1970, my life as it was known to me. It began in a hospital room in Monterey where I was preparing to die, if I so chose. But now it is the silence, a preparation, a womb-like listening. I am listening."

What could I say? There was something trance-like and mysterious about her words; I wondered if she was on some kind of medication, or if the monastic setting had gone to her head. I had had a roommate once who converted to Eastern thought and practices, changed his name from Greg to Arbind and before he took his vow of silence and confined himself to a portable chalkboard, spoke in the formal and strangely obsequious manner of his guru or his yoga gang or the books on consciousness he was always thumbing through. There were phrases I still remember . . . *I grovel in mortification*, or *verily, it is the noble eightfold path*, or *union with the unpleasant is painful*, and *there is a path to walk on, there is walking being done, but there is no traveler*. Greg had been dazzled out of his own speech patterns.

"I am living now in silence," my mother repeated, "and your coming here does not startle it, but seems to soothe me deeper into this time even as I lean back into the past. So that I can tell you. That is why you have come, I know. To ask the question that only my listening for the first time can answer."

I wondered briefly if she were entirely sane.

"I am living now in a place of silence, and this time that you have asked about is a foreign land. My past, the people, I, or she, just a character, while you, Eamon, you are . . . so real."

She actually reached over and touched my hair. I could hardly stand it.

"Won't anyone ask me a question? I remember that thought . . . it came, and came again . . . will no one ask me a question? At last you have asked. You have come . . . you were coming anyway, but that's okay," she made a gesture with her hand, a graceful turning, down to up, "you have come here, Eamon, and you have asked by your coming."

"Kate."

I watched her wince. Then reconsidering, she gave her head an almost imperceptible shake. "But that's right," she said, putting up her hand to stop any apology. "Kate. No, it's right. Kate Riley, that is my name. Not mother or mom, or mummy as I used to call my own. I haven't the privilege to cry, even, have I?"

But she did cry, just a little, in the kitchen over the teakettle where I might not have seen if I hadn't been wishing for it. The living room couch separated the two spaces, and I was lounging at an angle, my arm resting with casual intent along the back, my knee cocked up across the cushion, and everything in the arrangement of my body meant to communicate the scintilla of interest I had managed to summon for her and this incidental visit.

Returning with her tea and a plate of sliced bread, still warm, and butter in a small crock, my mother looked me in the eye, not to atone but as if to confirm something she knew all along but would now accept fully.

"So. A beginning . . . anywhere will do," she said, a bitter twist of her mouth, an almost businesslike sigh. "They seem to be everywhere, beginnings. There is a little bit of the beginning in everything we do, an old dog who keeps scratching at the back door. I can hear him now . . ."

I saw that her hand was shaking. Her hands were fine, pale and fine, objects shaped by an artist who loved his work.

"We were stopped on a hill . . . that was a beginning, and an end, and a truth I had a chance to find. *For truths are sometimes detected first in a place remote from the one to which they apply* . . . I read that once. And there was a blind girl on the sidewalk. In a way, she started it all, and finished it, too. I was scheduled for brain surgery, which I knew I didn't need." She gave a bitter laugh, then gazed intently at my face, as if trying to remember the question. "You were in boarding school by then, not with the Jimenez family."

And so I listened to her story, what of it I could stand. It made a difference, but not enough of one. Too much time had passed. I had already learned how dangerous it was to care.

Marie

My mother did not want to be touched when she was dying. She drew her hand from mine and later, when they arrived, from my brothers', Eamon and Brendan. David was gone by then. They found him on his boat—he was a fisherman, in Alaska—they found him alone on his trawler twenty miles offshore with a boning knife struck through his heart and the sun gleaming off the steel grip. For a while they thought someone else had done it.

She did not use my name when I arrived, she retreated among the stone columns of the archetypical: "Daughter," she said. And so summoned, I listened to the space containing her significant silence.

My mother could not bear to be touched when she was dying. She was sixty-nine. Maybe she had had enough of touch, of men who didn't care because she couldn't finally care for herself. In truth, I was relieved. Her hands were warm and dry, a smear of yellowish antiseptic enveloping the bruised, blood-stained entry of the IV on the back of the right one, the nails dirty—she had been in hospital for almost two weeks and no one had cleaned them for her. Even so, her hands were still beautiful. But it was the sensation of a contagion, and of being allowed to avoid it, being told to avoid it, that brought relief. Whether it seemed that death itself was contagious, that in holding her hand I might catch it, or it catch me, or whether it was simply who my mother was, who she had been, I was afraid of contracting, I cannot honestly say. Some of both maybe. I was her only daughter. She was told that I was blind. It was, she said, one of the reasons she gave me up. Naturally, that made it worse. I used to hate her, to count her losses as my gains, but that was when I was younger and could still be hurt by imagination, by the dream I could never dream. It was Gregor Vancleve who found me, growing up with the Drummonds; Gregor who suspected my existence, and who wished for me and his son, Brendan, family—just that. Family.

Kate Riley was never meant to be a mother, mine or anyone's, only a daughter who would become a lover.

If she had been stronger, if her will had not swooned at the gates of desire, if she had not dropped to her knees before even the least and shabbiest of temptations; if she had not been so much a part and product of her times, of the confused or dissolving codes, the rush to modernity with its glorified standards of living clambering ever up; if she had not acted always in the service of her own idolatry and had been able to reach beyond her own moment in time into the moments of others, and into the future: then she might have recognized both her insignificance and her importance. By what measures, swift and desperate, she descended into abjectness! It was a tactic that failed. And the mystery of the time element, the ways in which it stood still for her even as it ran out, beginning with her father, with her Poppy, and ending there, and after that ending again and again—with me, cast off because she could not forgive herself or Jan or her mother or even the Prairies themselves for not being world enough to keep Poppy and his love alive. To keep Kate alive.

They say that repetition is forgetting in its most spellbinding form. People who survive car accidents replay those raw, nonnegotiable moments hurtling through time, and somehow the time, because it is pure, because it hasn't been tamed, is both compressed and blown apart, like the universe itself expanding and contracting, again and again, each detail horrendously animate and scarified into a psyche that stutters, that cannot move on. The needle stuck. A hundred times I asked myself, "What was she after, my mother?" Until at last I heard the answer in the question itself—she was after. After Poppy. And all that followed his death was a vain reaching backward to before.

Hers was a life of insatiability, of infinite lack.

It was not easy to humiliate my mother because she kept so few ideals. Men leaving her—that constituted her primary exposure to humiliation. Also, suggestions that she was lower class, that, having come from the Prairies, she could be nothing more than cousin to a sodbuster. Once, in her later years, she took a music appreciation course—this was when she was making efforts to improve herself—at a community college north of the city, and after class one day she tried to purchase a recording of *La Bohème*, which she pronounced La Boheem. When the clerk corrected her—probably a pallid, wiry, unformed male with too much education and not enough masculinity, a late model version of the rejectamenta of her glory days—she apparently suffered a sudden and complete mortification, her face red, her temper pyrotechnic. It was David who reported this to us; David was terribly sensitive. It was just the sort of sad little anecdote he was always collecting. Until he had collected so many that it broke his heart.

They say that you have to have a knowledge of sin in order to find redemption. My mother possessed that knowledge, claimed it fully, but she would not accept redemption, preferring, finally, moral anarchy. They say that love is a homesickness, and I suppose for her this was so, since she had only ever had a home within the encircling arms of Poppy's life. She would insist that she had loved many, but in truth men composed not her heart but her identity, the color and content, the very breadth of Kate's self. And armed with a man, it was Kate she meant to love, and Ramona Moon she kept trying to accept. Oh, yes, I heard all about Ramona Moon.

My mother died a fat woman. I cannot think of anything, any other condition or state of affairs, she would have preferred less. Even to say it brings tears. When she learned that she was dying the first thing she did was launch a new diet—it was reflexive. For her, the equation was simple: each pound of fat subtracted that much love, or perhaps it only kept her from the incremental and inexorable realization that, fat or thin, she had rendered herself unlovable. She wanted—as we all do—to die loved. In love.

I count her losses, though it was only the earliest of them that mattered, that counted.

At some point during the two weeks of her ultimate leave-taking her kidneys failed. They would not give her any fluids, still hoping that one or both of them would kick back in. The doctor said: "Her condition is not compatible with life." He said: "She is actively dying." It was 2000, and the language of death had changed since her childhood, but still not enough to conceal the truth. She had already signed the documents before I had even arrived, declining resuscitation, rejecting years of dialysis and dependency. It surprised me. But then, I suppose she figured that there was no one on whom she could depend. I sat at her bedside in the ICU, studiously not holding her hand, which lay huddled by her hip like a small hurt child who would have no consolation. Her expressions kept shifting, one to another, like those sped-up films of clouds and weather. The morphine had dropped her just below the surface of consciousness, but she was having a busy time of it down there, mucking about with her memories and the vestiges of an existence. She smiled, frowned, looked dubious, impressed, sad, sexy, even angry, her lips thinning to a pale line of contempt—all in silence, a silent film of Kate Riley's life as performed by her facial muscles. They call it a deathwatch, my sitting there beside her as she died, but it was evidence of her life I witnessed, the signs and traces of signs that whatever it had been, her life, her experiences, it had surely *been*.

Eamon and Brendan spent most of that long last night in the ICU lounge, watching the television. Every hour or so I checked in on the two of them, these sons who were satisfied to let their mother go under my watchful eyes. After all, they had had enough of her, and I had had none. "Do you want to sit with her?" I asked. Something funny had just occurred on the TV and their smiles were still faintly in evidence. "Is she conscious?" Eamon asked. I told them no. Then they both shrugged, a genetically identical shrug, I noticed, not unpleased with our relationship, or with the duty they were proud to confer upon their older sister. Honestly, to sit beside her as she died, her hand extracted from mine just as she had extracted herself at my birth, her face communicating to me so much of what she had felt throughout her life, offered a strange and vast sort of contentment. I was her audience of one. At last. The she-child Kate Riley could not bear to love.

A male nurse came in to check her catheter and the still-empty bag that hung alongside her bed, and then, in an act of kind practicality, he began to spread Vaseline on her parched lips. His touch brought her up from the morphine depths.

"Some Vaseline. For your lips," he told her with a smile.

"Piss off," she said.

Piss off.

He glanced over at me, with pity for what he imagined to be my embarrassment, or perhaps with pity that I had such a mother, or perhaps pity because he could not share his amusement with me, the daughter. For at her words, he had smiled again, a tiny acknowledgment of a large and conspicuous reality. He was alive, employed, muscular; this dying fat woman whose useless catheter he had just pinched—she could not touch him. Her condition was not compatible with life.

UNIVERSITY OF NEBRASKA PRESS

Also of interest in the Flyover Fiction series:

The Floor of the Sky
By Pamela Carter Joern

In the Nebraska Sandhills, nothing is more sacred than the bond of family and land—and nothing is more capable of causing deep wounds. In Pamela Carter Joern's riveting novel, Toby Jenkins, an aging widow, is on the verge of losing her family's ranch when her granddaughter Lila—a city girl, sixteen and pregnant—shows up for the summer.

ISBN: 0-8032-7631-1; 978-0-8032-7631-4 (paper)

The Mover of Bones
By Robert Vivian

In one hand, Jesse Breedlove holds a bottle of Cuervo Gold— or what's left of it—in the other, the shovel with which he has just unearthed the bones of a small girl buried in the cellar of a Catholic church in Omaha, Nebraska. So begins Breedlove's odyssey across the literal and mythical landscapes of America.

ISBN: 0-8032-4679-X; 978-0-8032-4679-9 (cloth)

Skin
By Kellie Wells

What happens when the spirit exceeds the limits of the skin? More troubling yet, what happens if it doesn't? These are the questions the inhabitants of What Cheer, Kansas, must finally face as their paths cross and recross in an ever more intriguing—and perhaps liberating—puzzle.

ISBN: 0-8032-4824-5; 978-0-8032-4824-3 (cloth)

Order online at www.nebraskapress.unl.edu or call 1-800-755-1105. Mention the code "BOFOX" to receive a 20% discount.